Matthew Kneale

English Passengers

Matthew Kneale lives in Italy. *English Passengers* is
his North American debut.

English Passengers

MATTHEW KNEALE

ANCHOR CANADA

National Library of Canada Cataloguing in Publication Data

Kneale, Matthew, 1960–
English passengers

ISBN 0-385-65866-4

I. Title.

PR6061.N37E544 2001   823'.914   C2001-901454-6

Cover art:
(water) Shinya Inoue/Photonica
(ship) courtesy of the Granger Collection
Cover design: Eric Fuentecilla
Printed and bound in the USA

Published in Canada by
Anchor Canada, a division of
Random House of Canada Limited

Visit Random House of Canada Limited's website:
www.randomhouse.ca

Published by arrangement with Nan A. Talese/Doubleday

BVG 10 9 8 7 6 5 4 3 2 1

CONTENTS

⟴

Note of Thanks

I WOULD LIKE to thank Southern Arts, and also the Arts Council of England, for the grants they have kindly provided. This novel would not have been possible without their generous help.

Note on Language

ONE OF THE CHARACTERS in this novel is a Tasmanian aboriginal. When I wrote his sections my intention was to portray someone intelligent and interested in words, who is from a culture wholly remote from that of white men but has been educated by them, absorbing English phrases, both formal and informal, that were common in the 1830s. He does not sound like a modern mainland Australia aboriginal speaker, nor is meant to: my hope was to depict a particular character from this distant time.

English
Passengers

A PROOF

AGAINST THE ATHEISMS OF GEOLOGY

THE TRUTH OF THE CHRONOLOGY OF THE BIBLE CONCLUSIVELY SHOWN

WITH

A NEW AND IMPORTANT REVELATION

THAT THE

Garden of Eden

WAS NOT, AS SUPPOSED, LOCATED IN THE REGION OF ARABIA,
BUT WAS INSTEAD IN AUSTRALIA, ON THE ISLAND

OF

TASMANIA

(THAT WAS FORMERLY KNOWN AS VAN DIEMEN'S LAND)

Including a full and extended explanation of the

THEORY OF DIVINE REFRIGERATION

BY

THE REVEREND GEOFFREY WILSON, M.A. CANTAB.

PRINTED BY J. P. TERENCE

52 PATERNOSTER SQUARE

LONDON 1856

CHAPTER ONE

———➤◆◀———

Captain Illiam Quillian Kewley
JUNE 1857

SAY A MAN catches a bullet through his skull in somebody's war, so where's the beginning of that? You might say that's easy. That little moment has its start the day our hero goes marching off to fight with his new soldier friends, all clever and smirking and waving at the girls. But does it, though? Why not the moment he first takes the shilling, his mouth hanging wide open like a harvest frog as he listens to the sergeant's flatterings? Or how about that bright sunny morning when he's just turned six and sees soldiers striding down the village street, fierce and jangling? But then why not go right back, all the way, to that long, still night when a little baby is born, staring and new, with tiniest little hands? Hands you'd never think would grow strong enough one day to lift a heavy gun, and put a bullet through our poor dead friend's brain.

If I had to choose a beginning for all these little curiosities that have been happening themselves at me, well, I'd probably pick that morning when we were journeying northwards from a certain discreet French port, where tobacco and brandy were as cheap as could be. Not that it seemed much like the beginning of anything at the time, but almost the end, or so I was hoping. The wind was steady, the ship was taking her weather nicely, and as we went about our work I dare say every man aboard was having a fine time dreaming money he hadn't yet got, and what pleasures it might buy him. Some will have been spending it faster than a piss over the side, dreaming themselves a rush of drink and smoke, then perhaps a loan of a sulky female's body. A few might have dreamed every penny on a new jacket or boots, to dazzle Peel City with fashion for a day or two. Others would have kept cautious, dreaming it on rent paid and wives quieted.

And Illiam Quillian Kewley?

As the *Sincerity* jumped and juddered with the waves I was dreaming Castle Street on a Saturday morning, all bustle and everyone scrutineering everyone else, with Ealisad walking at my side in a fine new dress, both of us holding our heads high as Lords, and nobody saying, "Look see, there's Kewleys–don't you know they used to be somebody." Or I dreamed my great-grandfather, Juan, who I never met, but who was known as Big Kewley on account of being the only Kewley ever to make money rather than lose it. There he was, clear as day, leaning out of heaven with a telescope, and calling out in a voice loud as thunder, "Put a sight on him, Illiam Quillian, my own great-grandson. Now there's a man who can."

Then all of a sudden our dreamings were interrupted. Tom Teare was calling down from the masthead, where he was keeping watch. "Sail. Sail on the port bow."

Not that anyone thought much on his shout then. The English Channel is hardly the quietest stretch of ocean, so there seemed nothing too worrying in discovering another ship creeping along. The boys went on scrubbing down the deck, while chief mate Brew and myself carried on standing on the quarterdeck, making sure they kept at it.

But you should know a little about the *Sincerity*, as there was a wonder all made of wood if ever there was one. Truly, you couldn't imagine a vessel that looked more normal from the outside. I dare say she was a little old–her prow was round and blunt and well out of fashion, and her quarterdeck was too high for modern tastes–but otherwise she seemed as ordinary as seawater. I'd wager you could've spent all day aboard and still been none the wiser. Unless, that is, you had a particular eye for the measure of things. Or you happened to take a look above the inside top rim of the door to the pantry.

And that would be hardly likely.

In my great-grandfather Big Kewley's day, now, such cleverness was never called for. The Isle of Man was still free and independent then, having yet to be bought by interfering English politicians, and as a free and independent land she took it upon herself to have her own free and independent duties on brandy and tobacco and such, meaning she had hardly any at all. Truly, that was the golden age of Man Island. Vessels sailed into her ports direct from every corner of the world, from Europe and Africa, from Indies West and East. Why, her harbour quays were so piled with barrels and casks that a man could hardly reach his own ship. What's more, every cheap, dutiless drop of spirit or leaf of tobacco was as legal as King George himself.

Naturally it seemed a shame to softhearted Manxmen, such as my great-grandfather, to go hogging such plenty all to themselves when there were poor desperate Englishmen, Irishmen, Scotsmen and Welshmen wailing and moaning at the scandalous cost of their taxed liquor. It seemed just kindness to load up a skiff on a moonless night and slip across the sea to some quiet edge of Ireland or Scotland—or for that matter England or Wales, as Man Island sits clean between all four—and help them out. Forget all this fashionable talk of free trade, as it's nothing but English mimicking. My great-grandfather was free trading before it was even invented.

But I'm drifting off from that beginning we had. Tom Teare's second shout came just a moment or two after his first. "That ship on the port bow. Looks like she's a cutter."

Now here I think we all took a little notice. Not that there was anything clear or certain, but this was definitely worse than just being sail. You see, though there are many ships that *might* be a cutter, there's one kind in particular that *always* is, and this was exactly the kind that we didn't want to meet. Nobody said anything—the boys carried on scrubbing and slooshing like before, and Brew and myself kept watching—but we were all thinking trouble.

This little jaunt in the *Sincerity* was taking a chance, I dare say, but still it had seemed worth the risk. The sad truth of it is there never was a family so clever at letting it all slip through their fingers as Kewleys. When Big Kewley died he left farms, half a dozen town houses, an inn and boats enough to take half Peel for a jaunt round the harbour, but by the time it got to me there was just the house we lived in—and that with its roof—together with a farm that was half stones, a shop in the wrong street and a little grubby inn that never paid. It wasn't even as if it had all gone on gambling and high women, which would at least have had a touch of the hero. No, the Kewleys were careful, sober people, but with a terrible taste for litigating wills, and a perfect eye for a rotten buy. Why, I can't say I'd done any better than the rest of them. Even with my captain's wages sailing dirty little vessels back and forth across the Irish Sea with cattle bones and such, I wasn't even stemming the tide. I knew if I didn't do something before long it would all be gone, and Kewleys would be begging on Big Street like any set of poor mucks.

Then one day I heard how a merchant vessel had sailed into Ramsey harbour bankrupt. Port dues were owing and she was coming up for auction, while the word was she'd go cheaper than dirty weather. That got me wondering. The fact was there was only one way Kewleys had ever got themselves rich, so perhaps I should give it another try? It was true that the old trade was long out of fashion nowadays, but that didn't mean it wouldn't pay. At least I should take a look. So I rode across to Ramsey to put a sight on this stranded ship. A battered old vessel she was, with a high quarterdeck like you hardly saw anymore, and even a little toy of a cannon on the prow to scare the seagulls, but I never minded. Why, just looking at her I could feel hope getting into my lungs. I could just see myself there, shouting orders from her deck, my own ship, that would make me rich enough to buy half Douglas town.

Within the week I'd taken her, too, and was looking into selling off those last few scrapings of the great Kewley fortune. My wife was never pleased, of course. Sweet delight of my life though Ealisad is, when it comes to risk she's one of those watchful, weighing kinds of female who won't venture tuppence though it could catch her fifty guineas. I did try to win her round for sure. I told her a little about the clever things that could be done with a ship, especially by Manxmen from Peel City. I told her of cousin Rob, who'd been in the English navy and married an Englishwoman, and now caught eels and such near Maldon town–that was hardly a spit from London itself–where he lived in an old house sat on an empty stretch of shore, handy as could be, so he'd even joked about what might be done there when he last paid us a visit. I told her how much a fellow might expect to catch from one voyage of this particular kind, and how it was only doing those Englishmen a favour besides, and so was moral as could be in its way. Not that it did any good. All I got back was black looks and Scripture talk.

"You'll have us all walking the houses begging for ha'pennies, mark my words," she'd say, "or in gaol."

"Don't you worry," I told her, "it'll be as easy as kicking pebbles on the beach. You just wait. Three months from now you'll have a fine new carriage to take you off to church on Sunday."

Of course things never do turn out quite as you expect. It took more than three months just to get the ship ready. First there was bringing her round to Peel, where all was more discreet. Then there was finding all that certain extra timber I needed, that had to be from a boat freshly broken up, and one just a little smaller than the *Sincerity* herself. Next there was getting the timber fitted, and repairs done besides. There was finding the crew, who had to be just right every one of them, meaning they had to be Manxmen from Peel City, as no others could be trusted. Finally, when ship and men were all set, there was the showing cargo, which was salted herring, Manx as could be. All of this cost a good few pennies, and though I had had paid a sweet price for the *Sincerity* herself, I was running short by the end and even had to borrow more from Dan Gawne the Castletown brewer. By late May, though, all was finished complete.

What a send-off that we had. Why, it seemed as if half Peel was there, standing on the quays and the herring boats, all staring, and perhaps waving a hat if they had one. Then again we were quite a sight. The *Sincerity* looked fine as Christmas with her new canvas, her fresh ropes and paintwork, and even her figurehead was gleaming as if new, peering away at the horizon through her dark curls, with just a hint of a winking. I'd bought myself a fresh set of clothes and a cap to match, and as I stood on the deck I felt fine and brave as could be. The only thing to spoil it all, in fact, was when I saw the Bishop of Man pushing his way through the throng towards us.

"Captain Kewley, is it?" he asked. "I understand you're sailing south."

The Bishop of Man, I should tell, was an Englishman named Chalmers, being a huffy old scriss always peering down his nose at the world. There were some persons said he'd got himself all in sulks because he'd not been given a fine airy cathedral in Winchester or Canterbury to lord it over, but had been shut away on a small country full of Methodists mumbling some language he couldn't understand. Not that I'm saying it was true, but there were persons said so. Now he was all sweetness, of course, seeing as he was questing after a favour.

"I have to go to Port St. Mary, you see. The roads being so very poor I wondered if I might make a little passage aboard your vessel."

I can't say I much wanted him aboard, even just for the hour or the two it would take us to reach Port St. Mary, but it's hardly easy saying no to bishops. Besides, if there was one man in Peel City who wouldn't be in the know as to what particular kind of ship that the *Sincerity* happened to be, it was him, so there'd be no great harm. Or so it seemed at the time. Up he climbed onto the deck, in his purple and his silly-looking straw hat to keep the sun off his fine Englishman's head.

Soon after that it was time to be away. As the wise man says, *keep a good wind waiting and it's nothing you'll be eating*. I called out for the bowline to be let go and the two towing boats started off, pulling away till their tow ropes snapped taut. Then the *Sincerity* gave a kind of shudder and a little strip of water opened up between her and the quay. I recall thinking that, though we were hardly a yard gone, we were started now, after all these weeks of waiting, and then I dropped into wondering about the mysteries of how things would turn out, and what thoughts I'd be thinking when I returned. Not that I guessed even a glimmer of the truth of it, of course. If I had, I would probably have jumped straight back ashore. I gave a wave to Ealisad, though she hardly waved back, being still in her huff, and then the crews of the two boats pulled at their oars and slowly the harbour began to change its shape, till it was scrinched up small behind us, and its waving bodies were hardly bodies anymore but just a crowd. After that there was no time for looking, as we were out in the swell, rocking nicely, and there was work to be done. The tow ropes were let go, the boats were brought up, and the boys were scampering aloft to let go a sheet or two and catch the wind. Soon the last sight of Peel was gone complete, and it was time to twist your head about and give a thought to what was next.

It was then that the Bishop of Man started getting himself bored. I suppose now he had monkeyed a passage out of us he could cast off his charm, and soon he was yawning and strutting his way about the deck as if he'd been suffering shipboard life for months. It was the creatures he found to amuse himself. There weren't very many aboard—I reckoned we'd only need fresh meat for a week or two and money was close, so I had got us just a dozen chickens, one sheep and a pig–but still they were enough for the bishop. There he was in his purple and his silly straw hat, clucking at the chickens and poking his fingers through into the coop, or trying to stroke the sheep, which didn't like him. He must've thought himself a proper St. Francis. Not that any of that was so bad. No, what was bad came just after.

"What a splendid pig."

It mightn't seem much to one who doesn't know, but it was to those that did. Not that I ever trouble myself with any foolish superstition, for sure, but I dare say some aboard did, and they'd have told you, certain as death, that there are particular words that must never be spoken aboard a Manx boat when she's out at sea or it'll be bad luck all voyage. Though I'm hardly an expert, like I've said, there's some persons insist you mustn't say rabbit but instead *pommit*. Likewise for herring you must always say *child*. For a cat you say *scraper*. For a mouse you say *lonnag*. The wind is *Old Bags*. Rats are *Uncles* or *Big Fellows*. *Ree Yn Laa*–that's King of the day in English–is the sun, while *Ben-rein Nyhoie*, which means Queen of the night, is the moon. *Blue Judith*'s a mermaid. *Blue John*'s the sea. And you must never, ever say pig, but always *swiney*.

Of course, mistakes will happen, and the bad luck can be stopped easy enough if the proper thing is done. Whoever spoke wrongly should, as I've heard, shout "cold iron" and then touch the ship's cold iron as quick as he can. This is hardly difficult after all, and so might as well be done, if only to quieten any that have such foolish beliefs. The trouble was that in this case it had been said by a foreigner, and a bishop besides. Consequently we none of us said a word, though one or two might have given him looks, and he might have noticed them too. Certainly he left the pig alone quick enough, and I recall that he went below soon after-wards, complaining of the sun, till we reached Port St. Mary and were rid ourselves of the old scriss.

Not that I was bothered by any of this myself, of course, having no time for such windiness, but I dare say there might have been one or two aboard who were troubled that such a thing had happened just as the *Sincerity* set sail on this, her first voyage as a Manx ship of particular purpose. So there were more than a few words said about Bishop Chalmers when, just fifteen days later, Tom Teare gave his third shout down from the masthead.

"The cutter, she's turning towards us now." Well, that left no doubting.

In my experience once bad luck gets started on a man it will go on, and Captain Clarke of the coast guard cutter HMS *Dolphin* was bad luck pure as air. As his vessel bore down at us I had hopes we might catch some addled old gent thinking of his retirement, all belly and gout yawning at the paperwork, but no, not at all, the Captain Clarke who stepped aboard the *Sincerity's* deck was one of those shiny-buttons Englishmen, all peering out of his uniform at the world, hungry to find what laws it's gone and broken. Why, there wasn't even a "good morning" out of him as he glanced about him, six marines following just behind in case he should feel lonely. All he said was "Captain . . . ?"

"Kewley," I obliged, handing him the ship's papers.

"Registered port Peel City, Isle of Man," he read, giving me a little knowing glance when he got to Isle of Man, as if to say, *I know all about that little spot.* "Sailing to Maldon, Essex, with salted herring." Now he played the actor a little, shaking his shiny-button head and pretending himself mystified. "I must say I'm a little surprised at your destination. Unless I'm very much mistaken Maldon is a fishing port. Are you sure they'll be interested in a boatload of herring?"

I gave him a shrug. "There's fish and there's fish."

Of course it wasn't the cargo he was really interested in. That was just starting. "What troubles me, Captain, is your position. Your voyage is from Peel to Maldon, is it not? So why, I wonder, should we discover your ship sailing northwards from the direction of France?"

I had an answer ready, at least of a kind. "We were hit by a squall just yesterday. It must have blown us thirty miles away to south." As it happened, there *had* been a bit of dirty weather the day before, and it *had* been from the north. As the wise man says, *choose your lies like you choose your wife, with care.*

Not that it did any good. Clarke showed his claws now, which he was always intending. "Captain Kewley, I must ask you if, contrary to your documents, you have broken your journey at a foreign port? I would advise you to answer with great caution, as any mistruth shall certainly be found out, and shall lead you to be fined so heavily that you will soon wish you had never gone to sea."

There was only one reply I could give and I gave it, with as much offended dignity as I could find. "Certainly we have not."

"Do you have any cargo aboard other than the salted herring listed here?"

"That neither."

He seemed pleased, like a hound that's smelt rabbits, and straightaway turned to his six boys in scarlet. "I want this ship searched and searched well."

So there we were. Matters weren't turning out quite as easy as kicking pebbles on a beach after all. Not that he had us yet, for sure, but it was a proper worry, while I hated the notion of my ship being poked at and prodded by strangers like some common street harlot. I'd taken what precautions I could to keep her fancies clothed, though this was nothing much more than making sure that everyone was kept busy, there being nothing like idleness to make a body nervous, while the last thing we wanted was some fit of stammering or a hasty glance in the wrong direction. Juan Brew, the chief mate, and Parrick Kinvig, the second, were shouting out orders like seven devils, making their boys jump around the deck with chores, or scamper up aloft to trim the sheets. China Clucas, the ship's giant, was at the wheel, while belowdecks in the workshop Chalse Christian the carpenter was sawing away at a piece of wood and Ritchie Moore the sailmaker was having a good sew at his canvas, while Mylchreest the steward was tidying the cabins.

That just left Rob Quayle, the cook, who was set to cleaning out the pigsty, this being the safest chore for him. Quayles, I should tell, were well known for being strange articles, being odds every one of them. Rob Quayle's father had died when he was only a babe–from pure screaming madness as some persons said–and so he was brought up by his mother, who kept a rotten little house down by the herring salting sheds and earned her pennies washing other bodies' dirty clothes. Whether it was this made Rob Quayle strange, or he just took his strangeness from the rest of those Quayles, that I wouldn't like to guess, but strange he was for sure, with his long face and worrying eyes, keeping to himself and thinking everyone was talking about him, which quite often they were. No, it was hardly a surprise he was soft as butter for the company of creatures. It was the swiney that the Bishop of Man had called pig that he made his best friend, and in the two short weeks we'd been out from Peel they already seemed proper family, so hardly an hour went by without Quayle going over to talk to it or feed it a choice scrap he'd found. As for the pig himself, you couldn't imagine a more conceited beast. The better its food, the fuller it got with high notions of itself, till Quayle was going half mad thinking up things it wouldn't turn up its snout at and leave.

"There's only one thing that swiney hasn't tasted," was the joke that went round, and it was a joke Quayle hated. "And that's a nice leg of pork."

Not that we were any of us in a mood for jokes now, as Captain Clarke set his marines poking about the ship. They started in the ship's hold, which was danger, but could be handy too, as our cargo might work in our favour. I had chosen this with some care, there being few things dirtier, slippier and generally more stinking than fifty barrels of salted herring. Captain Clarke did what he could, standing well back when his soldiers started opening up barrels, but the fact is there's no escaping a mighty dose of fish. As the redcoats emptied them out onto pieces of sailcloth, a proper mighty stink filled the air, and little specks of oil and skin and bone went splattering this way and that, jumping a surprising distance, so they sprayed over the marines, and even caught Captain Clarke's shiny uniform and shoes. Well, he didn't like that at all, for sure, but it never stopped him, more was the shame. Even when his boys had been through two dozen barrels, the hold was fuggier than dog's breath and not a scran of anything had been found, still he was keen as mustard.

"That'll do, Sergeant," he called out, as if he was having himself a fine old time. "Let's start on the rest of the ship."

That was a worry. So round the vessel they traipsed, groping and prodding, with me following behind keeping watch. First to the fo'c'sle, where the soldiers went through the crew's sea chests and poked at the hammocks and clothes hanging up to dry. Next to the work cabin, where Chalse Christian the carpenter and Ritchie Moore the sailmaker were looking sombre with their pieces of wood and canvas. It was in the pantry I got a proper scare. Clarke took himself a peek—nothing so bad there–but then, rather than just content himself with a sight of biscuits and beef and such, he had to go and put his hands round the top of the doorframe and sort of lean himself in. For a moment I couldn't tell if he might've accidentally fingered that certain piece of cord that hung there. Only when he swung himself back out, looking as sour as before, did I breathe more freely. Then we got to the dining cabin. This might be the finish of us or could save us altogether. You see, I'd given a good deal of thought to this particular spot, thinking there's nothing better suited to keeping a lady's honour protected from dirty rummagers than a good dose of high finery. What was more, it worked, and a sight better than those salted herring. Even as Captain Clarke stepped inside I could see his face beginning to soften a little.

"What a collection you have."

I went with the wind. "It's a hobby of mine, I suppose. I've always been an admirer."

Now he was roaming the room peering at them one by one. "The Albert is very good. Where did you find them?"

"In Peel City. There's a good deal of interest on the island." I can't say this was exactly true. In fact there was no interest on the island except from passing Englishmen, so I'd had to send as far as Liverpool to find the prints. But as I saw it, if I was to be a patriot, then why not the whole Island of Man with me? "My favourite is the Victoria. Now there's royalty, is there not?"

"The way she leans upon the lion is very natural." For the first time since he had come aboard there was a civility in the man's voice, as if I might deserve to be treated as a full human creature rather than as a mere lawbreaker unproved. "And it's unusual to see so many of the children displayed all at once."

As it happened, I had taken a little trouble over these, learning them every one by heart. "Victoria, Albert Edward, Alfred, Alice, Helena, Louise, Arthur and little Leopold," I recited. "I'm looking out a Beatrice of course, though I dare say she'll need to have a few more months on her before we'll see her picture."

"The two busts are also very good." He had a peer at the one of Victoria, which was fastened to the top of a tall hollow block against the wall. Fortunately he didn't look too long. Would you know it, he was looking doubtful, even a little guilty. I suppose the man simply could not imagine that a fellow who knew by heart the names of all nine royal children would think of cheating Queen Victoria's own loyal customs. That was the end of his interest in the search, for sure. He had the marines poke around the cabin a little, but when the sergeant tried to look behind the print of Albert, Clarke turned quite huffy.

"I think that's enough," he said sharply, as if inspecting the ship had all been the poor body's idea, and a mighty rotten one besides. "You can return to the boat now."

Well, here was a sweet moment to savour. If you happen to come from a small country of the world, like Man Island, you can't go expecting too many victories over foreigners—Waterloos and Bannockburns and such—but this seemed not so far off in its way. There we'd been, invaded, occupied and staring disaster in the nose, and now our enemies were fleeing away back to where they'd come from. Why, by the time we were back on the deck, and were stood by the pigsty, watching the marines lower themselves over the side, Clarke was almost apologizing.

"I hope your fish will not have been spoiled, Captain?"

It was all I could do not to look too pleased. "Ah, I'm sure they'll be fine enough."

"Well, I must thank you for your cooperation, and I hope you've not been inconvenienced." With that he stepped back towards the ladder so he could join the marines in the boat below.

We were as close as that, truly we were. Go on, Captain Clarke, just get yourself and your snurly fish-splattered uniform off my deck and be gone. Away with you, so we can save ourselves all that trouble and journeying and hiding in cellars and worse—much worse—besides. Why, the very thought of it makes me quite shake with wanting. But no. There he is, already so well over the side that he's just shoulders and a head, when he has to give that final glance in my direction, you know, for politeness—as if I wanted the big snot's smile—and it was done. All of a sudden I realized he was looking just a little too long. Now he was having a frown, his eyes all beady and wondering. That wasn't good. Next he was pulling himself back onto the deck, and I knew we had trouble.

"What's that you've got there?"

It wasn't me he was asking but Quayle, the cook, and Quayle looked like he'd been patted on the head with lightning. "Just cheese," he stuttered, "for the swiney here."

Clarke peeled the cheese from his hand—a mighty chunk it was, and all foreign-looking in its shape—and took a deep sniff. "And where might this cheese be from?"

I guessed quick enough what was up. There had been a row of shops right by the quay of that certain discreet port, and Quayle must have slipped across without anybody noticing. Seeing how the silly fritlag would only stammer us into worse trouble, I shot him a look to quiet him. "Peel, wasn't it?"

"So this is Manx cheese, is it?" Clarke turned it over, and then his face went all sort of white and he held it up for me to see. "And I suppose this is Manx writing?"

Would you believe it, there was a big tear of French newspaper stuck to the underside, that it had been wrapped in. I knew Quayle was a windy dawd of a one but still I could hardly believe he had been so stupid as this. And all for that useless lump of swiney.

Clarke had himself a quick stare at the paper. "This is dated just four days ago." You'd have hardly recognized him as the same man as a minute before. Quite gone was all his shiny-buttons cheeriness. Now his voice was sort of breathish and his face had gone quite pinched with fury. Sad to say, I'm sure he wouldn't have been half so bad if I hadn't managed to catch him so nicely with the prints of Queen Victoria and all her babes. He had been duped and he knew it, and there's nothing your uniformed Englishman hates more than being shown stupid by foreigners.

I had to say something. "Wasn't there a fishing boat we ran into? You must've bought the cheese off them, mustn't you, Quayle?"

Quayle nodded weakly. He'd have agreed if I'd said he'd bought it off some passing shark. Not that it made much difference now, as Clarke wasn't going to believe a word I said, though it was seven times true. Besides, buying goods off a foreign ship without declaring it was almost as much breaking the law as buying them from a foreign port.

"I think," he said, icy as hoarfrost, "that it's time you took yourselves to London, so you may have a little chat with some gentlemen from Her

Majesty's customs." Then he peered over the side to call back his marines from the boat. "The *Dolphin* will escort you," he added, all sarcastic, "just to make sure you don't get lost."

So off we went, quiet as lambs, with a coast guard cutter just behind, and the six marines stretched out on our deck, smoking pipes and having themselves a good few laughs about Manxmen and cheese. There was nothing to be done about it, either, except to tell Quayle that he was to cook us for our dinner a fine feed of fresh roasted *pork*. Of course, there were some aboard remarked how strange it was that the creature that had caused us this trouble was the exact same one that the Bishop of Man had called pig. Not that I was one to trouble myself over any such foolishness, but then again, it was a little curious.

By dusk the coast was clear in sight. A long day it had been, too. Looking at that black English shore, all our dreamings of jink and rum and rented females were long gone. My thoughts were all of searches and questions, of fines and confiscations, of bankruptcy. Perhaps even a spell in gaol.

What we actually got, of course, could hardly have been more different.

The Reverend Geoffrey Wilson
JUNE 1857

THAT NIGHT I WALKED in Diemen's Land. Through the furthest wilderness I strode, where no Christian had yet trod. Before me rose up cliffs steep as fortress walls, though these were like no ordinary cliffs, being white and smooth as polished alabaster. Humble yet fearless, I began to climb, surmounting boulders and chasms, reaching ever higher, till finally I stood upon a mighty peak and, there before me, miraculous to behold, lay the greenest land that ever was: a lush yet ordered abundance, a garden in the wilderness, lost these six thousand years. As I looked upon it, filled with awe and wonder, every distant fern and stream and flower seemed to murmur to me, "come hither, sweet vicar, come hither, and make haste."

Then I woke and found myself in my sister-in-law's house in Highgate. Early morning summer sunlight caught the curtains with a delicate brightness, transforming this most ordinary of scenes, filling me with a warming light of truth, and giving to my premonition—for premonition it surely had been—a sense of something confirmed.

"Louisa," I gently called to my wife. "I have just had a most extraordinary dream. I do believe it is a sign."

My dear wife, though she is filled with fine and noble qualities, is not easily drawn by the visionary. "Oh good," she murmured, without great attention, then returned to sleep.

Early though the hour was, I rose from bed without delay. Twenty-six years as a parish priest in rural Yorkshire had been more than long enough to imbue me with the ways of country people, and could not be gainsaid by a few weeks in lazy London. In this case my promptness proved most opportune. Hardly had I set to work on my correspondence when there was a knock at the door and the housemaid, once she had been raised from her slumber, admitted Jonah Childs's coachman, who had brought a note from his master across town in Clapham.

Dear Mr. Wilson,

Can you come here at eleven? There is someone it is imperative that you meet with regard to the expedition. Please inform by return if this is inconvenient.

Also, bring Renshaw.

Yours as ever,
Jonah Childs

The note's simple directness was wholly characteristic of that noble man, as was its hour of arrival: he must have decided upon the meeting in the middle of the night, having the coachman roused—the idle fellow was visibly sulking—and sending him on his way there and then. Jonah Childs was never one for the slow or the round and about, being nothing less than a fountain of enthusiasm. To know him, indeed, was to be constantly delighted by his warm and excitable nature, his exuberance, his sudden and unexpected bursts of laughter. There were some, it is true, who considered him rather too changeable for their liking, yet I saw this never as a fault, but rather as a quality of charm, resembling the weather on a delightful spring day, when the wind may suddenly and unexpectedly alter its direction, transforming rain into sunshine.

The truth was that without Jonah Childs's extraordinary kindness the whole expedition would have been impossible, and I believe the Garden of Eden might never be found at all, at least in my lifetime. The man had been nothing less than a power of generosity, a gift from God, and in consequence any little annoyances that might be suffered were of little account. While it was, I admit, far from wholly convenient for me to to be called so suddenly to his home in Clapham, I never for a moment considered declining his invitation. It might, besides, prove of no small importance to learn the identity of this mysterious "somebody" he wished me to meet. Mr. Childs was so unpredictable of spirit that there was no telling what might be in his thoughts.

"Tell your master I look forward to visiting at eleven," I informed his servant.

The morning promised a hot day, being already well warm by half past eight. As my cab journeyed down from Highgate hill, London dimly glinting in the distance through its own dust, I considered how richly unpredictable life could be. Never in my wildest dreams would I have imagined, even a few months previously, that I might find myself in such a situation as this: my life wholly revolutionized, parish duties exchanged for hurried preparations for—now only ten days away—an epic journey of discovery.

I cannot say the change was wholly unwelcome. Twenty-six years is a long time to remain a vicar in rural Yorkshire, and while I was honoured to perform my humble priestly duties, and found the parishioners—in their direct way—wholly charming, I must confess that there were moments when I did wonder if I had not been intended to perform some greater service on this earth. My student work had been, though I say it myself, not without promise, while I sprang—if somewhat distantly—from one of the older families of Kent, which had included within its ranks two bishops. I began my ministry with some zeal, endeavouring to improve the lives of my flock by launching a little campaign to have the alehouse open only three days in the week instead of seven, and offering—as a nobler recompense—two extra church services. Sadly this little initiative was answered, in certain quarters, with something like hostility.

Attendances at my normal Sunday services actually declined, while I felt myself regarded sometimes with frosty glances in the village.

If this were not troubling enough, I found myself also increasingly concerned for the happiness of my dear wife. She had been brought up in exhilarating Manchester—she would often reminisce about its many colourful shops—and did not find life in this quiet corner of Yorkshire always easy. For a time she was distracted by the demands of our seven children, but as these grew older and more independent, her stoicism seemed slowly to wane. The main source of her distress was, charmingly, her noble loyalty to myself. Often she would recall one of my teachers during my Canterbury days, with whom I had enjoyed some splendid theological duels, in which I had acquitted myself, I must confess, by no means poorly. The man had later gone on to become a man of some influence in the Church, and she felt, perhaps foolishly, he might have helped me find some more exacting toil. Hard though I struggled to reassure her that such things were quite beyond our own poor under-standing, still she would raise the matter ever and again, even to the point of weariness. Being much troubled by her unhappiness, which I seemed powerless to alleviate, I became increasingly drawn to taking long walks, along the cliffs or across the moors, so my senses might be refreshed by the bracing Yorkshire wind. It never occurred to me, of course, that I might be walking upon the very answer to my many questions.

My interest began as the merest foolishness: a simple pleasure in collecting pebbles, the more pleasing of which I would bring home and place on the mantelpiece. After a time I developed a curiosity about their colours, which varied so wondrously, which led me onwards to observ-ing the hues of the cliffs and soils of the area. From here I took the great leap of purchasing a bag and tiny pick for the collection of samples, and all at once I discovered myself to be a man with *a pastime,* that even took me on little journeys of discovery about the county. Naturally I never expected anything to come of this enchanting pursuit beyond the knowl-edge and simple pleasure it already provided.

One morning I visited our nearest town to purchase a replacement for a lamp that had broken, only to find that the shop was closed. A little annoyed to have wasted my journey, I drifted into a nearby bookseller's, and soon chanced upon a newly published volume on geology. How close I came to replacing the book upon its shelf, considering its price too high. What drove me to make so rash a purchase? Merest chance? Or did some distant voice murmur words of encouragement? Of such mysteries are formed life itself. That same afternoon I applied myself to reading and received a mighty shock. Even in the very first chapter the author—supposedly a geologist of repute—brazenly asserted that Silurian limestone was no less than one hundred thousand years of age. This was despite the fact that the Bible tells, and with great clarity, that the earth was created a mere six thousand years ago.

This was not mere error, this was slander. This was a most poisonous assault upon the good name of the Scriptures. As I sat thus by the fire, the cup of tea by my side grown cold, my wife working upon her knitting, needles clicking, my heart began to beat faster, and suddenly I knew myself to be in the midst of one of those rarest of moments, that are like some dazzling hilltop vista in the midst of the slow walk of life. A great truth began to pour through my soul, like some charge of electricity. All these long years in Yorkshire had not been wasted, far from it. I was simply being prepared for the great task now revealed to me: to right this terrible wrong, and prevent weak minds from being led astray by this vile falsehood.

From that moment idle pastime was turned to deadly earnest, as I endeavoured to make a kind of machine of myself, to defend this great cause. I read every volume on the subject that I could find, only to discover that more than a few others were tainted with the same calumny as my opponent. My enemies were stronger than I had supposed. Still I strove not to lose heart, recalling to mind the story of little David and mighty Goliath. I began conducting investigations of my own, journeying even outside Yorkshire, as far as Wales and Cornwall. I studied. I pondered. I studied again. Half-formed thoughts began to crystallize into lines of reason. Vague assumptions took on a clear, fighting form. Finally I felt ready to put pen to paper and attempt my very first pamphlet, which I had printed at my own expense: *False questions honestly answered: the new theory of divine refrigeration fully explained.* Little did I imagine as I looked upon the results of my labours, stacked ready to be sent to periodicals and men of influence, where these sheets of paper might finally take me. Publication is a powerful thing. It can bring a man all manner of unlooked-for events, making friends and enemies of perfect strangers, and much more besides.

My opponents' first argument was that the rocks of the earth–which are generally agreed to have once been in a hot and melted state–would have required far longer to lose their heat than the Scriptures described. My reply was that the earth had indeed cooled at great speed, being made possible by a process I termed *Divine Refrigeration*. Seeing as our Lord had enjoyed the power to create the world, it seemed only logical, after all, that he would also have had the power to alter its temperature. This left only the atheist geologists' second claim, which concerned the vanished creatures. My adversaries had fussed greatly about these, especially a defunct animal named the trilobite–that resembles nothing so much as a giant wood louse–whose remains are sometimes found in Silurian limestone, and which they claimed must have existed in some long-past era. The explanation, however, seemed nothing less than obvious. The earth had originally been created with a huge variety of animals dwelling upon it, extending from the useful–such as horses and trusty dogs–to the simply ludicrous, such as this tiresome specimen. Naturally, with time, many of the less satisfactory animals–and what could be less satisfactory than a giant wood louse?–had simply vanished away. A good deal of them, I proposed, would have succumbed during the great flood.

One would have thought this might be an end to the matter, but no, my suggestions seemed only to feed the flames. Within weeks a countering piece appeared, not by my original adversary but by another of this many-headed hydra. What, my new critic demanded, of the first plants and animals? Genesis states that these were placed upon the earth within two days of the earth having been formed. Surely, he insisted, even divine refrigeration could not cool a world of molten rocks so quickly.

Thus was the Garden of Eden brought into the fray.

My staunchest ally in this desperate battle was the Good Book itself. Although the Scriptures possess the answer to every question that may be asked, they do not always surrender these easily. Sometimes the faith of the reader is tested with an ingenious puzzle, for which there are provided clever clues, and thus it was here. The Bible tells us that man and the animals at first dwelled only in one place—in all likelihood not even an especially large place—being the Garden of Eden. Here lay our answer. I surmised that Eden had lain upon a unique form of rock, one that was wholly impervious to heat, and which floated upon the rest like a great raft, probably surrounded by clouds of steamy vapour. Genesis does not tell us how long it was that Adam and Eve lived contentedly in the Garden before the serpent went about his wicked work, but men seemed to have lived to a great age then and it was surely a good number of years. By the time they were finally banished, the rest of the earth would have had ample time to be cooled by refrigeration, and plants and animals would have spread far and wide across its surface. This was the thesis of my second pamphlet: *The Geology of Eden considered*.

It seems, however, there is no silencing critics. If this is true, they cried, in letters to periodicals, and as many as two articles, then where is this special form of rock? Why has it not been found?

For some time I struggled with this problem, and I will admit I struggled in vain. Studies and reading brought no relief, likewise the letters I wrote to those few intrepid fellows who had travelled in remoter regions of Arabia, where I still supposed Eden must lie. Those were difficult weeks, and I confess I came close to abandoning the matter altogether, deciding, with the greatest reluctance, that there was nothing to be done but simply to wait for future discoveries to prove my case.

Then, one day, I received a most unexpected piece of correspondence. The sender, who had been following my writings with interest, explained that he had previously lived for some years as a sheep farmer upon the remote island of Van Diemen's Land, that has lately been renamed Tasmania, and lies just southwards of Australia. His farm had lain on high ground on the very edge of the settled area and he related how, on clear days, he could glimpse the distant mountains of the wilderness beyond. Though he had travelled extensively in other parts of the globe he had never seen anything remotely similar to these. The peaks, he said, were like ruined fortresses, almost as if they were all that remained of some wondrous city, built upon a scale greater than could be aspired to by mere man, that had lain forgotten for thousands of years. As if this were not already curious enough, he insisted that exploration of the colony had been largely confined to the coast and that, with the exception of aboriginal black men, not a soul had yet explored this distant wasteland.

All at once my mind was set racing. Genesis, in that famous passage, which had, I realized, often left me slightly puzzled, states that four rivers flowed out from Eden. One is the Pison, which is unknown, a second is the Gihon, also unknown, which is said to flow to Ethiopia. A third is named the Hiddekel, *which goeth towards the east of Assyria*, and lastly there is the Euphrates. I have told how the Bible sometimes offers its knowledge in the manner of a puzzler testing his audience. A simple glance at the map shows that it is quite impossible for rivers to flow from the same source to both Ethiopia and Assyria, as the two lands are nearly completely divided by ocean, being connected only by a narrow stretch of the peninsula of Sinai, itself a notorious desert. The more I considered the matter, the more I came to conclude that the passage could signify only one thing, and I was astonished that I had never realized it before. *Look elsewhere*, the Scriptures were urging. *Look to some other place altogether*. But where? *To the east of Assyria*. Suddenly all was dazzlingly clear. East of Assyria? Why not far to the east, as far even as Tasmania?

This was not proof, of course. My next step was to try to discover the names of the rivers of that distant island. I sought the aboriginal names, their replacements by white settlers being far too recent, though these proved far from easy to obtain, the aborigines having been, most unfortunately, all but extinguished. My interest being whetted, however, I would accept no discouragement but persevered, writing to any men I could think of who might have spent time in that distant colony, and urging them, if they could not help me themselves, to provide the names of others who might. Little by little names began to come, and looking upon these, I quickly became struck by what I saw. They were not identical to those of the Bible—with the hazards of time it was inevitable that changes in pronunciation would have occurred—but still I found myself nothing less than amazed.

Biblical Name	Aboriginal Name
Euphrates	Ghe Pyrrenne
Gihon	Gonovar
Pihon	Pewunger
Hiddekel	Liddywydeve

Where, one might ask, do these four rivers originate? Why, in exactly the region of mountain wilderness that my farming friend had glimpsed from afar!

Naturally I felt I had no choice but to make these findings available to the public. Thus appeared my third pamphlet: *A proof against the atheisms of Geology: the truth of the chronology of the Bible finally and conclusively shown.* I suppose I had anticipated the piece might attract a response and yet the scale of this quite took me aback. All at once our home was no longer the remote haven it had been, and frequently the postman was quite weighed down with correspondence. Callers would arrive, sometimes unannounced, one from as far as Edinburgh. Even the local population began to regard us with a certain dour curiosity, while my wife, who had never previously shown great interest in my geological pursuit, began quite to enjoy this little fame we had discovered.

The letters were not, sad to say, all supportive. I was especially wounded by the fact that, for the first time, I found fellow churchmen ranged against me, obstinate in their reluctance to abandon their conviction that Eden lay in the Holy Land. For every critical letter received, however, I had at least one other in support. What was more, a great number of these asked the same excited question, a question which, oddly enough, had never occurred to me till then: *when was an expedition planned for Van Diemen's Land?* There was no doubting its pertinence, as the whole great subject could never be finally proved except by such a means. While I little considered this to be my own concern, feeling my role was that of a humble forger of ideas rather than explorer, I did write to the Geographical Society, to alert them to this vital issue. In the event, however, they showed only a most disappointing interest, dazzled, as they were, by curiosity to find the source of that dreary river the Nile. Altogether the matter would likely have progressed no further, had not a letter arrived at the rectory one fine Thursday morning, enclosed within it a train ticket to London.

> Dear Mr. Wilson,
> Your pamphlet I have read. Your notions I applaud. Eden must be found. I believe I may be the man to make it happen.
> I await your visit.
> Sincerely yours,
>
>   Jonah Childs

It was a remarkable missive. Then again I was soon to learn this was a remarkable man. Well do I recall that wondrous first meeting between us in Clapham, Mr. Childs's eyes shining with excitement as he asked his questions, which he did with such enthusiastic rapidity that I hardly began to reply to one when I would find myself met with its successor. Such was his passion to see the Scriptures defended that I feared he might be moved even to tears. After only a few minutes' discussion he began scribbling a list of estimated costs, which he added together with a sudden flourish.

"This I will gladly meet, and more besides if it should prove necessary."

I was dumbfounded, nothing less. Never before had I witnessed such mighty, and godly, generosity. I endeavoured to convey my humble thanks.

"You must go, of course," he then declared. "You came up with the notion. You know the rocks. You must go."

It was a suggestion I had not considered. I was most honoured at the thought and yet, if truth be told, I was most doubtful. I had never journeyed overseas before, nor even travelled on a ship, excepting river ferries. There was also my dear wife to consider. In the event it was she, brave little poppet, who decided the matter. When, the next day, I assured her I would happily remain with her in peaceful Yorkshire if that were her wish, she quite threw up her hands.

"But you must go, Geoffrey. It is your destiny. Don't you worry about me. I have the children, and my sister too, to keep me company."

Thereafter matters proceeded apace. Mr. Childs felt that a man of experience was required to lead the expedition and, after some consideration, the task was awarded to Major Henry Stanford: a tall, quick-eyed soldier, who had battled variously against Chinese pirates, Sikh warriors and more, as well as famously traversing Mesopotamia entirely alone, enduring such great hardship that he had been obliged to eat his own mule. He knew nothing of geology, it was true, and little of the Scriptures, but this aside, I supposed he would make a most adequate leader. He lost no time transforming our aspirations into reality, making arrangements and purchasing stores. It was he who chartered our ship, the *Caroline*. This was a most excellent vessel, which had been constructed to carry naval stores, and had served in the recent war with Russia before being sold into private hands, while her crew had as fine a military history as their craft, being a robust and fearless assembly of Portsmouth men.

Ten more days and we would be lodged within her, and our expedition would have begun. The very thought fired me with excitement as the cab made its way across London. I had directed the driver to take me first to Hampstead, to the home of Timothy Renshaw, the expedition's botanist, who Jonah Childs had requested I bring. Timothy's father was a dour man of modest origins who had made himself a fortune from the manufacturing of plaster, and the family home was large, not to say ostentatious. Timothy's mother, by contrast, was a most cultured woman of good Herefordshire family, and it was she I was shown in to see. I observed she seemed a touch uneasy.

"Timothy is just coming. I'm afraid he has been feeling a little unwell."

The fellow shuffled into the room soon afterwards, looking wan, with discernible shadows beneath his eyes. His appearance confirmed my suspicion that his suffering was wholly self-inflicted. The boy had quite a reputation for ill living, being a great worry to his parents for his late nights upon the town, and I assumed these excesses were not unconnected with his parents' eagerness to have him join our expedition.

"What's up?" he asked, without offering so much as a good morning to myself. When I explained that his company was expected at Clapham, and shortly, he put on the dreariest of voices. "That's awkward. I had things to do." Seeing his mother's sharp look, however, he gave a shrug. "But I suppose if I must . . ."

I confess he had never been my ideal choice for this great venture. Mr. Childs had been determined that we must have a scientist, feeling that no expedition was complete without, but acquiring one proved no easy matter. Scientists, it seemed, are a tribe greatly swayed by fashion, and the dismal jungles of South America were the preferred destination of the moment rather than distant Tasmania. It was just as we were beginning to lose hope, indeed, that we received a letter from Mr. Renshaw, whose wife had learned of our expedition from a female cousin of Mr. Childs she knew through her church. Accompanying Mr. Renshaw's letter was a reference from the eminent botanist Dr. Dyson, who had been engaged in instructing Timothy, and who praised his student's work upon cold-climate plants—especially thistles—describing him as "a rising talent in this rare field." It was only when I met the younger Renshaw that I found myself wondering if Dyson's praise were not double-edged, and if the rareness of his field might be a subtle qualification upon his rising talent. Jonah Childs, however, unpredictable as ever, seemed to find every satisfaction with the sullen fellow.

"I do believe the Lord himself has sent him to us," he declared, after the interview, eyes shining. "So serious, so mature beyond his years. He will be a credit to the expedition."

I kept my doubts to myself, as in my experience it was ill advised to try to dissuade Mr. Childs from one of his enthusiasms. Kindly though he was, his was a complex nature, and if contradicted his mood could change with surprising speed, from exhilaration to profound disappointment, or worse. On the one or two occasions when I had been unwise enough to oppose him, such as over his suggestion that we might use Tasmanian native wallabies as pack animals, he had, though he acceded to my view, grown quite resentful, even leading me to fear—doubtless foolishly—that he might lose interest in the venture altogether.

"This is slow," remarked Renshaw with a kind of dreary satisfaction, as the cab ground to a halt once more. The journey had been swift enough till we passed around Trafalgar Square, where we became mired in traffic. This was hardly unusual, delay being as common a feature of

London roads as fish in rivers, but as time passed, and the recriminations of nearby drivers grew louder and more torrid, I began to grow concerned.

"What's the trouble?" I called up to the cab driver.

"Some going on at Horse Guards Parade."

Craning my neck past Renshaw, I saw there was indeed a great commotion in front of the army headquarters, with carriages littering the road in profusion, and a large crowd was gathered, many of them in uniform. A strange sort of assembly they made, at once agitated and subdued.

"It hardly looks like a parade," I ventured.

Renshaw shrugged. "Must be some new war."

It seemed a remark both foolish and lacking in taste, and I was on the point of reprimanding him when the cab lurched forwards and began to proceed once more upon its way. Fortunately the roads southwards from Westminster proved empty enough, and it was not long before we were rumbling down a lane towards Jonah Childs's home, which was one of a row of houses marooned in fields, being an advance colony of ever-spreading London. It was only with care that one might discern signs of the great trading enterprise that was Childs and Company: the portrait of Jonah's father above the stairs, depicted in some faraway land, amid a scene of trees industriously felled, and ships awaiting their transportation, or the splendid reproduction of HMS *Victory* just beneath, constructed, so I had learned, from no fewer than twenty-two kinds of wood.

"Mr. Wilson. Oh, and Mr. Renshaw too. How splendid!" Mr. Childs was irrepressible as we were shown into the study. "Our other guest has already arrived."

So this was the mysterious "somebody." He was a heavy-shaped sort of man, intense of expression, even to the point of cheerlessness. Only when we shook hands did his face come to life with a brief smile, while even then there was something defensory about his manner, as if he felt some need to fend off imagined disapproval. A lingering London harshness to his speech suggested this was a man who had, like Timothy Renshaw's father, raised himself from modest beginnings.

"May I introduce the eminent surgeon Dr. Potter," Childs explained.

"He is a friend of Dr. Kite, who did such wonders for my poor sister's feet." He broke into a nervous smile. "Dr. Potter has kindly offered his services for our expedition. Isn't that splendid?"

I will not have a word said against Mr. Childs, whose character is beyond any reproach, and yet I confess I did wish he would refrain from making important arrangements without first consulting the views of others. It was not that I objected to this Dr. Potter, or his origins–I am never one to pay any heed to such trifles as a man's birth, which are, besides, of little account in the eyes of the Lord–but I was more than a little concerned that such a great change was being proposed so shortly before our departure. There was, if nothing else, a danger of hastiness. I glanced towards Renshaw, but he was yawning at his own shoes, wholly uninterested in the matter.

Potter regarded me coolly. "I have long had a scientific interest in Tasmania, and so I was naturally most interested when I learned of your expedition."

"Has Major Stanford been informed?" I asked. Our leader was away upon some windy hillside of Dartmoor, testing the new tents.

Childs nodded. "He was most delighted to hear you would have a physician." All at once a frown appeared upon his brow. "You don't seem very pleased, Vicar."

It seemed hardly useful, or wise, to object. I attempted a smile. "I'm sure Dr. Potter will prove a great asset."

Jonah's face broke into a delighted smile. "But that's splendid. Why, now I can show you the other little surprise I have."

For a moment I wondered if I was about to be introduced to further new members of the venture: a team of camel drivers, perhaps. Fortunately this was not the case. Childs led us in a polite straggle to an adjoining room where, laid upon a packing case, were six shining new rifles and a revolving pistol.

"I have a cousin who owns a small factory in Birmingham that makes a part for them," he explained. He picked up one of the rifles and aimed it carefully at a nearby wall. "They are the latest military issue, and quite as good as anything except sporting guns, so he told me, being of the new expanding-bullet type."

The lure of guns: I confess I myself felt it, though all my teaching warned me otherwise. As for the others, they were quite captivated. Potter examined the pistol almost as if in a trance, then took one of the rifles, abruptly threw it in the air and caught it again, like some excited boy. Even Renshaw was ensnared, carefully handling one of the weapons though it was almost as tall as himself. "Do the bullets actually expand?"

Potter knew. "They change shape. At first they're spherical, so they can drop easily down the barrel, but the metal's soft, and when the charge goes off it blows them sort of flattish. That way they exactly fit the bore of the gun barrel, and spin nicely. It's the spinning that makes the gun so accurate."

Renshaw did not understand what bore was, and this prompted Potter to point one of the rifles in turn directly at each of our eyes, so we could make out the gently spiralling grooves in the barrel, all of which he did with a certain zest.

I felt a need to deflate the moment. "Please do thank your cousin. It will be a great reassurance to have such fine weapons with us, I'm sure, though I trust we will have no cause to put them to use."

"I hope you're right," answered Childs, his mood suddenly sombre. "Although I must say I'm not so sure. After the news today I was more than pleased you'd have these fellows with you."

I was mystified, as were Renshaw and the doctor. "What news?"

Childs seemed taken aback. "I assumed you'd heard. There's been a terrible rebellion by the Bengal army. Delhi has fallen and hundreds of poor women and children are feared brutally murdered."

There is news and news. Most of it catches our sympathies only modestly, and though it may cause in us brief joy or sorrow, its distant protagonists soon fade from thought. This, however, was different. Here, surely, was catastrophe on a monstrous scale. I recalled those angry, anxious faces outside Horse Guards Parade—well did I understand them now—and for a moment it was almost as if I could hear the terrified cries of innocents, carried magically across the miles, from those cruel and dusty plains.

"The news takes a month to arrive," added Childs, "so there's no knowing what may have occurred by now."

Dr. Potter carefully replaced his gun upon the floor and for a moment we all stood in thoughtful silence. It was Renshaw who broke our solemn reverie, showing–as ever–his talent for misjudgment.

"That could make trouble for your plans."

Captain Illiam Quillian Kewley
JUNE 1857

THREE LONG DAYS we had those London customs boys groping their way about the *Sincerity*, all stiff and snurly and hardly speaking a word. They weren't my favourites, those three days. They had put us in one of those new sealed docks, and there was nothing to do but wait, listening to the terrible mad din of London spilling over that high wall like a threat. All the while my poor vessel was poked and scrutinized in a way that was terrible to behold, and I was thinking it only takes one find, or one fool of a body getting himself into a scare . . .

Truly, there's no thoroughness like customs' thoroughness. First they had us move all the barrels onto the quayside and tip out the herring. Next they checked all our stores, down to every cask of hardtack in the pantry, as well as the chicken coop, the sheep pen and the boat where Quayle's pig had been. They went through everyone's sea chests, and took the prints of Victoria and her brood out of their frames. They even had a try at my uniform, scrinching up the cap, I suppose in case I had a few ounces of tobacco hidden inside. Then, when they'd done with all that, they started right over again, now tapping and banging their way round the vessel, now pulling up a floorboard, now making little fires to see where the smoke went. Worse was the interviews. One by one each of us was taken off alone to the dining cabin for his little chat. Stories were checked, particularly my foolish blurt about the boat Quayle was supposed to have bought his cheese off. All the while they were threatening and coaxing and hoping someone would bust and go off like a rocket.

"We're going to find the stuff soon enough anyway," was their sneer. "You may as well make it easier on yourself by telling us now."

Three whole days. And what did they find after all this fuss?

Not a thing.

I could hardly believe it myself. I mean, I knew we had a wonder made of wood, and that the crew were every one of Manxmen from Peel City, but still I never thought the *Sincerity* would keep herself so tight and virginal as she did. This was the very cream of Her Majesty's Royal English Spying and Conniving Customs Service, after all, and in their own dread nest of London too. And us just a shipload of poor, ignorant souls from Man Island, smallest country in all the wide world. Not that I'm one to go talking miracles, but it did seem out of the ordinary. Why, I almost wondered if giving that Bishop Chalmers his ride had earned us a favour after all.

Well, there was a thing to celebrate. Not that I'm much of a one for foolishness, but there was no stopping the rest of them after those three long days. Down the hold we went that evening where nobody could spy, with everyone speaking Manx just in case. Drinking? Well, there might have been a little. Singing? I dare say. Toasts? That there's no denying. *"Boiys da dooine as baase da eease,"* we called out, which means in English *"Life to men and death to fish,"* and is about herring, as are all Manx toasts. Then it was *"Death to the head that never wore hair"* and *"Here's death to our best friend."* Meaning herring, of course.

I dare say there's always a price to be paid for that sort of night. In this case, though, the price did seem higher than was fair. Stumbling out of my cabin the next morning with a sore head, made sorer by that din of London roaring out like some great fight with wheel carts, what did I find waiting on the deck but a stranger, perched nice and comfortable on a coil of rope, smoking his pipe. "Captain Kewley?" He got up in a gradual sort of way, as if I wasn't worth any hurry. "My name's Parish." With that he reached into his pocket and handed me a letter. I guessed from its mean, interfering scribble that this was customs poison. Nor was I wrong.

"The Board of Customs," it announced, "has decided that, on the evidence of the foreign goods discovered aboard the *Sincerity*"—this being Quayle's cheese—"that the merchant ship *Sincerity* broke her journey from Peel City to Maldon at a foreign port, for which she had no entitlement, and which her master repeatedly denied to an officer of Her Majesty's coast guard. In consequence of these actions it has been decided that her master"–this being me–"is to pay a statutory fine of two hundred pounds."

Two hundred pounds. That was as much as many men would hope to earn themselves in ten years. Two hundred pounds that we didn't have. There were also port fees, which were high, being London–where we hadn't wanted to go–and were rising with each day we stayed. Lastly there was ninepence duty for the cheese. This wasn't real law, mind. This was just raw revenge for their being beaten. Forget all their talk, there's no bad losers like Englishmen, especially Englishmen in uniforms. No wonder all those Indian Hindoos had mutinied against them with the likes of this going on. I wished them good luck.

"I'm to stay here till it's paid," explained Parish in a leaning sort of way. "Just to see how you're doing, you know."

I knew all right. He was there to spy. Having failed to find a thing through all their searching, the customs were now hoping to smoke us out with fines and watching.

I did what I could. I wrote a letter that same day to Dan Gawne, the Castletown brewer. I had hopes of that letter. Seeing as Gawne had already lent us jink, I supposed he might be scared into giving out more, just to get it back, while it seemed to me we were a fair enough risk, as if we could just get free of this gaol dock and away to Maldon we'd have money enough for anyone. In the meantime we did all the selling we could, to agents in the dock and other vessels too. First went the salted herring, though they didn't catch very much, as they'd been out of their barrels twice now and it showed. Next went any spare ship's stores, even down to the chickens that were left. Why, I'd even have peddled the prints of Victoria, Albert and the eight babes if there'd been a buyer. It was never enough, though. When all was done and I counted out the jink, we were still eighty-three pounds short. Then Gawne's answer arrived, being short as could be.

Sell the ship and pay me what you owe.

That was no reply. That was just a low rottenness flung over oceans. As if I'd sell the *Sincerity*. As if I even could, considering what her new owners would find inside her. We called Gawne some names that morning, I can tell you. Scrissag. Scrawl. Sleetchy old scraper. Hibernator.

Castletown snot. Fat muck of a fritlag. Big slug, all sitting on his shillings with his little crab of a wife, snurly and high as if they thought they were somebody.

Not that it made any difference. Within the hour we were in worse trouble than ever, when two of the starboard watch, Tom Hudson and Rob Kneale, jumped ship, doing so clean in front of the whole crew, springing over the side with their sea chests as if they never cared. "No, thanks," they jeered, when I ordered them back. "We'd rather find a boat that can pay." With other vessels this wouldn't have mattered, and would even have had its uses as their wages could be kept, but the *Sincerity* wasn't other vessels and all her crew had to be Manxmen from Peel City. All of a sudden I knew it was time to be taking a chance, and a big one too. As the wise man says, *it's no good betting pennies when the dice have snatched your horse and your house.*

Now if a body goes knocking around ships he will hear things, including chatter about places he's never seen and never expects to, and I'd heard talk about London, including the name of a particular inn that was near the docks, where certain people might be found and certain arrangements made, as it was said. Perhaps, I reasoned, I could get us a loan out of someone as part of an arrangement. It would be a good enough deal after all. Once we were free, those certain somebodies could have our cargo at a most reasonable price. There were dangers in such a venture of course. Most of all we didn't know who to trust among all these Englishmen foreigners, and there was the fear we'd been getting help from a gang of customs officers in disguise, as they were known to play such tricks. For all this, it had to be tried.

First I needed to get some samples. I sent Kinvig up to distract the spy Parish with a bit of talk, just as a precaution, and had Brew set the boys working at something noisy too, while I made my way down to those certain secret places that the *Sincerity* had kept so pure from customs' eyes. First I went to her pantry and reached above the rim of the doorframe, to that certain piece of cord that Captain Clarke had so narrowly missed, which I gave a gentle tug. The answering click didn't come from nearby but from the storeroom next door. Not that you'd have known what it was that had clicked there unless you happened to go looking behind a particular coil of rope at the panel just behind, which was suddenly a touch loose. Which I did. And d'you know, out it swung, to reveal a couple of pieces of cable just asking to be pulled. Which I did too. Now what did we have now but two more clicks, from the dining cabin. Sure enough, the two busts, of Albert and Victoria, seemed somehow a touch less anchored. Have a close look and you'd notice the hollow blocks they were fastened onto were a little loose, and give one a push and you'd get a smartest surprise, as the hinged trap door in the floorboards swung open so tidy and smooth.

Now I'll tell you why all those serious-faced customs men never found a thing. It was because the *Sincerity* wasn't just some piece of cheap faked-up carpentry, no. From the dining-cabin floor down, the *Sincerity* was two entire vessels, one inside the other. The inner hull was those timbers I'd bought from the boat that was being broken up, and though I'd had it thinned out little, still it didn't sound hollow if you gave it a thump. It even looked weathered and damp, just like it should. As for the gap between these two hulls, this was no more than eighteen inches– more and the hold would have looked too curious–but eighteen inches right round the body of a ship holds a mighty store of bales of tobacco and flasks of brandy. Not to mention those certain pieces of French painted glass that I had taken at the same time. A pleasure it was to look down upon it all, stretching into the dark, all tidy and valuable, with that rich smell of wood and leaf and spirit to sweeten your nostrils.

I only needed enough to show, of course: a few ounces of tobacco in a tin, a small flask of brandy, and one of the bits of painted glass, which were small enough. I slipped these into my coat pocket, then restored the *Sincerity* to decency, and made my way back up to the deck where Parish was still talking with Kinvig, seeming none too interested in what I was up to. I gave a nod to chief mate Brew to follow, Brew being a clever fellow, for all his pale dozy eyes looking slow as cheese. All those Brews were proper brains, and certain ones said they were too sharp altogether, and that you should *never trust a Brew at the fair*. Not that I was one to take notice of the likes of them, for sure. The other one I took along was China Clucas, who was always handy to have about, being the ship's giant, and strong as seven oxen.

Luck we were needing and luck we were getting. The three of us strolled across to the gate, gentle as babes, flapping our arms to show we weren't carrying anything, and were waved through by the guards with hardly a glance. All at once we were in that London which I'd hardly put a sight on till now. Not that I was one to be scared by a bit of dirt and noise. I decided we should walk, just in case the cabs were spying for the customs, and we set off at a jaunty step.

"Want someone to show you the way, mister?" This came from a lad, if you could call him that, as he was more a ball of grubby rags with little hungry eyes peeping out. "I'll show you the way for a penny."

How he guessed we were strangers I couldn't have said, as we'd been making our faces miserable and ordinary as any Londoners'. The thought came to me, though, that he might be handy enough. "A penny, eh? Very well then. It's the Waterman's Arms we're seeking."

"I know it," he fairly sang. "Just follow me."

"I hope he's not working for the customs," murmured Brew.

I had to laugh at that, as it wasn't often Brew came up with such a bit of raw foolishness. "Aw, man," I told him, "next you'll be seeing customs spies in the fishes themselves."

It was all we could do to keep up with our guide as he led us from one stinking street to another, and we walked further, and further again, till I began to wonder if he really knew the way or if he'd just told us so to try and earn his penny. Finally he took us along a narrow alley and into a dirty little court overlooked by wild, leaning houses, and here he just stopped. By now my patience was running thin.

"You're lost, aren't you?" I told him. "We've not all day to waste, you know."

Rather than just answer, like you'd expect, he did a curious thing, giving out a loud shout. "Daa! Maa!"

In a moment a little crazed body of an old man stepped out from one of the houses, leaning himself on a long grey stick, all mad hair and eyes that didn't look at you but stared somewhere off to the side. He looked too ancient to be anyone's father. I was thinking he'd help us find the Waterman's Arms, but then all at once the lad turned at me and spat out a cry. "Oi! Where's my two guineas?"

I suppose it should've been funny, but it wasn't quite. The only one to laugh was China Clucas, who always was the slow one. Next thing he was stooping down to be on a level with the creature. "Aw, man, you know it was just a penny you're getting."

I could see the lad drawing in a power of breath. Next thing he was all noise, yelling out, "Thieves," just as if he was one big whistle. Suddenly there was a whole throng of them creeping out at us, all shouting out their claim on the little fritlag. There was his "mother," who looked younger than he did, and his "brother," who looked older than the mother, as well as uncles and aunts, and some more that weren't specified. A very close family they seemed, too. Their one wish, as they straggled out, was that we should give their relative back his four, no five guineas that we'd stolen off him. Well, it was clear as glass what this was about.

"Let's get out of here," I called out.

Most of them were no bigger than the lad himself and for a moment I thought we might escape nice and stately. Slow, we started, and mostly backwards, back out of the court and down the alley, with China holding the line. We were all right till we reached the street, where there was more room for them. All at once the lad sank his teeth into China's leg, and while the poor gorm was distracted the little old man scelped him one with his stick, and when I tried to help him, two others were ripping at my pockets. At that we just ran, a sort of howl rising up behind to hurry us on as we took the street at a full gallop, dodging past loiterers—especially the ones with outstretched arms—and on. All of a sudden I caught sight of a big plain building that could only be a chapel. The door was open and someone was going inside. "Over there," I yelled.

A moment later I was inside, huffing and panting at the back of a sermon. A popular one it was, too, being full to standing with sober people in poor clothes, some giving me dirty looks for being so clattering and out of breath when their preacher was droning. China was just behind, squeezing into the congregation as best he could, but of chief mate Brew there was no sign.

"Did you see what happened to him?" I whispered, catching myself a "shhhh."

China shrugged, then rubbed his leg where he had been bit. I suppose we should really have gone back out and had a search, but there was the worry they might all still be there. Besides, I reckoned he should be able to take care of himself, with all that cleverness of his. "We'll look a bit later," I said, and China looked happy enough with that.

"These terrible events in India," expounded the preacher, who was a tidy little fellow in spectacles, "are nothing other than the first step upon the road to that battle that shall end all battles."

So he was an Armageddon man. Well, I don't mind a bit of fire and brimstone, though it's hardly my favourite. Manxmen, I should explain, aren't always so pure as to their Scriptures, and there's many will go to two or three different churches all on the same Sunday, especially if there's not much else to do. It seems a shame, after all, to keep just to one when your Anglicans have the best singing, Romans come top for smoke and smells and for theatre you couldn't beat a hellfire body like this one. There it came, sure enough, "Armageddon," and just a few years down the road too, so he promised. The man had a clever trick of bringing things nicely up to the moment. According to him, Gog, ruler of Rosh, Mezhek and Thuval was none other than the Tsar himself, of Russia, Muscovy and Siberia. As to the final battle, which would be followed by pestilences and apocalypses and such, this was to be fought between Russians and Englishmen, like the little squabble they'd just had in that Crimea, but a hundredfold nastier.

"Who shall be swept away by this great judgment, this mighty tide of destruction?" Ah, we all knew the answer to that one. Sinners. He had a whole list, giving a little pause between each so we'd not miss any by mistake. Fornicators and drunkards. Breakers of the Holy Sabbath. Papists and followers of Dr. Pusey. The Turk and all worshippers of the infidel Mohammed. The black savage who had never acknowledged the glory of Christ. The Jew, who murdered Christ our Saviour. And any others who'd been remiss confessing their sins and begging for pardon. The congregation were rapt as babes, having themselves a fine time as he danced them this way and that with his words. First there was a mighty tingle of fear as they wondered if they'd confessed enough, or if it might be themselves who'd be burning forever. Next there was the sweet relief of hearing that they'd probably not be on the bad list after all, so long as they went careful. Finally, and best of all, they'd have a smug little ponder of all those rich Lords and Ladies, and Kings and Emperors who, for all their fine clothes and carriages, were beyond saving, and would soon be knocked off their high perches clean into hell. It was strong stuff. Though I'm no end-of-the-world man myself, just hearing it told with such certainty did pull at me a scran, throwing up little doubts and wonderings.

"Let's be off now," I whispered.

It was as if China never heard. I saw he was staring at the preacher wide-eyed with fear, hooked like a fish to his words. Then again, that one always was a fool for being persuaded, soft gorm of a body that he was. When I gave him a nudge he actually turned his back on me. Well, discipline aboard Manx boats may be thin as milk compared to your English or American vessels, Man Island being too small for the formal, but there are limits. I gave him a jab in the ribs. "Crewman Clucas, I'm ordering you to come along."

I suppose it did come out a little loud. All at once one of the other listeners was giving a sharp tug at my jacket. "That's enough. If you can't stay quiet then you should go."

The trouble was that the cloth lining had already been ripped half to pieces by those low dirts of robbers reaching into my pockets. All at once I felt something give and fall. Now, if there's one sound that will carry nicely, it's breaking glass, and even our friend in the spectacles went quiet for a moment. Likewise there's no smell like brandy to catch the nostrils, and everyone nearby was peering round to see what was doing. A fine little sight there was for them, too. Next to a smashed flask of brandy was the tin of spilled tobacco, and next to that was the glass plate. This last was broken but it still wasn't hard to make out what was pictured on it, as it was nicely done and there are certain particular shapes that a man will notice. It was of a young miss, brave as could be, sat in a comfortable chair, smiling and holding a little kitten. As for clothes, well, she had a neat little bonnet and a fine pair of ankle boots with laces up to the top. And of course the kitten. But that was about as far as it went. The detail was very fine.

"Drunkard," hissed a voice.

"Fornicator," spat another.

Altogether it seemed like I'd not be doing too well on hellfire day after all. At least it got Clucas moving, though, and you couldn't have got him out of there quick enough. The other good thing was that as we stepped outside there was no sign of our friend in the rags or his many relations. The street was quiet, while just a few yards down, sunning himself on a wall, was that sly one chief mate Juan Brew. It was typical of the man. If all the world went stepping in dog muck he'd be the one to spy himself a guinea instead. Sometimes it was tempting just to give him a good kicking.

"D'you think it's true, though?" That big gorm Clucas had got himself in a proper blather. "Is Armageddon coming?"

"For you, certainly." My thoughts were on those samples the big walloper had gone and made me break. The fact was it was no small disaster. There was no point even trying to find the right Waterman's Arms now we had nothing to show.

To my surprise Brew seemed hardly bothered by the news of what had happened. "Ah, don't worry yourself, Captain. I've had an idea." He smiled. "Why don't we offer up the *Sincerity* for charter? Say we'll take a few passengers away off to some faraway spot of nowhere, wherever they'd like to go. That'd get us the jink to pay the fine."

"Charter?" I knew we were desperate, but still. There's ships that are for taking passengers and ships that aren't, and I knew which particular kind was the *Sincerity*.

"We wouldn't actually need to take them anywhere," Brew continued, sticking to his thought. "Once we're free from here and have some money for the cargo we can make up some story why we can't go after all, and give them back their pennies from our jink."

It was tempting just to say no, and put a hole in his cleverness. The truth was, though, that it wasn't such a bad idea.

The Reverend Geoffrey Wilson
JULY 1857

THE FIRST SIGN that anything might be amiss was the large cart that drew outside my sister-in-law's house, its burden concealed beneath a thick tarpaulin. I was busily engaged upon my correspondence and took little notice at first, assuming it must concern one of the neighbours, but then the housemaid called me.

"There's somebody asking for you, Mr. Wilson."

Waiting outside the door was the cart's driver: one of those dour London types who seem to be forever at work with their mouths, whether it be chewing, spitting, smoking a pipe or all three at once. "So where's it to go?" he asked, pointing to the cart.

I was pondering a suitably discouraging reply when his assistant pulled away the tarpaulin and revealed, neatly stacked, every one of our stores for the expedition. "But this is quite wrong," I told him sharply. "These belong aboard the *Caroline*."

The driver was still fumbling for documents when I saw Jonah Childs drive up in his carriage. As he clambered out, I saw the dejected look upon his face, and all was soon painfully clear. "I only heard myself this morning," he explained. "The Admiralty are sending her with munitions to Bombay."

We had no ship! As if this were not already disaster enough, he then shocked me with more bad news.

"Major Stanford has also been taken from us, I'm afraid. His regiment is sailing for Calcutta within the week."

Only two days more and we would have been already at sea, safe from any such misfortune. I felt the greatest sympathy, naturally, for the military in this, their hour of grave crisis, and yet still I could not help but wish they had not found another vessel to requisition, and another major. Was not our venture, after its own fashion, every bit as important as their campaigns against murderous rebels? If they were attempting to defend the rule of civilization, we were endeavouring to defend the very rock upon which was built that civilization: the Scriptures themselves.

It was a terrible blow. An expedition deprived of both leader and means of transportation was no expedition at all, but mere wishfulness. In the event I had little time to consider the problem, being faced with the practical matter of where the displaced stores were to be placed, as the cart driver was showing signs of impatience. While I had no wish to make a warehouse of my sister-in-law's home, where I was myself a guest, they could hardly be left in the street, and so there seemed little else to be done. "Put them in the parlour," I told him, seeing as this was the largest and least cluttered room.

Mr. Childs had sent word of the crisis to Renshaw and Dr. Potter, and they appeared soon afterwards. I suggested we all gather in the parlour, so we might keep an eye on the two workmen. It was a sad moment. The constant arrival of our stores, which soon began to form a small mountain in the centre of the room, provided an awful pertinence to our discussion, seeming almost to taunt us with their thwarted promise: the tents, the hammocks and horse saddles, and, not least, the seemingly limitless number of mule bags, which appeared plentiful enough for a small army.

"I'm afraid it won't be easy to find another vessel," declared Childs glumly. "I understand the Admiralty is requisitioning everything it can lay its hands on."

"What if we went by steamer?" suggested Potter. "I believe they now go as far as the Australian mainland."

I could not help but find it a little trying that this man, who had been a member of the expedition barely a week, was already lecturing us as to how it should be conducted. "It is essential that we have a vessel of our own," I told him firmly. "We may need it to transport us to some part of the Tasmanian wilderness, or to bring us supplies."

Renshaw yawned. "How about a foreign ship? They won't have been taken."

It was typical of the fellow to come up with so disloyal a notion. Childs, who is of a keenly patriotic disposition, gave him a reproving look. "Better to have no vessel at all than that. This is an English Christian expedition and as such it should not have to rely upon men of false belief. No, if nothing else is obtainable, then I am afraid we must simply consider postponing departure."

Here I had to intervene. "But that would mean we'd not arrive in Van Diemen's Land in time for the southern summer, which is the only suitable season to journey into the interior. The venture would have to be delayed by a whole year."

At this point the discussion faltered. The fact was, we had reached an impasse. It was essential we leave at once yet none of us could think of a means of doing so. For a time we stood thus in the parlour in unhappy silence, watching the arrival of ever more stores. By now the cart driver and his helper had finished with the bulkier objects and, perspiring from their exertions, were at work on consumables Major Stanford had purchased.

"There's some choice stuff here," observed Renshaw.

It did seem that Major Stanford had selected his supplies with an eye for both quantity and quality, not to say luxury. I found myself wondering if he might have been unduly concerned by a reluctance to repeat his unfortunate experience with the Mesopotamian mule. Before us appeared, variously, best potted ham, hermetically sealed salmon, hotchpotch from Aberdeen, and whole cases of sherry, whisky and champagne. Nor was there any danger that these would be consumed in discomfort, either, as the next stores included folding tables and chairs, table linen, crockery and some finest Sheffield silver cutlery. To complete the arrangements there was a large box of finest Cuban cigars.

"No wonder there were so many mule packs," murmured Renshaw.

Jonah Childs seemed little pleased, which was understandable seeing as it was he who had paid for it all. "I had no idea Major Stanford felt a need to be so commodiously supplied."

"Perhaps it's not entirely unfortunate that he has been called away," suggested Potter. "After all, he has no knowledge of Australia."

It struck me as more than a little impertinent of this new arrival to begin criticizing long-serving members of the venture, and yet, rather to my own surprise, Childs made no attempt to discourage the man. He even seemed to concur with his view. "That's certainly true. Mind you, I'm doubtful we would be able to find an Australian expert now, at such short notice."

Thus we passed on to the question of the leader, though the discussion remained of necessity rather tentative, the expedition itself being nothing else.

"Then again, do we need an explorer at all?" suggested Potter radically. "Such persons will be ten a penny in Tasmania itself, I'm sure. Perhaps we should be looking simply for a someone who possesses the right qualities of character. A man of determination and vigour. Of energy and decision. Of strength of body and mind."

It was perhaps my imagination, yet all at once I had the distinct

sensation that the doctor was not drawing some abstract profile of suitable leadership, but was subtly trying to recommend his own self. This
might seem unfair, and yet in the short time I had known him I had
observed he was a man of lively, even pushing nature. It was hardly a
prospect I could welcome. The fellow was doubtless admirable in his
own way and yet I was far from convinced of his fitness for this most
important task. Ours was no ordinary expedition, after all, but something
like a holy quest, in search of wonders of limitless significance. It would
be quite wrong to place at its head a man about whom almost nothing
was known, least of all his moral understanding. My concern, and it was
no small one, was that Mr. Childs, unpredictable enthusiast that he was,
might simply suggest the doctor as leader there and then.

"Surely," I proposed, "we should be looking for someone with a
proven commitment to principles behind this venture. Someone of
known moral purpose." I should make it clear that I had no wish to
suggest myself. To do so, would have been against my very nature, which
abhors any kind of self-advancement. The thought, indeed, had not even
occurred to me. I was simply concerned to define the correct qualities of
leadership, for the sake of the expedition.

"A geologist perhaps?" murmured Renshaw, quite unnecessarily,
glancing from Potter to myself with a provoking look.

Jonah Childs turned in my direction, seeming faintly surprised, as if
some notion had occurred to him for the first time. "Perhaps you yourself would be willing to take up the task, Vicar?"

Thus it was that, sudden and unsought for, this most difficult of
honours appeared before me. The suggestion was so unforeseen that I
found myself quite taken aback, assailed by troubling thoughts. How
could I even contemplate such a thing when there must be, surely, another far better suited? Yet where was he, though? It occurred to me that,
imperfect though I might consider myself, I was not wholly without
qualities that might prove of usefulness. I did have a knowledge of the
Scriptures, and of geology, as well as being possessed of some poor
understanding of the minds of men. So much was at stake, and so great
was the urgency! The others were stood watching me, awaiting my
reply. Could I? Should I? All at once I recalled my visionary dream of just

a few days before, and the cry I had heard: "Come hither, sweet vicar, come hither, and make haste."

There was my answer. "If you require me to lead this expedition," I declared quietly, "then I shall do it."

Dear Mr. Childs broke into a wide smile. "Bravo, Vicar, bravo!"

"We still need a boat," Renshaw insisted drearily.

In the event, a solution was nearer than we could ever have guessed. It was almost as if, having overcome one great hurdle, we had now earned a remedy to the other. Our saviour was none other than my own wife, who appeared through the door just a moment later, clutching a hatbox. "What is going on?" she demanded, regarding, with no little surprise, the great pile of expedition stores. Hardly had I begun to explain our predicament, however, when she waved her hand in dismissal, as if there could be nothing so foolish.

"But there was a ship for charter in this morning's newspaper," she declared, amazing us all. "It had a delightful name as I recall. I believe it was the *Chastity*."

CHAPTER TWO

Thirty-seven years earlier

Jack Harp
1820

IF IT HADN'T BEEN for the wind veering round northeasterly so sweet, then probably none of it would've ever happened and I'd still have that small rowboat. That is a thought.

The sealing season was done and supplies on the island were getting low, so it was time to take the big whaleboat over to George Town to call in on that penny-pinching bugger Bill Haskins. That whaleboat was a tidy vessel with a good sail on her and, though Ned was all foolishness at the tiller, so I even had to give him a cuffing or two, still it only took us two days.

Now, George Town is all well and good but it is taking a chance. Mostly you can trust them, as it's a small enough place, but you never do know what strangers might be passing through and who they might go talking to, while the last thing I was looking for was getting dropped back into prison clothes after all the trouble we'd had escaping free of them. So we didn't stop once but went straight over to Haskins. We hadn't been for a year, nearly, and first we just had ourselves a proper good look. He had some prettiest glass marbles, all different colours, like I hadn't seen since I was a lad back in Dorking in the old country. Also I found something for my cheek where my skinning knife had caught it a month back, leaving a proper gash of a cut that never would settle. I told Ned to stay quiet during the talk, as Ned was a fool for business, being only any use on the seals, and in the end I got us a good trade for our hides, with enough flour and tea and rum to last nicely, and the medicine for my cheek. There was a few coins over, too, and I did think of paying a call at the inn, and perhaps even take a turn with that Lill, but Ned was whining that we'd be noticed, so back in the boat we climbed.

Usually the journey back from George Town was a proper fight against the westerlies but this time we'd hardly set out when the breeze veered round to the northeast pretty as could be, which was a proper piece of luck. We couldn't have had an easier run and inside three days we were almost home. It was then, the wind keeping sweet, that I got to wondering about something else I might get besides tea and flour and rum. Ned, being a cowardly bugger, didn't much like the idea, having a scare of them that I was thinking of, but I won him round, calling him names and saying if we got two then he could have one all for himself. Ned was always one who could be talked along. He paid dear enough for it, too, in the end, as things turned out.

So we carried on clean past the island and then turned south along the coast that is mostly trees, till I saw smoke from one of their fires up ahead. After that we went careful. I took the sail down and took us close in to the shore to be less seen. It wasn't easy landing there, as the surf was wild, but in the end we beached her in a creek a mile or two distant from them. It was while we were hiding the boat in bushes that Ned came over with his scares, and bad too, so he was no use even after cuffing talk, so I left him there and went off alone, keeping myself hid in the trees. A good bitch I spotted straight off, too, diving off a rock for shellfish, not an inch of clothes on her, with a good pair of racks, and her fluff and crack showing like she was just waiting for it.

After that I went back to the boat and Ned till the time was right. We couldn't have a fire, of course, and that night was cold. A while before first light I went off, going quiet, finding my way by the moon till I saw their fire. There must have been thirty of them, all sleeping close to the blaze as they could without getting burned, as if they were scared of what might come out of the dark. That gave me a chuckle. I crept round to the gin I'd seen before, and hauled her up by the arm. Well, she was trouble, that piece, yelling and biting like some raw animal, and getting the others after me, too. I was expecting that, mind, and when they got close I put a bullet through the nearest, which scared the rest nicely, though it didn't stop her from squirming and such. Even when Ned and me got her in the boat she was carrying on worse than ever, so I quite worried she might capsize us and spill our stores over the side. I said to Ned, "We've got ourselves a right warrior here." She was that bad, in fact, that when we finally got back to the island I wouldn't have her in the cabin but fixed her with a chain outside, and even then she'd bite and scratch when I worked her. Ned wanted his turn but I told him no, as he'd not earned it.

Then I got a surprise. Just a few weeks later I found three barrels of the new flour were spoiled right through. That was trouble. We'd not last just on the rest, I knew, so I had to go back to George Town in the whaleboat to get my redress. Ned said he was feeling crook and stayed behind.

Bill Haskins moaned, which I knew he would, and said I must've let the flour get damp and that was why it had spoiled, which was never true. He did give me two barrels in the end, though, which was only part but was better than nothing and would be about enough to last us, I reckoned. What with other things that needed doing, and a night with that Lill at the inn besides—which was taking a risk, but I did it anyway— it was a ten days before I got back to the island.

I guessed something was wrong when I saw there was no smoke coming from the chimney. Sure enough, when I walked up to the cabin carrying one of the barrels of flour, what did I find lying just outside the door but Ned, with his trousers round his ankles and his head stove in like a bust pumpkin, the stone that had done it sat just nearby, all stained. He must have been there a time, as the birds had had themselves a good feed, especially his belly and face. The gin was gone of course and so was the small rowboat.

Well, it was no mystery to me what had happened. She'd tempted him. She'd learned a few words to speak, while I'd seen him watching her, and that silly sod Ned tempted easy as butter. Once she'd got him thirsting for her strong she must've witched him into opening up her lock and letting her free, and then, while he was busy getting his rewards, she'd have given him a tap with that stone. When I was putting him in the ground I saw his tackle had been got at nasty, which I reckoned was her rather than the birds.

D'you know I never could find that small rowboat. Three days I spent searching along the coast where she must have landed but there was never so much as a splinter. I reckoned she must've stove her in. Well, that did strike me as an unnecessary sort of act, and mean too.

This last seal season since has been a good one, mind, being as fine almost as I've known, so I'm hoping I might have enough skins to trade myself a new rowboat down at George Town. If there's one to be had, that is. I never do feel safe with just the one boat, you see, in case of accident. Who knows, if the wind's right I might even get myself another gin afterwards. She'd have to be less of the warrior this time, though.

Peevay
1824–28

ONCE WHEN I was small and always running hither and thither, and all the world was puzzles to confound, I got myself that little surprise. Even now that bugger does stir tenderest feelings deep inside my breast. Other fellows might lose their way after that ruination, never to find it after, but not me. I did endure. Then again, enduring always was my special skill.

That was in long-ago times, many summers past, before everything got changed, so it is hard to perceive that was just the same me as now. Why, I never even knew these words to speak then. But still I can recollect. Day I got my surprise was hot, blowflies were biting and everyone was stopped by a wide pool, shallow as your foot. Bigger children were splashing to be cool and stop the flies, and suddenly all I wanted was to get some of that splashing too. Into the pool I ran, fast like the wind. But below the water it was slippery, so my feet were skidding and down I fell, hard, with a grievous blow. Then, when I pulled myself up, feeling a sore knee, that hateful thing did occur.

Just there in the water, you see, all at once there was a stranger, and this stranger was like a monster. His face was almost ordinary but that just made him worse because his hair was so wrong. This was never the colour of hair at all, no, but pale like grass goes after hot days. His eyes stared at me. When I gave a start, the monster's face rippled.

For a moment I thought the others might have got monsters too. But when I looked they just had themselves, upside down.

Mongana saw. "Freak," he screamed. Mongana was my worst of all foes in those long-ago days. Mongana means blowfly and it was just so, as his best pleasure was stinging and biting. The little scut was two summers older and hated me ever since I could recollect, so his hatred was an always thing like wind in the trees. Often he would follow me, trying to trick me unawares with some kick or grievous blow, so I never went anywhere without a waddy stick to be ready. "D'you like what you see, freak?" he shouted. Then he splashed, and his splashing was as hating as his shout, and when the others splashed too I went away.

Later, when they'd left, I returned to the pool, just in case the monster was gone now. But when I walked into the water there he was still, staring up at me with those frightened eyes.

Of course the great mystery of those long-ago days was what in fuck happened to Mother and Father. Other children had theirs, unless they died, yet I had neither, nor even any distant recollection. When I asked I never got answers, but just angry looks and sometimes a grievous blow.

"Never you mind," Grandmother would say with eyes like cuts. Grandmother often was angry with me. She was my friend, my protector, my family, but though she was kindly, her kindness was always a little hating. It was just her way. It was she who gave me meat as we sat by the fire, popping it into my mouth with her long, bony fingers, but when she gave it she would scowl. "I don't know why I bother feed you. You're nothing but trouble." Likewise if we were all walking to some new place and I was crook, she was the one who kindly picked me up and carried me on her shoulders, but then she'd pinch my leg hard so it hurt. Sometimes I got so angry I hated her right back and would go off and sleep just by myself on the other side of the fire. But she was my family, so in the end I always did return. When I came back she wouldn't say a word but gave me food just like before.

Of course now, all these years later, I know why Grandmother was hating in her kindness. I don't blame her none, either. Why in scut not,

Grandmother? I might ponder. But when you're just small you never question the why of things. You just swallow them like air.

"Forget Mother," she said, when I provoked her with my asking, which I did often, as I never was one to give up a thing when I had begun. "She's gone and that's all." This was everything I ever could get from her.

But of course I wouldn't forget. I asked Tartoyen.

Now, Tartoyen was almost more my friend than Grandmother, though he was not my family. He had no sons, just daughters, and I did divine that was why even then. Tartoyen was a little fat and had lazy eyes, but he was clever and hardly got wrathful at all except when he was feeling crook, so everyone listened to what he said, and did it too, usually. He never grumbled that I was some little scut and just trouble, like Grandmother did. Sometimes he taught me new things, which was tidings of joy. Best of all, if he caught Mongana and other enemies trying to wound me with some grievous blow he would strike them down. But even Tartoyen got strange when I asked about Mother. His face would change, like he saw black rain clouds coming.

"She went away across the sea," was all he'd say, and he wouldn't look me in my face like usual but turned his head away. It was even worse if I asked about Father. Then his eyes would go narrow. "You don't have any father. You never did. Now stop bothering me with these things. Your mother's dead. If she was alive she'd come back."

Still I never did believe him quite. I did and I didn't, both at the same time. When we were stopped by the shore I would look out at the big noisy waves and dream Mother walking out of them. She was tall and fine and better than any mother those others had. In her hand she'd carry a rush basket filled with strange food from wherever she'd been across the sea—muttonfish big like stones, but sweet like honey, and roots blue as the sea—and she'd give these all to me, smiling in some tenderest way like Grandmother never did. Sometimes she'd bring Father with her but I never could see him well. That's a thing with dreaming. Sometimes your dreams are confounding and won't do what you want, even though they're yours. I did try hard but I could never make Father have arms or legs, so he just seemed to hang above the water, like a kind of cloud with a face.

If there was one enemy of my dreamings it was that little scut Mongana and his mother, whose name was Pagerly, as they would do anything to give me hardship. Pagerly would try and turn others against me by telling piss-poor falsehoods, saying I struck their babies with grievous blows when they weren't watching, or that I cursed them secretly and this was why they got crook. If I heard her saying such heinous stuff, then I'd shout, loud as I could, that she was just some lying scut and they shouldn't listen. Mostly they knew I was right, but only mostly, and I could see they never believed me all the way through into their deepest breasts. Sometimes I could feel their eyes on me, wondering.

Mongana was almost worse. He would say any poisoning thing just to cause me woe and spoil my dreamings. "Where's your mother, freak? Don't you know? I'll tell you. When she saw how ugly you were she tried to kill you and then she ran away to die."

"That's not true. She went away across the sea. Tartoyen said so."

But Mongana was hateful and his favourite game was to drop words in your ear like poison ants' eggs. "Tartoyen just says that so you won't cry."

Afterwards I tried to drown those words, like pissing on fire, but they would hatch and I felt their bites. When I sat by the sea and tried to dream Mother and Father it would go all wrong. Yes, she would step from the waves all tall and fine like before, but then she wouldn't smile at me at all, but would walk right past with a face like stone, as if she didn't want to know me now. That was hateful.

But time passed, and I did endure. As I told, enduring always was my special skill. I endured Mongana and on lucky days I even got the scut with some grievous blow. Why, with time I even thought less often about that mystery of what happened to Mother and Father.

Sometimes we stayed in some place and sometimes we walked again, hither and thither. In hot days we were in the bush and Tartoyen and the others hunted game, which we cooked on the fire. When cool winds came and bush was getting just ice and snow and so we went by the sea with its huge waves and noise, and we built huts lined with tea tree bark, where we'd stay warm, and we'd eat muttonfish or sometimes seal if we got one.

Little by little I began to recollect places where we went, till I knew those hills and mountains and even where the world stopped. Slowly slowly I could solve some of those puzzles to confound. Tartoyen took us to that valley in the hills where red ochre was and he showed me how he put it in his hair to make it so beautiful. He taught me how to know what weather was coming next, just from that hazy ring round the moon, or from the shape of clouds, and his ways were so clever he hardly ever was wrong. He showed me how to make spears sharp with fire and my teeth—so sharp they'd almost catch in rock—and how to throw them too, though I was still too small to throw them far. I learned how to follow animals from the marks they left, and to know which tree possum climbed by the scratch he left on the bark with his claws. And I learned about KANUNNAH, who was ugly and heinous with his long hanging head and stripes on his back, and who was our hated foe. Kanunnah would kill you if you did not spear him first and most of all he liked to eat children. Quite often we saw kanunnah though he ran away when he saw we were so many.

Also I learned of WRAGGEOWRAPPER, who was ugly and tall and came in the darkness sometimes, fast like the wind, and shrieked like trees creaking. Wraggeowrapper would stare at us when we slept and was a most grievous foe because you never could see him. He would make men go mad if he caught them at night away from the fire, but we were too clever and stayed near. When we sat so in the dark, after our eating, Tartoyen told us stories—secret stories that I will not say even now—about the moon and sun, and how everyone got made, from men and wallaby to seal and kangaroo rat and so. Also he told who was in those rocks and mountains and stars, and how they went there. Until, by and by, I could hear stories as we walked across the world, and divine how it got so, till I knew world as if he was some family fellow of mine.

Sometimes we met TARKINER, who were southwards of the world. Tarkiner were almost friends, and three women of ours came from them, though some words they spoke were strange, and they did things that were just piss-poor foolish, like getting fearful if we put mutton-fish in the fire to cook, as they said this would make the rains come, which it never would. If we met them at the edge of the world we would stop sometimes and tell any news, and in the night we would camp together and stay awake late to see who was best at dances, Tarkiner or us, though it was always us.

Also there were ROINGIN, who were northwards and were our foes. They always were this ever since anyone could remember, being heinous scuts who couldn't be trusted if you turned your back just to piss against a tree. Tartoyen told us stories of old wars with Roingin and how they never did win except by low cheating. Even lately there was some battle, where Gonar's uncle got speared in his leg, one of theirs too, and some others speared too, though I was too small to recollect this. Mostly we kept away from that end of the world and when we went near we spoke little and went carefully. We never were scared of Roingin, of course, as they were only cowards, but they were more than us, as Roingin were famous for being many. Once when we were at the edge of the world I saw them, that whole mob, plenty of them, sitting by the sea eating muttonfish, which was interesting. They saw us too, of course, but they pretended they never did, while Tartoyen made everybody stay quiet and so we went away without any war that time. Afterwards Gonar said we were foolish not to fight Roingin and spear them dead, as Gonar did love fighting better than everything, being angry like some fight got inside him and wouldn't let him rest. But others knew Tartoyen was right, as Roingin were so many.

So time passed. I grew taller, until, by and by, I did suppose I knew every thing now, and there were no mysteries to confound anymore. Of course in truth I knew piss-poor little. Why, I knew only half, and that whole other half was sat there waiting, like one kanunnah, licking his lips.

One day it was warm and there was rain but no wind, so drops fell straight like stones. We were in the bush, sitting quiet and watching meat cooking in the fire, and the smoke smelled good, as this was the first game we caught for days and we were hungry after eating just roots. Then Gonar, who went off to the edge of that clearing to do shittings, came running back and shouted in a whispering way, "Something's coming."

Now if something's coming and you don't know what it is there's no prudence just waiting for it to walk on you. Tartoyen signalled with his hands and we went away into trees without any noise, to a place some way off, with bushes to hide, though we could see between the leaves. Then twigs were breaking, telling us this something coming was clumsy. In fact it was three somethings. No, I had never seen creatures so strange, I do recollect. They were the shape of men but only this. Their skin was not like skin at all but was the colour of stone, and loose, so it flapped. Even their feet were ugly, too big and with no toes. Worst, though, were their faces. These were coloured like raw meat, with no alive look in them. Up they walked through the rain, which was getting heavy now, so it made the trees clap. They stopped when they saw the fire and meat, but then they ran towards it, very fast and grabbing.

I looked at Tartoyen and to my surprise I saw he looked just woeful. Then I saw everyone was woeful now, even Gonar, who would fight the wind itself. That was some puzzle to confound and made me curious. "What are they?" I whispered.

D'you know Tartoyen went angry, like I never saw him go angry before. "Ghosts," he said, like I said something bad about him. "Dead men jumped up."

When everything's got suddenly strange, one more strange thing seems almost usual. So this was what happened to dead ones, I did suppose. It was scaring but also interesting. I did observe those ghosts didn't look happy being dead but were restless, like they had bad aches inside. Also they were too hungry. They never stopped to see who made that fire but just started eating the meat. Our meat. Its cooking wasn't finished and it must have been hot as burning but they just tore off big pieces and put them in their mouths, very rude. Death gave them some big appetite I did divine.

Here were many mysteries to confound. So I tried to surmise why Tartoyen never told me about these ghosts before, though he told me everything else. Also I pondered if ghosts could die, though this seemed impossible when they were already dead. I was thinking so, rain was clapping, and others were watching ghosts eat our meat when all suddenly I saw Mongana's mother give me a hating look, sharper than spears. Sometimes you do just know a heinous awful something is going to happen, and sure enough, now she pointed right at my face.

"It's his fault."

All at once every one of them was looking at me. I didn't understand. "What d'you mean?"

For a moment nobody said a word and the only sound was that rain clapping quicker and quicker, making the leaves shiver. Then Mongana's mother gave Tartoyen a look that was full of scornings, which was strange too, as he was Tartoyen and no one did that usually. "Go on, tell him."

I supposed Tartoyen would give her words like some grievous blow, but no, he just closed his eyes like his head ached and never spoke a word. Grandmother did instead, yes, whispering like some snarl, "Leave him alone."

But there is no trap like a mystery to confound. Even if you know the answer is some terrible hardship to endure, still you must hear. "Tell me."

Tartoyen he let out a big breath and sort of sagged, like belly meat. "Your father was like them. A ghost."

That was some mystery to confound, bigger than any other. How could I be the child of some dead man? Yet those looks of others told me it must be so, as they were changed now, as if I was some piss-poor strange fellow, or Roingin. Then I did recollect that long-ago afternoon, and that stranger looking up from the shallow pool. So I could divine this truth. Yes, that was ghosts' hair I had, and ghosts' monster face. This was some terrible thing. All this while here I was, breathing and eating for years, and mostly things stayed just the same. Days came and went and I thought I knew everything. Then all at once, quick as slipping and falling, I found every day of it was really just some hateful foolishness. Suddenly I got angry, and I most of all I got angry with Tartoyen, who was supposed to be my good friend.

"Why didn't you tell me?" I didn't even whisper it. I hardly cared if those ghosts came and killed us all.

Tartoyen didn't answer me but just looked at the ground, where a little grey beetle was walking over some leaf.

"You lied to me. You said I had no father."

Tartoyen closed his eyes. "He wasn't like a father. He just came one time in the night and took away your mother."

Now I saw Grandmother pointed her long, bony finger at Tartoyen's face. "You let him steal her from me. You all did."

D'you know, they all looked shamed. All because they didn't kill Father that long time ago. The only one who wasn't, and was just hating, was Mongana's mother, Pagerly. "My husband fought him even if none of you did. Don't you forget that," she snarled. "He wasn't scared of any ghost. He was brave when you were cowards. And his ghost"–she pointed at me–"killed him for it with his thunder noise."

Mongana was crying.

So I learned why they both hated me all this while. Mongana's father got killed by Father. It was all bad, very bad. Still I had to know more, even if it was just worse. "What happened to Mother?"

Grandmother shrugged. "She escaped from the ghost's island and came back to us. But by then anger got inside her and wouldn't let her rest. So one day, after you were born, she went away to kill him. I tried to make her stay but there was no telling your mother what to do."

That was when Pagerly gave me a gleeful look, as if she had some special hating thing for me. "She wanted to kill you, Peevay. She wanted to smash your head against a tree. She said so. She would have, too, if she hadn't been so weak."

That was the very worst thing of them all, I do recollect, and I felt quite weak with piss-poor woeful feelings deep inside my breast. Mongana was right after all. Mother wanted to kill me. She never would step from the sea with special food just for me.

So finally ended that mystery of what in fuck happened to Mother and Father. I saw others watching me, and their looks were as if I was different now, not quite like them, which was heinous. All of a sudden everything in all the whole world was just spoiled, and it was all my fault besides. All I wanted was to put it back like it had been just before, when we were sat around the fire, quiet and ordinary and waiting for meat.

"Look, they've gone," said Gonar.

I'd forgotten about the ghosts. Sure enough when we peered through the trees there was no sign. Carefully we left those bushes and returned to the fire. Ghosts' tracks went away running, as if they heard our talkings and got scared. There was hardly any meat left except for just bones.

Tartoyen looked up, like dark clouds had passed. "Let's find some more game."

So he and some others went away to hunt. The rest of us started collecting wood for that fire. All was quiet and people were just doing ordinary things, like everything was the same, but of course it wasn't really. I couldn't forget Mongana's mother's words, saying how Mother wanted to kill me, or the way they all looked at me like I was different from them. When others weren't watching, I suddenly walked away, but slow, as if I must go pissing or so. Once I was out of their sight I started running. Away I went, faster and faster, till it was as if the trees and bushes were running too, and wind was on my face, and ground could hardly even happen quick enough to catch my feet, and I felt good right through to my bones to be getting away. Down a valley I went, jumping across a small stream, then up that other side and on, till I was gasping and my heart was clapping faster than the rain. Even then I never stopped, but I ran through trees and bushes that cut my legs, hither and thither, till finally I could go no further, and I dropped down by that old log.

So I lay there, waiting. Of course I never had been all alone before and soon it was curious. Everything was so still. I lay by the log and listened to birds singing and trees moving and they all seemed very loud. By and by my heartfelt desire was for Tartoyen and Grandmother and others to come and find me, and to be piss-poor sorry for what they said, crying and telling me Mother never wanted to kill me after all, which was just lies. Yes, and they could give Mongana and his mother some grievous blows besides, very hard. So it would be almost as if nothing ever happened after all, and those dread feelings deep inside my breast could just go away.

But that was one vain hope. There were no footsteps, no shouts. Nothing happened at all, except for flies biting and birds calling. Finally it got dark and I knew they wouldn't come. Suddenly I detested them so I hardly cared that I was alone and had no fire. I even wanted kanunnah to come with his long ugly head and kill me with his teeth. Or Wraggeowrapper to drop down from the trees and make me go mad. Truly, I didn't give one scut about either.

But kanunnah and Wraggeowrapper didn't come. In fact nothing happened. I just fell asleep.

Next day everything was just the same except that I decided to die. I ate nothing and drank nothing and made myself a good bed to die on, out of moss and grass and fern leaves, just beside the log. Then I waited. But it's not so easy just to die like that. I was itchy where the flies bit and the bushes scratched, and my hands wouldn't keep still. Also I couldn't decide whether to die lying on my side or on my back. Till finally it was dark, and again I fell asleep.

Then, on the third day, something most curious and confounding happened. I awoke and it was just getting light, with a red sky like blood. I was thirsty and hungry. But most of all, even though nothing was new, I got blissful, so much that it was as if I never had been blissful before. Why, I felt weak as if I was crook with some great good fortune and tidings of joy, and it wouldn't let me keep still so my hands were shaking. That was one puzzle to confound. I wanted to shout and surprise the trees and biting flies. I wanted to be alive whatever Mongana or his mother said. I wanted to be alive even if no single pisser in all the world, friend or hated foe, wanted me to be alive. That still does confound me even in these long-after days, when all world is so changed. Perhaps it was just because I was so hungry. Or it was that I had discovered my special skill, which was to endure. For that was surely what I had found.

So I decided to go and find the others, as I never even hated those buggers anymore. Not that this was easy. It was some time since I ran away to that log and even then I paid piss-poor heed whither I was going, while this part of the world was all forest, and thick too, so I never could see any hill or rock or other friendly thing to tell me the way. Those trees were worrisome. One moment I would think I knew them, and was saved, then I would see they were telling grievous falsehoods and were just different trees making themselves look the same. Also I felt light in my head from being hungry so my feet kept catching the ground and making me stumble.

Finally I reached a path, and though I didn't recognize which one it was I saw there were footmarks. They looked fresh, just a day or so old, and were enough for all my ones, which was interesting, so I followed, pondering what I would say to them all when I found them, and what they would say to me. I never had been alone like this before and now I felt very brave. I followed them until I could hear birds fighting, which meant something bad, so I went carefully. Sure enough, just ahead that path went into a big clearing and there, looking through leaves, I saw a big crowd of birds, pecking and tugging. It was those three ghosts they were eating. They had spears in them, plenty of them, and were in different places in that clearing as if they tried to run away. So now I knew you could kill them even though they were dead. Why, I felt a little sad for them, though they ate our meat and caused me so much heinous trouble. I threw a stone and made the birds go away, though they just went a short way off, jumping and waiting.

This was a puzzle to confound. Tartoyen let them go away before, saying we must hunt game instead, so who speared them like this? I went close to look, as it was interesting even after what the birds did. Are you Father? I did ponder. Or you? One had hair just like mine, and when I touched this it felt the same too. Another still had one eye, which was blue as cold days' sky. Then, when I touched their skin, which was the colour of stone, I saw that it was not really their skin at all but a false one. Beneath was real and this was pale like their raw meat faces. At least my skin was human colour.

Though it was interesting I was too hungry to stay long. So I threw another stone at the birds and then went on along the path again, following those footmarks. Then, by and by, I smelt a smell, which was the best, finest and most delicious smell, of smoke from a campfire, where meat might be cooking. When you are hungry as piss, your nose will find it, yes, though it comes from behind whole mountains. Hunger makes your eyes tired, you see, and your ears too, but your nose is cleverer than ever.

Well, that smell gave me strength to make my tired feet walk onwards, till I reached the top of a hill, and there, rising up from the forest, I saw a thin stick of smoke. That was great good fortune and tidings of joy. Yes, I thought, now I am saved. So down I ran, fast as the wind.

George Baines, Employee of the New World Land Company
1828

Dearest Father,

I am sadly conscious of the many weeks that have passed since I wrote to you last, and hope you will not think your son neglectful, but you will know how infrequently a boat is sent from this most remote of places. As to my news, I know hardly where to begin, so great have been the changes to the settlement—and to my own circumstances—that have occurred. I cannot say all has been easy. Often have I thought of you, gazing upon a class of pupils through your spectacles, so stern and wise, and always knowing, with such seeming ease, what is right.

The final journey from Hobart town—which is hardly more than a sprawling seaport village—was less bad than I had feared, and I was not nearly so seasick as I was coming from England. More troubling altogether was the state of the settlement that was to be my new home. While I knew this had been in existence hardly a year, still I was taken aback by what I found. Aside from Company House, which had been brought down in pieces especially from England, and seemed quite splendid, all the rest was composed of the simplest bark huts, without even floorboards or plasterwork to keep out the wind. I did my best to accept this simplicity without complaint, but to think instead of my enthusiasm for the prospects of this great new company, and my own part within it, until, as winter turned to spring and the winds began to grow kindlier, I became gradually quite accustomed to my primitive little home. I also became more used to the landscape. This is never Dorset, being in every way wilder and less formed, yet it is not without its own charm. I developed a particular affection for the eucalyptuses, that are known here as gum trees. These grow in profusion and possess a wonderful lightness of colour—the way their delicate leaves flutter in the breeze quite raises the spirit—while their tangy scent seems the very essence of this strange land.

The other company men were friendly enough for the most part. The stockkeepers, who are the foot soldiers of the establishment, and are a tough breed, treated me with more charity than they treated each other, I imagine on account of my youth, and they even gave me a nickname, "the Little Preacher," because I seemed so serious of expression. It became something of a joke that I wished to reform their ways, which, of course, was far beyond my intention, and even Mr. Charles, the chairman, joined in the game. "Still not got them singing hymns, Mr. Baines?" he would call out when he passed me.

I was assigned as an assistant to Mr. Pierce, the company agriculturist. This man was not greatly liked within the settlement, and the stockkeepers in particular made no secret of the fact that I had, as they put it, "drawn the short straw," talking of Mr. Pierce as "a strange one" and "not right in his head." I remained reluctant to give credence to such views, considering it was better to make my own opinion of the man–this being a course you yourself have always advocated–though I confess I found Mr. Pierce did seem a most curious fellow. His face was usually graced with frowns and looks of puzzlement, as if he was too much given to thinking for his own good. He seemed to have as little time for the others as they had for him, though towards myself he was always kindly and patient. My duties mostly took the form of accompanying him on tours of inspection, walking across the company lands to visit the various stockkeepers and attending to any animals that were sick. These walks could be tiring, especially when the weather was bad–which it so often is here–but they were a most effective means of learning about my adopted home, there being, I believe, no better way to get to know a land than to walk across it, feeling its earth beneath your feet and smelling its scents.

It was on my second such expedition that we came upon some of the Van Diemen's Land natives. We were crossing an area of open grassland when we caught sight of some sixty of the fellows idling beside a campfire, and I must tell you they were quite the strangest creatures I have ever set eyes upon. They were tall, and some might have even have called them handsome in their savage way, though all, male and female, were in a state of utter nakedness. If their appearance were not startling enough it was rendered more so by the curious way they arranged their hair: the men had theirs stained with some form of red-coloured substance, so it fell in thick strands, like scarlet ropes, while the women kept their heads close-shaven so they were almost hairless (a style which could hardly have been described as ladylike).

I would gladly have kept a good distance from the creatures. Mr. Pierce, however, insisted on approaching them–he claimed to have done so several times before, without ever suffering injury–while I, as his assistant, had little choice but to follow. In the event, fortunately, they proved friendly enough in their way, even giving us some meat from a wallaby they had killed and cooked upon their fire, and which did not taste so bad as one might think. Mr. Pierce, who had learned some of their names during his earlier encounters, insisted we remain sitting with them for a good while, even to the neglect of our work, as he attempted to learn words of their language. If truth be told I was more than a little impatient to leave. There seemed no knowing what really lay in their thoughts as they sat around us, so strange and numerous, sometimes touching my hair or my clothes to satiate their curiosity. For all I knew they might be secretly planning to murder us with their spears, which they had with them in great quantity, and which were fearsome instruments, light yet sharp as needles, so they looked as if they would pierce thickest leather.

When we finally walked back through the rain Mr. Pierce would talk of nothing else but what capital fellows they were. I believe I had never seen him so animated, indeed, clapping his large hands in the air with excitement. I even found his excitability a little troubling. Curious though the natives might be, they hardly seemed the chief concern of a company officer with duties to perform. His partiality would, I believe, have been of less concern to me had it not been for the antagonism between himself and the stockkeepers. As we walked, he insisted on confiding in me that he thought them "ruffians" who "belonged in gaol." Hearing the man's resentment of his fellows, I could not help but wonder if, in some strange way, his lonely enthusiasm for the natives was another expression of this same antipathy. It was a thought that I kept to myself.

It was not long afterwards that I came down with a fever that confined me to my hut. Mr. Charles, the company chairman, and his wife could not have been kinder. They came to visit several times when I was bad, Mrs. Charles bringing me soup to help keep up my strength, and insisting that if I was not better directly I should come and stay in Company House. This was a most generous thought. The building would probably seem of little account to you, Father, who are quite spoiled for architecture, but the longer I remained in the settlement, the finer it appeared, with its verandah and hallway and glass in every window. It was, indeed, the one object that gave our rough settlement an aura of civilization. In the event I soon began to improve, and so never had need to stay there, and yet I do believe the very thought of this grand and kindly sanctuary helped greatly in my recovery.

Then one afternoon, as I was sitting on a log outside my hut, convalescing in the spring sunshine, I heard shouting and, glancing up, I saw a most curious sight. Into the settlement was striding Mr. Pierce, before him Higgs and Sutton, two of the stockkeepers. Mr. Pierce was quite white with fury, and was driving the pair like some angry dog herding sheep, while they cursed as only stockkeepers know how. As Mr. Pierce passed, he waved at me to follow, which I did readily enough—being more than a little curious—to the door of Company House. Mr. Charles emerged to find himself the adjudicator of a most heated discussion. Mr. Pierce, quite stuttering with anger, claimed that he had found the bodies of two aborigines, both of them buried—though poorly—within fifty yards of the stockkeepers' hut. Examining these he had found them both to have been shot to death. What was more, he claimed on several previous occasions to have seen the two stockkeepers trying to tempt native women into their hut in a way that he claimed would certainly have provoked their menfolk.

"They're murderers, nothing less," he exclaimed, "and they must be taken to Hobart as murderers and hanged."

Higgs and Sutton were equally vehement in their denials, insisting that they had seen several wild-looking men who they supposed must be runaway convicts, and that these must have been responsible. This seemed hardly a very plausible claim. It was true that there is a penal colony on this side of the island at Macquarie Harbour, to the south along the coast, and it was likewise true that convicts have been known sometimes to escape, yet the distance is great and the terrain notoriously difficult, and as far as is known all escapees had either returned voluntarily or perished of cold and want. It was far more likely that the stockkeepers had killed the blacks. While I felt sympathy for Mr. Pierce, I am afraid his wild talk of hanging hardly added to his case. The two wanted teaching a good lesson, certainly, but they were men we all knew.

Mr. Charles did his best to calm matters. "I have made it clear before now I will not permit cruelty to the native population," he insisted, "and this will be looked into with the utmost care."

It seemed a most reasonable reply and yet Mr. Pierce still remained unsatisfied. "They will be dismissed?"

Mr. Charles considered this hardly proper. "They have not been proved guilty and so must have a right to be considered innocent."

His answer elicited a little nod of thanks from the two.

In truth I suspected the chairman's thoughts were less concerned with principles of justice than the needs of the settlement, there being already barely enough men to keep all in order. Mr. Pierce, though, showed little interest in *such practicalities. He grew red in the face and began shouting quite needlessly, stammering that this was, "evil permitted, which is no better than evil done." Such language was hardly respectful, and yet Mr. Charles took it calmly enough, reminding him that it was several weeks before the next boat from Hobart was due, and suggesting that we all attempt to forget the matter until then.*

In the event, this proved hardly possible, as only a few days later matters took quite another turn, when one of the stockkeepers observed a group of blacks deliberately killing some of the sheep. He tried to scare them away, only to himself receive a slight spear wound to the leg. Thirty-five animals were butchered that day, while by the end of that week we had lost a further sixty-four. Our entire herd numbered fewer than five hundred, all of which had been brought hither with the greatest difficulty and expense. What was more, we were expecting the ship Champion *to arrive direct from England within the next two months, bringing animals of a type not yet to be found in Van Diemen's Land, and which were intended as breeding stock. Their loss was not to be contemplated.*

The days which followed were tense indeed. Mr. Charles was often to be seen strolling through the settlement, his fine, noble brow furrowed with worry. He took what measures he could. All were instructed to carry arms at all times, and two men were posted to guard the settlement day and night. The animals and stockkeepers were all moved northwards, closer to the settlement, so that they could be more easily safeguarded: an arrangement that could of necessity only be temporary, the grassland being of limited extent. Such precautions would seem nothing less than essential and yet, I am sad to say, there remained one officer who insisted, and loudly so, that they were wholly misguided: Mr. Pierce. It was as if the man deliberately sought ever greater extremity of opinion, until he could be satisfied by nothing short of plain wrongheadedness. He even opposed the requirement that weapons be carried at all times, his justification being that this was in itself a form of provocation. His suggestion was that we should instead endeavour to communicate with the natives, and persuade them of our regret at what had occurred, while he even offered to go himself, and try and use the few words of their language he had learned. Mr. Charles was not persuaded, needless to say, having the wisdom to see that such behaviour would win nothing more peaceable than a shower of spears.

Presently all seemed to grow quieter once again. A week went by without any further incidents, or even sightings of the natives, then another, and I began to hope that Mr. Charles's prompt measures had been effective. In time Mr. Pierce and myself even resumed our tours of inspection, which were now much shortened, the animals being brought nearer. As we walked, Mr. Pierce was forever complaining of his gun, as if to carry it were some form of unjust punishment.

"Useless damnable thing," he would grumble, rapidly blinking in that curious way of his. "I'd happily fling it away. But that would hardly do, now would it? No, good Mr. Charles would never like that at all." With this he would look at me in a signifying sort of way, as if to include me in his dissatisfaction. Though he never expected me to join in his tirades, still they left me feeling most awkward, as if to listen at all was somehow to condone his words.

Then one morning we saw that some sheep had strayed beyond the new fence, back into the lands from which they had been moved. It was hardly a disaster. The number of animals was not great, and we soon found the breakage in the fence through which they had escaped, and effected a repair. What was more surprising was that all had occurred within the clear view of one of the stockkeepers' huts. It was that belonging to Sutton and Higgs.

"They will regret this," Mr. Pierce declared, with some satisfaction.

Such was his strength of feeling that I found myself frequently trying to placate him. "They probably haven't been gone long. They may be at Smith and Crane's hut, getting some materials to mend the fence."

"Then let us find them."

When we reached the next hut, however, we were surprised to discover that this was also unoccupied. Even when we climbed a hillock just nearby we could see not one stockkeeper, though their animals were near, and several of them should have been visible.

All at once I began to feel troubled. "What can have happened?"

Mr. Pierce was dismissive, though I observed his look was uneasy. "We've seen no sign of anything wrong. I would say this is merely a case of gross neglectfulness. Mr. Charles must certainly be informed, and informed without delay."

Hardly had we begun to retrace our steps towards the settlement, however, when there rang through the air an unmistakable sound: gunshots. They seemed to be coming from the northwest, from the direction of the sea, and, judging from their faintness, were some distance away. Their regularity indicated nothing less *than a battle, and as I listened there came into my mind an awful vision, of men fighting for their lives against a gang of murderous natives, hurling clouds of those light, needle-sharp spears. Mr. Pierce said not a word but simply turned about, looking pale, and began marching towards the din. Thus we hurried onwards, my heart pounding, my gun at the ready, and my thoughts much troubled by how little practice I had had in the use of weapons.*

We were still far off when, all at once, the shots ceased. "I hope we're not too late," I remarked.

Mr. Pierce nodded grimly.

Without the sound to guide us it was harder to be certain of our direction, but we proceeded as best we could, through a stretch of woodland and alongside a little stream, until finally we found ourselves on a little grassy headland above the sea. All was as calm as could be, with no sound besides the wind and the cries of the birds. I was quite wondering if we had reached the wrong place, or even if the gunshots might, after all, have some quite innocent explanation, when Mr. Pierce, who had reached a cluster of rocks near the edge, gave a shout: "Over here." As I grew near, I saw that on one of the stones, looking strangely neat, was what looked like the painted outline of a human hand, shining red. It wasn't yet dry.

Mr. Pierce was already clambering over the rocks beyond, and I heard him utter a kind of groan. I followed him, and suddenly all about me was blood. It glistened on leaves and blades of grass. It lay collected in scarlet rock pools. In a moment I was quite covered with the stuff, sticky on my hands and clothes. Only when I reached the cliff's edge did I discover its source. There, far below at the bottom of the precipice, they lay, lapped and tugged by the waves. I had never seen such a sight. Smashed limbs. Smashed heads. Insides spilled. All was brightest redness, as if from some scarlet spring bubbling up from the beneath.

Every one of them was a native. Together they must have formed half the tribe I had seen.

I will confess that, apart from the very horror of the discovery, my first feeling was a kind of weak relief that they were not, after all, men I knew. It may seem callous, but in a remote place such as this a man does feel strong loyalty to his fellows. The feeling was short-lived, however, quickly turning to greatest disgust, as I began to contemplate what had been done.

Mr. Pierce, needless to say, was greatly distraught, sobbing openly, in a manner that was painful to behold, as he attempted to descend the cliff, though there seemed little enough purpose now, as there was no sign of life below. The tide was coming in, and I could see that some of the dead were already being gently lifted from their places by the waves. After several attempts, and my own urgent appeals, he finally acknowledged that the way was too steep, and he sat beside me, very still, murmuring to himself again and again, almost in the manner of a chant, "They shall be punished for this."

I could see now that, unlike myself, he had been fearing exactly such an occurrence from the first, as we had hurried towards the sound of gunshots. He had never for a moment supposed that it was company men who were in peril. I felt ashamed. Why, at that moment I do believe I felt almost as strongly as he. In a curious way the sight of the poor creatures bleeding and broken made them seem all the more pitiably familiar. Smash a man to pieces and he will look much the same, regardless of his skin or manner of speech.

If any faintest doubts remained in my mind as to who was responsible they were dispelled soon enough. We were barely halfway back to the settlement when we came upon them, ambling home without hurry: ten stockkeepers, Sutton at their head, and all of them carrying their guns with a kind of bravado. Some wore wet clothes, that I guessed had been hastily cleansed of the stains of their killing. I could hardly believe these were the same men that I had thought I knew and with whom I had joked.

"Murderers!" Mr. Pierce quite screeched. "Cowardly murderers."

They denied the deed, though such was their tone that it was hardly a denial at all. "Must be those convicts, busy again," Sutton declared, throwing a wink to Higgs.

"Then what, may I ask, are you all doing here?" Mr. Pierce demanded.

Sutton merely shrugged. "Off for a little bird hunting, we were. Shooting crows and such." Crows was a slang term for the aborigines, and this evoked a foul laugh from the rest.

"You shall be punished for what you have done, and well punished too," Mr. Pierce warned. "I will see to it, believe me."

Sutton gave him a foul look. "I'd say it's lucky you've got the Little Preacher with you."

Hearing my nickname spoken in such circumstances was strangely shocking. "My name is George Baines," I told him coldly, "and I will not have one such as you calling me anything else."

I dare say it was foolish to provoke them. I was answered with threatening stares, and one of the quieter of their number advised us to take ourselves back to the settlement directly, as he put it, "for your own good." Though it was hard to walk away with so much anger still inside one, there seemed little wisdom in lingering, as even Mr. Pierce acknowledged.

"Our fight is better fought elsewhere," he urged.

When we reached Company House we found Mr. Charles away, and his wife explained he was out inspecting some of the company lands. This was unfortunate and the hours that followed were difficult indeed, as we sat in the dining room, being sometimes brought tea by Mrs. Charles, listening to the clock tick, our thoughts still filled with horror. We both spoke hardly a word. Mr. Charles, when he finally arrived, seemed to divine our mood at once, his face turning grave. He listened patiently as Mr. Pierce recounted his terrible narrative.

"We should go there without delay," Mr. Pierce declared impatiently when he reached his story's end. "The tide was rising but there may still be some left there for you to see."

Mr. Charles frowned. "It will soon be dark."

"We can take lamps."

"John," urged Mr. Charles, raising his hand to calm him. "I know you feel most strongly about these poor people. I understand you are greatly distressed." His voice sank to a sad murmur. "Yet I will ask you to do one thing. Try, if you can, to cast this from your mind, just for the moment. There is the whole establishment to consider, and it cannot be managed without men. Believe me, I will ensure that this matter is dealt with most fully."

Mr. Pierce fell into blinking. "You mean to let them go unpunished?"

Mr. Charles gave him a thoughtful look. "I said no such thing. I am merely asking that you let me attend to this in my own way."

"Mr. Charles, I am afraid you leave me little choice." Mr. Pierce stood, a little shakily, so his chair scraped behind him, then gave my arm a tug, so I was obliged to stand also. "As of this moment I resign my post with the New World Land Company. If you will not enforce justice, then I will simply find it elsewhere. George and I will go to Hobart directly and bear witness to all we have seen, including, Mr. Charles, your own reluctance to do your duty."

His sudden announcement quite took me aback, and I confess my feelings were quite a storm. I shared his anger, most certainly, and likewise I shared his determination that something must be done, feeling no little disappointment at

Mr. Charles's cautious suggestions. To resign his post with the company, how-ever, seemed premature, even rash. It was most awkward that, merely by my very standing beside him, I seemed to have joined him in this action. Barbarous though the stockkeepers had been, had I not journeyed halfway across the world to be part of this venture? Somehow, almost by accident, I appeared to have turned my back upon these hopes. Much though I respected Mr. Pierce, I could not help but wish he had at least waited a while so we might discuss the matter.

Mr. Charles seemed aware of my predicament and threw me a brief sympa-thetic glance. "I hope we may talk of this again," he said as we passed towards the doorway, "when you have both had a chance to rest and reflect."

Rest and reflection could hardly have been further from Mr. Pierce's mind, and he fairly marched away from the settlement. "We must be gone from this place, George," he urged me. "When a body of men gives itself to evil, as these men have, then to remain with them is to join their wickedness, nothing less."

I tried to moderate his view. "They're not all them evil. Mr. Charles is not evil."

The remark seemed only to fortify his conviction. "Is he not protecting the murderers? It is like a malady. Every one of them is infected." All in a rush he was forming plans as to what we must do, and wild plans they seemed. "We must create our own wholly separate settlement, and remain there until we find transport away. If there are any untainted men, as you suppose—and which I doubt—then they can join us there." Abruptly he stopped and glanced about him. We had reached a stretch of empty land, just out of view of Company House and the rest of the settlement. "This will do," he declared abruptly. "We should begin by building a hut."

The day had been so terrible and now it felt somehow unreal. I looked about me at the place that he had chosen. The ground was damp underfoot, this being, I supposed, the reason for its remaining unused. "But how can we? We have no tools. We do not even know how to construct one."

"I have a knife," Mr. Pierce insisted, holding this up, though it was a small thing, better suited to peeling fruit than building huts. "Come along. We'll find some wood and cut it into shape."

We found logs, but most were rotten through with damp and fungus, while those that were not were far too irregular of shape to be easily assembled together. We had, besides, not a single nail. When I pointed this out, Mr. Pierce began carving a number of wooden pins with his knife—whistling with a kind of desperate cheerfulness as he did so—though I could not see how these would help. By then it was growing dark, and a cold wind was beginning to blow.

"We should have started by building a fire," I declared, suddenly angry.

Mr. Pierce seemed taken aback. "We will build one tomorrow."

I looked at the mess of branches we had assembled, which more resembled a bonfire than the elements of a hut, and suddenly I was filled with impatience. "This is all pure madness."

He looked hurt. "Then what do you propose?"

All at once I found I had made up my mind. My thoughts were all of my own hut, of food and warmth. "I'm going back."

I was quite taken aback by his reaction. He regarded me with the most profound astonishment. I suppose, having confided in me so often—though I had never wanted him to do so—he saw me as the one fellow to share, unquestionably, his own opinion. His face turned to fury. "Go then. As if I care whether you go or stay. Go and join the rest of them, and don't ever think of coming back."

I returned to my bark hut, feeling quite wretched. I was also very hungry and so lit a fire in the hut's little hearth, that I might begin preparing myself some tea and flour damper to eat. I had made only a little progress when Mr. Charles knocked upon the door.

"Mr. Pierce is still gone?" he asked.

I nodded, a little coolly.

"I had hoped to invite you both up to the house," he explained. "Mrs. Charles thought you might be hungry and has roasted some lamb." He cast an eye over my poor food. "Of course you may prefer to eat your own meal here. . . ."

I went. I was not sure why I did, but I know now. Before long I was sat at that fine wooden dining table, my stomach filled with meat and brandy. It was not Mr. Charles who raised the subject of Mr. Pierce, it was I. Mr. Charles merely sat in his place, kindly nodding and frowning at my words. Mr. Pierce, I insisted, simply would not listen to anyone else. He was too much the outsider, forever failing to work with his fellows. He had no sense of moderation, of loyalty. I do believe I hated him. It may seem strange to you, Father, seeing as he had done no wrong, and now, when I reflect upon the matter, I suspect that it was this very fact that lay at the heart of my anger. It was as if I hated him for being so right, and so forcing me into wrongness.

Mr. Charles listened quietly all the while, smiling thoughtfully at my words. Only later, when the meal was finished and the brandy bottle was nearly empty, did he cast me a thoughtful look and offer an opinion of his own. "Of course you'll be aware, George, that if Mr. Pierce has his way, and these men are tried in court, then the only thing that shall suffer is the company itself, which will be destroyed." He lit his pipe. "The men deserve punishment, most certainly, but not once in the short history of Van Diemen's Land has any white man been hanged for killing a black, regardless of what laws may say. What will result is a mighty outcry in England, and especially from our enemies. The hard work that has been done here will be of no account. Newspapers will shout. Shares will lose their value. From there it will be but a short step to bankruptcy. Of course all that is of no consequence to Mr. Pierce." He puffed at his pipe. "How much better if it could only have been left to me. As chairman I could easily make those men regret what they have done—nearly as much as if they were taken to Hobart—and I could do it quietly."

"Will you do so?" I asked.

"Not now. I will, though, once the Champion *arrives, and we have hands to spare."*

In truth I doubt if I even needed persuading. I had come here, after all, seeking complicity—to find company to shield me from that look of scorn Mr. Pierce had thrown me as I turned to go—and here it was. Thus, that very evening, I signed a short statement of lies. I bore witness to the fact that, to the best of my knowledge, no more than six natives had been killed, and these by men who had found themselves under sudden and unprovoked attack.

Mr. Pierce I did not see again for some time. As the days passed, my strange resentment gradually ebbed away, leaving me only a profound and painful shame, which was more than enough to dissuade me from paying a visit to that damp spot just nearby the settlement. My mind was only changed when, one day, I overheard some chatter among the stockkeepers.

"I don't know what he's eating," said one. "Rats, most likely."

The other laughed. "And not many of them, either, by the look of him. Who knows, with a little luck he mightn't trouble us much longer."

"Good riddance, that's what I say."

I returned to my hut directly and fetched a quantity of flour. Mr. Pierce I found sat beneath a kind of mat of branches and leaves suspended from two trees, his hair and beard all in dirty tufts, and his look wild, quite like some vagrant. Though I tried to speak to him several times he would not utter a word to me, let alone accept the flour. I left it near him, hoping he might eat some after I had gone.

It was not long afterwards that an American whaling vessel appeared in the harbour, sheltering from poor weather. Mr. Pierce hurried out to the shore the moment he saw it, and before long he had managed to arrange a passage to Launceston, at his own expense. Mr. Charles invited the ship's captain to Company House that same day, and I am afraid it is likely that, unknown to Mr. Pierce, my own written statement accompanied him on his journey.

It was only a week or so later the Champion *finally arrived, direct from England, and the whole world became suddenly and utterly changed. At a stroke our population was doubled, while a good number of the new arrivals had with them wives and even children, who brought to the settlement a long-overdue sense of domesticity. In spite of these welcome distractions I did not forget to remind Mr. Charles of his promise concerning the punishment of the stockkeepers.*

"I will deal with it the moment I can, don't worry," he promised, "but I cannot look at anything just yet. There is so much to be done just now."

This was hardly the reply I had hoped for, and yet there was no denying that he was very busy, the whole settlement being nothing else. The ship had brought four carpenters, and wood too, and new dwellings seemed everywhere to be springing up from the ground for the new arrivals, these being not the tents and bark huts of before, but proper houses. There were plans even for a church. More animals had also arrived, including the new breed of sheep, and there was a good deal of work to be done extending the company lands back to their old boundaries. It was in the midst of this that Mr. Charles said he would like me to take Mr. Pierce's place as the chief agricultural officer. I will not say I did not feel some misgivings. I certainly did. The fact was, though, that this was no little honour, especially seeing as I was so young. It would also, I reasoned, add to my own influence within the establishment, and so my ability to prevent any repetition of the terrible acts of before.

It was only a couple of weeks after the ship's arrival that the attack came. The settlement was still carefully guarded and how the aborigines reached Company House unobserved remained a mystery to us. The only one who even saw them, indeed, was Mrs. Charles. Excited by the wealth of foods brought by the Champion, *she had been working late preparing a cake when suddenly she found ten of them were strolling through the door, clutching firebrands. She was so terrified she could hardly utter a word. Miraculously they did her no harm, simply setting light to curtains and furniture, then quietly slipping away. She then managed to recover herself and warn her husband and the others in the house, though the flames spread too quickly to be quenched, and within an hour the beautiful building was quite lost. The next morning Sutton and two other stockkeepers were found speared to death near their huts.*

A search was mounted at once to find the aborigines. Mr. Charles issued strictest instructions that they must not, if possible, be harmed, but were to be brought back to the settlement alive, from where they would be sent to Launceston and delivered to official hands. In the event, they never were caught, and all that came of the pursuit was one sighting of two dozen blacks on a distant hillside, striding southwards. They were chased, but then the weather grew bad and their trail was lost. In truth I was far from displeased.

That was only a couple of weeks ago. It is not, however, the end of my news. I have not yet reached, in fact, the very matter that has made me suddenly wish to write to you, Father.

It is now late December, the southern spring is turning to summer, and when the weather is calm the evenings are delightfully warm and long. When my work is done I sometimes like to walk down to the seashore and to look upon the ocean. So I did four days ago, remaining there as the light slowly faded, from scarlet to pink to the deep blue of dusk. My way back took me through the length of the settlement, which is now cluttered with building materials and tools. I was halfway down this when I heard the utterance. This, I should say, was a laugh, nothing more. It rang out loud and calm. The voice I recognized at once as that of Mr. Charles. When I looked up I saw, through the gloom, that the man he was talking to was the stockkeeper Higgs.

It is a trifling thing, I dare say. Try as I may, though, I simply have not been able to rid it from my thoughts.

So now, Father, I have written it all, every part. It is for that very reason, I know, that this letter will never be sent.

Peevay
1828

INSTEAD OF GETTING meat cooking on the fire, which was my great desire, I got a war. I never saw one before, no, but I heard stories from Tartoyen, while some things you do understand even without knowing. This was no battle yet, but nearly, with mine on one side and Roingin on other. That was a mystery to confound, yes, as Roingin never could be here, in the world, but must stay in theirs, as everybody knew. Also they weren't enough. Roingin were famous for being many but now they were fewer than mine. Still I could see they were strong, as they had more spears. Tartoyen, Gonar and others of mine just had a few—some didn't have even one—while Roingin had two or three each. That was some grievous worry, yes, and I did ponder how mine could be so piss-poor foolish.

"You are cowards," sang Roingin, to make my ones fearful, "and we will kill you very soon."

"You are liars and cheats," mine sang back, "and today you will die."

This war was a slow thing, I did observe, and shaking spears and singing insults went on and on with no fighting, so I went round through the bushes to where Grandmother and other women of my ones were standing. Grandmother was rejoicing to see me, though she was cross too. Grandmother never could just be pleased.

"Peevay, where've you been?" she asked. "We looked everywhere for you."

That was pleasing. So they were sorry, I did divine. I asked her how this war happened, and she said it started the morning before, when they met Roingin just walking through the forest of the world—our world—as if it was their place and not ours at all. That was a fighting thing, of course, as it is a strongest law that everybody must stay in their place unless they are allowed.

"There nearly was a war then," said Grandmother, telling how they all got ready, spears pointing and so, but then Roingin asked to speak their story. Gonar said they must not, but Tartoyen never did love fighting much, so he did permit them. Roingin story was too woeful. Ghosts came to their land, they told, plenty of them, and with ghost animals too, that were small and stupid and coloured like snow. First these ghosts were friendly, but then they tried to steal Roingin women and fighting happened, just small. One day when Roingin were looking for seal to hunt, ghosts came suddenly with sticks with thunder noise, and killed everyone they could, half all Roingin, children and everyone, and threw them into the sea. Later Roingin killed some back, but now ghosts were too many, always more, and when ghosts came to hunt them, Roingin decided they must leave their own land or all get killed. That was some ruination, truly, as to leave your world was just impossible, like being dead. Or so I supposed then.

Gonar wanted to kill Roingin anyway, despite their story, but Tartoyen felt sad for them. So he said ours would not kill them after all if they went away to their land now and never came back. They agreed, yes, and looked as if they went, but then when my ones woke this morning they found spears were gone, except just a few, and they saw Roingin watching through the trees, and shouting to Tartoyen he must let them stay in the world after all. Tartoyen couldn't do that of course. In fact he was more wrathful than everyone now, even than Gonar, as Roingins' grievous betraying made him look just foolishness. So everybody got ready to fight.

"Go back to your world," my ones were chanting. "Go back to your world or you all will die."

Each side had one fighter who wanted to make the war start. Ours was Gonar, while Roingin's was a short one with killing eyes. Each would run forward bravely towards enemies by and by, to wave his spear in the air and start new chanting, but then he'd look back at the rest of his to divine if they were following, and they never were. So it was, once and again, and I don't know if it ever could start, no, except for that accident. This was quite funny at first. Their warrior made another grievous provocation, waving his spear and so, and when his others never came, again he went away, walking backwards so he could watch my ones still. It was this going backwards that was his ruination, as he never saw that root stuck in the ground, but just fell. Some of mine laughed, I do recollect, and I laughed too, but not Gonar. He was gleeful at this great good fortune and ran forward fast, throwing his spear like wind, straight into Roingin warrior, making a little tiny cutting sound, *chhhh*. That was a good wound he got, I did divine, in his belly, enough for any wallaby, and though he shouted and tried to get up he could not.

Other Roingin were angry now, of course, and ran forward at Gonar, who got two spears both together, one in his neck. This was woeful and caused tender feelings deep inside my breast, yes, as it was lamentable to see him speared thus. Now everyone was shouting and holding spears as if they might throw them, or stooping down behind some tree, and suddenly I feared this might be some terrible war, everyone dead, though I never heard of any such before.

That was when the noise came. Truly, I never heard anything like it ever before. Louder than thunder it went, but very sudden, so I hardly knew it when it was already finished, and my ears were humming like wind in rocks, as if I got hit by some grievous blow. For one moment I wondered if this was the sound of being dead and if I was a ghost now, but then I observed others were still alive, and looking surprised just like me.

Then I saw the strangers. I think they were there before, yes, and I never noticed because of the fighting. They were standing away by the trees, not many—fewer even than Roingin—but looking strong. At the front was a woman with a face that was hard like stone, and in her hand she held a strange stick, that was long as a spear but thick like some waddy, with a thin end, all beautiful and shining. I could see smoke coming from it, though it wasn't burning, which was interesting, and made me think it was some magic thing. It was this woman who shouted at us.

"I won't let you fight each other. You must fight for me."

War was finished now, of course, stopped by everyone getting so surprised. Some ran away into trees, others just stood and stared. Then again it was some great mystery to confound. You see, this woman, who I never saw till now, spoke my ones' language.

Another puzzle to confound was that Grandmother was crying. Grandmother never cried.

"Who is she?" I asked.

Grandmother looked at me, and for the first time that I ever could recollect I observed there was no hating in her eyes. "Your mother."

So I finally saw her. She never was tall and beautiful like I thought, no, but was quite short with strong arms and legs, and quick eyes ready for some fight. Still I never minded. This was blissful and great good fortune. This was jubilation and tidings of joy. She had come to find me after all. I did not wait but ran, past mine, past Roingin, even past strange animals that I never saw before, that looked like kanunnah but small, and were called DOG ANIMALS, so I learned after. She never saw me till I was close. Then I grabbed her leg and shouted, "Mother."

Thus I got my worst grievous blow. Her eyes, which were gleeful before, turned cold like winter sea. Then she pushed me off, hard so my arms hurt, and turned away. Where she walked was interesting, yes. She went over to one boy, smaller than me, with little thin legs so he looked good for hitting, and d'you know she took the heinous little shit in her arms, as if he was some finest wondrous thing.

So it was I first saw Tayaleah, my never-guessed scut of a brother.

CHAPTER THREE

——»·«——

Captain Illiam Quillian Kewley
JULY 1857

AFTER THREE FULL WEEKS caught in that sealed dock like rats in a box, why, even the river Blackwater seemed paradise itself. It's the Blackwater that leads up to Maldon town, and a well-named stream it is too, as if it's mud you're looking for then this is just the spot for you. All that eastern shore of your England is mudflat land, being nothing more than a great nothing of wind, yelling birds and too much sky. And mud, of course. But after that London every last dirty scran of it seemed loveliness itself.

As the wise man says, though, *for every summer Sunday there's a winter wind to pay,* and in this case the cost of our freedom was plain for all to see, strutting about the ship as if they owned it. Total charge: three passengers. Worse, Englishmen all of them. I can't say I was happy about the arrangement. I dare say I'd expected the *Sincerity* to see a few humiliations in her time–to be nibbled by barnacles, shat on by gulls and poked and prodded by customs men–but never, not once, did I think she'd be reduced to the shame of passengers.

Strange articles of passengers they were, too. Truly, you never did see such a clever and pestful trio as these, all disagreeing with themselves and taking their great clever brains for a little stroll about the deck. I dare say it was hardly a surprise they were odds, mind, seeing as their quest was to discover themselves the Garden of Eden. The Garden of Eden! As if it couldn't just be left in the Bible where it belonged. They weren't even looking to find it in any sensible spot, but on some rotten island at the very ends of the earth, called Van Diemen's Land, or Tasmania, as it couldn't make up its mind. This was a mad fool of a place, by the sounds of it, all gaols and bluemen and worse, being nowhere any sensible fellow would venture near. It was there, and all the way back, too, that we were supposed to carrying the three snots. A whole year of Englishmen. What a thought that was. It was bad enough just taking them along the coast to Maldon.

Worst was mealtimes, when I had to suffer them in the dining cabin, with all their genteel little smirks and thank-yous and *I wonder if you could pass the salt, Captain?* The hardest to take was that vicar, Reverend Wilson, who was a thin, twittering sort of body, with a toothy smile that sat on his face all the time, like he never tired of himself. Truly, you never met a body so rich in his own importance, and watching him smirk and chew at his dinner it was hard not to think what a surprise he'd give to the fishes if he accidentally got dropped over the side. He was mean as could be, too. Truly, I don't think we could've found a more suspecting and penny-counting scrape if we'd trawled all London especially. It was all I could manage to coax enough charter money out of him to pay the customs fine, and even then he insisted on following me round the provision shops and such, peering over my shoulders as if I couldn't be trusted. Was that really enough casks of water for a journey to Australia? Enough biscuit? Enough chickens and sheep? In the end I had no choice but to stock up with half a shipload of food and water and creatures that we didn't want, quite as if we really did intend to take them to the ends of the earth. All the while we were loading up their own stores which were fancy as could be–champagne and best French brandy, choice meats and even silver cutlery to eat it all with–so we knew that, for all his moaning, this vicar was rich as the man that turned the rabbits all to gold.

Hardly a day seemed to go by without him calling at the sealed dock with some new fussing. He squawked so loud about sleeping quarters that I was sure he was after my own cabin. I was tempted to clear out Chalse Christian's carpentry workshop and fling them in there, but I supposed we'd never catch a penny out of them with that, so in the end it was the mates' cabins they had. I had Chalse Christian the carpenter rig up a top bunk in Brew's haunt, which would now be graced by Reverend Wilson and Dr. Potter. Second mate Kinvig's cabin, being nothing more than a cupboard with a porthole, I gave to the plants boy, Renshaw. Even then they were all three of them moaning and complaining, saying they wanted something more genteel, as if this was some passenger steamer. Nor were they the only ones playing huffy, as Brew and Kinvig were in a proper scowl at being slung into the fo'c'sle with the boys. Never you mind, I told them in Manx, it's only till we get to Maldon.

Finally there came that welcome morning when we were to be gone from the London dock. I'd have been happy slipping away nice and quiet, for sure, as in my book it's never clever to go catching the world's stares, but sadly that wasn't our Englishmen's way, and quite a crowd turned up to wave them good riddance. There were parsons, and newspapermen looking sharp. There was Jonah Childs, the moneybags, who had signed the charter agreement and given us our jink. A funny-looking body he was, tall as trees with a little tiny head so he looked like a bottle stuck on a pole, as he went round playing the big man, letting everyone have a little shake of his hand. Then there were the Reverend's children— a great stringy pack of them—and his wife and her sister too, who were a proper pair of wallopers, smiling away as if they couldn't wait for the old sleetch to be gone. Not that I blamed them any for that. Renshaw, the little plants boy, did hardly better, as his brother and father looked cheery as tombstones, while his mother was too far the other way, sobbing and fussing and pulling out a little present that she pretended she'd forgot, "for those cold nights in the mountains," though this turned out to be a dainty pair of gloves just right for supping tea with the Queen. It was the surgeon of the three, Potter, who did best with his goodbyes, catching himself half a hospital's worth of doctors, all making little speeches to one another at how grand it was he was going. They'd have a surprise when he came back inside a week.

Finally the ropes were let go, the boats hauled us out of the sealed port and a tug towed us down the river and away to the estuary. Grand as it felt to have the *Sincerity* back to a bit of ocean, it was rotten hard having those Englishmen aboard, all snooping and curious and noticing things. My fright was they might notice too much. The other little bother I had—and which I'd hardly troubled myself with till then, as there'd always been something worse to worry me—was how on earth we were going to unload that certain special cargo without catching their notice. Shifting casks of brandy by the dozen, along with sheaves of tobacco and some interesting pieces of French glass, will tend to cause a bit of fuss and noise, after all. It would have to be done somehow, though, as we couldn't give them back their charter money till we'd sold up.

"Perhaps we should just drop all three of them over the side," suggested Brew, smooth as milk. Sometimes I hardly knew if that one was joking. We didn't have to make up our minds, neither, as it turned out. The breeze was a southerly, which did with tacking, while Maldon wasn't far, and just that next afternoon we put a sight on the Blackwater. I had the boys drop anchor at the river mouth, thinking it just near enough to the town for us to look into our certain arrangements, while still handily out of view. Our passengers never liked this little surprise at all, of course, and the moment the Reverend heard the roar of the anchor chain go he was moaning and complaining.

"Maldon? But what on earth for? I've told you we can't afford any further delay."

"It's the ship's clock," I told him, as this seemed as good a reason as any. "We can't go sailing around the world with a broken clock, as we'd never know where we were. Why, there'd be nothing to stop us sailing clean into some part of Africa or Australia on a dark night that we'd never so much as guessed was there."

That quietened him. If there's one thing to settle passengers I dare say it's a bit of shipwreck talk. Besides, it was true enough, apart from a couple of little tiddling particulars that I'd forgot, such as that we had no intention of sailing anywhere further than Peel City, and the ship's clock worked nice as nip.

Next Potter, the surgeon, started up. "If it's so very important, then shouldn't we return to London and find a clockmaker of quality? We're still near, after all."

For just one moment I almost wondered if he was suspecting us. It hardly seemed likely, for sure, but you never did know, while exactly the very last place I wanted to put a sight on now was that London. I hardly could fathom that surgeon. He was a different pair of oars entirely from our friend the vicar, that was certain. If Reverend Wilson was skin and bones, Potter was purest meat, and likewise if Wilson was all talk and fuss and getting in everyone's way, then Potter was quietness, like a big badger you wouldn't quite trust.

"Maldon's a tidy little port," I told Potter. "Don't you worry, we'll have no trouble finding a good clock man there."

There was little enough they could do in any case, as it was my vessel. I had the boat lowered into that Blackwater, to go and find cousin Rob. Not that that turned out easy. I knew he lived near Maldon, but, as any fool will tell you, there's near and there's near, and the two are different as pigs and parakeets. "You can't miss it," he'd told me when he last visited Peel City. "It stands all alone by the shore, straight over from Northey Island." That had seemed clear enough at the time, but then directions usually do when you're still months and miles off from needing them. We'd written to each other once or twice since, making our certain arrangements, but I never thought to have him send us a map. Now that we were perched on the Blackwater, and Northey Island was dead ahead–looking like nothing but so much more mud–I wished I had.

"What about that over there to larboard?" called out Parrick Kinvig, the second mate. "That looks like a house."

It did too, fairly much. The weather was a touch misty and it was a good way off, so it was hardly more than a tiny speck of white above the mud. "I suppose it could be," I answered him.

"But I'm sure it is, Captain," insisted Kinvig, all huffy that I'd only said *could be*. Kinvig always was a scrowly one, being the kind that could stir trouble from angels themselves. There were persons said this crabbiness was on account of his father, who was a useless old body, and famous for drinking his horse and his cart in one summer at the inn, this being one of those things that nobody ever forgot. Other persons disagreed, saying Kinvig's rage came from his own tallness–which was no tallness at all, as he was a tiny mhinyag of a body, hardly higher off the ground than a child–there often being trouble in midgets, as was shown clear as glass by Emperor Bonaparte himself. I hardly cared, if truth be told, as it's the proper job of a second mate to be always in a rage, yelling and scelping at the boys to keep them from slacking. Why, the sign that a second mate knows his work is that he's hated worse than the devil himself, and here Parrick Kinvig was beauty as could be.

But I'm getting away from where I was, which was this house or such that he'd seen. Up to now I'd planned going to the right of Northey Island, as that looked the wider stream, but a building is a building and this was the only one that showed. "Very well, larboard it is," I said, adding, just to stop him getting too high, "and if it's no good then we'll know who to blame."

There's faster ways to travel than rowboats, I dare say, and even with China Clucas the ship's giant at the oars, still we were slow as snails. Little by little, as the afternoon snuffled off towards dusk, the building grew, from just a speck to a speck with edges, then to something like a matchbox with a roof, till finally there it was ahead of us with its sign swinging in the wind, a full-grown inn. That wasn't the best news, for sure, but it could have been worse, as if there's one place that's good for finding where somebody lives then it's an inn. We beached the boat, Kinvig went off to ask and a moment or two later he was squelching his way back. I guessed from his look that it was nothing good.

"They know him, right enough, and his house is just further along. But we'll not find him. He took himself off to Colchester, so they said, just a few days ago, and got himself murdered half to death in some knife fight. He's still there."

It was as if bad luck was following us about, like an old dog that won't be chased off. All at once I had no buyer, nor any way of finding one. I was low on jink and had three passengers expecting to be taken to the ends of the earth. The fact was if there was one thing I'd relied upon in this whole adventure it was cousin Rob. Not that I'm one to go hurling blame, but he was hardly making things easy for us. He'd known well enough that we were on our way, after all, and if we were a little late that was hardly our fault. All he'd had to do was sit quiet and wait like any sensible body, but no, he'd had to go dallying off to Colchester and tempt some passing knifeman to stick a blade into him.

"Perhaps we should go up to this Colchester and have a quest for him," said Kinvig.

I was in no mood to start chasing about, making ourselves noticed. "Even if we found him he'd probably only go and die on us." We could go straight on to Maldon and try our luck asking questions, in the hope that I'd find those certain bodies Rob had said were interested, but I could see trouble there. We didn't have a single name–Rob had been too canny to tell, I suppose for fear I might make a deal without him–while the customs knew we'd been going to Maldon, and might well be keeping watch. But there was something we could do. "Where did they say Rob's house was?"

Kinvig looked puzzled. "Just further round the island."

"Then let's be on our way."

Now, cousin Rob was hardly the kind to go collecting servants, while his Englishwoman wife would be away in Colchester at his bedside, so, as I saw it, his house was sure to be empty. Not that I want to seem unkindly, but we'd had an agreement, and he'd been the one to break it and drop us into blackest trouble. Why, we'd have been right as rain if the silly slug hadn't chosen to get himself stabbed. No, this was simple compensation. Why, if he made up his mind not to die after all, we might even think about giving him a few pennies back, if we felt kindly.

China and the rest put themselves to the oars and round Northey Island we went. It was a relief to have made up my mind and even the land seemed to give us the nod, growing cheerier as we went along, a distant Maldon spire or two peering out over the mud. After a time the shore became lined with a fine bank of trees, and just after there was a house, sitting all alone just like it should. It wasn't a bad size, neither.

"Where's his boat?" wondered Kinvig.

I guessed that quick enough. "He must've taken it to Colchester."

I left Vartin Clague in the boat to keep watch and across that mud we went. I gave a little knock at the door–just in case–and then, when nobody answered, we went round the side and played tugging at windows, till we found one that opened nicely, and there we were, in the sitting room.

Strange it is how just being in another man's house will set a body to mumbling, even though you know there's nobody there. "There's some choice stuff here," said Kinvig in a whisper.

He was right enough, I saw, as my eyes adjusted to the gloom. There was a fine table and chairs, and some grand pictures on the walls, of foreign boats with square sails and fellows sneaking about in strange hats carrying baskets on poles, looking like Chinamen. On the mantelpiece was a couple of model warships, neatly done too. This couldn't be just from catching eels. I reckoned Rob had been doing some trading on his own account, and doing nicely, too. There should be some jink to be found, for sure. We set to work, pulling open drawers and such, but mostly all we found was old papers and other uselessness. Finally, in the kitchen, I lit upon a stash of silver cutlery. It looked quality to me, while he'd hardly be needing such fuss croaking away his breath in Colchester.

"This'll have to do," I told the others. "Fill your pockets. And one of you take that clock while you're about it." A pretty little thing this was, sat on the mantelpiece next to the ships.

"Look here," said Kinvig as he scooped up some more spoons. "They've got some kind of letters on them."

"These too," agreed China, holding up a fork.

"HH," I read, this being more than the others could manage.

"And there's a little mark underneath," noticed Kinvig. "It looks like an anchor."

It hardly seemed worth paying much heed over. There was no telling where Rob would have got his things from, after all. "Never you mind about that. Just get it back to the boat."

The fact was I still hadn't quite given up hope of finding some actual jink, so while the others shuffled their way back over the window, clanking with heavy pockets, I took myself upstairs to have a little look. It was mighty dark up there, but I could just make out a door and find the handle, so open it I did. Inside I made out a bed, being a big jumble of blankets as if it hadn't been made since Rob had jaunted himself off to Colchester. There was no sign of any chest or such, which was a disappointment, but I spied a couple of fine candleholders on the mantelpiece, and it was one of these I was taking a look at, in fact—trying to see if it was solid silver or just plate, which would hardly be worth troubling over—when all of a sudden a most curious thing happened. Over from the bed a voice called out, being a snapped, military sort of voice, and it said, "What the devil are you doing, Phillips?"

Just seven words, that was all, but what a lot seven words can tell a man. First of all these seven told of how that bed wasn't quite so empty as it had looked. Second they put me nicely in the know about a fellow named Phillips, who sounded as if he was some rat of a servant, and, as far as I could guess, must either be having his night off or was a very sound sleeper. Lastly, and sweetest of all, there was the little gem of a discovery that I wasn't in cousin Rob's house at all, and never had been.

All in all I thought it best to leave the candleholder, whether it was silver or not. Out through the door I went and behind me I heard what wasn't any kind of word at all, but a kind of well-spoken howl. Well, given the right day I can be swift enough on my feet. Down those stairs I went, leaping three at a time, then through that sitting-room window clean as a ball through a barrel, and till I was dashing away towards the river. The rest of them hadn't yet reached the boat and were taking daintiest little steps to keep from slipping in the mud. They stopped and looked round when they saw me coming in my chase, and looked like they were about to start asking foolish questions—which I was in no mood to stop and answer—but fortunately just that moment there was a bright flash from the upstairs window of the house, and also a mighty bang, that settled their curiosity nice as nip. Mud and speed are never a good match, I dare say, and it cost us a few nasty slips—as well as several forks and spoons—but finally we got ourselves into the boat and pushed off from the shore.

After that we just rowed fast as devils, too busy for chatter. Nobody said a word when, just a little further round the island, we passed a wretched-looking cottage, standing all alone, with an old rowboat sat upside down and eel nets draped from posts. But I gave a good hard stare at Kinvig, seeing as he'd been the one who asked at the inn.

It took a good while to make our way back down the Blackwater, and all the while I was sat at the tiller, staring at the boys with their bulging pockets that clinked as they rowed, and the more I looked, the less happy I was. By the time the ship came into view I'd already made up my mind, at least half, anyway, while the other half was soon settled by the passengers. I'd hoped they'd be all abed, you see, dreaming their clever Englishmen's dreams, and that we'd at least get ourselves aboard nice and quietly, but no, they never would make themselves so convenient. There they were, all leaning on the rail to watch. It was the Reverend had the quickest eyes.

"A clock!" he called out when we were still fifty yards away. "They've found a clock. Hurrah! Our troubles are over."

Renshaw, the plants boy, was more doubtful. "Are you sure that's the right kind?"

If there was one thing I didn't want to be just then it was interesting, but interesting we were. As we clambered onto the deck, they were all eyes.

"But, Captain, how did you get so covered in mud?" wondered Dr. Potter, in that watching way of his.

I just shrugged.

"And you've found some new cutlery for the ship's table," observed the Reverend. "I must say I'm very glad. I didn't wish to complain, but the rest was rather poor."

Bad luck? Why, we had enough of it to fill up half the ocean. It wouldn't be long before our friend with the gun had the whole neighbourhood started, and once they found our footmarks in the mud they'd be racing down that river Blackwater fast as dogs that have smelt rabbit. If we hurled the clock and every knife and fork clean over the side we still had three witnesses against us, and all of them respectable as royalty. The more I thought on it, the worse it looked. Even fleeing wouldn't be safe, as this sort of foolishness was sure to catch the eye of newspapers. It's not every day, after all, that a house is tidied up straight out from the ocean, Viking style. All it would take would be for one of our Englishmen passengers to put a sight on the wrong page of the wrong paper and we'd be cooked as herrings on the fire. Running a bit of contraband was one thing, but housebreaking was quite another. That was gaol, or even transportation. That was ruin, for sure.

Not that we were finished yet. Nobody could find us guilty if we weren't here, and one little thing, at least, was on our side. The wind. There was a lovely sea breeze pulling clear away from Maldon and out towards the ocean. If we could just keep away long enough, then who'd remember or care about a few soup spoons? As to where, well, I never even had to choose, as it had been chosen already. "Brew," I called out. "We're weighing anchor."

"Maldon?" he asked. "We'll never get up river in this breeze."

"Tasmania."

For once Brew lost his smooth look.

CHAPTER FOUR

Jack Harp
1821–24

WHEN THE SEALING SEASON was done I set off for George Town in the whaleboat just like usual, and all the way I was wondering if I'd find a small rowboat as good as the one I lost to that gin, which had been a handy little thing. The tide was going out nicely when I arrived, so I beached the boat and took myself across to that penny-pinching bugger Bill Haskins. Haskins loaned me his cart to bring over the skins, which I needed what with Ned being gone, and once I had them all on his floor we started our money talk, which went sweet enough, too. He said he knew of a rowboat going that was a tidy vessel and had just had a fresh bit of varnish. His offer for the skins was better than I'd hoped and was enough for the rowboat and the stores I needed with even a little keeping money on top. He couldn't get hold of the silver till the next day, so he said, nor the man who had the rowboat to sell, but he gave me a Spanish dollar and a couple of French coins to keep me floating till then, which seemed only right.

After sitting alone on that island nearly a full twelvemonth I was feeling more than ready for a bit of company. By evening I'd had a good fill of rum at the inn and a taste of that Lill, besides, in the room at the back. I won't say Lill was anything special, being ripe past her best, and sour of temper too, making a proper fuss if I got a little rough, but she was a fair bit of leather and after so long I was in no mood for complaining. I was just thinking of having myself another turn, in fact, when those redcoats bastards burst in, all boots and muskets and calling me escaped. I gave them what trouble I could, dropping one against the wall so his head got a crack, and giving another a bloody mouth, but they were too many and had me in the end.

By then I was thinking, and my thoughts weren't pretty, neither. I gave Lill a stare but she looked all surprise, so I reckoned it wasn't her. As they started hauling me away, I called out to that redcoat officer, "Who was it then? What bastard sent you after me?" He never said a word, of course, but he sort of blinked, which told me enough. All at once I knew who it was had snitched on me, clear as daylight.

It was rough being back in convict clothes when I thought I'd got free of them for good. Being escaped, and violent too, I was put on the roads, which was bad, especially in the cold weather. That was two years and then I got into a fight with an officer with too much mouth on him, and I was sent to Hobart on the warehouses they were building, which was bad too. The talk going round was it would get no better, as there was a new governor come, Alder, who was known for being a proper martinet, and wanted every one of us flogged into quietness. That sounded trouble, no denying. Not that I gave it much thought. What I did think about, and often too, was my old friend Bill Haskins and what a clever cove he'd been to catch himself a whole boatload of sealskins for just one Spanish dollar and a couple of French coins.

Peevay
1828

MOTHER'S HEARTFELT DESIRE deep inside her breast was that we should go out from the world to kill Father. It seemed woeful, yes, and scaring besides, to go away into some heinous unknown place, where stories in rocks and hills were not ours. Some of mine, such as Grandmother and Tartoyen, said they wouldn't go, which was ruination, as it meant we must get cut in two, like some tree chopped by lightning, and everyone must choose staying or going. Mongana and his mother were keeping there, and Grandmother said I must stay too, as I was too young for fighting and she and Tartoyen would look after me, but still I wanted to go with Mother. I did believe I could win her tender cherishings, you see, as they were my own deserving. Hadn't I waited for her all those summers, and dreamed her walking so pretty from the sea? Worst, if I stayed I would be giving her to Tayaleah, my little scut of a never-guessed brother.

Tayaleah means owl but in truth he never was like any, as that is some strong, swooping thing while he was weakly, with his thin legs and looking always fearful. It was a mystery to confound that Mother could give him her adorings, but so she did. When Tayaleah tried to make a spear and it was piss-poor blunt and wouldn't throw, Mother said it was the best spear. Also when Tayaleah climbed some easy tree hunting possum—who probably wasn't even there—Mother said he was bravest boy. Even at night by the fire she did cradle his little snivelly head and keep him safe from cold and dark. This made me frenzied, yes, as that cradling was mine not his. That little pisser should be vanished, killed to nowhere, and it was my heartfelt desire deep inside my breast to spear him dead. He was so weakly that I surmised this would be easy, too, except for Mother. She stayed with him always and gave me hating looks if I went near. Tayaleah knew I had revilings for him and I could see his fright of me, and yet he never was hateful back, which was some puzzle to confound. Why, I never even heard him say heinous lies about me to Mother, though she would believe anything he told. I suppose there was just no wrath in him, even for enemies. No, I think I would almost have liked him better if he was raging, as then we would be fine foes.

Finally the time came to go away. That was lamentable. It was hard to leave so many of my ones, even ones I hated, like Mongana and his mother. Roingin were cut in two also, and goodbyes were long and slow, while even dog animals Mother brought went quiet, like they knew this was some mournful thing. Then Mother said we must go now and we began, some walking almost backwards so they could look still. By and by that big mob cracked and became two, like fingers unsticking. Shouts got loud and wavings bigger as we went further. Then suddenly we were in trees, others were getting hidden and all I could see was this new mob, that was Mother's mob.

Mother did try and kill Father before, of course, but she was confounded. Years before, when I was just some new baby, she went back to the shore near Father's island, but then she couldn't find Father's boat, which she hid before. Probably sea took it. That was some grievous blow for Mother, as Father's island was far and even with a bark canoe she couldn't go just alone. So she walked beside the sea by and by, making spears and hunting game, and watching for some other boat, though she never found any. Once she got chased by white scuts, and later she slipped and hurt one leg in rocks so she couldn't hunt game, so she got hungry and sick. By then she walked so far she was beyond Roingin world, and reached some place which we hardly knew even in stories. I think she would be dead, too, except that she met another mob, whose name was TOMMEGINER, who were eating muttonfish by the sea.

Tommeginer almost speared her for being strange, but when they heard her woeful tale they felt sad for her by and by, and gave her food to eat. They told her how ghosts came stealing their women sometimes, and killing everyone for no reason, so they were fighting a war with them, though this was hard. Mother never was scared of ghosts because she knew them, and she said they weren't dead fellows jumped up like Tommeginer thought, but just some heinous pissers from beyond the sea. She told how they could be killed easily and how she killed one herself just with a stone. So they never called them ghosts anymore, but num, which was their word for those white men.

So Mother joined their war. She learned about dog animals that Tommeginer got from white men, and which were clever at smelling but greedy for food and fuckings and so. She even took one Tommeginer as husband, and he was father of that little shit Tayaleah. Soon she learned fighting cleverly–better than other Tommeginer–and when their clever-est fellow got killed she chose their way, which was some impossible thing, yes, as she was woman, and foreigner too. One day they speared two white scuts in their hut and she got their magic stick that killed with its noise, and is called GUN. When she was on Father's island, fixed to the wall of his hut long before, she saw Father make his GUN ready for killing seals, and she did try to recollect this, until she learned how to make it work, with powder and killing stones. That was wondrous to other Tommeginer, and great good fortune and tidings of joy, as it meant she could use white men's magic against them. She killed one very finely, in his head, and always Tommeginer could see white scuts' fright when they saw her carrying that gun. She kept it carefully, with wood in the end to stop rain getting inside.

Then one day coughing sickness arrived. Many Tommeginer got crook and died and Mother's new husband was one. Later, when they were so weak, num came in the night and killed plenty of them, all together, so Mother and some others were lucky to flee. That was a worst grievous blow. After then Mother told Tommeginer who were still living that they must leave their world now, as it got too woeful and killing to stay, and so they did. For many days they went, hunting game and so, till finally they found footmarks of us, and Roingin too. This was interesting to Mother, as she did want to meet her old fellows, and also to get new ones to fight her wars.

So here I was, in her mob. Those were woeful days I can recollect. I missed Grandmother giving me food with her long, bony fingers, and I missed her more when I got tired from walking and there was nobody to carry me high on shoulders for a time. I missed Tartoyen with his stories and teachings and his kindly looks, as I never got any such from Mother, even after days passed and I hoped she might get better to me. So I felt alone with these many strangers, until I even got some tender feelings deep inside my breast about Father, who we were going to kill. Yes, others said he was some heinous scut and so, but still he was Father, and my only one, and sometimes I did suppose he might be kindlier than Mother. But then my thinking would go hither and thither, like some tree branch blowing in the storm. Now I was sad for him and hoping he might escape us after all. Now I was thinking how clever I would be if I could kill him dead myself. That was a fine dream, yes. There I was spearing him quick in his belly, snicky snick, everyone was full of wonder and surprise, and even Mother was pleased, so she never scorned me anymore but gave me all her cherishings, while Tayaleah got left alone in some cold place and nobody cared.

By and by we reached the last edge of our world and stepped across into places I never saw before, which felt strange. Roingin were pleased, as this was theirs–they were always pointing at some place or hill they did recollect–but they were also fearful and watching for white scuts who threw their fellows off that cliff into the sea. Mother said we must not fight these ones now, heinous though they were, as they were too many. CHOOSE THE WAR THAT YOU WILL WIN was Mother's thought, and she said it often. But she let us make sticks sharp as spears that we hid in small holes in the path, pointing upwards so they might step there and get our surprise. Always we went carefully, watching far ahead. Days were bad, always raining, which Mother said was best, as num white men hated rain and would just wait in their huts without ever knowing we were near. She was right, too, and we never saw any. Soon we reached the sea, all still alive, and I could discern islands, one far away, low and grey like some cloud. When Mother looked at this her face went hard like stone, so I knew it must be Father's.

Rain was falling but wind was quiet, which was lucky, as it meant sea was not too angry, and also Father should stay inside his hut like other whites, so we could kill him more easily. So we started making bark canoes, enough to carry us all, even babies, as Mother said it was too dangerous leaving anyone behind. Only dog animals stayed, and when canoes were finished and we pushed them into great waves they got fretful, howling and running along the shore hither and thither. I never went on any bark canoe in the sea before and it was some fearful thing, yes. Waves made it jump and fall like a leaf in big winds, and I held on hard, pondering all the while that I might fall away into that ocean, or bark canoe might break into nothing. Sky was dark and sea was too, so it looked deep as if it had no bottom and was just more water forever, so it was scaring to think that this canoe and us were like some beetle on some wide lake. Also I feared huge whale creatures that I saw playing before, and which might jump up and bite my feet, which were dipping. But they never did. By and by Father's island got nearer till finally we were close enough to see all. Boat was there and hut had smoke coming up, which was great good fortune, as it meant he was inside.

Mother made us stop on another side of the island, even though this was further, so Father would not hear us. Then we went carefully. When we got near we could observe two women were behind that hut, both tied with shining strands that Mother said were called CHAINS, and which made her spit at the ground, very angry. Tommeginer got blissful when they saw these women, as they whispered they were Tommeginer too, but disappeared long before, so everyone thought they were dead.

Mother made strong faces to make Tommeginer stay quiet, and two women too, as they were filled with tidings of joy to see each other. So we went near, small steps, very careful, until, ready with spears and Mother's gun, we opened that door so quickly and, in our mighty rush, we went within.

It was dark in there, smoky too, and smelling of fish and seal fat, but that fire made light to see, just enough. In one place were sealskins, plenty of them, so I hardly could believe so many seals could get dead so. Also I saw other white men's things which were interesting, such as wooden ones like tree stumps, whose name was CASKS, and strange ones standing on legs on the floor, whose name was STOOLS. That hum whitefellow was sitting on one of these. He was surprised to see us of course, very so, and his mouth fell open like some broken shell. Just for a moment he looked away to a wall where GUN was leaning, like Mother's but smaller, but this was too far, so he just sat still. Thus we won this war without anybody killed. Yes, everything was great good fortune and tidings of joy except for that one heinous thing.

Mother made a scowling face. "It's not him."

That was hardship to endure, yes, and we all got tender feelings for poor Mother, whose dear desire was always to kill Father. Also it was some mystery to confound, as this was Father's island, so he should be here. Mother started talking to this fellow in his own words—which she learned when she was here on this island with Father, fixed to that wall—and sometimes we pricked him with spear to make him answer quicker. It was interesting to hear white men's talk, yes, as I never heard it before, and I observed it never was said properly but was just murmured, like wombat coughing. Now, of course, I can speak those words myself, and better than Mother ever could, so they hardly are words to me anymore but just thinkings that are said, but in that long ago time they were new and curious. Another interesting thing was that she spoke Father's name, which I never heard before, and sounded strange like no real name ever did. This name was JACK.

"Where's Jack?" she said, once and again. "Where's ugly whitefellow with big cut on him?" So she drew line on her face with her finger to show. But that num just looked at floor and said he didn't know. He told that he came to this island two summers before—fleeing from some other num–and though hut was already built here it was empty, for a long time so he thought, and no other white man ever came. Next we brought the two Tommeginer women he kept outside, and they spat and hit his face for all those hateful, heinous doings he did, but still they said he was correct and that they never saw any other white man but him. Mother was mournful, I do recollect. Even when others took the white man outside and speared him dead to please her, still she never would smile.

The next morning we took the white man's boat, which was bigger than canoes so my legs stayed inside. Two Tommeginer women were so happy to be escaped they sang all that way, and dogs on the cliff were pleased too, shouting as we came near. Still Mother stayed angry that she couldn't kill Father. When some of my ones said we should go back, to find Tartoyen and Grandmother and those others, she looked hard like stone and said no. "We came here to fight, didn't we?" she told, waving her guns, as she had two now. Mother could be scaring when she was angry, yes, and though some fellows gave each other looks, nobody did confound her, or even try. So we never went south but east, across Roingin world, for more war.

*Sir Charles Moray, Secretary for Colonies, London, to George
Alder, Governor of Van Diemen's Land*
1828

Sir, I write to you concerned as to the plight of the aboriginal race of His Majesty's Colony of Van Diemen's Land. It is my understanding that, as a consequence of violence between these and the white population, the blacks' numbers have become greatly reduced, so much so that they are now entirely extinguished in many districts. I have been advised that, if matters continue on their present course, the native population of the island will, before long, be entirely extirpated.

It is imperative that such an eventuality be avoided. Though lawless aggression against colonists cannot, naturally, be permitted, it is nothing less than essential that the good name of His Majesty's Government be protected. The destruction of this aboriginal nation, however remote its station and savage its nature, would form an indelible stain upon the reputation of this country, and would most certainly be used by foreign powers seeking to cause embarrassment to His Majesty and his representatives. You are, in consequence, required to do all in your power to endeavour to preserve the blacks, at least in sufficient numbers to assure their continued survival.

George Alder, Governor of Van Diemen's Land, to Sir Charles Moray, Secretary for Colonies, London
1828

Sir, in your last communication–which took close to five months to arrive, the transport ship Aphrodite *having struck windless weather–you expressed your alarm regarding the fate of the natives of this island. You may rest assured that this is a matter upon which I feel no less strongly than you yourself, having been concerned as to the plight of this unhappy race since ever I arrived upon this colony, four years ago. I have, indeed, made every effort to protect and improve them, though this has proved, I regret to say, far from easy to achieve.*

The blacks, you must understand, have no comprehension of what I may term system, *this being the very root of order. Despite their wandering and elusive ways I have hoped that they might show some curiosity towards this mighty and civilized society that has appeared so suddenly in their midst–in our agriculture and manufacturing, our complex laws and processes–but I am afraid I have been disappointed. They have likewise maintained a savage resistance to their own spiritual advancement, though there are more than a few good men in the colony who would happily help them from their state of moral darkness.*

In spite of such discouragements I have made every effort to ensure they are preserved. You will recall that I organized a most extensive campaign to apprehend the runaway convicts who comprised the natives' chief persecutors (most of whom, I may add, escaped in the time of my predecessors) and that this proved so effective that nearly all such men, including some of notorious character, have been captured or killed. By the time this was completed, however, the aborigines had become bent on revenge, venting their wrath upon any white they could discover, whether guilty or innocent, while this in turn caused some among the free settlers to answer violence with violence. Once again I responded promptly, issuing not one but several proclamations, commanding the whites to treat their black neighbours only with kindness, and warning them that any unprovoked killing would be answered with the harshest punishment. The truth is, however, that it is not easy to control the population of an island that is as large as Ireland and as mountainous and inhospitable as Scotland. It appears some among the white settlers have continued with their aggressions, in spite of my proclamations, while the blacks most certainly have. The colonial government has had no choice but to send parties of soldiers in pursuit of native raiders—though they are rarely found—while some among the settlers have organized hunting parties of their own. Thus, despite all my efforts, the colony has slipped ever further into a state of warfare.

Matters have not been helped by the activities of a small group of men of property, who have made themselves enemies of the colonial government, and have lately sought to tarnish the reputation of His Majesty's representatives by playing on the fears of the free population and suggesting they are not protected against the violence of the blacks. Meetings of protest have been held and attacks have appeared in the Colonial Times, *many of them directed, and most poisonously so, even at my own self. While I care little for my own reputation in this matter I have felt great alarm at this undermining of the authority of His Majesty's Government. Any land whose population is comprised largely of convicts and convicts freed, is, by its very nature, little less than a tinderbox, while if the forces of property fall into conflict with their own government it must be feared that the convict will seize his chance and mutiny. The havoc wreaked would certainly be terrible indeed, and could quite consume this colony.*

Such a situation, I may assure you, shall not be permitted to occur. Prompt action is needed and prompt action has been taken. I met last week with my most senior officers of government, including the colonial secretary and the chief police magistrate, and we were all agreed that, sad though it may be, the two races dwelling upon this island are now wholly beyond reconciliation. I considered the only possible means to end the conflict between them is to divide the colony into two entirely separate realms. This important decision is already being put into effect. A full and detailed proclamation has been drafted, announcing that henceforth the aborigines must leave the settled districts, and are to dwell only in the areas of the west, and also the northeast of the island. It is, I feel, a more than fair arrangement. These two areas together form nearly one half the total land of the island, and while it is true that they are comprised largely of wild, mountainous country, which yields less in the way of sustenance than the rest, the natives appear now so greatly reduced in their numbers that I have no doubt it will prove amply sufficient for their needs. These districts have suffered few, if any, incursions by white men, being for the most part still unexplored, thus ensuring that the blacks will be able to remain there safe and undisturbed. In this way their continued survival as a race–which is, as I have already remarked, of such great concern to myself–will be assured.

I am glad to report that even in a few short days this policy has shown some success. The rising passions of the settlers seem already blunted, and the reputation of the island's government, and my own self, has been considerably restored. There are still difficulties to be overcome, I will not deny. It will not be easy to alert the aborigines of the new arrangement, though here too I am doing all that is in my power to be done. Copies of the proclamation are being printed in great numbers, lengthy though the document is, and these will be distributed all about island, so they may be nailed to gum trees on the peripheries of the settled districts. There are one or two natives who were captured at a tender age in the past, and were taught their letters to some extent, though they later escaped, and it is to be hoped that these may explain the document to their fellows. Attempts will be made to apprehend others, who will be instructed as to the island's division and then released into the forests to spread their news. If some among the blacks continue to insist on remaining in the areas reserved for the whites, and on launching their attacks, no option will remain but to impose martial law and have these sought out until they desist.

The arrangement will doubtless take some little time to become established and yet I hope and believe that it will prove a most important and useful step towards establishing peace on this colony. It is a radical change, and I remain most optimistic that it will, in time, provide an enduring means for the protection and preservation of the unfortunate blacks, quite as you have, sir, so eloquently urged.

Peevay
1829

WEATHER STAYED WOEFUL, all strong wind and noisy rain, so we never met any white men to kill us as we went looking for war. Thus we went hither and thither, day after day, hunting and walking, till my feet were sore and even dog animals got tired. By and by we were gone right through Roingins' world and into Tommeginers', though this was just empty now, as Tommeginer were all with us or killed.

Then one morning we walked out from mountains, and parrot and cockatoo were calling, wombat dirt was there on that track, telling us we were near good land. Just after we found one puzzle to confound. Stuck on wattle tree was a tiny spear made from shining stuff like Mother's gun, very beautiful, and hanging from it was some strangest thing. This was like some dried skin, but thin and easy to tear like leaf, and when wind came it moved, like dead bird's wing. Black lines were on it, like pictures of nothing, plenty of them, so they covered that whole thing.

"That's just some white men's shit," said Mother, as if we were foolish fellows to be so curious. We all wanted to burn this new thing but Mother said no. "It means white men are near. If we make fire, then they'll know we're coming."

Nobody answered her. Nobody ever did. We were Mother's mob now, and Mother knew more about white men than anyone. Also she was scaring. She was right about them being close, yes. We went on, going carefully, trying to make dog animals be quiet—which was hard as they always were too wayward—and soon we found another white man's shit thing just the same, this time stuck on eucalyptus. Next there were trees cut down, and on the path were num footmarks with no toes. After this was a clearing, very large, with a wall all made from wood, and strange animals stuck inside, that Mother said were white men's animals whose name was SHEEP. I never saw these before, no, and they were interesting. They were fat and also stupid, running all together hither and thither, with short legs so they couldn't jump or climb trees or burrow, and I did observe that white man made them white just like himself. We wanted to spear them, as this would be easy as pissing on a stone we did surmise, but again Mother said no, we must go carefully. Then, just afterwards, walking quietly through trees, we saw that white men's hut.

This was more interesting even than the animals. It was made from tree bark, I did observe, and it had a special hole in the roof that pulled smoke out like some rope as if there was some magic thing. Of course now I know all these whitefellows' tricks and they're only ordinary. That hole was just a CHIMNEY. Likewise the white men's thing stuck on wattle tree was only PAPER, and its pictures of nothing were WRIT-ING, which I can do myself, as any one will tell. But when you don't know suchlike they are a curiosity. White men like to think you're stupid when you don't know some new thing he has, but in fact that's just his foolishness. He doesn't want to know that our ones can learn his clever-ness quick as he can, because deep down inside his breast white man WANTS our ones to be stupid.

I was still watching the smoke and wondering how it went when all of a sudden one very fat white man came out of the hut, walked over to a pile of wood and had his pissing. "I saw that one before," said one Tommeginer, whose name was Lacklay, whispering so excited. "He killed my sister."

Truth was Mother would do for those scuts whoever they were, but Lacklay's talk was useful, as it meant we could be angrier, which is important in fighting. So we got ready. I was quite fearful, I do recollect, as this was my first war with white men, while I was still just short then, and too small to do any dangerous wounding. Still I did want to be some great hero, and show Mother how I was brave and better than that Tayaleah, with his weakly thin legs. So I made myself brave.

Soon fat white scut went back into his hut and we went to the edge of the trees. Truly, that war was too easy. Mother and Lacklay went carefully, getting behind hut without making any sound, and then they put their fire sticks to the bark till it was burning. Then we all waited. Fire was quick, yes, and soon it was loud like branches snapping, and smoke was blown in wind like some crazy thing. White men knew what was happening of course. They did not run out but looked round the door, two of them. Fat one fired his gun once, but without killing any-body, so we just stood and watched while Mother called out in their own words to confound them.

"Come out, you fuckers, so we can kill you." And so.

This talk did scare them, yes, and so did Mother's gun, which she pointed at them by and by, so they stayed in their hut till fire was too hot and their faces got black, when suddenly they just ran out without car-ing, fat one trying to hit us with his gun like it was a waddy stick. Mother fired her gun now, and Lacklay fired the other, which Mother gave him, and though they missed, it never mattered, as we threw spears, and though my one didn't hit, others did, and soon those pissers were falling and getting finished with waddy sticks.

So it was done. Heinous thing was that Mother never did give me her praising like she should. No, she just told how brave Tayaleah was, though he did nothing but hide in the trees and watch. That was a hardship to endure. Mostly, though, that war was great good fortune. White scuts were killed just so, with none of us dead, and we even had the fat one's gun now, though its wooden end was broken. Yes, we had tidings of joy as we walked away from that burnt hut. Mother let us spear white men's animals now, which was too easy, just like we thought, and soon we reached forest once again, where we went quickly, sometimes singing, sometimes firing some piece of bush to see if game ran out, till we got two wallabies. Yes, we were joyous heroes that day.

When it was getting dark we stopped by some stream, made a big fire to cook wallabies and ate meat till we were full. Afterwards we danced a dance that we called White Men's Dance, which was our new invention, first dance just of Mother's tribe. At the start we danced fat one going out for his pissing and never knowing we were near. Then we danced us, going carefully, and Mother and Lacklay firing their hut. Finally we danced white scuts looking out, so scared, and then running hither and thither and getting speared dead. That was a fine dance and we played it many times. After, when it was late and we all were tired, we slept.

Now, in these long-after days, when that time feels too far away, like some dream story that never was, I do believe I heard them coming. Probably I heard something, yes, as I was already awake and curious even before it started. Perhaps it was some small noise, like a twig breaking or dog animal growling. Anyway it was good, as it made me readier. Probably that tiny noise let me live all these years.

Sound that came next made me deaf as if my head was in water. I knew that sound now, of course, as I heard Mother's, and the fat white man's too. Next, just for one tiny moment, all was quiet, and I hoped it was not any heinous thing after all, but just some foolishness with our guns. But then others fired, plenty of them, and there was screaming and dog animals were yelping. That was heinous. Our fire was gone weak but still I could observe that Lacklay was shot, very bad, and others too.

White men were coming, walking slow from the dark, in one big circle all around, watching so carefully, some putting another bullet in the end of their guns, others holding sticks and killing knives.

I do believe if they shot Mother soonest then probably we would all be dead. Yes, if there was one grievous error they made, this was it. Probably they fired at men first, thinking these were most dangerous, which was some great foolishness. I was near Mother and now I saw her looking at one place in that circle of white men, where it got stretched, and there was just one scut, very big. So she lifted her gun and shot, and all of a sudden he was gone and there was a fine hole. I do recall how everything went slow after that, almost as if it was never happening at all, and never would, but somehow my legs did move by and by, which was great good fortune, and so I started, not standing but just scampering, hands like feet, past nearly dead Lacklay, past another, then into trees. I could hear some coming after but I never paid heed, running like wind, never minding if I hit some tree or scratching leaves, just going fast as I ever could go. Being so small did help, yes, as I could go beneath. On I went, and on again, till finally I must stop, from tiredness, and when I listened all I could hear was my own breathing, so quick and fearing. Then I hid in that same place by and by, crawling into some bush, just keeping still and being alive.

Noises in the forest were a puzzle to confound. Sometimes twigs broke or leaves scraped and it was hard to tell if these were my ones, white scuts, or just some wallaby going hither and thither. Finally sky began to get lighter and when I looked all about I saw no foes. So by and by I left my hiding place and went on, going so carefully. Soon I saw footmarks with toes, so I knew they were ours. That was great good fortune. Quietly, quietly I followed, careful like some hunter, till I reached our fire and sleeping place of that night before. Truly, that already seemed like some long-ago time.

Fire was finished now, except for tiny smoke and ashes smell that makes you sneeze. There was another smell, besides, too hateful. Yes, my ones were there, some wailing, some just standing and looking. So I saw we were less than half Mother's mob of yesterday, which was woeful. Round the fire were dead ones, plenty of them, shot or heads smashed, or cut with killing knives. Worst, though, was the fire, where babies were, thrown and burnt. For some while I just watched and pondered this place.

But you must know this truth, which is a heinous thing. Those feelings deep inside my breast were not only lamenting, you see. No, even now there was one small part that was tidings of joy. Perhaps you think that is impossible, and that I must be some vile fellow, hateful to behold. Perhaps I am. But please, I urge, do know me. What made me so, you see, was Mother. There she was, looking and searching in that fire dirt and going in the trees, calling again and again, one word, always the same, like some animal that's got caught in a clever trap and cannot get free.

"Tayaleah. Tayaleah."

The little shit was vanished, you see, nowhere to be found.

CHAPTER FIVE

Captain Illiam Quillian Kewley
JULY 1857

I DARE SAY there was bound to be some fussing from the boys when they learned that they weren't on their way back to Man Island after all, but were now bound for furthest Australia. The ones that had scolds for wives–these being, fortunately, a good portion–weren't so bad, but the rest got themselves into a proper huff, wailing and threatening in Manx, till I had to tell the Englishmen that they were wanting more pay. Why, I even worried they might curdle completely, and that I'd find myself set adrift in a boat, the Captain Bligh of Peel City. There's nothing like a fear of gaols, though, to bring a man around. After a day had passed they grew quieter, and before long they were just in sulks, which was their natural, everyday state.

Three days' sailing and we were off the Isle of Wight, with no sight of our good friend Captain Clarke of Her Majesty's coast guard cutter *Dolphin*, nor any oceangoing bloodhounds sniffing for Maldon furniture. The wind was blowing nicely and at this rate it wouldn't be long before we were past the Scillies and safely out of range of Englishness, excepting, that was, the Englishness we had aboard. Curious it was to walk on the quarterdeck, knowing it would soon be lurching about under some strange tropical skies, the like of which none of us had seen, nor much wanted to neither. My worry was Ealisad. Hadn't I promised I'd be back within the month, with jink enough to spoil her better than Queen Victoria? It'd be weeks before I could so much as send a letter and tell her I'd be the odd year late. I'd not be easily forgiven for that. Not that there was much to be done about it, mind, so I tried not to think on it, keeping myself busy with the ship. There was enough to do, besides, as I needed to be sure we really were ready to go playing Captain Cook. Fortunately the *Sincerity* was in a good state, having been nearly murdered to death with repairs in Peel, so she had new yards and canvas, and spares enough for a hurricane or two. Why, for that matter she even had a spare hull to help her float. Thanks to our fussing vicar we had fresh water and eatables to last, and proper documents, too. It was only when we were well out to sea, in fact, and I started wondering about laying down a course for the rest of the voyage, that I remembered the one little item that we were lacking.

Charts.

I blamed the Reverend. The silly scriss had fussed us all across London buying every kind of store, so why hadn't he thought to moan me into a mapmaker's shop and finished the job? It was pure neglectfulness. Trouble it meant, no denying. A ship's captain needs charts like a lawyer needs sin, as to go sailing about the globe without is dropping right back to Chris Columbus himself, who mistook America for India. Even the chief mate, Brew, who was smooth enough to smile his way through his own funeral, fretted at that one.

"We'll just have to put in somewhere," he said, all frowns. "Portsmouth isn't far."

It was never so easy, though. Portsmouth was customs men, and would also be a stroll around the town for our three passengers, which meant newspapers for them to stare at.

"Let's put a sight on the chart locker," I told him. "You never know, we might be lucky."

I'd never given any serious study to this spot before, just piling my own charts of the Irish Sea, English Channel and such on top of what was left there, and now I took a more careful look I found it was a proper mess, looking as if it hadn't been cleared out for half a dozen captains. First was a thick layer of pencil drawings, all of the same ill-tempered-looking cat, which I guessed was the leavings of a heavy dose of sea boredom. Next was worse, being a pile of rhyming verse, all concerned with passionate Spaniards named Alphonse and Esmeralda, who were forever stabbing at one another and dancing in the moonlight. After that were pages of scribbled figures, together with a long, crabby document blaming pennies lost on some long-forgotten chief mate. Finally, under this, I found a few charts.

One of these caught my eye straight off, being nothing other than a handy little portrait of the Cape Colony, where we now hoped to find ourselves in a couple of months, and might even sell a few certain casks of something to whatever Africans were loafing about there. The map was hardly recent, still marking the place as Dutch—which Brew said took us back to Napoleon himself—nor was it especially pretty, looking as if its owner had used it as a plate for his dinner once or twice, but for all that a chart was a chart.

We were less lucky with the West Indies, which was a mighty shame seeing as they were our first halt. We had to go across the Atlantic to catch the breezes southwards to the Cape, and it was part of our agreement with the Englishmen—an agreement which I'd hardly troubled myself with at the time, seeing as I thought we were only going to Essex—that we were to call in at Jamaica. All that I could discover that even pictured the island was a map of the whole world, and this was a Mercator besides, which meant Norway was as long as my hand while whole of the Caribbean hardly covered two penny pieces.

"We'll hardly find our way into Kingston harbour with that," said Brew, screwing up his face.

I had a little thought. "Perhaps we don't need to."

The Reverend Geoffrey Wilson
JULY–AUGUST 1857

THREE DAYS into our journey Captain Kewley and his chief mate, Brew, suddenly strode into the cabin without so much as knocking at the door. Hardly had I begun to register my displeasure at this invasion of my privacy, when the Captain began trying to persuade me that we should not, as planned, drop anchor at Jamaica.

"It's just that I remembered the chase you were in to get to Tasmania, you see, Vicar, while the fact is we never need to go there. We've got supplies enough to carry us to Africa nicely."

While I regard myself as a man ever open to suggestions, I confess that this particular proposal held little appeal. In the first place I felt that an agreement, once entered upon, should be properly adhered to by both parties, if only as a matter of principle, while it had been amply clear that we were to stop at Kingston. There was, in truth also another consideration. Ever since the *Sincerity* had reached open waters and so encountered the full motion of the seas, the pleasing prospect of our first landfall had been greatly—even ceaselessly—in my thoughts. The possibility of this now becoming even further removed, and of my remaining aboard ship continuously for two months or more, was therefore far from welcome.

"I believe we should keep to our original course," I told the Captain firmly.

"It's to your own advantage," Kewley insisted.

Assistance came to me from an unexpected quarter. Potter's head loomed down from his bunk bed. "But we must call in at Jamaica," he declared simply. "Besides, I cannot believe it would add so greatly to our journey, seeing as we have to go near."

I must confess I had found the behaviour of the expedition surgeon far from helpful—a matter which I will recount more fully later—and yet his words at this moment were welcome enough. Kewley tried to threaten us with sea technicalities, but when I warned him that I might be forced to reconsider the charter fee that we had agreed, his face, which normally displayed a kind of beaming slyness, quite scowled. "I'll see what I can do," he promised sourly, and with this he and Brew marched away, grumbling to one another in that infuriating language of theirs.

I am never one, I must insist, to indulge in self-pity—I have, indeed, observed that this quality can be as much the undoing of a man as drink, leading him into ever greater aimlessness and despond—and yet I confess the days after we departed from the river Blackwater had hardly been my happiest. The start of my difficulties was, I believe, the dinner we were served the evening we set sail, which was excessively fatty, while matters were not helped when, on retiring that night, I found the cabin became filled with a most noxious smell, much like some terrible gaseous pond, and which, I was later told, was caused by water in the bilges becoming disturbed by the movement of the ship. It was true that the *Sincerity* was rolling and pitching ever more wildly. Within the hour the wind seemed to be blowing little less than a full gale, and, feeling suddenly unwell, I found myself journeying up to the deck, shivering stoically by the rail in my nightshirt and overcoat.

Sadly this proved only the first of many such visits. The weather seemed obstinately resolved to grow worse rather than better, and by morning waves were crashing against the bow so hard that the whole vessel reverberated with their force, and that a man more lacking in courage than myself might almost have feared that the ship would capsize altogether, or simply fragment into so many splinters. Rather to my surprise my two colleagues appeared unaffected by the fatty dinner, and would both greedily march off to the dining cabin on every occasion. Despite my discomfort I was most happy for them, naturally, though I did take exception to the way Dr. Potter would insist on loudly describing the meals he had just consumed, even though it must have been evident that I was feeling still delicate.

Apart from sickness, the other matter that was much in my thoughts was sleep, or rather my own lack of this essential sustenance. I do believe that, with the exception of a field of battle, there is hardly a place on earth more poorly suited to the gaining of rest than a sailing ship. Every night, just as I was falling into much-needed dreaming, there would be some shout in Manx and all at once the ceiling of the cabin would shudder with the stamping of heavy boots, so loud that it sounded as if the crew were revenging themselves upon some tiny scampering creatures. Next they would then set to work upon some operation of the ship, such as bringing round the sails to obtain a change of direction, which could occur numerous times in one single night. Timbers would creak, ropes and blocks would squeal, officers would bellow, boots would thump and the crew themselves would begin singing at the top of their voices, seeming unable to tug at any rope without wailing some unspeakable shanty song.

I tried my best to induce the Manxmen to show a little consideration but it was to no avail. When I struck upon the ceiling of the cabin with a stick they pretended not to hear. When I asked Captain Kewley, in a most friendly manner, if his crew could not engage more quietly in their

nocturnal operations, he was nothing less than uncivil. Nor did the behaviour of my two fellow passengers, I regret to say, help matters. While
I am never someone to judge others with undue harshness, and it is my
greatest delight to find goodness in my fellow men, I confess I found my
patience increasingly strained. Though Renshaw had a tiny cabin of his
own, the wooden partition that divided this from ours was of such poor
construction that there were large gaps between the timbers, and one
could hear his every movement, while frequently during the night I
would be disturbed by the sound of his fidgeting with his person in some
curious, twitching way, quite as if he had some ailment. Dr. Potter was
more distracting still, and would insist on keeping a light burning late
into the night so he could scribble notes in his notebook with that infuri-
atingly scratching quill. "I'll just be another moment, Vicar," was his ever
repeated cry when I requested, with all the gentleness I could muster,
that he cease.

I did my best to regard the man charitably, despite his many provo-
cations. When he insisted on draping his clothes, that he had just
washed, around the edge of his bunk, so they dripped seawater directly
onto my own cot, leaving large damp places, I told myself this was not
the result of some lawless nature, but only of his having been brought up
without the advantage of fine manners. I even thought to help him improve himself, drawing up a few simple rules with regard to domestic
matters, which I then placed in written form on the wall just above his
own berth, so he might observe them with convenience. One might have
supposed he would welcome such a kindness, but no, he instead showed
a maddening forgetfulness as to my little suggestions—a forgetfulness so
pronounced that I could not help but doubt its sincerity—while he would
insist on referring to them as "the parson's laws," in a tone of voice that
was little less than offensive.

Some men might have answered such behaviour with anger, but I
preferred to seek solace through faith. These were days of much praying,
and I found myself often moved to seek guidance from Him with regard
to my two colleagues—often in their own presence—perhaps dwelling
upon some little trait of character of theirs that might, I believed, with
His help, find improvement. Thus I would pray that Potter would find in
his heart greater kindliness and consideration towards his fellow men,

and that Renshaw would sleep soundly without disturbing any with his restlessness. I did have hopes that these humble efforts might help them both to find a greater understanding of themselves, and that, with time, they might even join me in these little ministrations. To my regret, however, they seemed wholly to ignore my endeavours, quite as if they had not heard me at all.

My humble efforts did not go entirely unheard, however. It seemed beyond mere chance that, as I prayed, I found my own life aboard the ship growing slowly less burdensome. Little by little my sickness began to pass until finally the great day came when I made my way to the dining cabin, with its many delightful, if cheap, prints of the royal family (a man could find no keener monarchist than Captain Kewley), where I dined for the very first time since leaving Essex. The lurching of the vessel, likewise, became less strange to me, until I was able to walk from place to place quite without suddenly clutching for support, and even the nightly din of work upon the deck grew less irksome, until it was hardly more distracting to my sleep than so much birdsong. Before long the prospect of the many miles and months of voyaging ahead seemed of little account, as I became accustomed to living upon this vessel, viewing it hardly as a machine of travel, but rather as my home.

By then our steady progress southwestwards had begun to bring noticeable changes, which resembled the alterations of the seasons, but strangely intermixed, as if May and September were occurring at one and the same time. While the sun grew stronger—care soon had to be taken if one did not wish to suffer a pinkened nose—the hours of daylight steadily shrank. Time itself seemed fluid, indeed, in this strange liquid world. Every midday a curious ritual was performed, when the Captain and his two mates—the smooth fellow Brew and the small, angry one, Kinvig—would stand side by side, pointing their sextants southwards. Finally, when each had lowered his device, Captain Kewley would call out, "Noon it is," and at once the bell would ring out eight times, hourly sandglasses would be set, and the new ship's day would begin. Without fail the hands of my watch would require adjustment by a minute or two to match this new noon.

I found myself much intrigued by the many curious ways of shipboard life. Why, I quite wished I could understand the crew's strange

Celtic language—vile though it sounded—as they frequently spoke it when I was near, and always with such cheerful laughter that I would gladly have given a penny to know the subject of their happy bantering. They were, I observed, a people of strong and yet puzzling traditions. They quite insisted, for example, that we must never call the pigs aboard the vessel by their correct name, but should instead refer to them always as "swineys," as a matter of some seagoing protocol, though this seemed a most foolish requirement, and I quite wondered if they might be playing a joke upon their new passengers. Then again I observed the *Sincerity* to be a place of no small formality, where every man had his exact post, quite as in some court of law. The Captain and the chief mate, Brew, would be found on the quarterdeck, to the rear of the vessel, where Kewley would have pride of place on the windward side, giving him a clear view forwards, with all the great sails billowing away. This was despite the fact that he himself rarely issued an order to the crew, such work being the preserve of Mr. Brew, who had to suffer the leeward side of the deck, from where it was hard to see anything except vast curtains of canvas stretching up to heaven. If, however, the Captain went below, then Brew would at once usurp his position.

Forward of the quarterdeck one would find the crew, and the second mate, Kinvig, angrily issuing instructions. His rank seemed much inferior to Brew's and he was often required to clamber into the rigging with the crew, while Brew hardly stirred from his comfortable spot upon deck. Further forward still lay the galley, a kind of rough hut upon the deck, which was the workplace of the cook, Quayle: a moody soul, who seemed to find companionship only in the shipboard animals. These beasts, I should explain, were numerous—at least at the start of the journey—and were housed in the various ship's boats, though it did occur to me that this was not the best arrangement, as, were the *Sincerity* to strike disaster, it would be no easy thing speedily to remove four bullocks from the long boat.

Prevention is better than cure, of course, and I was ever impressed by the concern shown towards the maintenance of the ship, which seemed to consume the majority of the working time of the crew. The deck was thoroughly scrubbed down as many as three times each day, which struck me as obsessively cleanly, until I learned that it was to prevent the planks from shrinking, which would permit water to seep below. To the same end the crewmen were frequently to be found hammering strands of old rope between the planks and pouring on hot pitch as a seal. Each and every rope of the ship's rigging was regularly examined, and perhaps painted with tar, while constant adjustments were made to maintain their tautness: a painstaking business, as the ropes formed quite a cat's cradle, and to tighten one invariably meant altering half a dozen others thereafter. There were frequent expeditions aloft to oil the blocks, through which the ropes moved, or to chip and repaint the ironwork. It seemed, altogether, that no sooner had some lengthy chore been completed than the order would be given for it to be begun all over again.

When not busy with such drudgery the crew either would be found in a state of semi-somnolence, dozing in the sun and smoking pipes, or would be high in the rigging, engaged in some display of skill worthy of circus acrobats. Often and again they would clamber, in hardly more than an instant, to a dizzy height above the deck, where it was a mystery to me how they managed to cling on at all. On one occasion the ship met an especially heavy swell that caused it to roll like a fearful seesaw, wildly tipping from side to side, so that the ends of the yards actually dipped into the ocean, and though it was hard for me even to keep my place just upon the deck, still the crew carried on quite as usual. One of them, whose place was at the very edge of the mainsail spar, was repeatedly plunged waist-deep in seawater, only to find himself a moment later propelled skywards as the vessel righted itself, until he was higher almost than the crow's nest, with the whole ship leaning crazily beneath him. All the while he was quietly at work fastening a rope.·

It was, as it happened, as I looked upon the men on that day, and witnessed their perilous toil, that a most pleasing notion occurred to me. I dare say that for many men there is some special activity that is essential if they are to feel a sense of completion in life. For some this may be adventure, or the pursuit of wealth. For others it might be family bliss and the comfort of routine. As for myself, nothing is quite so pleasing as the prospect of honest work, through which I may bring a little joy and comfort into the lives of others.

I wasted no time but mentioned my idea to Captain Kewley that same afternoon. Convincing the Captain of anything was never easy, as, like his compatriots, he possessed an obstinate reluctance to be impressed by another's enthusiasm. A favourite word of the Manxmen was *middling*, which they used to display a seemingly limitless absence of concern in anything. If some furious typhoon were to strike, threatening to sink the ship, they would likely say only that it was *middling bad weather*. If there occurred a wondrous tropical sunset with colours to dazzle the eyes, it would be only *middling fine*. Why, if the four angels of destruction themselves were to appear before a Manxman, toppling mountains like so many flowerpots, I dare say he would think them only *middling troublesome*. With this in mind, I should not perhaps have been surprised by Kewley's response to my proposal.

"Sunday sermons, eh?"

"I feel it is nothing less than my duty," I explained. "These men who face danger every day would, I believe, find no little comfort in their being brought closer to the word of God."

Kewley frowned. "I dare say it's harmless enough."

It was, at least, no prohibition, and this was enough for my purpose. I set to work with cheerful determination. Before I could begin labouring on the sermon itself there were a number of small matters to which I had to attend. It seemed only right, for example, that I should be provided with a few simple shelves placed in the cabin, on which I might keep my books, my papers and writing implements. Likewise, the table in the dining cabin being irretrievably gashed and stained with grease for my purposes, I proposed that a tiny desk be attached to the dining cabin wall. The Captain, though he grumbled, eventually agreed to have the carpenter work upon these, and soon afterwards it occurred to me that it would be delightful to have a little platform constructed, perhaps upon the quarterdeck, together with a stand for the Good Book itself, which would serve as a kind of sea pulpit and sea lectern. What was more, it seemed only logical to have constructed a number of simple yet sturdy benches, so the crew might listen in modest comfort. Here, however, the Captain proved wholly uncooperative.

"I'm not having any deck of mine turned into some floating chapel," he insisted, in a tone of voice that was, I regret to tell, hardly polite. "This is a ship, not a preaching house."

Sad to say, he was not the only one whose help in these little matters proved wanting. Dr. Potter became quite sulky when my little writing desk was set onto the wall, as–by purest chance–it happened to lie just behind his place at the dining table, and he made the greatest fuss that it interfered with his sitting. His mood did not even improve later when I tried to raise his spirits, sitting down beside him on his cot and quietly praying for the Lord to help us to find that kindliness that lay somewhere in every man's heart. In fact he seemed if anything to grow worse. It was about this time, indeed, that I began to wonder if such a man was suited to take part in an expedition of such great importance as our own.

Dr. Thomas Potter
AUGUST 1857

The Celtic Type

The Celtic Type (instance: Manx) is altogether inferior in physique to the Saxon, being smaller, darker and lacking in strength. Typically the forehead is sloping, showing evidence of the "snout" characteristic, noted by Pearson as an indication of inferior intelligence. The skull is marked by deep eye sockets, expressing tendencies of servitude. Cranial type: G.

As to his general character, the Celt is wanting in the industriousness and nobility of spirit of his Saxon neighbour, his dominating characteristic being indolence. He is content to wait upon events rather than moulding them, and suffers a fatal patience, hoping that fortune may smile upon him. In his favour it can be observed that the Celt possesses a rude sense of creativity (instance: songs and stories). He also possesses a simple physical courage, which has provided him with his most enduring role, as the foot soldier of the Saxon.

The moral qualities of the Celt are poor, being characterized by idleness and resignation. Towards foreigners he is clannish and habitually secretive, preferring to converse in his own primitive tongue (instance: Manx) though he may be perfectly capable of speaking in English.

In conclusion, the Celt has his place at the lowest station within the European Division. This is indicated not only by his physical and moral qualities but also in his dismal history, which is typified by disorder, disunity and decline. It may be assumed that within the womb the development of the Celtic embryo is arrested after no more than thirty-six weeks, or a full three weeks sooner than the Saxon.

The Norman Type

The Norman (instance: priesthood, aristocracy and monarchy of England) is similar in physique to the Saxon, though on close examination he will be found to be <u>slighter</u> and altogether lacking in the latter's rugged hardiness. His complexion is pale, and his hair often inclines to reddishness. His facial shape is typically long and narrow, indicating <u>arrogance</u>. Cranial type: D.

The character of the Norman is one of <u>decline</u>. He has ever relied on <u>inherited</u> advantage, a state of affairs dating back to the lucky accident of conquest. He is <u>idle</u> and lacking in any spirit of industry or application. Likewise he is prone to weaknesses from which sturdier types would not suffer (instance: seasickness). He is entirely without creative talents.

The morality of the Norman is poor, being typified by concealed <u>selfishness</u>. His dominating characteristic is <u>cunning</u>. He strives to maintain himself at an exalted station within society through <u>scheming manipulation</u> with others of his race. Any display of moral purpose will be fabrication. The Norman is, most of all, of a <u>parasitical</u> nature, feeding upon the simple kindliness of nobler types.

In conclusion, the Norman place is hardly higher than the Celt within the European Division. The development of the Norman embryo can be assumed to be arrested after thirty-seven weeks, or two weeks fewer than the Saxon. The Norman's enduring control of that <u>triple curse</u> of Aristocracy, Priesthood and Monarchy can be ascribed not to his ability but to the great abhorrence, among his Saxon subjects, of any form of disorder.

Timothy Renshaw
AUGUST 1857

SO THERE WE WERE, stood on the deck in the hot sun, waiting for the wondrous joy of Wilson's sermon. The one consolation was that at least there would be something to keep my eyes occupied while the old goat stuttered on. The lookout had called out the news just an hour or two before, with a great shout of "Land ho." It was hard to see what he was crowing about at first, the day being so hazy, and only when I screwed up my eyes tight could I make out a faint line just above where the horizon should be. With time, though, the line grew darker and easier to catch until, quite suddenly, it turned itself into a good-sized piece of land, not even very far away, with cliffs and hills.

It might not sound much to anyone spoilt for solid ground, I dare say, but after all those weeks without anything to look upon except wind and water and seabirds, it was as welcome as could be. Others may like the thought of sitting aboard some ship for months at a time, but not me, and I would have given more than a little to be magicked to Haymarket, for a drop of fine liquor and perhaps a little intimate company from the wrong kind of female.

The company I had could hardly have been more different. It seemed ever to be my fate to be surrounded by people who thought they knew every answer. My parents, and my brother Jeremy too, were always ready to deliver a disapproving lecture upon the virtue of hard work and my need to improve myself, while my fellow expedition members delighted in exactly the same game. The one point upon which they seemed agreed, indeed, was that I was lazy and foolish and should be treated as their junior. Wilson was the worst, and was forever making scornful remarks as to my reluctance to raise myself from sleep at the hour of dawn.

It was not as if I had even wanted to come on this voyage.

"A little hardship should knock some sense into you," my father had promised kindly.

My mother was not to be outdone. "It is our hope that it may also help you gain a greater sense of the spiritual."

All I had gained till now was a greater sense of boredom. Six weeks we had been sailing, and still we were hardly started. I had long read the few books I had brought, and read them once again. I would have borrowed more, but Wilson had only the driest tomes, either theological or geological, while Potter had brought no books at all, seeming content to scribble his endless notes. I even tried to pass time by making friends with the Manxmen, but with no great success. They might join me in smoking a pipe or two, but they would always keep themselves a little distant, and would suddenly break into Manx among themselves, as if to discourage me from remaining too long.

Land was a welcome enough sight, certainly. I wondered how many days I would have still to wait before I might stride into Kingston, and be free of my tiresome colleagues.

"So which of the Indies is this?" I asked the Captain as we regarded the new shore. I was hoping it might be Jamaica itself.

Kewley, rather to my surprise, seemed not greatly interested. "One of them, I dare say."

"D'you think we shall make land today?" asked the vicar.

"I very much doubt it."

Wilson looked even pleased. All he seemed to care about was that nothing should interfere with his sermonizing. All day he had been busy thinking up new ways to make a nuisance of himself, clucking and fussing. His chief demand had been that a temporary stand be created on the quarterdeck, so he could play the giant parson at everyone. As if he were not bothersome enough already. "I'm simply concerned," he told Kewley, pressing his hands tight together as if he were trying to squeeze out some kind of juice, "that the men may not be able to hear me clearly."

The Captain, to be fair, did not give up without a fight. "They hear *me* well enough."

"It would seem hardly fitting for the word of God to be bellowed out like some shipboard order," answered Wilson, twittering at his little joke. "Surely it would be possible to devise some temporary arrangement, perhaps made from a few of the cases containing our stores?" Next he gave his toothy smile, which, in my experience indicated he was getting ready to stab. Nor was I mistaken. "Unless, that is, you feel your men should not benefit from a little Christian instruction."

There it was, the vicar's killing thrust. Kewley could hardly protest further without making himself look like some Antichrist. He frowned at the sea, knowing himself beaten, then grumbled assent.

Wilson beamed. "I'll just need four of your men. It won't take them a moment."

Potter had sat himself on a coil of rope just below the quarterdeck, writing in his notebook and I supposed this was where he planned to remain. The spot was almost out of view from the temporary pulpit, so Wilson would not be able to see if he was listening, while the doctor could never be accused of hiding away and playing heathen. I was surprised to see him making even this careful concession, in truth, so bad had matters become between the two. There had been times when I had hoped I would have proper hitting fight to watch, especially on that morning when Wilson sat next to the doctor in the dining cabin and started praying for "all men" to "overcome their petty hatreds and listen to the words of wisdom of their brothers." Potter's face looked dark with rage. Mind you, he'd given as good as he got, especially at the start, when Wilson had been seasick and Potter had driven him half mad with goading. That was purest Potter. If Wilson would annoy to death with his pushing and twittering, Potter was all quiet danger.

"Oh no, I'm afraid that one won't do at all. What about one of the cases of champagne?" Wilson said this with a touch of sadness, quite as if it were he who would be heaving and sweating crates up the stairs. A champagne case was duly brought and laid beside the others on the quarterdeck, but still he was not satisfied, peering at it from different angles, then having it moved from one side to another, only to shake his head again. "Perhaps one of the ones with cutlery?" Finally, though, even he could think of no reasons for fussing and he declared his platform ready.

The Manxmen seemed divided over the question of his service. Some, such as the Captain himself, looked none too pleased at this sudden interference in their Sunday, which had previously been a preserve of lounging and pipe smoking. Others, though, appeared content enough, and gathered themselves beneath the quarterdeck, bright-eyed at the treat ahead. I had never seen Wilson at work before and, rather to my surprise, he showed himself to be quite a player, acting out his drama. First he raised his hands in the air to make everyone hushed. Then, when there was no sound except the wind, the birds and the light flapping of the sails, he suddenly changed his mind, shook his head and stepped back down from his platform. For a moment he stood at the rail, cupping his chin in his hand and frowning at the ocean, so we could all observe his state of contemplation, and then, just as some in the congregation were beginning to fidget, at once he clapped his hands together, as if he had found the answer to whatever question that had been annoying him, and he jumped back to his place.

"As you all will know," he declared, "there is no greater mystery than the sea." Now he leant forward onto an upturned case of portable soup that acted as his lectern, so he could stare at us more thoroughly. "The sea! The sea! That great wilderness which . . ."

It was bad luck for him, there was no denying. Just when he had caught the moment nicely there was a cry from the topmast, ringing out clear in the light breeze. "Sail. Sail to the northwest."

The Captain looked pleased at this chance for a little belittling, and strode straight up onto the vicar's platform, all but pushing him to one side. "Teare, bring my telescope." Wilson himself had to smile and look as if he never minded.

This new ship must have emerged from behind a headland of the island, as it was not very far off, being easily near enough to be seen from the deck. It was a large schooner, with two triangular sails, both coloured grey. As for direction, it was pursuing a course parallel to our own. His telescope brought, the Captain retired to the rear of the quarterdeck to take a good look.

This time Wilson did not trouble us with another miming act but simply leant forward onto the lectern. "As all of you will know, there is no greater mystery than the sea. The sea! The sea! That great wilderness which appears to possess . . ."

It was not his day. All at once the Captain strode back onto the platform looking fierce, and, without so much as a by-your-leave, bellowed out an order in Manx. Whatever this was, it could hardly have been better calculated to wreck the proceedings. In an instant every member of Wilson's congregation was dispersed, some scampering up the rigging, others gathering about the base of the mainmast unfastening the ends of ropes. I could not help but wonder if this were a case of deliberate wrecking, a suspicion evidently shared by Wilson himself.

"Captain, is this really necessary?"

"It may be and it may not, but I'm taking no chances with a ship like that." With this mystery Kewley handed his telescope to the vicar.

"It seems an ordinary enough vessel."

"She'd be more ordinary still," said Kewley, with too much patience, "if she carried a flag or two from her masts and had a name and port painted on her prow."

Shielding my eyes, I could just make out that the mast was bare and the prow was black and nameless.

Wilson seemed still unimpressed. "There's probably some quite harmless explanation."

Kewley shrugged. "Let's hope so."

By now the crew had begun to pull the yards about and China Clucas was turning the wheel spokes, bringing the ship slowly round, until she was veering away from the other vessel. All eyes looked aft. For a moment all seemed well, but then the two grey sails began gradually to change shape, until she was once again aligned behind and parallel to us: a narrow strip of dark woodwork with a great expanse of grey sailcloth stretching out above. For a second or two we all remained silent. Then Brew bellowed to the crew, and they jumped into activity, unfurling more canvas.

"It looks a poor sort of vessel," Potter declared, almost petulantly. "I'm sure we will outrun her."

It was a pleasing thought, but, as matters turned out, well wide of the mark: as I watched, it was soon evident that they were gaining upon us, if slowly, in the light wind. How strange it felt to be stood thus at the rail, among the smells of pitch and wood and damp that were now grown so commonplace, knowing that just a mile or so distant was a vessel filled with strangers, who were hoping to rob, or even murder, us all. It was no catastrophe I had imagined. Nightmares of storms and shipwreck I had had, but never had I thought we might find ourselves pursued by some form of freebooter pirates. I felt my pulse quicken, and yet I found myself also somehow unmoved. I wondered, with some shock, if I was simply numbed, or if I even cared what fate might be awaiting me. Potter also seemed subdued, quite slumping over the rail, and only Wilson had lost none of his spirit.

"Have no fear," he called out to any who would listen. "I will use all powers to intercede with them. I will beg them to treat us mercifully. I will tell them of our Christian purpose. God will help us."

I was, in truth, far from sure his mediation would improve our prospects. Captain Kewley was engaged in more practical measures. He had the crew form a human chain, lowering buckets over the side and then passing them along the deck and up into the rigging, so seawater could be hurled against the sails.

"It helps the canvas catch the wind," Brew explained. "In a light breeze like this it could make a good difference."

How effective an advantage this might be, sadly we never discovered, as within only a few moments our pursuers could be observed doing exactly the same. Their advance upon us seemed undiminished. Borrowing the Captain's telescope, I could now see their vessel in some little detail, its deck crowded with dark figures. These, a little to my surprise, showed no signs of shouting or working themselves into some frenzy, simply standing thus, unnervingly still. Among them there was a constant glinting, as the sunlight caught bright metal strips by the dozen. Cutlasses?

"D'you think they may be freed slaves?" I wondered.

"They cannot be," insisted Potter, suddenly animated. "Slaves would never show such resourcefulness."

Captain Kewley shrugged grimly. "I can't see it much matters what their profession was."

"Perhaps we should lower a couple of boats and try and haul ourselves out of trouble," suggested the chief mate, Brew.

Kewley shook his head. "By the time we've cleared out the creatures they'd be on us. Besides, the wind looks like it's freshening again." This was true enough. As he spoke, another gust came, flapping the sails into greater life. Kewley frowned. "Can we get that cannon going?"

"We've no shot," Brew answered grimly.

"How are we for guns, then?"

"There's a couple of old muskets in the stores locker, but I'm not sure they'll fire."

My only surprise was that nobody had thought of it sooner. I suppose we had been so preoccupied with escape that we had hardly been thinking of anything else. "What about the rifles?" I asked.

Suddenly we were all hurrying. It was not until this moment, curiously enough, when something could finally be done, that I felt something like panic. All at once I felt myself seized by a curious clumsiness, bumping my way down the stairway quite as if I were drunk. The case was heavy as a coffin but eventually Potter, two Manxmen and I managed to haul it up to the deck. Kinvig, the little second mate, ripped open the lid with a hook, and we found ourselves staring at six gleaming rifles and a revolving pistol.

Potter frowned at a cartridge as it sat, trembling slightly, between his fingers. "I'm sure there was some trick with these. Let me see . . ." He ripped at the greasy paper with his teeth and black powder poured out. When the paper was torn further, the grey nose of a bullet became visible. "But that can't be right. The bullet is pointing at the charge."

"Perhaps it was made wrongly," I wondered. I tried a cartridge each, fumbling with the paper, but it was just the same. If it was dropped down the barrel powder-first, as it must be for firing, then the bullet would be shot out pointing backwards, which would hardly do. There's little worse than trying to think through clever puzzles when time's running short and your mind's full of fears of being murdered, and it was sorely tempting just to despair and think everything impossible. Glancing back, I could see the men on the sloop's deck quite clearly now, as they stood regarding us, so still. Most were holding cutlasses, but some had what looked like grappling hooks.

It was Wilson, of all people, who had the answer. "Wasn't there something about pouring the powder out and then turning the bullet round?"

"That was it." Potter emptied the powder into the barrel of his gun, then tried the bullet, which was still wrapped in its cartridge paper. It fitted nicely. Using the spindly ram to press it well home, he raised the gun and aimed it, for some reason, at the mizzenmast. All at once there was a violent report—causing squeals of alarm from the pigs and sheep—and a small cloud of smoke filled the air. As for the mizzenmast, this now had a mightiest hole smashed into it, quite as if it had been punched by some metal fist.

Captain Kewley gave him a hard look. "I thought it was their vessel we were shooting?"

"At least it shows it works, and very well too." Glancing aft, Potter now looked disappointed. "They've lain down. How cowardly."

Sure enough, our tormentors had all now vanished from sight, though their vessel continued its progress just as before. An instant later a shot rang out and a bullet whizzed through the air somewhere above our heads, causing us also to drop to the deck.

"What about the Reverend's pulpit?" called out Brew.

The platform could hardly have been better suited to our needs, it was true, and we all hurried behind its shelter. Still it was hard to know what we should do.

"Perhaps we should just shoot at their vessel," proposed Potter. "The bullet seemed to cause a good bit of damage."

"It might only make them more violent towards us," insisted Wilson, who seemed to be looking forward to the chance of lecturing them into mercy.

Captain Kewley looked thoughtful for a moment. "I suppose we could aim at their wheel. That's the part that might notice."

It was visible enough–though the helmsman had dropped out of sight, guiding it, I imagined, from below–and so we began. Wilson refused to take part, protesting that it was no business for a man of God, but I took a rifle, as did Potter, the Captain and three more of the Manxmen, while the little second mate, Kinvig, took the revolving pistol. I had never fired a gun before and cannot say I found it much of a pleasure. First there was the biting into the cartridge, which gave one a mouthful of grease, and the pouring in of the powder. Next came the fiddly business of placing the ram into the end of the long barrel, so one could push home cartridge and its bullet, this last being surprisingly large and heavy. Then there was the awkwardness of keeping the gun aimed against the motion of the ship, and all the while taking care not to accidentally shoot our own helmsman, the huge fellow Clucas, who was lying flat grasping the lowermost spokes of the wheel. Finally there was the firing, which jolted one's shoulder hard as could be, caused a fine ringing in one's ear and filled the air with smoke. For all this it seemed a good deal better than being robbed and murdered, and soon we had going a proper fusillade. As to the guns, they were quite as fearsome as Jonah Childs had promised, and every time the smoke cleared away the woodwork about their wheel looked a good deal more smashed. Their shots, by contrast, were few and seemed to come hardly near us. Thus we fired away, round after round, till the ammunition box was a good deal emptier, yet still they gained on us, the freshening wind speeding their progress. Then, just when I was supposing we would have to try and shoot them as they jumped aboard, the chief mate Brew gave out a shout.

"Some of them are standing up."

I saw a number of them had done so, and were hurriedly working on the booms of the triangular sails.

"Let's have them," said Potter, lunging for another cartridge from the box. "They'll be easy as can be."

"Where's the need?" answered the Captain. "It looks as if they're trying to turn away. We must've scared them off."

He was right, and as we watched, the other vessel began gradually to turn away towards the wind, the crew hauling the two sails round as she moved. The other Manxmen began cheering, and in a moment we were all letting out a roar.

"It could just be a trap," Potter insisted. "They're still very close. I say we fire once more, just to be certain."

"We might as well," agreed the little second mate, Kinvig, who appeared to be enjoying his taste of warfare. So, as much from habit as decision, we loaded our guns once again.

"Fire," shouted the doctor.

We did so all together, almost in the manner of some squad of execution. It was then that something most curious happened. Our pursuers' rearmost boom suddenly and violently swung free from its place, doing so with such speed that it caught two unwary crewmen, knocking them clean over the side. In an instant it was swinging back, the canvas above wildly flapping, and the vessel's deck became a scene of pandemonium, as crewmen tried to catch the boom's rope, only to dive away as the spar beat round upon them once again.

"I rather think," said Kewley coolly, "that one of us has shot away their boom's block."

All at once I felt quite weak. I dare say some form of subdued fear had finally bubbled over, while I felt also a little sickened by the thought of the wrecking we had done. I could not help but wonder if, during the last few minutes, I had unwittingly killed someone.

Dr. Potter was untroubled by any such worries. "We have conquered them," he declared in triumph.

Wilson had to outdo him, needless to say. "We have been delivered," he added, in a correcting tone of voice. "I believe it would be only fitting if we held a little service of thanks, that we might . . ."

Before he could say another word Kewley waved his arm to interrupt. "But tell me, shall I set us a course for Cape Colony? It doesn't seem safe to stay in these waters, after all, that are filled with pirates and marauders."

Potter opened his mouth just a fraction, but then seemed to change his mind. Wilson merely shrugged, while I was too shocked to care greatly. So it was that, grinning as if he had pulled a white rabbit from his cap, the Captain shouted out orders, and the crew went about their work setting a new course, away from whatever joys might be found in Kingston, Jamaica, and south, towards Africa.

CHAPTER SIX

––→•◆•←––

John Harris, Van Diemen's Land Settler and Landowner
1829

IT WAS a fine summer's evening, I had finished my day's work and was sitting on the verandah, enjoying a quiet smoke, when I heard a curious yowling noise, and all at once Peters, the cook, came marching up, dragging behind him a little pickaninny.

"I found him in the cool store hiding behind some sacks," Peters explained. "He was chewing at some piece of meat he'd stolen, though it was plain raw."

It was no mystery where the creature had sprung from. A mob of his kind had speared two stockmen over by Black Bluff just a few days before. Heathcote had got up some fellows to give chase, and they managed to find the scoundrels that same night and give them a good punishing, but I heard some had escaped.

"Spotted any others?" I asked.

"Just this."

I had never seen one so close before and an ugly little thing he seemed. I have no time for thieves, nor savages either, and I was just about to call over one of the hands, to have the creature slung off my land, when the door behind me opened and out stepped Lucy. I sometimes think there is no limit to the foolishness of women. In hardly an instant she was kneeling down beside the little brute, cooing and calling him a poor little baby–though he looked at least seven–and saying how he seemed starved with such thin legs, and should be bathed. When I tried to put her right she turned all high and mighty, quite the baronet's daughter that she is, and simply took him by the hand and led him inside. I hoped he might give her a bite but he never did, more was the pity, I suppose being too scared, and within the hour she had dug out some of Charlie's old clothes to dress him in–which looked comical as could be–and was feeding him half the larder. I was sure he would bolt once he had some food inside him, but no, he seemed to have taken to Lucy, just as she had to him, and before I knew it she was insisting we should keep the little rascal.

Here I drew the line. Lucy being Lucy, there followed a proper battle, and though she hurled all she could at me, from tears to the money her father had lent, I stood my ground. I told her fair and square that the thing could not be done unless it were done properly, and that if he were to be kept he must be useful, by which I meant he must know his letters. In truth my thought had been simply to get him gone–I was sure she would soon forget him once he was–and I never intended anything more than the Hobart Orphans' School. Lucy, though, would have none of the place, insisting he would never last a week there–which was probably right, in truth–and so, after being bombarded by a good deal more weeping, I finally suggested we send him to Mr. Grigson in Bristol. Grigson owed me a favour or two after all the trade I had brought him, and it seemed hardly much to ask that he take a day or two from his trading to find a tutor for the boy.

That settled, I decided the creature had better have a name. Lucy said he called himself Tayaley or some such nonsense, which was no name at all, so I gave him George, after the King, and then Vandiemen, from his place of birth, making George Vandiemen, which I thought rather clever. Next I looked into ship sailings, and I wrote a letter to Grigson, explaining the matter and assuring him the boy did not bite, as well as also ordering a new plough to replace the one that went just before Christmas. With this I sent ten pounds, which would be enough for two years' board and tutoring, especially as I had made it clear he required nothing fancy, but only his letters, anything else being just waste, as he would never understand.

Finally the day came when he was sat atop the cart ready to be carried away to Hobart. Lucy was all tears, of course, and kept making him repeat English words she had taught him, till the driver cracked his whip and the cart rolled away. She was bad for a few days after, but with time her spirits began to return. Ten pounds was a lot to waste on such foolishness, but I supposed it was worth it to be rid of the little brute. Why, I'll confess I even felt a little curiosity as to what some dusty Bristol schoolmaster would make of one of our wild Van Diemen's Land savages.

George Alder, Governor of Van Diemen's Land, to Mr. Smithson of the Prison Committee of the Society of Friends, London
1829

I was greatly pleased to receive your enquiry regarding the present state of the penal system of this colony. It is my hope, indeed, that this may one day prove of some small little interest to students of mankind, both in England and elsewhere across the globe. Since the earliest of times one of the greatest mysteries to trouble philosophers has been why men turn to vice, and how they may be made to reform themselves. What could be more useful in this great struggle than a land populated by men of proven wickedness, and where it is possible to experiment upon them in a scientific manner? It has been this prospect that has formed my chief concern here, and during my five years as governor my wish and purpose has been to devise an effective mechanism *for the improvement of men: a dependable and unerring engine to correct those who have strayed from the path of righteousness.*

Much has already been set in motion. The convict who arrives in Van Diemen's Land will soon realize, if he is attentive, that he has been placed upon a kind of moral chessboard, and that his progress upon this depends entirely upon his own conduct. If his behaviour is goodly and honest he will rise, slowly but surely, and his circumstances shall grow ever less harsh, until finally he reaches the uppermost of the seven levels of punishment, and is issued with his ticket-of-leave, which marks the beginning of his transition to full freedom within the colony.

Let him err, however, and he will quickly know of his mistake. Watch him fall, so swiftly, with every new misdeed or act of insolence that he commits. First his ticket-of-leave is taken from him and he is assigned to work upon some farm. Next he plunges once again, labouring on public works of increasing severity, from buildings to road making, then to a chain gang, struggling in the sun and wind. Misbehave once more and he will reach the full misery of life within a separate penal settlement, such as Macquarie Harbour on the remote west coast, where he toils, shackled, waist-deep in icy seawater, pushing at giant logs, and feeling the lash upon his back if he slackens even for a moment. Thus he has reached the final and seventh level of punishment, below which none may pass, unless to be hanged, and so face the justice of Him, greatest of all judges. Our convict may rescue himself even now, however, if he will only learn from his adventure. If he will reform his behaviour he will begin rising once again— though it may take no small while—back through all the seven levels, until finally he finds himself rewarded with his freedom within the colony. Let him perform some act of unusual goodness, indeed, and he may leap several stages, or even, in a few rare cases, all of them in one bound.

The machinery of punishment may appear upon first sight to be harsh in its severity, but in truth it is never so. It is, at heart, no different from a school classroom, being but a means for the shaping and enlightenment of human minds: a mighty engine of betterment, designed to bring the happiness that follows improvement. For such a system to prove effective it is of course essential that it be universally acknowledged as fair. To this end I have made strenuous efforts to prevent any bullying of convicts by officers or over-seers, and I have likewise acted firmly against any instances of favouritism or leniency. It is, after all, a function of this colony to retain a terrifying rep-utation in faraway London or Glasgow, so foolish men may be deterred from the temptation of crime. It is also important that the island's machinery of punishment is known to be entirely inescapable, so convicts will not be dis-tracted from their improvement by foolish hopes. To this purpose I have cre-ated a most effective machinery of policing, including constant checks of identity and travel passes throughout the settled districts. I have also estab-lished what I believe may be one of the most thorough arrangements for the assembling of information yet devised in any land. Exhaustive records are kept on all men dwelling within the colony, free and fettered, in a set of mighty volumes known as the Black Books. These contain physical descrip-tions, as well as a most detailed summary of moral progress. Each and every change to a convict's status within the seven levels of punishment is carefully recorded, together with its reason. This mighty store of information is con-stantly revised and increased, while both convict and settler are encouraged to add to the government's knowledge by reporting any curious or suspicious behaviour they have observed in their neighbours. If every man abroad is perceived as a potential informant for the colonial administration, it may be hoped that even the wickedest fellows will show caution, and righteousness shall everywhere prevail.

This arrangement has, I will admit, been a cause of some difficulty. The free settlers have shown no little resentment at being treated in a manner similar to the criminals, and some of the wealthier, swollen by the arrogance of their fortune, have made themselves my enemies. I find little sympathy for their objections. It is essential, after all, to keep detailed records of free settlers, if simply to prevent an escaped felon from masquerading as one of their number. There is also another, more profound reason for their inclusion within this great experiment, there being much to be learned from the histories of all those in the colony. I can think of more than a few instances of men who smugly came to Van Diemen's Land as free subjects, only to be found out for some hidden wickedness and speedily dispatched to Macquarie Island. It is nothing less than purest arrogance on the settlers' part to regard themselves as irrevocably innocent. Since the time of Adam and Eve, after all, can anyone regard himself as free of the stain of sinfulness?

I have, indeed, found myself sometimes musing if one day a mighty machinery of justice of this kind might be extended even to a free society, with levels not only of punishment but of reward, so that every single aspect of men's lives could precisely reflect the virtue of their conduct. If a sufficiently ingenious system could be devised for the assembling of information it might be possible to alter the status of each subject with regularity, even every month, so all would be constantly made aware of their moral progress. How fine it would be to have men rewarded not for their greed or cunning, but for their acts of virtue. The arrangement might be administered with such subtlety that even those who have not yet broken any law—liars, cheats, seducers and more—could be made to reap the harvest of their wickedness.

Such thoughts are, however, mere reveries. It is still too soon even to pronounce upon the success or otherwise of this present system. I may say, however, that indications are promising, and it remains my hope that the work done on this faraway island may in some small way help men towards a better future age, when wickedness and criminality shall become wholly and finally vanquished.

Jack Harp
1824–30

AFTER I WAS TAKEN at George Town I was four years in stinking convict clothes, on the roads and in those Hobart warehouses, and then one day I got hauled before some office scribble with a little waxy moustache who told me I'd been improved. So I was put on a farm near Launceston milking cows and shearing sheep. That was luck, as it happened, the owner being soft as mush. On Christmas Day he gave us pudding and even sat down with us to eat it, too, and it was this caused the trouble, so I heard. Some sod must've squealed that we were being treated too gentle, as within the month we were all chucked off to other farms. Mine wouldn't have been so bad except for the bugger of a master, who'd got it in his head that every felon there was fingering his wife–though there was no reason, as she was an ugly old sow–and would scratch out any reason to give you a beating. Show a moment's slowness or a laugh he didn't understand and out would come the lash. I put up with it for a while but then one day he came screaming murder saying I'd milked the cow wrong and made her sick, which was plain lies, and I wasn't having, so rather than just wait for my beating I started on him first, giving him an answering which he'd not forget in a hurry. So I wasn't improved after all, as I got told, but was worse, and that was why I was put on the bridge.

That bridge was worse than all the rest put together. The work was bad, being shifting and cutting great blocks of stone, while every night we had to sleep in boxes stacked up like coffins that were too low even for proper sitting up, and got hot as murder in the warm weather. Worse, the overseer was a bastard of a lasher, while the rest of them in gaol clothes were lame creepers every one of them. I got so wild all I could think of was changing that overseer's face like he deserved, or bolting, and sometimes I was inches close to making a run for it into the bush, chains and all. I never quite did, though. I bided my time.

No talk was allowed at the bridge, so news was hard to come by, but we always caught it in the end. The first I heard about the Line was from a farmer who stopped to water his horse. I could see he'd worn gaol clothes in his time, just from his looking at us, as the settlers hardly will notice a man if he's got chains about his ankles. He never talked to us, knowing that might have made trouble, but to the guard, though he spoke loud enough for all the riverbank to hear.

"Looks like the governor and his army will have to ferry themselves over this one," he said, squinting at that stump of a bridge sticking out from the riverbank, like the leavings of somebody's arm, which was all we'd done till now. "When they come through, chasing blacks."

That was enough to start a good bit of chatter through the coffin doors that night, with jokes aplenty about Governor Alder playing Napoleon against the crows. After that I heard the guards murmuring about it to each other sometimes, and calling it the Black Line. It sounded as if it would be a proper fuss, too, with soldiers and settlers by the thousand marching across Van Diemen's Land to scare those blacks into their trap. That got me thinking. Mostly I thought how an army like that will need all sorts of jobs doing, and how any of them would be better than chipping away at stone. What's more, with so many fellows about, a cove might just disappear and never be missed. Not that I said anything of this to those others. A good thought like that should be hid nicely in a man's head, like a road-found dollar sewn into his coat hem. Besides, they never deserved any favours from me, that crowd.

So when the overseer started telling how some of us were needed for an expedition I was readier than any, and shouted out my name quick as could be. It was that quickness got me picked.

It felt sweet to be saying goodbye to that bridge, even with a chain clanking at my feet. Us who were going were got up soon after dawn, and then we had to stand waiting while the soldiers had their breakfast. That was when one of the those buggers that were staying thought he'd have a joke, and called out from his coffin, "Mind you don't get a spear in your guts." That started them all up, laughing from behind their little coffin doors as loud as they could manage, though it was just rage really, at our getting away. I wasn't having that. I started making this noise that was something like *ck*, and I gave a nudge to the creepers in front of me till they did the same, and soon they'd all started up, *ck, ck, ck,* till we couldn't have sounded more like so many poor miseries chipping away at a heap of rocks, which was what those others would be doing for the next hours and months. That gave a good laugh. I was about to chuck a pebble or two, just for good measure, but then the officers were walking back from their breakfast.

It just took us a little chain clanking and we were round the hill and that foul little stretch of river was gone. It was slow going, and after a few hours we stopped by the shore so the officers could have themselves a little rest and a smoke. That was welcome, and I was lying in the grass, catching my breath and rubbing my ankles where the chains had bit, when I looked up and there he was, riding along the road towards us, all fine and proper in his high saddle, quite the gentleman. My guess was he was on his way to Launceston to sign up for the Black Line like a good King's subject. It was my old friend Bill Haskins.

He didn't notice me, I suppose just seeing another gang in convict clothes, but steered his horse to the river for a sip. He did pay attention just after, mind. That was when I got myself up from the grass, picked up a stone, stepped quietly over, helped him down off his high seat and then gave him back a little change for that Spanish dollar and two French coins. I'm still not sure how much I managed before the redcoats grabbed me but I got in a good bit of work and I like to think I put out that fucker's eye. I suppose it might seem a foolish thing to do, and certainly it wasn't showing myself improved, but still I can't say I felt regretful, even though it meant I missed the Line.

Of course, I didn't know then where that little bit of payment would take me.

Ben Hayes, Van Diemen's Land Farmer
1830

IF A FELLOW was looking for a good ripe sniff of gun oil then this was the place for him. In all my days I never seen so many muskets all at one time. Ranged along the walls, they were, and leaning against the cases they had been sprung from, filling the air with that newly oiled smell.

The depot had been got up at Oatlands, on the main roadway to Launceston. I had passed through there before and found it a quiet enough spot, just a roadside inn and a few houses, but that day it was lively as could be. Aside from soldiers and convicts there were volunteers like myself by the score, and the throng of the place quite took me back to Norwich on market day. Everywhere you looked there were halloos firing off quicker than crackers on Guy Fawkes Night, as fellows spotted some face they hadn't seen for a month or a year. I had ridden down with Sam Ferris, Sam being a neighbour of ours, and a Norfolk man too—which is as fine a testimonial as I can think of—and a cheery morning of greetings and news we had. Then we went to get our weapons, which meant a good while of standing waiting. Even when I finally got my musket it was a rough sort of thing, so I was glad I'd brought along two pistols of my own. With it came a pair of handcuffs and a small heap of ammunition that I counted.

"Is that all I get?" I said to the army clerk, though it was more for Sam, as he always was one for having a bit of sport.

"Thirty rounds is the issue," said the clerk, looking sour.

I held up the handcuffs. "What if I give you these back, which I won't be needing anyway, in exchange for another thirty? That way if I miss once I'll still bag fifty-nine of the buggers."

Sam had himself a good laugh at that. As we walked back out into the spring sunshine, who should we see riding up but the governor himself, playing general, though he was really too pale and scrawny for the part, looking more like some bloody preacher strayed onto a horse. A pair of his officers told everyone to hush and then he gave us all a little speech, thanking us for our help, which nobody minded, though he spoilt it all with some bleating about the blacks, and how we mustn't harm a hair on their heads, but coax them over with kindly words. "Think of yourselves as beaters engaged in a grouse hunt," I think he said. Well, if it was applause he was after he got hardly more than a patter, and that was more than he deserved. The fact was he'd never have done a thing if people like me hadn't started kicking up such a fuss that he got scared.

In the evening Sam and me made for the inn. We weren't the only ones, of course, and a merry spot it was, packed to the walls and out into the roadway, everyone knowing this was their last chance for drinking before we began our big stroll through the bush.

"What we should do," I told Sam, "is down one rum for each bloody crow we'll bag."

That got him laughing. "It wouldn't be fair. Why, we'd drink the whole place dry."

A sore head I had the next day when we started. The thing about plodding along, step after step, is that it will lull a man into daydreaming. Try as I would, it was hard to keep forever scanning the land ahead, and looking for trouble behind every bush, as my thoughts would wander, perhaps to that storehouse I was looking to build, or to where the price of wool might swing next. Then all at once I'd come awake sharpish at something moving up ahead and my heart would be going faster than a steam hammer. I'd crouch low and tug the gun off my shoulder, and peer round to see if Sam was in sight, or Pete Tanner, who was off to my left, and sometimes they were both vanished, the land having pulled us apart or trees having got in the way, which was a worry. Then I'd look again and see it had all been some foolishness, just a roo, or a branch caught by the wind. It wasn't that I was frightened, for sure, but being so tired all the time will make a man jittery.

That was the fault of the bloody governor, as you couldn't imagine a venture worse organized. For a start we didn't even have tents. Here we were, a proper army, as he'd told us in his speech, and we were left to spend our nights on the ground like so many beggars. I never did get a proper sleep, as there was always some stone or root to punish the ribs, or the rain would start pelting down, finding its way through the mess of branches and leaves that we rigged up as shelters. It was hard, besides, not to keep awake listening. The more days that passed and miles we walked, the more a man would get to wondering if a few hundred savages were bunched up just ahead, perhaps even that crazed Amazon bitch that I'd heard talk of, who swore like a trooper and would cut at a man in ways that weren't to be thought of. That wasn't proper warfaring, that was plain bleeding savagery. Still it was the sort of thing that would come to a man sometimes, especially in the middle of the night.

I wasn't the only one who was watchful in the dark, either. One time when it was cloudy and there was no more light than in a box, I was just dropping off to sleep when all of a sudden a musket went off, quick as death, over to the east. That had Sam and me on our feet fast enough. For a moment all was quiet, but then suddenly guns started firing off as if this was a proper battle, and from the hill we were stopped on we could watch flashes spitting away in the darkness, as far as we could see. At a moment like that it's not easy to keep quietly staring ahead into a wall of black nothing. I couldn't hear anyone coming but that didn't mean they weren't there, and the way I saw it there might have been five hundred bloody savages creeping up and thinking we were a gap in the line, so it was sense itself for Sam and me to let off a few rounds, just to warn them away. Finally all went quiet again. Still I can't say I caught much sleep.

The next morning I expected to hear two dozen blacks had been brought down, but no. Soon after light word passed down the line that all that was found was a few possum prints, which seemed a proper mystery.

There wasn't much to be done about it, mind, so we packed up and went on our way once more.

Peevay
1830

MOTHER MADE US go about for days near the fire where we'd all got so killed, looking for Tayaleah, though this was some grievous peril as num white men might come back any moment and kill us more. All the while she wailed and called Tayaleah's name. My worry was that he might step out from some trees and I'd never be free of the little scut after all, but fortunately he never did, and finally Mother let us leave that terrible place. It was my hope that now he was vanished she would give me her cherishings like she should, but this was just some vain hope. No, she just gave me hating looks almost as if it was me who vanished him, while he got more adorings than when he was here. Always she was recollecting how clever and brave he was, while nobody said this was just foolishness, as they were too scared of getting her angry.

So we went on with our war, going east or south, hither and thither, further and again, till even the forest was strange, with trees I never saw before. That was sad, and often at night I dreamed of the world where I knew all blossom scents, where I could tell the stories inside every rock and river and where Tartoyen and Grandmother were quietly dwelling if they weren't killed yet. Sometimes we said we wanted to go back, but Mother said it never mattered where we went now because every land in all the world was the same, and everything was just war with white scuts. She was right, yes, as white scuts were everywhere. Hardly one day passed when we did not see one, perhaps far away, chasing sheep or sitting on his tall laughing animal that was called HORSE. If they were in some small place and were few we would fight them. Sometimes we killed them and sometimes they killed us. A few times we found others of ours, lost from their ones, and speaking strangely, and we got more, but mostly we got fewer.

After every war Mother made us walk fast and very far, so they would not catch us all like before. Also she said we never could make big fires anymore, as these would tell num white scuts where we were, and we could only make some small fire put in a hole in the ground, so it hardly did warm us. Those were cold times and hungry too. Sometimes we'd pass many days just eating roots, which never made you feel full. Still, num didn't kill us in the night anymore, so I suppose Mother was clever in her thinkings.

Then one day I went with Heedeek to hunt without fire, which meant going into forest early, when day was hardly started, and then standing in some bush very still, listening for wallaby's long feet as he jumped. Heedeek was grown but only just and he never had any wife yet. He had thick hair, coloured red, unless we had no ochre, and it fell all round, like water dropping over some fat stone. He was a little clumsy, tripping on tree roots or kicking branches from the fire when he passed, but he was always kindly to me and never called me heinous names like Mother did. So he got like my old brother.

Heedeek wasn't a clever hunter, no, and often going with him was just waiting and nothing ever speared, but this morning was different, so

I did surmise. Yes, I stood for just a short time, cold as I must not move or make noise, when suddenly leaves were rustling and some branch was going snap. This was great good fortune, I divined, as others waiting by the fire were hungry for meat, and perhaps I could be their fine hero. From its crashing, so loud, I guessed this must be some fat wallaby, or even kanunnah, who was a little frightening, but we could eat him still. Heedeek gave me a silent look to point where this animal was coming, across that clearing, and I gave him one back to say yes. Then I crouched down behind bushes and got ready with my spear. Sure enough, leaves moved, just where we thought. But then, instead of any wallaby or kanunnah, out walked scut white man holding his gun and killing knife.

That was one puzzle to confound, as white scuts never came in forest. I pondered that perhaps he was hunting game like us, but this was foolishness, as every wallaby would hear his noise, and smell his stink too, which was strong so I could smell it even from this far place. Soon there was another mystery to confuse. He did not go through clear places, like any clever one, no, but walked straight forth as if he was on some empty hill. Soon he was having a great fight with trees, swinging his killing knife to try and make his road. I knew he must be doing this for some long time, too, as his dead skin, which was coloured red like blood, got torn and flapping like leaves, so you could see his real skin beneath, and even this was scratched all over, like possums climbed him.

Heedeek made a sign with his spear that said I'll go round that way and spear him if I can, but you stay still, which was interesting but scaring besides, as white scut had his gun. In the end, though, it never happened. Just when Heedeek was creeping off to start his killing, more tree breaking sound started, now from another side. Sure enough, when I looked through leaves I saw another white scut, also coloured red, and then I could hear more noises besides, far away. That was heinous trouble, no denying. Heedeek looked at me, pointing his spear to where Mother and the others were waiting, and so we went back, going carefully.

Mother was interested. "Let's go up higher where we can see," she told Heedeek, as even still she would not speak to me, being too hating, and waving her strong short arms she led the way out of the forest and up some hill just behind. There we lay down flat so white scuts wouldn't see, and we tried to make the dog animals go flat too. Surely enough trees started quaking and then one num stepped out, shook himself and pulled leaves and so from his hair and his dead skin, shouting with wrath as if something bit him. Then more trees shook and another stepped out, and another too, till all at once it seemed as if that whole forest was trembling and spitting out white scuts, all carrying one gun, far as we could see. So we gave looks at each other. We knew, you see, what this was. These white scuts never were just hunting wallaby. They were hunting us. So we began fleeing.

One good thing was that those num were slow as mud while we were fast. Away we went, like the wind, and by dark we were so far that their fires were just small like sparks in the night. Those fires were plentiful, though, so we knew these were many more even than those ones that came out from the forest, which was one heinous puzzle to confound. Truly, this was some giant creeping of white scuts, all across the land.

Still Mother was not despairing. "We'll just have to go round them," she said as we sat by that small, cold fire hidden in its hole.

All that next day we went so, going fast, with dog animals hurrying round our feet as if this was some fine game. Soon we felt hungry and wearful besides, but still we went again, away from white buggers but also around. By and by I felt safer, as we were gone so far I divined we must be past them. Then, woeful tidings, we went over some hill and there they were still, plenty of them, walking towards us in their line, slow as ants.

"Perhaps they're just the same ones," said Heedeek, hoping. "Perhaps they just followed us."

Mother saw more cleverly. "No. Those others were red like blood. These are brown."

That was lamentable. Up until then I never had pondered how many white scuts there were in the world, as we never did see many all together, but now I could surmise there was no finish to these hateful buggers, and I knew we never would be rid of them even if we fought forever and ever and never died. Even Mother looked woeful that moment. Not that there was much time for desponding, no, as those scuts were just coming nearer all the while. So we hurried away once more, as fast as we could, though that land was just bald rocks and I surmised they must see us. Rain fell and we were cold and hungry, so my feet hurt and my head got weak and floating. Finally we stopped, all falling down panting, just too tired to run further. Mother set two watching for white scuts coming, and then we had our talking.

Heedeek, who was always careful, thought we should go around again. "Maybe they're not so many as they seem."

"You saw their fires," Mother told him, folding her arms and looking at him as if he was just some piss-poor foolishness. "We'll just get more tired and hungry and still they'll be coming. No, it's better to fight them now."

Nobody wanted to fight these whites, as they were so many that we knew this was dying, which was heinous, but she was right, I could surmise. Besides, Mother was frightening, especially when she was angry, so being killed seemed almost easier than saying no. Mother let us rest a short while, but then she took her spear and got to her feet. So she started going straight back towards white scuts, first slow, then faster, and all the while we followed.

Ben Hayes, Van Diemen's Land Farmer
1830

FOR TWO DAYS we crossed farmland, which was sweet. I slept one night in a fine dry barn, and sometimes the women would see us coming and run out with hot milk and fresh bread, which tasted better than Christmas goose. It didn't last, though. Before long we struck bush that was thick like it only knows how in Van Diemen's Land, with thorns that tore our clothes and then tore us, so soon everyone was ripped halfway to rags, with so many scars it looked like they'd been napping on bloody bayonets. My worry was my boots, which were getting so bad that I had to tie them with strips from my shirt just to keep the soles on. I hated my pack by then. It is a fact that what seems light as daisies for a minute becomes heavy as rocks when you're hauling it mile after mile, so hardly a moment passed when I wasn't wishing I could fling away those handcuffs, and that I'd never brought those two pistols of mine.

We slept a night in forest, and the next day we climbed into high open country, which was welcome apart from the cold wind. It was that same afternoon that I saw them. I had stopped a moment to shift my pack and try to get more comfortable–though it never did any good–and when I looked up, there they were, two dozen or more of the buggers, scampering away over the next hill. I just froze. I glanced across to Sam and he was just the same. Then we looked at each other and sort of laughed. Not that it was funny.

We passed the word along and then kept going like before. Soon after it started raining, which was bad, as my clothes had barely dried off properly from the last wetting. It was coming on towards dusk when the shout went down the line to stop. Usually we made camp in just pairs, but this time, what with having seen those blacks, and so many too, this didn't feel quite safe, and we ended being six. I suppose it did leave a bit of gap to eastwards, but the way we saw it, if they did start trouble at least we'd be enough to fight. Now Pete Tanner was one of those fellows who can get a flame out of pure pond water and soon he had a merry little blaze going, in spite of the wet that was still coming down all around. Well, there's nothing better to warm the bones than a fire. We cooked some flour into damper, while Sam pulled out a small possum that he'd bagged with his musket that morning, and once we'd got his coat off he was soon doing nicely, smelling sweet as could be.

The way I look on it now it was the rain that was to blame, as, this being dusk, it did make it hard for a man to see far. Besides, it was so chilly that only a fool would stray off from that blaze we had going. We'd set a watch, for sure, but those blacks must've had some way of making themselves hardly visible, as he only saw them when it was nearly too late. All of a sudden there they were, running like the wind through the little valley just below us. Trouble they looked, too. Up at the front was a one that I could only think must be that Amazon I'd heard tell of. Stark naked she was, and holding a fowling piece in her hand. That was a shock, truly, as nobody'd said anything about them having guns. Why, we should've been warned. Behind her was another strange one, just a boy, and black as the rest, though his hair was pale as straw.

Well, we took up our guns quick enough, though it was hard to catch them in our sights what with all their running and jiggling. I was ready to fire, that's the truth, and I would've too if one of the others had only given a shout, like I was expecting for them to do. None of them did. The fact was it was a worry that we might miss, especially with the blacks being so invisible in the dusk, as then they might come back at us, including that Amazon with her gun. Everything went quiet, so all you could hear was the rain and the crackle of the possum roasting on the fire, and inside half a moment they'd scampered away nearly out of range.

Sam was the one who finally spoke. "I suppose we should go after them." The way he spoke made it sound like a question.

Nobody answered, but nobody moved either. We just stood watching. A moment later they'd reached trees and were gone from sight.

"If we go after them that'd leave a gap in the line," said Pete Tanner.

Sam chewed on his cheek a little, which was his habit. "Besides, there's no telling if our guns would ever fire in this wet."

Soon after, we went back to sitting round the fire, where it was warm. The damper and that possum were tasty as could be, and later we brewed up some tea in the billy. That night we set a proper watch, with fellows staying awake in turns, just like the proper army. Nobody saw anything, mind.

It wasn't that we ever decided to stay quiet about what happened, it was just that none of us said anything. There hardly seemed much purpose.

George Alder, Governor of Van Diemen's Land
1830

ONCE BREAKFAST WAS DONE with and all was packed up once more, our mighty march resumed, with a great jangling of billies, water bottles and muskets. It was only now, as we approached the end of this great campaign, and the narrowness of the land brought together these two thousand men, who had been strung out half across the island, that they finally, by their concentration, assumed the appearance of an army. A brave little army they looked, too, in their ragged clothes and boots. What noble work they had done, to traverse this harsh land, and without suffering a single casualty, excepting those few who had died from mishap, or accidentally shot one another. Their great task was almost done. My chief concern now was that they should remember to treat the aborigines with gentle forcefulness, as I had urged.

Ned, my chief police magistrate, who is quite a worrier, feared that we might not have enough pairs of handcuffs. "The reports I have had say there could be as many as four entire tribes trapped."

"If we run short, then we can always use rope from the tents," I suggested. My attention being then distracted by the sound of shouting behind me, I glanced back and caught sight of a man who could hardly have looked more out of place in this wild spot if he had sought to do so: he bore no weapons, and rather than wearing rough outdoors clothes was dressed in a coat and top hat which would have been more appropriate for a visit to church. As he drew nearer, I recognized him as John Pierce. It was, I supposed, hardly a great surprise, as the man was an infamous maker of nuisance. He had once been employed as an agricultural officer by the New World Land Company, only to abandon his work and appear in Hobart, uttering the wildest claims of cruelties done to the blacks by his colleagues. Fortunately his employer, Mr. Charles, who is a most goodly fellow, had already written to warn me of the man, who he explained had grown quite demented, and had taken to living wildly in the bush like some vagrant. Pierce came several times to Government House with his denunciations, and once he even attempted to accost me in the street, so I was sorely tempted to have him arrested.

Observing me, he spurred on his horse, calling out in a frenzied voice. "Governor Alder, I demand that this operation be stopped this moment. You are committing deliberate murder here, nothing less."

He was a most curious-looking fellow, with eyes that were forever blinking and a wounded expression that almost made one wonder if he might break into tears. Demented though he was, I supposed I must give him some answer. "Mr. Pierce, you are thoroughly mistaken. There will be no murder here." I began to tell him of the three hundred pairs of handcuffs we had prepared, and of the careful instructions I had given to the men, though it was to no avail. I dare say there is no arguing with a madman.

"Your handcuffs are mere pretence," he insisted. "Your intention, though you seek to hide it behind the contraptions of justice, is only too evident. I will not be removed. I will bear witness to this massacre so it can never be denied."

I was fast growing weary of the fellow. "Mr. Pierce," I informed him. "I never suggested you should be removed, but if you continue to make a nuisance of yourself, and to disrupt this most important military operation, then you certainly shall be."

It was then that, rather to my puzzlement, I saw he had fallen into silence, and was now staring ahead with a look of profound surprise. I followed his look. While I had been arguing with the fellow we must have ridden over a ridge, as now a fine view stretched out ahead. It was an exhilarating spot, with gulls hanging high in the wind and the crash of waves all around. To the left lay the sea, to the right also, with the thick line of men glinting and stamping away in each direction, as far as the shores. In front of us lay a wide expanse of open grassland, rolling gently down to the water, and looking a little like some wild part of the Devonshire coast. we had reached the very end of the peninsular, and our great march.

"It is a miracle," Pierce murmured.

The most noticeable thing about the scene, I should explain, was that it was wholly and utterly empty of aborigines.

Peevay
1830–31

TIME PASSED, summer came and our fleeing and fighting went on like before. Then one day we found a cider gum tree. This was good tidings, yes, as they never are usual. We cut his bark so gum dripped out into a hollow we made, mixing with water and getting changed into some sweet stuff which makes you foolish and dizzy. This was a good one, too, with enough for everybody, and soon we were laughing and so. All except Mother. Truth was Mother never was the same after that great creeping of num white scuts. Even though nothing happened, and they just stood there by their fire watching, and never killed us after all, still Mother got afflicted, worse than I ever saw her before, and even long after, her look was like stone. I supposed it was because she knew we never could win now, and she wished we got killed then, just so, all finished.

We were still sitting round the cider gum when Cordeve, who was keeping watch that time, called out. "Look there. It's my sister!"

Cordeve was Tommeginer and I never even knew he had any sister, but there she was, yes, walking through trees, with two other women I never saw before. That was great good fortune, truly, as we never saw any but white scuts all this long while, ever since we became Mother's tribe, so it was joyous to find others like us were still alive. Usually Cordeve was just quiet but now he was gleeful and tidings of joy, running to these new ones. He got near, too, when suddenly his friendliness turned to a fighting run, and he raised his spear for throwing. "Watch out," he shouted. "Behind you."

There coming after his sister, you see, was one white man. He was a puzzle to confound, yes. He had no gun or killing knife, and just stood there, short and fat and easy to hit, and smiling too. I think Cordeve would spear him, too, but then his sister didn't go away like anyone would expect, but ran back to stand before this num and be his guard. "Stop!" she called. "He's my friend."

Yes, that was strange, but strangest thing came just after. All at once that num white scut shouted to us, and d'you know he never shouted to us in white man's talk at all, but in Tommeginer language. He didn't speak very properly, truly, as his words were wrong and stupid, like baby's, but still, whoever did hear of some white man speaking like us? "Don't be frightened," he told. "I only want to help you. My name is Robson."

"You must listen to him," said Cordeve's sister, very beseeching. "He can save us."

This Robson was smiling now, as if we were foolish children. I suppose we were staring in mighty surprise at his knowing our own words. "She's right. I know of a place where you'll all be safe. A fine place where there are plenty of kangaroo to hunt and no bad white men can hurt you. I can take you there." He reached into his dead skin, which was dirty, and pulled out some shiny round things of different colours, like flat stones. "These are for you. They're called buttons."

His words were interesting, yes, as in truth I was too tired of always hurrying and fighting and being cold and hungry. Besides we were not many now and probably we would all be killed quite soon. Cordeve was going up to take one of the coloured things that were called buttons, and I thought I might too, as they were pleasing, but then Mother gave her hating look.

"Don't go near," she told. "No white pisser brings anything but killing." So she turned to white man Robson. "Go away and leave us alone or I'll kill you."

Robson never seemed to hear her words at all, just smiling as if he never believed her. I suppose he never did know Mother. "We have meat for you if you are hungry," he said, just smiling. "Plenty of it. And a fine warm fire to sit beside."

"And there are many others with us who you'll know," said Cordeve's sister.

All of a sudden Mother just raised her gun and fired. I never did surmise if she wanted to miss that fellow or if she was just confounded. Probably she was confounded. Though he wasn't killed, still he was mightily fearful, and I recollect he went like some spider, crouching, running away and holding up his hands to stop anyone hitting him—though nobody was—all at the same time. Cordeve's sister and the other two women went with him, running away into bushes, and then Cordeve went too, calling out his sister's name. I suppose he was sad to lose her so quick after she got found.

"We must go away from here," said Mother.

So we went away. I did ponder, as we walked, that maybe this white man could save us like he said. Probably some others wondered too. Still nobody said anything to Mother, as no one ever did. All the while she was looking angry and calling us to go faster, as if she was more fearful of this one white scut with his smile and speaking Tommeginer language than all those others in the great creeping, with their guns and killing knives. By and by we reached a high place, and when we stopped and looked back there were tails of smoke from fire sticks, so we knew he wasn't scared by getting nearly killed, but was coming after us still. Those smokes were several, too, so we surmised there must be plenty of our ones with him, just like Cordeve's sister said.

So we were fleeing again, and this time it was from our own too, and not just num. This was much harder. When we looked back they always were close after us, so ours were watching our tracks, and seeing them even though we went carefully, which num never could. Even then I think we could evade them easily, except that coughing sickness came. I never had seen this till then, though I had heard of it as some heinous thing, and more killing even than white scuts. On that second day of fleeing it caught Cordeve's cousin, whose name was Lawerick. After just a few hours he was hot and gasping, and by evening he was spitting out white stuff like bird shit, and was so crook he hardly could speak. That same night two others got sick besides. One was Mother.

A thing about Mother was she never would yield. If my skill was enduring, then hers was just going on by and by. Some other would know we must stop now as we were just ruination, but not Mother. Next morning her eyes were faint and her step was stiff, but still she never paid any heed. "We must go to the river," she declared.

I soon saw her bold intention. First, when we got to the river, we put out all fire sticks except just one and put them in bushes, and we hid our tracks by brushing them with leaves. Then we stepped into the stream, though it was cold, and we began walking, shouting at the dog animals to try and make them stay in the water too. All day we followed that stream, though our feet got numb and were often cut by sharp stones, and Lawerick and Mother and those others got more crook all the while. Finally we came to a place where all was big rocks, smooth and flat like big shells, and Mother said we could go out onto these, as they showed no tracks. Behind was a small forest and this was where we went, wiping our footmarks so foes wouldn't see.

I supposed we were safe now, but still we were getting sicker by and by. Mother said we couldn't have any campfire here, even in a hole, as enemies would smell its smoke, and that night was cold. In the morning Lawerick was very bad, moaning and such, and though his eyes were open he didn't know anybody. He died soon after, and his dying started a big fight, I do recollect, as his brother said we must burn him, which was correct, but Mother said no even to this.

"We'll put him in the forest now and burn him later, when they're far away," she told. Lawerick's brother was too angry, saying animals might find that body and eat it, but he was alone in his talk, and so Lawerick got put in the forest like Mother desired.

Later that day clouds went and warm sun shone, which was better, and everyone who wasn't bad with coughing sickness went searching for roots to eat just nearby. I went with Heedeek. We found some, and though they weren't so many still it was more food than we had since we started our fleeing, and we ate hungrily and then gave some to the others that were crook, who were six now. It is pleasing to eat when you are hungry, and afterwards everyone lay down to rest.

Everyone except me.

I was thinking, you see, of that white man's warm fire and his meat to eat, and how blissful these things would be. Then I was thinking of his promised place with kangaroo to hunt, where we would be safe, I did surmise. For a time I looked at those others as they slept, and then, very quietly, I went away. Nearby was a tree that was tall, and so I climbed, going high till I reached just thin branches which leaned as I held them. From that place I could see half of everywhere, so it looked. Over to westwards were mountains, sharp like cutting stones. Near to eastwards was that same cold river where we walked to be hidden. And there, to southwards, were thin lines of smoke like rope. These were never so near as before now, and as I watched, holding on to those branches till my arms ached, I saw they were moving away from us now. Yes, I could divine, Mother's walking in the stream had worked and they had missed us. When I climbed down I went over to Mother, who was hot and coughing in her sleep. I took some root I found, which was large and just good for eating, and I put this near her hand, just as some kindly thing. Next I went over to the small fire stick that was all the fire Mother let us have now.

It was too easy. Fire stick was stuck in the ground, but stupidly, so gum tree leaves were not far above. I looked but others weren't watching. For a time I just stood there, pondering. Then gently I moved that branch till fire took it.

That was all it did need.

CHAPTER SEVEN

Timothy Renshaw
AUGUST–SEPTEMBER 1857

THE SURPRISE of nearly being murdered by pirates had a quietening effect on all aboard the *Sincerity*, myself included, and for a time even Dr. Potter and Mr. Wilson treated each other with something approaching civility. It did not last, needless to say. Once we crossed the equator our vicar began to look restless, and it was then he started praying aloud at first light, which he called "dawn godliness." That drove me halfway to distraction, as his moaning came straight through the holes in the partition wall, while Potter didn't look pleased at all. Soon after that there was the business of the mug of tea that was found on the vicar's Bible, which was answered in turn by a new and longer list of parson's laws. Even that wasn't enough for Wilson, and in his next Sunday sermon he insisted on lecturing us about how we must look deep into our hearts and cast out all envy and wickedness, hurling, as he spoke, little saintly smiles in the doctor's direction. When the sermon moved next to praising the virtue of deference, and saying how it was the God-given duty of those "of junior station" to obey their "natural betters," Potter's face turned quite clenched.

It was that sermon that decided the next course of their little war. The moment it was finished the doctor marched across to Captain Kewley, while Wilson—who had seen his rage—followed just behind. I went too, being curious. Their feud was the nearest thing there was aboard the *Sincerity* to something happening, while, finding each party quite as annoying as the other, as I did, I suppose it afforded me some faint satisfaction to watch them assail one another.

"It occurs to me," Potter began, "that it might be of interest to the crew if I delivered a few educational lectures, perhaps on scientific matters."

Wilson cut in before Kewley had a chance to answer. "What a generous thought, Doctor. Though I should say that such a thing would hardly be suitable for the Sabbath, when we prefer to reflect upon the spiritual."

His thinking, I supposed, was that Kewley would not want lectures cluttering up the ship's workdays, and so Potter's proposal would be squeezed nicely into oblivion. He was probably right, too. Where he made his mistake was in being so very pushing. A weary look passed across Kewley's face. "I don't see why we shouldn't have room for his talk as well as yours, Vicar. After all, the doctor's science is also part of the good Lord's world, is it not?"

Wilson wriggled his best but, I was pleased to see, the Captain would have none of his bullying. So it was that the ship became quite a library of scribbling, as my two colleagues worked upon their discourses like swordsmen sharpening their blades, each casting his face into the most serious expression, as if to demonstrate the superiority of his work over the other's.

It was early that same week that the weather began to change. The wind had been blowing strongly until then, propelling us swiftly southwards, and already the sun had begun to lose a little of its strength, its light turning subtly whiter, reminding us that we were venturing towards a part of the world where the season was still late wintertime. On the Thursday the wind backed round from the southwest, feeling suddenly chilly, and troubling the crew with a good work with the sails. Then on the Saturday morning it dropped away to nothing and we found ourselves becalmed, and that night the fog came. By Sunday morning the vessel was encased tighter than a hand in a glove. The light was so dim and the air so still that it felt almost as if we were not at sea at all, but were inside some kind of murky room. When one looked out over the side, the water was visible only for a few yards, while upwards the masts and sails vanished into the whiteness.

It was around noon that we heard a loud splash off the port bow, sudden and shocking in the stillness. We all hurried to the rail, though we could see nothing but fog. Captain Kewley even called out, "Ahoy there," but there came no answer. Only when we stood, carefully listening, did we become aware of a sound from the same direction, faint and rhythmic, deep and low.

"It's creatures," said Kewley in a whisper.

It seemed there were a good number of them, and as we listened their breathing grew slowly louder, until it extended all about the vessel, as if we were in the middle of some huge ocean dormitory. The beasts none of them ventured close enough to be seen, and I could only presume they must be some form of whale or grampus. It may seem foolish and yet I found their invisible presence unsettling, while even the Manxmen, who I would have expected to be used to such oddities, went about their work with furtive looks, speaking in lowered voices, quite as if the huge animals were listening.

Our two Sunday lecturers, by contrast, seemed little interested, being both far more concerned with the discourses they were to give, leafing hurriedly through their notes, or disagreeing with one another over the construction of the temporary pulpit. Dr. Potter was to speak first. He forwent Wilson's dramatic preamble, simply marching onto the platform, from where he peered down at us with a serious look. "My lecture today concerns the process of animal magnetism, that is also known as mesmerism," he declared solemnly, pausing for a moment as one of the creatures produced a faint blowing sound, eerie through the fog, "and will be concluded with a practical demonstration of this most important process, in which I hope to reveal great secrets of the soul of man."

His intention was, I supposed, to outshine Wilson's sermonizing, and perhaps to deliver a few stabs along the way. To this end his choice seemed clever enough, mesmerism being a phenomenon of great popularity, which had filled more than a few music halls with eager watchers, delighted by the spectacle of some poor fool believing himself a donkey or bereft of a leg. I was quite intrigued myself, in fact, having never guessed the doctor was a practitioner of such an art. Rather to my surprise, however, the Manxmen seemed little pleased. For a moment I assumed they were still troubled by the presence of the sea creatures, but no, from their looks they seemed to be regarding the doctor with real dislike. I could only imagine they feared some form of joke might be played upon them. Wilson, who was sitting on a coil of rope well away from the proceedings–having insisted that "sadly" he could not listen as he must attend to his sermon–had also observed the crew's displeasure, and was visibly smirking.

Potter himself pressed on regardless. The first part of his discourse dealt with something he termed "the geography of the mind." It was a subject I knew little about, and I found it interesting enough in its way. He asserted that the brain was divided into many segments, almost in the manner of an orange, each of which contained one "impulse," many of these being a moral quality. These varied no less than human character itself, extending from wisdom to a fondness for sweet food, and from anger to a fear of heights. The power of each impetus would alter from one man to the next, and their strength or weakness would, when combined together, define the moral character of each individual. Thus a man with pronounced impulses of bravery and loyalty would make an excellent soldier, while another, who was weak in honesty and strong in greed, would likely fall into thieving. Between different races of men, as the doctor told us, variety was far greater still, as the very structure of the brain would alter. Thus we learned that the Chinese possessed a unique impulse of delight in bright colours, while among savages of Africa there was a complete absence of the impulse of civilization.

"It is mesmerism that can unlock these wonders of the mind," Potter explained. "Each impulse of the brain extends to the skull, and so, once a man is brought into the correct state of entrancement, the different elements of his brain can be made to reveal themselves simply by touches of the operator's fingers, in a fashion remarkable to behold. It is, indeed, quite as if one is playing upon the keys of an organ. Press upon the segment of fear and the subject will at once show signs of great alarm, perhaps believing that a fearful chasm has opened up in front of him. Try deceitfulness and his every utterance will be untrue. Touch confession and he will admit to all manner of secrets. Ten minutes of mesmerism can reveal a man far more truthfully than months studying his apparent nature."

Some of the crewmen, I noticed, were showing signs of restlessness, tapping their feet upon the deck.

"Mesmerism pays no heed to titles or other grand frippery. Enchant a pauper and you may discover him to be wiser than a lord," Potter continued, undeterred. He cast a sudden glance towards the vicar: "And a simple butcher's boy may be found richer in virtue than a priest."

So there was his first stab. Wilson's smirk vanished and he buried himself in his notes.

Pleased with this little piece of violence, Potter stepped to the front of the temporary pulpit and peered down through the fog. "This, I hope, will have made clear the theory behind this most important process. The moment has now come to offer a practical demonstration, so you may see for yourselves, and for this I must ask for the assistance of a volunteer."

I had expected that this might prove awkward and I was not wrong. Potter smiled, and waited, only to find himself answered with a wall of silence. Soon the creaking timbers and water lapping against the ship's side seemed loud indeed. The doctor looked quite taken aback.

"Surely there is somebody?" Just as he was beginning to look a touch alarmed, the chief mate raised his hand. Potter broke into a smile. "Thank you, Mr. Brew."

"Ah, but I'm not offering," Brew declared, grinning in a way that looked hardly reassuring. "I'm just asking what'll happen to the lucky body that does. Will you have him strip himself naked thinking he's a bunny rabbit?"

The crew let go a faint ripple of snickering.

Potter looked troubled. The very last thing he wanted was for his lecture to be turned into some kind of joke. He attempted to retrieve the mood of seriousness as best he could, assuring us all, with an awkward smile, "I have not the slightest interest in theatrical games. The fact is that mesmerism, besides being an invaluable tool of science, is also a most natural state in which to enter, being wonderfully calming to the nerves. While some persons are more susceptible than others, I do believe that there is hardly a single man or woman who cannot safely be brought into such a condition."

The Manxmen did not laugh at this little speech, it was true, but none of them volunteered either. So it was that the doctor made the mistake of trying to reassure us further. "It is; indeed, a process quite as

normal and healthy as sleep. Why, there are numerous recorded instances even of animals becoming mesmerized, while in some cases
that I . . ."

He got no further. Up went Brew's hand like a semaphore arm.
"Animals, did you say?" He tilted his head to one side, all dangerous
innocence. "Well, there's a thing, is there not? I wonder, Doctor, could
you mesmerize one of the swineys for us then? You know, just so we can
see how it's done."

This brought more than just looks and snickering. Mylchreest, the
steward, uttered a curious squeaking giggle and this was enough to un-
leash all the rest. I will admit I laughed myself, while Wilson turned
about on his coil of rope, clearly delighting in the spectacle. As for
Potter, he was beginning to look greatly disconcerted. He had intended
this occasion to be one when he would revenge himself on his enemy,
and instead found himself humiliated before the whole ship, caught in
that purgatory between feigned seriousness and open ridicule. It was
quite a sight, especially in one who, until now, I had never seen lose
command of himself.

"I'm not sure that would be useful," he declared, with the stiffest of
smiles.

He would have been wiser just to say a very plain no. As it was,
Brew pretended to take his words as some form of encouragement, nod-
ding his head as if in agreement. "Wouldn't we all love to see it, though,
Doctor?" He glanced about him, stirring the rest into agreement.

"But I have no experience of any such thing," Potter declared
weakly.

"Ah, you're doing yourself down," said Brew, now maliciously supportive. "A clever fellow like you would manage it easier than kicking."

I believe the doctor would have wriggled his way free even then had
it not been for Captain Kewley. Until this moment he had kept aloof
from the whole matter, but now he gave the surgeon a sly look. "Come
along, Doctor," he called out in a cheerful voice. "We're far too interested
to be put off now. Mesmerize a swiney for us, there's a good fellow."

Potter threw the Captain a desperate glance, I suppose hoping he
might show pity and make a joke of his suggestion, but it was in vain.
The rest of the crew were already urging him on with shouts and cheers,

and so, with as much enthusiasm as a condemned man strolling to his gibbet, he began making his way forwards through the fog. Wilson left his coil of rope to follow, as did I. Reaching the boat that served as the pigsty, the doctor looked crushed. Why, I would have felt quite sorry for him if I had not had to suffer his company through all those long weeks.

The reason that a pig had been proposed rather than any other creature was simple enough. We had eaten almost all the rest. All the bullocks were gone, and the chickens too, while of the sheep only one sorry specimen survived. Pigs were usually kept till last, being regarded as the best sailors, and three of the four animals still remained, all berthed in the main boat. As Potter and his audience gathered around this, the poor beasts showed some alarm, cowering and snorting, which was hardly surprising seeing as they had witnessed so many of their fellow animals being taken, one by one, to the front of the vessel and noisily dispatched from this world.

"Don't you go crowding them," the cook, Quayle, protested, seeming the only one displeased by the turn of events. "I won't have them upset."

Of the three beasts, two were sows while the third was a male, huge and sagging, with the most disquieting eyes: mournfully alert, as if he understood only too plainly the temporary nature of his situation. Potter stroked his beard, seeming now resigned to attempting the task forced upon him.

"The method I will use," he announced cautiously, "is the same as I have employed upon men, though there is no certainty that it will prove as effective on animals."

It was the male he picked, I suppose because this seemed the most humanlike of the three. He reached out towards the creature, looking it firmly in the eye, and then began passing his hands about its head in a kind of stroking movement, though without ever quite touching its skin. Whether this was part of his technique, or simple avoidance of the mud and worse with which the animal was caked, was hard to know. As for the pig itself, it flinched away at first, but then gradually seemed to grow calmer, and after a time appeared even to be quite enjoying the process, meeting the doctor's mesmerizing stare with a dozy look of its own. Gradually the movements of Potter's hands extended, until they reached halfway down the creature's back and he was leaning right into the boat. Then, peering determinedly at the beast, he drew back.

"The animal," he announced, suddenly proud, "is now entranced."

This won a hush of respect, and surprise too. Before the doctor could proceed any further, though, the creature uttered a loud snort and began sniffing among the pieces of muck and old food at the bottom of the boat. Potter ignored the sniggers that followed, now looking serious. It seemed the exercise had now caught his curiosity, causing him to forget his earlier reluctance. "There is another method that I can try which may prove more suitable to animals," he declared. "This involves the subject intently staring at an object until entranced."

My curiosity was how the pig would know that he was supposed to stare at anything. In the event, I never discovered. Potter's mistake, as I see it now, was that he did not arrange matters before he started. He was too impatient to place the creature once again into a receptive state– which he did with the same stroking and staring as before–and it was only when the animal began to respond, looking dozy, that he troubled himself with what mesmerizing object he would use.

"What I now need," he said in a soft voice, never turning from the pig's small, doleful eyes, "is something bright and reflective. Anything of polished metal will do."

For a moment the Manxmen looked at one another, uncertain. Then the chief mate, Brew, reached to his waistband. It is possible, of course, that his choice was just accident, but considering the man's character this seemed unlikely. He passed the object into the outstretched hand and then, as Potter brought this before him, both he and the pig found themselves looking at a long, shining knife.

The doctor saw the danger at once, pulling the blade back to hide it from the animal's sight, but it was too late. I had no idea that a pig could make so great a noise. All at once the air became filled with a hideous squealing: a sound of pure, rawest fear. At the same instant he began plunging irresistibly about the longboat, quite like some steam locomotive, with the sows following just behind, their pen rocking violently from side to side, hay spilling into the air like coal dust, and the metal tubs that held their food banging and crashing as they were hurled back and forth. The Manxmen did their best to retrieve the situation, leaning forward with outstretched arms, but the fact is that three pigs in full flight are not easily stopped, especially when they are slippery with mud and dung. The wiser policy might well have been simply to leave the poor creatures be, as every grabbing hand encouraged their panic. Finally, though, the sows were halted, and then China Clucas, the ship's giant, managed to catch the main beast by its tail, and though all three screeched dreadfully, the scene in the pen began to show signs of greater calm.

As to what followed, even now I could not say if it bore any connection with what had just occurred, or if it was merely a coincidence of timing. It seemed to follow, certainly, but the mind will sometimes play tricks at such a moment of excitement, seeing unconnected events as so many links in a chain. In truth I could not even say if sea creatures possess the power of hearing, let alone if they concern themselves with sounds emerging from beyond their watery domain. The fact remained, however, that hardly had the pigs been stilled when there was a momentous watery crash from somewhere beyond the port bow. We never saw what ocean acrobatics the beast had got up to, on account of the fog, but the consequence was clear as could be. The ship, which had been still as land, began suddenly and violently rolling.

For a moment I thought we had suffered nothing worse than surprise. A ship, after all, is well used to a bit of tipping. Then, though, I became aware of the excited chattering in Manx on the further side of the boat, and realized they were all looking at Clucas' arm, which he was holding with his hand in a curious way, and I saw blood was spilling out between his fingers. The pig he had caught had toppled clean against him when the ship rolled, and he must have caught his wrist against a jagged corner of the creatures' water tub. Clucas himself looked pale as a ghost.

It is curious how swiftly a mood can alter. One moment we were engaged upon what was, if truth be told, an unkind joke. Half an instant later all were grave faces. The greatest change, though, came to Potter. All at once he was transformed from dupe to hero.

"Have my case brought," he commanded. So he set to work.

The sea creatures did not stay long after that, and the fog was gone by the next morning. As for Clucas, within just a day or two he was recovered enough to sit quietly on deck in the cool sunshine, offering respectful greetings to his saviour whenever he came near. It was perhaps hardly a surprise that, from that afternoon, nobody, including Brew, tried to make a joke of the doctor. Potter even treated us to another lecture the next Sunday—this one on the benefits of vegetarianism—and, much to Wilson's annoyance, his audience stood through the whole thing quiet as lambs.

The Reverend Geoffrey Wilson
OCTOBER 1857

FINALLY, AFTER nearly three full months at sea, we made our first landfall at Cape Colony, upon the most southerly point of Africa. This, I am glad to say, proved a most delightful spot, lodged prettily beneath the wide massif of Table Mountain. The streets are wide and the white-painted houses are charmingly decorated with pot plants and creepers, whose colourful flowers quite dazzle the eye. As to the population, though the native Africans seemed somewhat shy, and the Boers were a little rough in their manners, those colonists who hailed from English shores displayed a cultured gentility all the more creditable in this distant place.

Among my first undertakings was to visit the post office. Before we left London it had caught my notice that the steamer service to this corner of the world would generally outpace any sailing vessel by several weeks, and so I had told my dear wife that she could write to me here, considering that this might bring her some comfort in her loneliness. I had anticipated quite a little library of letters awaiting me and was, I confess, a little surprised to find only one envelope in her hand, though there were no fewer than four from busy Jonah Childs. His missives were full of helpful notions, reporting of how he had had word from an old friend of his by the name of Rider, who was now a colonel in the Cape Colony militia, and who had insisted we call upon him. It was pleasing to know that I would be received by one of the highest of the colony's society. I was further flattered to hear that our arrival in Tasmania was now warmly awaited by none other than that island's governor, who it seemed was an acquaintance of one of Mr. Childs's many cousins. As to my wife's news, her single letter was somewhat brief, concerning itself mostly with a new dress shop in Highgate that she had discovered. Any slight disappointment I felt, however, was quickly dispelled. She was, I realized, simply endeavouring not to worry me with her own distress, brave little poppet that she is.

It was as I was about to leave the post office that I saw, striding in through the door, Dr. Potter. It was hardly a happy meeting. He offered me only the curtest reply to my greetings, while I could not help but notice that he was holding a letter, whose address he seemed to be trying to conceal, though I could clearly see between his fingers the words "Mr. Jonah Ch . . ." I dare say it was his right to communicate to whoever he wished, and yet I felt it would have been only courteous to consult myself, as leader of this expedition, before writing to our patron. As it was, I was left wondering what such secrecy could signify.

I sent my card to Colonel Rider the next morning. A note arrived at the lodging house by return, addressed to myself, and inviting "the Reverend Geoffrey Wilson and any members of the Van Diemen's Land Expedition who may be agreeable" to dine at the castle, where the colony's militia were stationed. I mentioned the matter to Renshaw when he finally emerged from his sleeping, and if I did not also tell Potter this was only because, as had so often been the case since we arrived, he was nowhere to be found, being away on some mysterious business of his own. The colonel's words "and any members of the Van Diemen's Land Expedition" seemed, besides, hardly to require the presence of us all, while I had no wish to overwhelm him with our numbers. The whole matter would have ended there had not Renshaw—quite needlessly—spoken of it to the doctor that evening. Potter's reaction was hardly to be credited. One moment he was whining like a spoilt child and the next he was blustering like a bully, insisting that he should have been asked too, and insinuating that I had somehow conspired to have him excluded. I was wholly satisfied with my own conduct, naturally, and yet, faced with this display of near-hysteria, I considered it wisest to have him to join us. I wrote to the colonel informing him we would now be three.

I soon regretted this charity. Hardly had we been welcomed by the colonel and his officers, and taken our places at table, when Potter began behaving in a manner that I can only describe as deliberately provoking. When Colonel Rider, a stiff but gentle fellow, inquired about our journey from London, he insisted on relating, in a tone of falsest commiseration, that I had suffered greatly from seasickness, even claiming that he had quite feared for my survival. This was despite the fact that he knew full well I had suffered only from poor food. Likewise when we began discussing Tasmania, he dwelt at length on the harshness of the wilderness, which he said was "rough country even for a fit young fellow like myself to go exploring, let alone anyone else." I fought back keenly enough, suggesting, over the lamb and mint sauce, how it was a great shame that he had so little knowledge of geology or theology, and so would be left wholly in the dark as we set about our exploration. I also related my experiences of walking across the hills of Yorkshire, subtly implying that I was at least as well prepared for the venture as the doctor, whose life had been spent in dank hospital rooms.

It was only when we had returned to our lodgings, as I lay in bed, considering the evening's events, that I suddenly grasped the doctor's true intention. How slow can be the forces of goodness that, of their very nature, can barely perceive wicked designs. Potter's purpose was more than mere insult, far more. The man, I realized with alarm, sought nothing less than to depose me from my rightful place as leader of this expedition. It was not Colonel Rider who was his real concern, but Jonah Childs. The colonel was sure to write to his old friend, and promptly, giving a full account of his impressions of us. What if he had been convinced by Potter's poisonous suggestions? There was also the letter I had seen Potter about to post, whose address he had attempted to conceal. I was, I now saw, being attacked upon two fronts, as the doctor endeavoured to turn our patron against me, even from this great distance. What made this especially troubling was Mr. Childs's own nature, that was so prone to sudden changes of mind. Had he not come close to appointing the doctor once already, I recalled unhappily, as we stood among the expedition's stores in my sister-in-law's parlour in Highgate?

I slept little that night. My mind was a frenzy of steamers. The mail service from Cape Colony to England took no more than five weeks. A letter sent directly from London to Melbourne in Victoria, as I recalled, took ten. The final journey from there to Hobart would, I imagined, require no more than a few days. Sixteen weeks in all. It was my hope that we would already have set forth into the wilderness of Tasmania before this time had elapsed, but this was far from assured. If the *Sincerity* suffered unexpected delay, as well she might, or we met with difficulties when organizing the expedition, there would be time enough for Mr. Childs—his mind poisoned with malicious falsehood—to write and command me to relinquish my office of leader, and to place Potter himself in my stead. It was something that I could not and would not permit.

Dr. Thomas Potter
OCTOBER 1857

Cape Colony

Town = of greatest interest to self re <u>notions</u> as possesses quite <u>remarkable</u> variety of <u>types</u>. Among world's greatest instances? Self spent many hours carefully observing. Soon came to new + unexpected conclusions. E.g. watched <u>Boers</u> visiting from outlying farms and noted they = <u>braggardly</u> + surprisingly <u>sluggish</u>: ride giant wagons (oxen) that = v. <u>slow</u>. Cf. <u>English</u> colonists = quick and energetic, filled with winning confidence. <u>New notion</u>: Dutch not Saxon Type as self previously supposed but in fact = <u>Belgic Celts</u>. Would explain absence moral fortitude + history of <u>decline</u>.

Races present of Cape Colony = as follows, listed by precedence:

1. British: Type = Saxon. Status = <u>natural rulers of colony</u>.
2. Boers: Type = Belgic Celtic. Status = <u>assistants</u> to British.
3. Malays: Type = Oriental. Status = farm labourers + <u>servants</u>.
4. Hindoos: Type = Indian Asiatic. Status = as Malays but <u>lower</u>.
5. Native Africans = Type: Negro. Status = <u>low</u>.
6. Hottentots: Type = lower Negro. Status = low and <u>brutal</u>.

11th October

Most satisfactory day. Began with news from <u>India</u>. Report in local newspaper indicates fighting continues v. fiercely, yet appears mutiny has not spread beyond Delhi + other areas of the north. British forces rallying well. Self feel certain rebellion will <u>fail</u>, though it may take much time, suffering etc. etc. This = quite as self <u>anticipated</u>.

Visited home of Dr. Louis Clive (he = fellow surgeon, introduction given by Dr. P.). Clive = excellent fellow + v. interesting on <u>Hottentots</u>. Told self these = among v. <u>lowest types</u>, barely of mankind. Self stayed to dinner with much joking. Clive v. interested re own <u>notions</u>, and most encouraging. Also v. helpful re obtaining <u>specimens</u>.

Wilson in sitting room when self returned to lodging house, giving self strangest + most malevolent <u>look</u>. Self beginning to wonder if he actually <u>losing his sanity</u>, especially after his scheming to prevent self joining he + Renshaw to dine with Col. Rider (though evening proved dull enough). <u>Dementia</u> = leading characteristic of <u>Norman Type</u>, indicating characteristic <u>decadence</u> and <u>depravity</u>? Matter = v. pertinent re <u>notions</u>. For moment, however, self have little time to study he, as chief concern = <u>specimens</u>.

Captain Illiam Quillian Kewley
OCTOBER 1857

WE HEARD the bad news even before we'd stepped onto dry land. Once the pilot was safely aboard and had started guiding us towards the harbour of that Cape Colony–a showy-looking place, lurking beneath a wide mountain, flat like a piano–I thought I might as well chance a little careful asking.

"So how is it for pennies here? Will we be rich men or paupers compared to where we've come from?"

He shrugged. "That depends on what you're buying."

"Well, let's say a night of lodgings. Or perhaps a bottle of French brandy?"

"The lodgings won't be cheap," he answered cheerily, "but you'll do handsomely on the brandy. Then you'll know this is a free port."

Ah, but I didn't. A free port? Well there was a useless, rotten piece of news. Truly, there's none like Englishmen to find some new way of cheating a man out of his livelihood. I ask you. What was the point of annoying the world with customs men, coast guard cutters and other trouble if you leave a mighty gaping hole in it all, with not a penny of duty demanded on anything? Not that I'm saying I missed those revenue boys, but if we had to suffer them, then we should suffer them here too, like we expected. Why, it was nothing less than a disgrace. After all the fuss we'd gone to building the *Sincerity* like she was, and packing her full with that certain discreet cargo, it was worth no more here than if we'd stacked every bottle in the main hold, for all the world to see, like any plodding fool of a merchant. Where was the fairness in that?

It had us well spiked, besides. I had been relying on us slipping the *Sincerity* away to some quiet cove so she might open up her treasures and catch her reward. I'd reckoned this would be a handy place to do it, too, seeing as it was a busy corner of the earth, while, from the look of it on our chart of the world, that Hobart of the Englishmen would be worse than useless, being just a speck on the edge of nowhere. But now I found we'd been tricked into stopping in a land of cheap dirts.

As the wise man says, though, *there's no sense weeping over the herring you never saw*, and I tried to cast it from my thoughts as best I could, attending instead to harbour chores, which were plentiful enough to keep me busy. First there was the paperwork to settle, and then I had to order in new water casks and food that we needed, which took a good few days to arrive. All the while the boys were whining and fussing for their wages and to be let on shore to make some trouble. I held them off as long as I could, but in the end I had to give way, handing out some pennies and letting them go hurrying down the gangway with their hungry looks. I kept a couple of them back, and China Clucas too, whose arm was fairly healed after the pig, to load up the last of the water casks, and the beasts I'd bought to keep us fed for the next piece of voyaging. This they did slower than snails, being all huffy at having to stay.

I didn't tarry longer to watch. I left Kinvig to give them a yelling now and then, while Brew and me went off to find some decent charts, just so we'd be able to know which part of Australia we were staring at. Here, at least, we struck some luck. The first ones we saw were nothing less than robbery, being costly as if they'd been drawn with gold, but then we came across a little den of a shop, where I found a fine little map of Van Diemen's Land—or Tasmania as they were calling it now—that was going for a quarter the price of the rest. It was a touch old, I dare say, having the year 1830 stamped at the top, but there seemed no harm in that. The coastline was clear enough, while any new roads or towns that might have happened inland were pure fuss to Manxmen in a boat. The shopman had another of all Australia, also a touch old, which would be handy too, if just to stop us sailing clean into it by mistake some dark night, and I was able to cog him down nicely and get us a good price for the two together.

There's cheer in a bargain and I found my spirits, which had been dropped low by all that free-port cheating, lifted nicely. I even thought we might as well put a little sight of this Africa, seeing as we were here, and so we took a stroll about the town. A skittish sort of place it was, I'd noticed. When we first arrived it had been cold as could be, with a breeze chill enough for any Ramsey January—quite the surprise for this Africa, that was famous for being hot as ovens—but then the wind had swung round northwards and all of a sudden summer had come, bright and hot as you liked. Now we were back to cold once more. Another curiosity was the fatness of the locals. Truly I never did see such a place for fellows carrying their own lard. First I wondered if it was a handy way of keeping themselves warm in this cold wind, as if they'd grown themselves coats on the inside, but then we went to a tavern for a try of some Africa food and there was the answer. Fish we had, but the poor things were half drowned to death in purest grease. When I asked the innkeeper—one of those Dutchman Africans, and as swelled as any of them—he told us proudly that it was best sheep-tail fat. A few months of that would load a man nicely.

The Indian and bluemen Africans must have been eating something else, being mostly thin as rakes. Quiet these were, too, as if they didn't want to get themselves too noticed. Nor was this surprising, I dare say, seeing as the Dutchman and Englishman Africans treated them like proper dirts, sneering and yelling at them in a way that wasn't pretty to watch. Man Island has its portion of snots, for sure—most of them Englishmen or Scotsmen ruined by having some foolish lordly title before their names—but this was seven times worse. This wasn't just a few old sticks thinking themselves high, but seemed one half of the town scoffing and tormenting at the other.

Brew was more interested in the shops. "Have you seen all that mining gear they're selling?" he wondered as we had a peer round one of these, though I could hardly miss it, as there was half a room of the stuff, from bellows and buckets to tents and portable forges. High on the wall behind was a large sign.

GOLD PROSPECTORS BOUND FOR VICTORIA, BUY HERE!
OUR PRICES ARE LOWER THAN IN ALL AUSTRALIA.

"What of it?"

Brew took on one of his clever, knowing looks. "Perhaps we should take some for ourselves. It might make us a tidy few pennies. Besides, it seems a rotten waste sailing all that way with nothing in the hold but ballast and such."

"Except," I answered, surprised at the man's foolishness, "that we've no spare money to pay for it, and we're never going to Victoria at all, but to Tasmania."

The fact was Brew was the sort of fellow who did think a thing through, and it was rare to catch him out stupid. "Why shouldn't we go to Victoria, though? We could make up any old story to tell the Englishmen and they'd never know the difference. They're saying Victoria has gold popping out of the ground like rabbits in springtime, so it would be just the place to get a good price for our cargo."

"What of the money we'd need? After stores and port fees and a few pennies for the crew we've nothing to spare to go purchasing mining gear."

"That's easy. We just peddle those forks and such that we caught back in Maldon. They'd sell well enough in a town like this."

The awful fact was that it wasn't a bad idea. I made a play of shrugs and playing doubtful, just to keep him from getting too high, but I came round in the end. So we went back to the ship to get a few pieces of silverware as samples, and then started looking for a shop. If it was cheapness we'd been wanting with charts, now we were after dearness itself, and we settled on a place that was all silver candlesticks and dainty little tables in the window, with a snurly sort of a fellow peering out from behind the counter. I could see he was interested when we showed him the wares, though he tried to look as if he never cared.

"I might find use for these, I suppose," he said, peering at the spoon and fork I'd handed him. "D'you have the full set?"

"All but one or two," I answered, remembering those that had dropped in the Blackwater mud when their owner had started shooting his gun at us. "But they'd hardly be missed, the many that there are. Why, there's half a crate of them back aboard the ship."

"Indeed?" He gave the pieces another scrutiny, and it was then that his eyes turned sort of narrow. "Where did you get these?"

If there's one thing sets a Manxman careful it's questions. "One of those London markets."

"Which one?"

I shrugged as if I could hardly trouble myself to remember. "Does it matter?"

"It might." All at once he was all beady eyes and cleverness. "It may be purest coincidence, yet I read something in the English paper only the other day about an unfortunate gentleman who was robbed of his silverware. Unless I'm mistaken his name was Howarth, Admiral Henry Howarth." He held up the spoon, pointing with his finger at the letters HH. "His home was not far from London, I believe, being somewhere by the sea."

I managed to keep my smile burning nicely. "Is that so?" I was all lost in mystery. How could he have seen any such thing? Then it came to me clear as glass. The steamers. Hadn't I seen them myself, cluttering up the harbour, all belching out their nasty smoke? They'd have been rushing past us in their hurry for all these weeks, bringing their mail and newspapers and trouble. "Of course there'll be fellows by the thousands and millions with names starting HH."

"There'll be some, certainly." The shopman gave a careful sort of look. "It was a most unhappy business, as I recall. According to the *Times* he had been a commander in the last Chinese war, while the cutlery that was taken had been forged from silver from a captured Chinese vessel. It was a great loss to him."

As if we'd not had enough rotten fortune already, now it turned out we'd been tricked into robbing some hero.

"Do you have any proof of previous ownership? A document of sale, perhaps?"

There are times to linger and this was not one. I threw a look to Brew. "Have we now?"

Brew was cross with himself for being so foolish. "D'you know, I clean forgot to bring it."

I was all forgiveness. "Ah, then we'd best go back and find it now." I threw the shopman a broad Manx smile and reached out to take the fork and spoon he had. "We'll not be long." For just a moment, and a bad moment it was, too, he looked as if he might try to keep hold of them, but finally he let them go.

"A fine piece of cleverness that was," I growled at Brew as we stepped out into the street.

It was a rare thing to scrape shame out of Brew, what with his braininess, but I saw a little creeping from him now. "It was just bad luck," he whined. "Besides, he won't do anything."

Just wondering made me take a glance back, though I at once wished I hadn't. There, stood like a sneak in his doorway, was the shopman, giving us a proper study. I made a little play of peering past him at something else entirely, though there was nothing much further down the street, as it happened, besides an old dog cocking its leg at a fence.

We were walking on now, and at good pace. "Even if he tells someone there's little they can do," insisted Brew, slipping back a peg. "Why, he doesn't even know who we are."

He knew enough, mind. "We told him we had a ship, though, and that the silver was aboard."

Brew's head fell at that. "But he doesn't know her name. No policeman will want to go searching every ship that's in just on a scran of a chance like that."

Or wouldn't he? The shopman could tell him what we looked like, while it wouldn't help that the business had been such a newspaper fuss, with hero admirals and Chinamen's wars to catch the eye. That sort of foolishness might well tempt a policeman, even an African one. All at once I was thinking breezes. It was only today that the wind had swung round southerly and given us the chance to sail away from here. If it veered back to a warm northerly, which it might do any moment for all I knew, then we'd be caught tighter than the bear that tried to climb the chimney. Why, we could be stuck here for days or weeks. By the time we'd reached the ship I'd made up my mind.

"I'm taking no chances." I waved Kinvig over. "We're sailing today."

The trouble was that it was never so easy. For a start there were still two dozen water casks waiting on the quay to be loaded, as well as a small zoo of creatures. As I watched, China Clucas and the other two boys were hauling up a trussed swiney by a pulley, which they did slow as treacle, being still in their huff at being made to stay. Aside from that, and far worse too, there was the little matter of finding the crew.

"They'll be drinking," said Brew.

"Or whoring," added Kinvig.

"Or both."

I doubted I'd given them enough pennies for both. Not that it helped much. "You'd better go and look for them," I told Kinvig. "There can't be many spots where they'd be."

He'd hardly turned to go when Brew thought up a new worry. "What about the passengers?"

What indeed? Their lodging house was just across the quay from the ship and I'd seen them all strutting off that morning. Being Englishmen they'd never do anything easy to guess, like finding a pretty whore to soothe away the day, and they might be up to any madness. I gave a shrug. "I'll have Kinvig ask at their lodgings. If they're nowhere to be found we may just have to leave their stores on the quay and go without them." They wouldn't like that any, for sure, and would be fussing and shouting and calling us all manner of names, but still this seemed sweeter than to chance spending the rest of my days rotting in some African dungeon. "Now I'd best pay the port fees, or we'll never be let out."

It was just as I was about to step down onto the quay when China Clucas called out, "I heard you. You want to sneak away without the Englishmen."

There's few things worse than when a fellow without much brain in his skull starts trying to play clever. He gave me a stubborn, knowing sort of look. I gave him a stern stare. "Didn't I tell you to shift those casks? Now get to work."

A wounded look came into his eyes. "It's not right going leaving the doctor behind. It's just not right."

The Reverend Geoffrey Wilson
OCTOBER 1857

I HAD ALREADY been waiting nearly an hour to see Colonel Rider. While this delay was more than a little annoying, it had at least permitted me to practise in my thoughts the discourse which I would give him. First I would endeavour to win him to my side, which I would do by telling him how I hoped to draw upon his great expertise as a leader of men. Next I would permit myself to grow troubled, relaying my doubts regarding Dr. Potter's soundness of mind, and recounting his more strange and vindictive actions during the voyage from London, paying particular attention to his attempt to mesmerize a pig. Finally I would offer my confidence, reporting how I feared that the doctor felt resentment at not having been appointed as the expedition's leader. This done, I would give no further opinions myself, but simply request the colonel's advice. While I have no interest in the trickery of strategies, naturally I have lived long enough to know how important it is to set forth one's views in a form that will win others to one's side.

Hearing footsteps and voices, I supposed I was finally to be admitted to see the colonel. Sadly it was not to be. "Mr. Brew? This is a surprise."

"Ah, thank goodness, Reverend. Your landlady said I'd find you here. The Captain's saying we must sail today. You're to come at once."

It was a demand as unreasonable as it was unexpected. Only the morning before, the Captain had said we would remain at Cape Colony for at least several more days. "But why?"

"There's no missing a breeze like this," Brew insisted. "If it shifts back, then we could be stuck here for weeks and months or more. You wouldn't want to be stuck here still Christmastime, now would you, Reverend."

"The Captain never mentioned this danger before."

"Ah, but that was before the breeze changed."

Infuriating though it was, there seemed little that could be done. Offering my excuses to the sergeant outside, I took my leave of the castle, quite wishing I had never informed our landlady of my destination of the morning. I had only done so, indeed, because I supposed she might find some small pleasure in knowing she had such distinguished guests.

Brew had a cab waiting. It was only as the vehicle was rumbling into motion that he asked his next question. "I don't suppose you know where the other two may be?"

There seemed no limit to the man. So I had been dragged from my own urgent purpose though the whereabouts of Renshaw and the doctor were still unknown. I might find myself waiting hours for them to return, when all the while I could be talking to Colonel Rider. "I have not the slightest idea," I told him with some coolness.

His face fell. "That's bad."

In the event the whereabouts of one of my colleagues was discovered soon enough. As the cab turned into the port I saw a straggling line of men ahead, whom I recognized as members of the ship's crew. Thus it appeared that the vessel was far from ready to depart after all, despite Brew's claims. The men could hardly have looked less prepared for resuming their duties, their hair and clothes wild as if they had lately sprung from their beds, while some were staggering as they walked, evidently drunk. All in all I would have more than a little to say to the Captain about this matter. It was only as the cab drew level with the men that, greatly to my own surprise, I saw Renshaw was walking sullenly alongside them. For a moment I thought he had injured his leg in some fashion, as he was walking with a limp, but then I realized he was missing one of his shoes.

"What on earth has happened to you, Renshaw?" I called out to him from the cab window.

He merely shrugged, though one of the crewmen, giving me a curious look, called out, "Fishing, he's been, Vicar, and at the same pretty riverbank as have we all. That's where he lost his boot."

What he meant I had no idea and no great curiosity, being far more concerned with the ill-mannered way in which I had been treated. Reaching our lodgings, I saw all our belongings had already been packed and were waiting in the hall, and as soon as I had paid the bill I had the cab take me across to the *Sincerity*. Kewley, I saw, stood on the main deck.

"Captain, I believe you owe me an explanation as to why we have had to leave so suddenly, not to say inconveniently."

The gall of the man. He did not answer but turned away from me, shielding his eyes to regard the port. "Ah, there he is. And about time, too."

Following his look, I saw another cab was drawing into view, through whose window was just visible the dour face of Dr. Potter. After his recent behaviour I would have felt no great sadness if he had contrived to have himself left behind. Seeing the frantic wavings from the ship's crew, he directed his driver to the quay beside the vessel, where he at once clambered out and, with the help of the driver and the ship's strongman Clucas, who had hurried down to greet him, he began unloading a number of wooden packing cases. Kewley, I was annoyed to see, seemed hopeful of using this distraction to make an escape, striding away to the quarterdeck. I had no intention of obliging him and followed.

"Captain, you have not explained the suddenness of this departure."

Luck was not on my side. He was just turning his grumpy gaze upon me when we were interrupted once again, this time by an uproarious sound of barking. The port was a popular haunt for stray dogs, that were often to be seen scavenging for food, and a pack of these were showing great interest in Potter's new luggage.

"Off with you," Potter shouted angrily, waving his stick. Though the animals scampered away it was only by a few yards, and they continued to bark keenly at the boxes.

"What have you got in there, Doctor?" Renshaw called out as the first of these was carried onto the deck.

Potter gave him a cool look. "Specimens. Specimens for my studies."

"Not cats, is it?" shouted out one of the crewmen, to some laughter.

I turned once again to Kewley. "Captain, may I ask you once again to explain . . ."

It is an injustice of this world that any protest, however rightful it may be, will tend to lose its potency by repetition. Kewley appeared to have lost all sense of awkwardness, quite brushing my complaint aside.

"Not now, Vicar. I have to attend to the ship. If you'll excuse me I must ask you to clear yourself off the quarterdeck."

Greatly irritated, I had no choice but to step down to the main deck and bide my time until the ship had been got under way. I sat upon a coil of rope, only to find myself at once moved on by the second mate, Kinvig. I had never seen the Manxmen, who were usually the slowest of creatures, displaying such lively animation. Above, some were already at work hurriedly loosening the sails, while others had lowered a boat to bring the vessel around. In a moment the *Sincerity* was free of her berth and had been turned into the breeze. Before long the boat was hauled up and the three topsails were being unleashed and tied into place, giving the vessel a tug of movement. The crewmen on the deck pulled the yards round till they were angled to catch the wind, and soon we were making progress towards the open sea. It was only then that I noticed a puzzling sight behind us. There on the quayside, just where the *Sincerity* had been berthed, there stood two fellows, both waving excitedly in our direction.

Potter had seen them too. "Who on earth are they?" he called up to Kewley.

"Them?" The Captain rubbed his chin with his hand, squinting at the pair. "Ah, they'll be well-wishers."

Their waving seemed somehow not quite right. "Are you sure?"

Rather than answer he turned and gave a great shout. "Come along, boys, give a wave to the well-wishers." After a moment's hesitation the whole vessel, from deck to highest rigging, became bedecked with waving arms. Curiously enough this appeared to diminish rather than add to the enthusiasm of those on the shore.

Thus it was we began our journey eastwards across the Southern Ocean towards Tasmania.

CHAPTER EIGHT

—————◆◆◆—————

Nathaniel Stebbings, Bristol Schoolmaster, to John Harris,
Van Diemen's Land Settler and Landowner

—————————

Rose House, Bristol   *12th October 1832*

Mr. Harris,

It is with more than a little sadness that I must bid farewell to young George as he returns to his native land. It seems hardly possible that he has been with Mother and myself fully two years, so quickly has the time passed.

When Mr. Grigson first came to call at Rose House and suggested the arrangement, I confess I found myself not a little uncertain. For all my experience as a teacher I could hardly claim any expertise in the instruction of wild black boys from the furthermost antipodes, and I shall not deny I came close to declining so curious a proposition. In the event, I am more than happy that I took the decision I did, as matters have turned out better than I could ever have expected. True enough, the lad was quite difficult at first. He showed an aversion to sitting still which proved hard to overcome, and would sometimes jump to his feet even in the middle of dinner, a habit which was cured only by constant reproach. He was also restless at night, often crying out in strange wild words of his own language, until he had roused all the household with his mysterious nightmares. With time, however, he grew more accustomed to his new home, and he is now a most well-behaved and likeable child. He has developed a particular affection for Mother's maidservant, Mrs. Cleghorn–a Welsh woman of warmest character–to whom he will cling about the waist quite as if she were some tree in a gale, showing such a visible reluctance to ever let go that she finds it no easy matter to attend to her duties.

As to the boy's studies, here again I found myself surprised, as he has *applied himself well and progressed at a good pace. You will find he now speaks English with fluency, although he has difficulty still with prepositions and some of the past tenses. Likewise he writes a clear and neat hand, though his spelling still needs further practice. Altogether his memory is good and he has got off his Psalms very well.*

My greatest delight, however, has concerned his Arithmetic. While in other subjects he is able rather than remarkable, here he has shown no small aptitude. He learned his multiplication tables with greater ease almost than his alphabet, which is most unusual, and has progressed so quickly with long multiplication and division that I have started him upon geometry. He seems to find a pure and simple enchantment in numbers, quite as if they are toys for his amusement. More than a few times I have found him writing out sums in his own time, almost with a secrecy, as if this were his personal pleasure. My surprise at his skills has been all the greater as it was in this subject, more than any, that it might have been expected he would find difficulty.

If I have written at some length about George's talent for Arithmetic this is not without purpose. The fact is that it is my wish that I may impress upon you the value of continuing him in his studies. I hope you will not find it impertinent, but I cannot help but wonder if you might reconsider your intention, as reported to me by Mr. Grigson, of having him work in some simple capacity upon your farm. My fear is that in associating with persons far less educated than himself, he will come to forget his own learning. In view of the great progress he has made this would be no small waste. With encouragement and further instruction I do believe George could be well suited to some official post, perhaps in the service of the colonial government. Employment in an office would likewise be more favourable to his health, as I have observed his constitution is far from strong. I have provided him with all his writing and ciphering books so his present state of knowledge may be clearly shown, and it occurs to me that these might be of no little interest to the island's governor.

It is left to me only to hope that you may find time to send us a letter now and then, that we may hear of the little fellow's progress. I fear Mrs. Cleghorn will give Mother and myself no peace if she is not provided with news of "my George," as she refers to him. Likewise should you discover any further such unfortunates who would benefit from a course of lessons here I would, naturally, be most pleased to offer my own services for their instruction.

Jack Harp
1830–37

EIGHTEEN OF US there were sat in that stinking ship's hold, listening to the roar of chain as the anchor was let go, which meant we had surely arrived somewhere. It was sweet enough to step on the deck and feel the breeze, as it had been close as death down below. We were stopped in a narrow bay, I saw, the shore just wild trees and not a sign of men. This was hardly a surprise, mind, as we were the lucky bleeders supposed to get this new misery town started. It was sheltered by hills and had a little yellow beach, and I thought it a pretty enough spot in its way, this Port Arthur, as it was to be called. I'd have time to think on that prettiness again, of course, as it turned out.

Within a couple of days we'd built huts and a storehouse, and we had ourselves a fine little gaol village. After that we started work, which was cutting down the giant trees and sawing them into pieces, or hauling them through the harbour–which was cold as winter–and soon there were other buggers arriving to share our delight. I'd never been snared in a penal colony before, but I'd heard talk of what went on at Macquarie Harbour–stories that would scare the devil himself–and I wasn't one to go waiting for it to happen to me. I reckoned the best way to stop trouble was to make it, and so I set about getting myself a name, which meant giving out hard looks and cracking any head that gave one back. I had to be careful of the guards, as to be seen was to catch a lashing, but it could be done in the quiet of the forest sometimes, or in the huts at night, and though I got caught and lashed once or twice I thought it was worth paying that price. I was careful never to forget any lip I was given, so my name was kept right, and I'd settle any bother in the end, even if it was weeks later. That served me well enough, too, at least through the first year or so, till the Macquarie Harbour boys blew in.

It was the whole lot of them we got, as Macquarie Harbour was being closed down for good. I suppose some office scribbler reckoned our Port Arthur could be made even worse. Proper hard cases they were, those buggers, with killing in their every glance, being the kind that would as soon get themselves hanged than stomach a sneer or slight, and from the moment they arrived in the settlement–which was quite a little town of huts and saw pits by then–they were out to govern the place as if it was their own toy. They did too, fairly much, the commander and his creepers of soldiers running as scared of them as everyone else, so they hardly troubled if some poor bastard got beaten half to death or worse. I did what I could. I tried keeping out of their way, and I tried looking crazed too, and not a man to trouble, but it made no difference as they had me marked down as someone to cut down to size. All in all I don't rightly care to recall what went on in those times.

The one good thing about those Macquarie boys was that they got us some fishing. After a while the store ran short, so our rations were cut, and they took themselves into a right temper at this, threatening all manner of joy if they weren't given more to eat, till the commander ran scared and told us we must feed ourselves. Work hours were cut and we were told to catch some fishing and start growing vegetables. That was sweet, too, as nothing felt so bad when you were sat by the water with a line, or digging in seed potatoes. I wasn't the only bugger to find it so, neither, and even those Macquarie boys got slowed down nicely. Why, it got so that the commander had to let his soldiers go fishing as well, as they were getting jealous of their own prisoners.

All good things must come to an end, so it's said, and with Port Arthur the good things stopped with a little Christmas gift we got, this being a visit by George Alder himself, governor of Van Diemen's Land. I'd heard a good deal about this fellow from the others, as he was often the subject of nighttime chattering in the penitentiary huts, when coves thought up all kinds of violent mishaps a great man like that should take care to avoid. There he was, stepping from his rowboat, a little troop of guards and creepers nursing him along. A bloodless face he had, almost as if he was crook, and eyes with no laugh in them, that made me think of purity vicars, or snakes studying at mice. He didn't look much pleased with what he saw as he snooped about, but kept grim as Sunday, scowling almost as if we'd let him down.

After that little visit changes came thick and fast. We got a new commander, who was one of those military Irishmen that cackle at cannonballs, and it was him that put a stop to our fishing and gardens. Our plants were all taken up and put together in one big field, which meant they weren't ours anymore and only a few lucky crawlers got to work on them. Then there were the new uniforms, all different according to how improved we were. Any coves that were thought on their path to salvation wore grey, while the rest of us that weren't were in cheery yellow. As for any poor bleeders who'd somehow managed to get worse, these were different again, having yellow suits with a prettiest pattern drawn across them, all made out of the word "felon," as well as a handsome pair of leg shackles to show off.

Another change was that tobacco was outlawed. In truth this caused more trouble than all the rest, as it drove the Macquarie boys half to madness, so they were always looking out for someone to punish. If you fought back—which I did—this was frowned on by the commander and his redcoats as showing you still unimproved, and so I stayed in canary clothes all the while. That was trouble, as time was passing and I was getting mighty weary of chopping at trees, feeling a lash on my back and staring always at that little yellow beach. Besides, I was getting no younger, and my fear was that if I got stuck here another four years I'd not be able to fight my corner, and would be just dead meat to any enemy I'd notched up, there being more than a few of those.

Port Arthur was getting older too. Convicts by the hundred there were now, with more buggers coming all the while, and from just a few huts by the shore it was grown into quite a Manchester, with work sheds turning out every kind of article, from boots to lampposts. There was a dock where ships were made, and strong guarded, too, while away to northwards there was a little coal mine with cells underground, that was said to be such a delight that even the Macquarie Harbour boys tried to keep away. If for some reason a fellow tired of all this joy and decided to take a little walk alone into the bush, there was a fine new semaphore on the hill behind the commander's house, so that in just a few moments all Van Diemen's Land might know of his strolling. If our fellow was caught—which he generally would be—and was left weary from his adventures, or had caught a bullet in his gut, there was a little railway to carry him back, with carriages pulled not by steam engines but by convicts, these being more plentiful. Why, if his excursion proved too exciting for his nerves we even had an island of the dead for the poor bleeder, where he could be buried in a good Port Arthur coffin, that he might have worked on himself.

It might sound grand enough already, I dare say, but our military Irishman commander was dreaming of greater things still, being unhappy that his little kingdom was all made of wood, which would hardly do for the likes of us. So it was that anyone who'd been fortunate enough to work with stone–perhaps playing at making some bridge–was suddenly wanted. I'd never thought I'd be pleased to find myself chipping at rocks once again, but after all these years sawing trees with the likes of the Macquarie boys it seemed gentleness itself. First I was put building a guardhouse for the barracks, that was round like some bloody castle, and after that there was the new church we had to have, so some parson could tell us how wicked we were every Sunday, just in case we'd forgot. That church was a mighty piece of work, and took a full year of splitting our hands before it was done. By then I was beginning to get hopeful that I'd soon be bidding farewell to Port Arthur. The rock chippers were mostly creepers that I could scare with just a few words and looks, so it was easy enough to keep myself improved, and after just a few months I traded my canary yellow for my very first suit of grey. If I stayed quiet and bided my time I reckoned I'd soon be away making roads or such, which would be soft as milk after here.

My next job after the church looked quietness itself, being a fountain and other foolishness for an ornamental garden, that was the toy of our Irishman commander's wife. She'd only been married to the old brute a few months and was a tasty-looking piece, fresh and ripe as could be, with a sad sort of look in her eyes, I suppose from being stuck on the furthest edge of nowhere with nobody for company but soldiers and coves in chains. The talk was that this ornamental garden was her husband's stab at keeping her cheerful, and it seemed to be working, as most every day she came strolling out to fret herself with some new little change she wanted, as everything had to be just so. Not that we much minded being ordered, seeing as she was such a juicy little piece. She never went anywhere alone, always having a little troop of soldiers keeping watch, just in case anyone got any thoughts, as well they might. It was hard not to stare, as she had a fine tempting shape, even covered up like she was, and on hot days I was sure I caught a faint whiff of her musk, sweet and ready as could be. After all this time locked away that got me feeling quite faint-headed with dreaming up the rest of the picture, and how she'd squeal with a fine good working. Still I took only careful glances, being keen not to lose that grey suit of mine.

She hardly spoke to us stone chippers, keeping her words for a fellow named Sheppard, who was doing the cherubs. Sheppard wasn't much skilled at them, in truth, having only been picked because he'd once had a trade carving tombstones–which is hardly the same–and they never looked like flying babies so much as fat boys with something nasty flapping on their backs. The commander's wife took it very serious, though, and was forever peering at them and giving advice, for all the little difference it made. It was those cherubs caused all my trouble in a way. By now we were in January and it was hot as ovens, while chipping stone is thirsty work. I'd been working out in the sun a good few hours, hacking at stone blocks for the summerhouse we were making next, and I'd taken a good few swigs of water from the bucket to cool my throat. Water will as water will, and, seeing all was quiet, I took a stroll across to some bushes that were near.

Hardly had I got set when I heard a sort of gasp. There she was, the commander's little pet, all hot and damp in her corsets and such, just on the other side of that bush. She must have stepped back there so she could get a look at the cherubs from a distance. Her eyes were staring wide, almost as if she'd never seen one before. As for me, I never meant any trouble. It was just I was caught by surprise, so rather than put him away smartish, like I suppose I should, I just stared right back. That was my mistake. All at once she let out a scream loud enough to be heard in Hobart town and soldiers were running.

To be fair, she never did push to get me punished. I even heard talk that she asked her husband to let me off. Not that it made any difference. Probably he didn't much like the thought of her seeing any but his own, just in case she started getting too interested. Inside half a moment I'd traded my suit of grey for a yellow one with "felon" written all across it, and a handsome pair of leg irons to match. Nor was that the end of the commander's thank-you. The finish of it was the work gang I was put into, and most of all the gang's overseer, Ferguson, who was known as the keenest lasher in all Van Diemen's Land.

Ferguson's skill was in finding your worst spot and then pushing at it, day after day, till you'd be maddened into doing some wildness that would earn you a nice little spell on the triangles. His favourite was asking questions. "You look tired," he'd say, looking all sad, so that for a moment you wondered if he really was worried for you. "Perhaps you should have a little rest?"

The rule in the gangs was strictest silence, so if you were foolish enough to give an answer his smile would vanish as if it had never happened, he'd be stamping his foot and calling you every stinking name he could think of, and next he'd have the soldiers running over to haul you off to the triangles for your reward. Not that it was much better if you stayed dumb. Then the bastard would shake his head, as if he was surprised. "Well, if you're not tired I've just the job for you." This would be the very worst thing he could dream up, such as dragging double-sized logs, or standing waist-deep in cold harbour water, pushing timber to some boat. Even then he'd not be finished. When you were half dead from that, he'd come sidling up to you again.

"Something troubling you, is there?" he'd ask, all kindly concern. "I know it. You're worried you'll have to leave this little spot one day, and venture back into the world, with its wicked temptations. All that rum to drink and tobacco to smoke, and tasty young females lifting up their skirts." Then he'd peer so close that his face was a blur of nearness and bad breath. "Don't you fret yourself, Jack, as your old friend Ferguson will keep you safe. Why, I'll fix it so you don't have to leave till you're old to your bones, and those females won't annoy you with so much as a glance." Then he'd pat you on the shoulder as if he really was your friend, which was worst of all. "Your old mate Ferguson will see you right."

After being worked on this for a while there wasn't one in his gang that wasn't inches away from throwing a punch. If anyone did, then he'd be ready—he was a good watcher, was Ferguson—and would usually dodge out of the way without catching himself a mark, it being easy enough to skip out of range of a fellow with shackles round his ankles. Then he'd call up soldiers and have you hauled off, and he'd be smiling wide, as there was nothing he loved better than seeing one of his boys catch a stroking from the Port Arthur Cat.

But I should stop here a moment, as this was no ordinary lashing device. Of all the many ones on Van Diemen's Land this bugger had quite a name, and with good reason. Nine tails and eighty-one knots it had, and all of them soaked in salt water and dried in the sun, till they were purest wire. A hundred from this was enough to make pig's liver of any bastard's back. Still I will insist—and I'm quite the man to ask—that the part of being lashed that worked on a man's mind most was never the stinging, but something different altogether. It was that dangling helplessness. No feeling could compare to being tied fast to a wooden triangle quietly waiting for the lasher to catch his breath—they never liked to hurry themselves—and start his next run, while all the time not being able to do a thing to stop him. Even weeks later just the very remembrance of this delight could make a cove's head boil clean over, like milk in the pan, so the smallest thing, such as some fool blocking his way on the path, would set him kicking and punching.

This was just how Ferguson liked his gang to be, too, as then they were easy as lambs to rile into another beating, being all in circles, like snakes eating their own tails. He showed a particular interest in me—I dare say he liked to please his commander—and after a few months and several visits to the triangles I was well primed. I hardly caught a glimpse of my eyes in those days, being out of reach of pretty mirrors, but I'd wager that they were madder now than they ever had been when I was trying to look crazed.

Hardly an hour seemed to pass without my thinking of ways of bolting, and I was soon past caring how wild or foolish they were. Now, a stranger to Van Diemen's Land might think there'd not be many ways to step out of Arthur, but there were more than you might guess. The first, being the one that worked most often, was just to sit quietly and look harmless for months and years, till finally you got let out. The trouble with this bugger, of course, was that I'd given it a proper try already, while it had done me no good, and now my patience was too thin for such slow work. A second way was to come up with some daring act of improvement, such as betraying some little secret of your fellow convicts. The worry here was that snitching was so common a trade in Port Arthur that it was hard to get word of anyone's trouble-making, while if you just invented some plot and hung it round some bleeder's neck–which was done often enough, too–there was the worry that you'd be found out, and lashed rather than freed. A third and better road was to play the hero, perhaps saving some fool of a redcoat from drowning, or from getting mashed when a tree came down. This could work handsomely, and there were stories of men who'd jumped from chains to full pardon all in one leap in just this way, but sadly it was hardly the kind of thing you could rely upon, unless you arranged the drowning or the tree all yourself, which wouldn't be easy. Besides, the commander had me marked as his special enemy, so I'd need to perform a proper barrelload of miracles to win his forgiveness.

This takes me to the fourth route–one that was discussed a good deal in hushed voices–being to simply make a run for it into the bush. This was tried regularly enough, too, though not with much success, the difficulties being many. Even if you managed to chop through your chains with your axe and dodge the nearest soldiers, in half a moment the arms of the commander's semaphore would be waving and search parties would be out, while it was hard to get far on account of the ocean. The dirty piece of land Port Arthur was sat on was as close to being an island as a chunk of land can be, being joined to the rest of Van Diemen's Land only by a strip of dirt a few yards wide, called Eaglehawk Neck, and though I'd never seen this spot it was well known to be guarded more carefully even than the commander's wife's petticoat secrets. A whole troop of redcoats was posted there, together with a row of giant dogs on chains, while I heard that offal was slung into the sea alongside to tempt in sharks. Even if some bastard did manage to get past, there were miles of bush–all thorns and mud and nothing to eat–before he reached farmland. Bolters often gave themselves up freely, as just a few days of roaming made Port Arthur seem comfort itself. Still I was interested in this particular road, mostly because it was there all the while, so tempting, while I was too crazed by now to care much if it would work. We were working close to the railway at that time, and as I watched those little carts trundle by, pulled by their convicts, I'd keep a careful watch on whether soldiers were near, and play little games with myself of what I might do.

But I've left out the fifth and last way out of Port Arthur, which I also liked to think on. This had worries, certainly, but it also had the rare joy of being entirely and absolutely certain. Why, I'd seen more than a few buggers taking it, waving their farewells as they marched through the settlement, giving a jaunty shout of how they were looking forward to having their carriage ride through Hobart town and a smoke of tobacco. The method was simple as could be. You just chose some cove–any would do, though my choice would be friend Ferguson–and then waited till he was looking off into some other direction. Next you walked up to him, nice and quiet, raised up a rock, or your chopping axe if you had one, and gently carved open his skull. Within just a few days you'd find yourself saying goodbye to Port Arthur forever, and having a grand journey all the way to Hobart, for a cheery spell in gaol cells and courtrooms, and a final dangle from a rope. It was hardly the choicest way out, I'll admit. After a few months gadding back and forth between Ferguson's gang and the triangles, though, I was past playing choosy, and was ready to bag whichever chance first showed its face.

Julius Crane, Visiting Inspector of the London Prison Committee
1837

THE WAVES were tossing the vessel about like a leaf in a storm, and as I stood upon the deck, in a brief foray from the shelter of my cabin, there drifted up through the hatches faint cries and moans, together with a most dreadful odour. It was the smell of humanity that has been reduced almost to the animal. The thought of the huddle of convicts tethered below was greatly distressing to me, and not merely because of the physical discomfort they must be enduring. As I knew only too well, their being pressed all together in such proximity would be permitting a terrible process to occur among them–a process as inevitable as chemical osmosis–as criminality and lawlessness spread from the most evil to those still possessed of any lingering innocence. Given a few more days they would, I had no doubt, all be equally contaminated with wickedness.

"They should be brought on deck so they can get some air," I exclaimed.

Knowles, my unsought-for travelling companion, remained unmoved. "I'd rather keep them nicely shackled, Professor."

It was a game of his to call me by this title, though I had told him several times that I was nothing of the kind. Knowles, who was journeying to Port Arthur to conduct an inspection upon the establishment's water supply, was one of those beings who relishes his own pitiless views of mankind, which he seemed to regard in much the same manner as he might a defective system of plumbing. Since we had left Hobart I had learned to treat his remarks with a certain coolness, as to show feeling seemed only to fan the flames of his cynicism. "You have no sympathy for your fellow men," I told him, more as a rebuke than from any expectation that he might take notice.

"Ah, but I have, Professor." He cheerfully patted his chest, as if to point out the sympathy's exact whereabouts. "There it is, just below my desire not to have my throat cut."

It was typical of the man. "If they heard your talk," I told him, "I would hardly blame them for wishing to cut yours."

Another curious quality of Knowles was his eyes. He kept these so narrowed that at times only his moving about informed one that they were open at all, and that he was not in a state of profound sleep. This, when combined with his habitual absence of any facial expression, gave him the look of some scornfully squinting bear. At most, as that morning on the ship's deck, a faint flicker might pass across his face–a kind of twitch–which I had learned to recognize as laughter. "Don't think they'd stop at me," he declared cheerfully. "They'll not have been reading the same books as you, Professor, but ones of their own devising, which prize nothing so high as cutting the throat of a good Christian philanthropist such as yourself."

Four more days I had to endure his company as we remained sheltering from the gales in Pirates Bay. How gladly I would have spent those four days inspecting the Port Arthur settlement, rather than endure Knowles's insufferable goading. Already I had been greatly delayed during my journey from England, while I had prison settlements on the mainland to visit after this one. To make matters worse, we were, throughout this time, absurdly near to our destination. The ship was hove to just by Eaglehawk Neck, the narrow bridge of land that links Port Arthur to the remainder of Van Diemen's Land. As the days passed, I became unhappily familiar with the sight of this cruel-looking spot, with its guardhouse and the line of cruel-looking dogs held in place by chains, one of which was lodged several yards into the water, upon a curious little platform furnished with a kennel, I suppose to discourage any convicts from trying to creep through the shallows. I knew that it lay only a few brief hours' journey overland from the main penal settlement, and it was most infuriating to look upon it, so near that I could easily hear the barking of the dogs, and yet to remain stranded.

The difficulty lay with the ship's captain. "This is no weather for rowboats," he insisted whenever I asked, being as obstinate in this as he was in refusing to allow the poor convicts up from the hold. Even when the wind eventually swung round to a more helpful direction, still he would not let us land, now claiming that the delay of lowering a boat might cause him to miss his chance to sail. Thanks to his stubbornness it took a full two further days and nights of beating our way round the coast before, peering out through the dawn light, I at last gazed upon my quarry of Port Arthur.

I had never expected the settlement to be so large. From a distance the throng of sheds gave the impression of a shabby manufacturing town, while the sound of bugles and shouted commands added a military touch. As the ship drew nearer, the establishment's purpose became more sadly evident, with gangs of convicts clearly discernible, tramping back and forth in chains. Knowles speedily scuttled away to attend to his watery duties and I confess I was happy enough to be free of him. I myself was taken to see one of the establishment's officers who, I was pleased to note, treated me with polite helpfulness, this being not always the case when an inspecting visitor arrives at an institution he may later have call to criticize. I was shown to my quarters, introduced to a second officer who was to serve as my guide and was even provided with an invitation to dine that evening with the commander and his wife. Thus prepared, I could finally begin my work.

If there is any advantage to being greatly delayed it is that one is left primed with impatient determination, and I accomplished more in that first day than I ever could have expected. I visited almost every building frequented by convicts: every workshop and sleeping quarter, every kitchen and punishment cell. I also accompanied a chained work gang as they processed into the nearby forest to cut down trees. Most useful of all, however, was the chance I had to speak to some of the convicts, that I might learn what influence their punishment was having upon them. While most were too hardened to cooperate, and refused to give answers of more than a single word, some proved more loquacious, and while their replies were guarded, still they formed, in their way, a most useful testimony.

As to my impressions, I considered that the settlement was efficiently run, and seemed little to suffer from those habits of vengeful cruelty which are often the most detestable feature of such establishments. What it lacked, however, was that most essential element: a system of moral enlightenment. The tiny settlement school offered only a handful of lessons each week, while the library—a miserable affair—seemed to be visited only by those few convicts who were already educated, and so had least need of learning. As for the church, while this was a most impressive stone building to look upon, my conversation with convicts indicated that the pastor's influence was distressingly slight, many of the felons hardly troubling to conceal their scorn for the man, whom they referred to as the "god botherer."

Being thus untouched by improving influences, the malefactors were ruled only by the threat of harsh punishments, which were given out for even the slightest wrongdoing. Such a system was both crude and painfully cruel to witness, being not so much a mechanism for the transformation of men as the kind of brutish training that might be used upon a wild dog. Hardly less troubling was the freedom with which evil influences were permitted to spread from felon to felon. Only in the work gangs was a strict code of silence enforced, while in the penitentiary sleeping huts beds were not even separated by dividing walls, allowing evil chatter, and worse, to occur in the dark hours.

This was far indeed from the modern ideas of prison systems currently gaining ground in England and the United States. These new and admirable notions did not rely upon chains and whips, but instead employed the gentle force of silence. Felons were to be kept always separated from one another, and thus would be removed from all influences except hard work and Christian teaching, until these noble qualities could win over their minds. A prison settlement such as Port Arthur, where malefactors could mix freely, was, by contrast, hardly a place of moral improvement so much as a school for criminality, where pick-pockets might learn from housebreakers, and housebreakers from mur-derers, till all were surfeited with wickedness.

Such thoughts were far from the ideal preparation for a polite social gathering–especially one in the home of the very man I regarded as being most at fault, the commander of the establishment–and as I washed and dressed I would gladly have exchanged the approaching dinner even for the simplest fare. The moods of men are unpredictable, however, and by the time I was making my way through the muddy ways of the settlement towards the man's house–a most attractive build-ing, with a long verandah facing the water–I was surprised to feel my spirits beginning to rise. After so long spent aboard ship, and in the unhappy company of convicts, I suppose I was ready for a little domestic comfort. As I was shown inside, it was hard, certainly, to resist the spell of a clean and orderly home, graced with feminine taste.

My hosts were most welcoming. The commander's wife was young and charming, and displayed a disarming excitement at the prospect of this little social gathering in her home. I supposed life for her in this remote and harsh place was hardly diverting. Her husband–who I had expected to be a martinet every bit as crude as his notions–also proved most hospitable in his gruff way, quite thrusting a large glass of punch into my hand as I was shown into the parlour. My only disappointment, indeed, was the sight of Knowles, standing narrow-eyed in the corner, from where he gave me a barely perceptible wink. I suppose I should have guessed he too would be invited.

It was Knowles, needless to say, who insisted on goading me into a discussion of the one matter I had been determined to avoid: my own views upon the penal colony. By then we had progressed to sitting around the dining table, where three convicts–one of them a huge fellow with a face like a cliff–were attempting, with no great success, to play the part of domestic servants.

"So how do you like Port Arthur?" Knowles asked, regarding me with a taunting look through his near-closed eyes. "Are the robbers and knife men well enough spoiled for your tastes?"

I felt the wisest course was to say as little as possible. "I have hardly had time properly to consider all that I have seen."

It was the commander's wife, rather to my surprise, who pressed me further. "But we are all most curious as to your thoughts, Mr. Crane. Surely you must have reached some conclusions?"

There was something in the glance she cast at her husband which made me wonder if I had strayed into some area of disagreement between them. There seemed, certainly, a discernible tenseness. Having no wish to criticize my host in his own home, I chose my words with care. "I have been most impressed by the efficiency of the establishment. I will admit, though, to being a little surprised that more concern is not shown for the improvement of the convicts' minds."

The commander smiled warily. "And how would you suggest such a thing be done?"

"Speak with candour, Mr. Crane," added his wife, smiling a little sadly. "We would so much like to know your opinions."

My unsaid thoughts of that long day must have been weighing upon me, demanding voice, as it took no more than this for me to quite forget my caution and begin warmly recounting some of the latest notions in this sphere. I talked of those men of vision I admired, in both England and America. I endeavoured to explain the advantages of separation over corporal wounding, and of silence over chains. All the while Knowles regarded his napkin with a mocking stare. As for the commander, he listened patiently enough, though he looked more than a little doubtful. His wife, I was interested to see, quite beamed.

"But this is fascinating," she remarked, darting a glance at her husband. "Surely such things could be done here?"

"I'm afraid it's hardly so simple, my dear," the commander insisted. "For a start such matters are hardly in my power, being more the concern of the governor, and the Colonial Office in London. At present both are urging me to make the lives of convicts here ever harsher, so that Port Arthur may retain its fearsome reputation."

This brought Knowles into the fray. "What our kindly friend Mr. Crane doesn't understand is that His Majesty's colony of Van Diemen's Land is not intended to reform criminals, but simply to store them, like so much rubbish in a dust heap, so that England can be emptied of troublemakers once and for all." He sat back, well pleased with the vileness of his own views. "I'm not saying it's a pretty arrangement but it's the arrangement there is, and I for one see little advantage in wasting money and time worrying over the morals of a dung hill."

The commander cast him a look of faint amusement. I, however, was unable to respond with such levity. "If the sole purpose of the system is to empty England of troublemakers, as you say, then it hardly seems to be succeeding very well. After all these decades of exiling men to the ends of the earth one is quite as likely to have one's pocket picked in London or Glasgow as before. For that matter I feel a good deal safer here in Van Diemen's Land. The fact is, Knowles, that you perceive the whole matter entirely in the wrong way. It is not a question of banishing men, but finding a way of reforming them. Is not every man capable of being redeemed?"

"That's easy to say," Knowles answered cheerfully. "But a tiger cannot change his stripes."

The commander's wife shook her head. "My thinking is quite with Mr. Crane. I am sure that there are convicts here who are capable of great goodness."

I was delighted to find myself not alone. Knowles, however, seemed not at all troubled by this stiffening of the opposition ranged against him. "Perhaps we should have ourselves a little test," he declared, turning to the huge, cliff-faced convict, who was in the act of placing upon the table a dish of stuffed mushrooms, all arranged in the pattern of a flower. "You there, could you tell us what brought you to this place?"

The man was greatly startled, glancing about the table, doubtless in the hope of discerning what hidden dangers might lie in the question. A nod from the commander helped to reassure him. "I was taken for robbing a baker's shop in Great Yarmouth High Street."

Knowles sat back in his chair like a judge. "And would you do the same again?"

The convict frowned for a moment, puzzling through the words. Finally he shook his head. "How could I? Not now. I'd never get back to Yarmouth from here."

His answer could hardly have been more unfortunate. Somehow it missed the point so completely as to be favourable to Knowles's views, though ludicrously so. Even the commander's wife, my new ally, could not conceal her amusement, while her husband quite lost himself in laughing. Knowles, naturally, was insufferable.

"What did I tell you, Mr. Crane?" he roared.

It was, in truth, a most unfairly phrased question. The convict should have been asked if he now saw the error of his ways, rather than if he would commit his crime again. There is, sadly, little so poisonous to logical debate as laughter, and, though I tried my best, it proved quite impossible to return to the serious matter at hand. When I walked back to my quarters that evening I was left with a sense of profound frustration. I had had an opportunity to champion ideas of the greatest importance, only to find myself thwarted by foolishness.

As if this were not annoyance enough, I learned the next day that I was to suffer the company of my persecutor during my return journey back to Hobart. It seemed Knowles had finished his work as speedily as had I, and it was assumed we would wish to journey as a party. The weather had taken a turn for the worse once again, and the commander thought it wiser to return to Hobart not by sea but overland.

"You can take our train," he declared, adding, with some pride, "I'm told it is the only railway in all the Southern Hemisphere."

Train was hardly the word that came to mind when, the next morning, I stood in the windy rain, looking upon the device. Though it ran on rails it had more the appearance of the kind of small cart used in quarries having only two seats, one in front of the other. As for propulsion, it had not even the dignity of a pit pony, being driven by four fearsome-looking convicts, who pushed at bars extending from its sides.

"So what are you here for then?" Knowles asked one of the convict drivers as he climbed into his seat, at the same time giving me a provoking wink. "Talking in church, was it?"

The man, understandably enough, gave no answer but to faintly scowl. In a moment he and his fellows began pushing the little carriage down the track, first at a walk, then a trot and finally at running pace, causing it to trundle away swiftly. The vehicle lacked any shelter from the elements, and I saw this was destined to be a most wet journey. Of greater concern to me, however, was the vehicle's safety. I had journeyed on steam trains on several occasions without experiencing the slightest alarm, but this had none of the weight and stability of such machines. The wooden rails were of a most rough manufacture, causing the carriage to shake and jar a good deal, while on downward slopes it would hurtle along at alarming speed. On one corner we came close to springing free completely.

"D'you think this is safe?" I remarked to Knowles, who had the advantage of the rearmost seat.

I suppose I should not have expected he would give a serious reply. "Safe?" he asked in a goading voice. "How could it be anything else when we are being driven by angels such as these?" He glanced at the four men, who were now engaged in pushing us up a long, gradual slope, the exertion causing them to pant. "What d'you make of them, Professor?" he asked, quite as if they could not hear. "Schoolteachers, would you say? And each and every one of them a victim of mistaken identity?"

It seemed hardly wise to provoke the men seeing as we were in their hands, and I was considering telling him so, when I saw we had reached the top of a little ridge. Before us the ground fell away abruptly, descending for a considerable distance, and in the distance I could see a gang of chained convicts working at cutting down trees beside the track. The pushers set the cart in motion with a heave and in a moment we were quickly gathering speed. All the while the four pressed at the bars with greatest determination, until they could hardly run to keep up, whereupon, at the very last moment, they hurled themselves onto the sides of the vehicle, their own weight seeming to add further to our headlong progress. All at once I had not the slightest doubt we were about to suffer a mighty accident.

"The brake!" I cried out.

One of the convicts, whose face was marked by a huge scar across his forehead, sullenly pointed to a kind of wooden crowbar fixed above one of the wheels, though he made no effort to apply it, merely turning away. Doubtless he was still angry at Knowles's mocking chatter. I had no intention of permitting the man's cruel cynicism, of all things, to cause my death, and as nobody else seemed willing to act, I did so myself. Clambering to my feet, I leant forwards and reached out for the brake lever. It seemed, unfortunately, that I had underestimated the effect my movement would have on the balance of the little vehicle, which at once began to lean to one side. I do believe all would have gone well enough even then, if only the others had thought to remain calm. Knowles himself uttered a sudden yelp, while the faces of the convicts, which had seemed so hard, turned suddenly pale, and they all began to lean in a contrary direction. While this might have seemed only sensible, the effect of their movement was greatly excessive, imbalancing the carriage even more the other way. In a moment it was swaying from side to side with ever greater wildness, until the inevitable occurred.

Whether the vehicle toppled over sideways, flew clean through the air or was tipped upwards upon its front wheels—or all three—I never will know. I recall the wheels uttering a desperate rasping sound, and after that all was incomprehensible hurtling and falling. I must have passed out for an instant. Coming to, I found myself beside the roots of a huge tree, and the only sounds I could hear were the wind in the trees, the pattering of rain upon the leaves and the whirring of the upturned carriage's wheels. Close by me was the slumped figure of Knowles, while next to him—entangled with him—was the prone form of someone not of our party. It appeared Knowles had flown clear into the fellow, knocking both unconscious. Each was bleeding from his injuries, though I was glad to see they still showed signs of breathing. As to myself, when I attempted to sit up I discovered that my left leg was injured, and likely broken. It was then, as I glanced around me, that I saw we were not alone. A gang of convicts—presumably the tree cutters I had observed before—stood nearby, staring.

It seemed essential to assert some authority over the men. "Where is your overseer?" I demanded.

"There." The speaker was a bulky fellow with a hairless dome of a head, a mighty scar across one cheek and the most troubling eyes, with dark rings beneath them, like a madman's. He was, I saw, pointing to the man entangled with Knowles. It was hardly a pleasing discovery. More encouraging was the sight of our four drivers, who I discerned were sprawled on the further side of the wooden railway tracks. They did not look greatly injured, while at least they were known to me. "These men must be taken back to the settlement at once," I called out. "They need help."

"Don't we all," answered one. At this the rest uttered faint yet malevolent laughter.

If matters were not already alarming enough, it was then that the fearsome-looking bald tree cutter stepped forwards to a flat rock and stretched his leg irons carefully over this. All at once he then raised up his axe and delivered a number of mighty blows, quite filling the forest with ringing. In a moment the chain was parted. With a clinking of trailing chains he began striding slowly towards us.

I thought it best to try and address him directly. "Please spare us. We have done you no harm. We need help."

He seemed not to hear. His fellows watching his every movement, he stepped past me till he stood above Knowles and the overseer. Next he raised his axe. My mind filled with horror and I turned away. Moments passed in silence, however, and when I finally looked again he was just as before, like some demonic statue, frowning at the two figures before him. He glanced at the little carriage, though this was broken beyond any usefulness. Then, to my amazement and wondrous relief, he suddenly hurled his axe away into the trees. Suddenly he was stooping, gathering up Knowles, and lifting him up, quite as easily as if he were some child.

"I'll get him safe, don't you worry."

Jack Harp
1837

IT WAS QUITE a stroll back to Port Arthur, especially carrying that fat bugger. I never got him all the way there in the end, being stopped by a group of soldiers just nearby, who took one look at my snapped shackles and the bleeding head of the cove I was carrying, and all but knocked me down on the spot. After that I was in a cell, wondering if I'd played things right or been the biggest fool in all Van Diemen's Land. Finally, though, an officer came along and said I had to go up to the hospital.

I had hope from the moment I walked in. There, lying in a bed was the fat bugger I'd carried. Also there was the commander himself, and the soft fool who'd called out to me to help. This last gave me a mighty hello, sitting up from his bed and holding out his hand for me to shake, though I wasn't sure if this was allowed. Truly, I couldn't have got a better preacher for me if I'd chosen one specially, and he wouldn't stop telling the others what a proper hero I was, and how I should never have been put in chains but should be rewarded. The commander didn't look much pleased, and neither did the fat cove I'd carried–which seemed hardly grateful–but it never mattered, what with my new friend singing my praises. D'you know, he pestered the commander into promising me a ticket-of-leave there and then. So I was pleased enough at how it had gone, even though I'd missed stoving in Ferguson's head.

Of course, ticket-of-leave is never full pardon but it's not far off. So long as I kept out of trouble and stayed in Diemen's Land I could do much as I liked. After all those years it was hard to believe it, especially coming so sudden. Still, it didn't take me long to make up my mind what to do with myself. I never have much liked towns, nor farms neither, while I'd had more than enough chipping at stones and cutting trees. No, I'd go back to one of those little islands, where I'd spent my hiding days. That hadn't been such a bad life, skinning seals and chewing mutton birds with nobody spying on you or telling you what to do. Why, I might even catch myself another little black miss, if there were still any left to find.

CHAPTER NINE

<hr>

Dr. Thomas Potter
NOVEMBER 1857

<u>29th November</u>

Land finally sighted this morning after forty-six days + much stormy weather. Loud cheering, singing etc. from crew. Wilson made all pray thanks.

Unfortunately then discovered this <u>not correct land after all</u>. Captain and mate studied sun with sextants, then announced coast not Van Diemen's Land but mainland of <u>Australia: Sincerity</u> off course northwards by <u>several hundred miles</u>. Kewley explained cause = <u>difficult sea currents</u> (self had no idea sea currents so troublesome). Said selves must put in at Melbourne, Port Phillip, for more water (fortunately v. near). Wilson v. annoyed as he impatient to begin expedition: scowling + giving me looks as if self = to blame, i.e. he exhibiting all = characteristics of <u>Norman derangement</u>. In fact change of plan = useful to self re collecting further <u>specimens</u>. Also believe old colleague <u>Dr. G.</u> now living in Melbourne: could be most helpful. And have need more <u>storage chests</u>.

Regret have neglected diary since Cape Colony, as have been much preoccupied with work on <u>notions</u>. Truly, this = wonderfully productive time. Do believe have felt spark of <u>inspiration</u>, no less: ideas forming & clarifying by the hour. Own interest advancing from mere <u>description</u> to <u>deduction</u>. This progress greatly due to most unexpected and useful instance re studies, i.e. <u>Manx crew</u> of <u>Sincerity</u>. Self suddenly realized most revealing study = here before self all this while.

Began with <u>chance</u> discovery. Self sitting on deck when overheard chief mate Brew scolding troublesome crewman as "Viking." Self = curious and so asked why? Brew = secretive as per usual, but reluctantly answering that in distant past Man Island = ruled by Norse (<u>Saxon</u> type). He poorly informed but believed Viking rule = <u>several hundred years</u> with much settlement. V. interesting. Self began questioning other crewmen about island. Replies often guarded or flippant, but nevertheless = revealing. Became clear that island, despite v. small size = riven by powerful <u>regional rivalries</u>. In particular ship's crew (all from Peel City) scorn those from every other area. Instances:

Ramsey town people called <u>Boasters</u> because claimed = arrogant.

Douglas town people called <u>Govags</u> (Mx for "dogfishes": reason unclear).

Sulby village people called <u>Cossacks</u> (reason v. unclear).

Cregneish village people called <u>Spaniards</u> re claim (doubtful) that all swam ashore from Spanish Armada. nb. Cregneish village also called China (reason unclear) + large crewman China Clucas so nicknamed because claimed he once had (fat) sweetheart from Cregneish/China village (he strongly denies).

Conclusion: situation may appear confused but in truth = v. simple: Manx not one nation but <u>two</u>: Celtic Type and Saxon Type (Vikings). Historical events + Norse language of Saxons may = forgotten but, remarkably, divisions remain strong—if unrecognized—in men's minds. Manx Celts and Saxons continuing to war with one another <u>without ever knowing</u>. Now that self = aware of matter, have observed many instances of <u>enmities</u> between two races of Manx, e.g. frequent bickering between crewmen, ill feeling between Captain (cunning + indolent i.e. Celtic Type) + China Clucas (strong + open i.e. Saxon Type).

This = of greatest importance. Here = potent evidence that separate races <u>cannot</u> and <u>will not intermix</u>. Discovery = of <u>fundamental importance</u> re notions. Self increasingly convinced that <u>types</u> not merely of importance to understanding re mankind, but in truth = the <u>key</u> to comprehending <u>all human history</u> + also <u>future destiny of men</u>. National revolutions of 1848 = clear indication of inevitable progression of events. Self can foresee future <u>great conflagration of nations</u> (own term) as World = embroiled in years of conflict, war + destruction etc. etc. Patience of stolid Saxon will finally snap. Normans' weakness and parasitism will be exposed and sorely <u>punished</u>. Weaker nations (e.g. black,

Indian, Oriental, Norman etc. etc.) will be swept away. New era will begin. May occur even <u>imminently</u>.

Have decided will revise jottings into full <u>manuscript</u>, with <u>view to</u> <u>publication</u>. Provisional title: *The destiny of Nations: being a consideration upon the different strengths and characteristics of the many races and types of man, and the likely consequences of their future struggles.* Feel this may prove of no little significance re understanding all mankind.

Captain Illiam Quillian Kewley
NOVEMBER–DECEMBER 1857

PORT PHILLIP BAY was a curious sort of spot, being so wide we couldn't even see the far shore, though it was every drop of it packed behind a little narrow bottleneck of an entrance. This was the very kind of spot you'd expect to find pilots loitering, and worse besides, and sure enough, as we passed between the headlands I saw a little house come into view, hidden nicely from the main ocean. More interesting even than the house, though, was the cutter. This had already spread its sails in the water just below, and was making good progress to a certain spot in the ocean where we'd shortly find ourselves. A handsomely stocked vessel she was, too, with a couple of cannon at her prow, six soldiers in prettiest red stood on her deck, and a uniformed Port Phillip Englishman besides, who, as soon as he was near enough, started wondering at the top of his voice if we might have a mind to heave to directly, so he could come aboard and tell us hello.

Well, I didn't need any schooling to tell me who he was. A wonderful thing it was that a fellow could steer a vessel clear halfway around the planet, till he was clean underneath the barnacles and weeds of his own ship's hull of four months before, and still he could catch himself just the same friendly greeting that he'd got on the other side. My only worry was that word might have been sent ahead of us from Cape Colony. I had thought of dropping those pieces of Maldon silver overboard, just to be safe, but it seemed a shame to fling good spending money into the ocean, so somehow they'd stayed all the while. It was too late now.

"Your papers, Captain?" This was our invader, Mr. Robins, tidal waiter for the Colony of Victoria, and was said with all the charm I'd come to expect of Her Majesty's servants, being no charm at all. A sullen child of a fellow he was–probably at his being posted on the edge of nowhere–and he scowled as if we'd sailed all the way from Man Island just to spoil his afternoon.

"We've nothing in the hold except stores and ballast," I told him. "The ship's been chartered by these gentlemen for their expedition." With this I pointed out the Reverend–beaming like your proper adventuring vicar–and Dr. Potter. I suppose I had noticed that tidal waiter Robins had the same high and snotty way of speaking as our passengers–I even wondered what trouble he'd got up to to get himself so banished–but still I never guessed how he'd change when he put a sight on some his own kind. Why, for once I was almost pleased to have those Englishmen aboard. Robins' face lit up like a lamp and all at once he and the Reverend were chattering away nineteen to the dozen, discovering distant cousins that might be neighbours or recalling some wondrous fine fellow that they both of them knew hardly at all. Next they were having a fine old Englishman's gossip–which Potter joined in as well– which was all fretting at the latest worries afflicting those poor Dukes and Princes who owned England. It was quite as if they'd all known each other for years.

"Will you be wanting to have a look round the ship then?" I asked when they let off for a moment, as I thought it only wise to offer. Truly, I need hardly have bothered. Our invader, Mr. Robins, troubled himself with the briefest of glances down one of the hatches, then returned to his feast of chatter. Finally, when he'd glutted himself fit to burst, he bid a reluctant farewell to his new friends, called away his six soldiers and let us be. That was just the kind of customs inspection I could grow to like.

He left us with a pilot, which was as well, too, as the chart I'd got cheap in Cape Colony had not a town or settlement marked. I could only suppose there'd been still nothing here when it was drawn, two dozen years before. When we finally came in sight of Melbourne, a couple of days later, I was surprised at the size of the place, seeing as it had only just happened. A great spread of a town it was, smearing all across that flat nothingness like some mighty spillage, with a few church spires and such poking up for grandeur. Why, it looked several times larger than Peel City, which struck me as hardly fair, seeing as Peel had been sitting there quiet and patient beside St. Patrick's Isle for as long as anyone knew. On the other hand, it was a good sign for us. If there was jink enough to build a whole city from nothing in hardly a moment, then we should get a fine old price for our certain cargo.

It was only as we got near that I noticed the ships. Scores of them there were, lining the sides of the little river harbour to rot, and a sad little mystery they made too with their peeling paint and their ropes and shrouds hanging slack. As it turned out, though, there was a kind of grim promise even here. While our passengers moaned themselves over the wrecked ship we were moored to—off to catch those lodging-house tub baths that they were always fussing about—I saw there was some old article on the shore, piling barrels onto a cart. It was him I asked what had caused the vessels to be abandoned.

"Gold," he cackled. "Or dreams of gold." He told how the crews, and even their officers, had all jumped ship and run away to the diggings to try and make their fortunes. "That was at the height of the madness, mind, when half the town was gone. Why, it got so that grand folks couldn't find themselves servants, and were down to cooking their dinners and washing their own underclothes. They didn't like that much, neither."

"Is gold still being found?" asked Brew.

The old fellow shrugged. "The diggings are long claimed, but that's not to say there mightn't be another strike somewhere else. There's rumours all the time."

I gave a nod to Brew—a licking-my-lips, jink-coloured nod—and he nodded back just the same. A land of gold. Why, I was even pleased now that Cape Colony had been a useless, cheating free port, as it meant we had the goods still to sell. Here we might catch gold enough for seven cargoes.

First, though, we had chores to do. *A new port is new work*, as the man says, and this Melbourne was no exception. I set the crew hauling up empty water casks from the hold, to keep them busy and stop them moaning about money to spend ashore, and I busied myself with the harbour paperwork, which, of course, brought another little visit from the customs. Fortunately this proved as harmless as the other had been, being a big fat slug of a body named Bowles, who seemed mostly made of beard, black and thick, that grew all up his face, almost to his eyes, so he looked as if he was hiding in a black hedge. Bowles hardly troubled us except to ask about our being Manx–which I could hardly deny–and if we had bought anything at Cape Colony, which I had no need to go telling stories about, seeing as we never had anyway. That done, he left us be, nice as nip. All in all I was beginning to like these Victoria revenue boys, and reckoned they should some of them be sent back to England, to tell that Captain Clarke and his friends how to behave.

It was not long after we saw the back of Bowles that we had another visitor. A little stob of a fellow he was, with too much smile in him. It's usual enough to have some harbour cheat climb onto your deck, offering flea-filled rooms or a choice bargain of liquor and females, and I hardly troubled myself as he clambered aboard. "Harry Fields." He held out a hand that was surprisingly large compared to the rest of him, as if it was where all his growing had gone. "Just arrived, are you? From the Cape, I'll wager."

"What if we are?"

My suspicion seemed almost to please him. "I arrange purchases. If you've anything to sell, I'm your man."

"What kind of anything?"

A scrinched, knowing sort of look came over him. "Who could say?"

Well, here was a thing. The fact was we needed a buyer of the right kind. Till now I'd been planning on asking about the town for Port Phillip Manxmen–which was always a hope, Manxmen being brave travellers–just in case somebody's cousin was here in Melbourne, and could set us on the right road. That would take time, though, while there was no guarantee there'd be even one. This little fellow Fields would be taking a risk, for sure, but that didn't mean he wasn't just what we needed. I glanced at Brew and he glanced at me. Now, one of the handy things about being a Manxman is that you never need to trouble yourself about being overheard if you've something quiet to say. While your Englishman must go through a whole bother of stepping out of the room or whispering like a plotter, your Manxman can simply chatter away in his own sweet tongue, safe in knowledge that there's hardly a soul on earth besides other Manxmen will understand a word. Irishmen and Highlander Scotsmen can catch some, to be true, but even they'll have trouble, while to your Englishman it's as clear as purest Chinese. So Brew and I never troubled to lower our voices, but discussed the body clean over his own head.

"He looks like a rotten cheating sleetch," I said, giving the fellow a smile, which he returned happily enough.

"Mind you, isn't that just the sort of fellow we're looking for?" answered Brew.

"He could be scrutineering for the customs."

Brew shrugged. "That's danger whoever we find."

This was true enough. All in all I decided this Fields was worth spying on, at the very least. "It's soon yet to be knowing if we've anything to sell, seeing as we're just arrived," I told him, "but is there somewhere we can find you, if we have a change of mind?"

He seemed content enough with that, did little Harry Fields, and gave us the name of a tavern where he spent his evenings. As he scuttled away, I called over Kinvig—who seemed the proper choice for blending into crowds, being such a little mhinyag himself—and sent him following.

Later that afternoon Brew and myself set off ourselves, and so we put our first sight on an Australian town. Tiring it was, too, that Melbourne, with its long straight streets and a faint smell of madness in the air, being the sort of place that drains all the soo out of a man and leaves him feeling thirsty and brittle for a fight. A patchy sort of place it was, almost as if its gold had dropped from the sky in tiny showers, drenching one spot but leaving another dry as bones. Here there'd be a building tall as Castle Rushen, all made from finest stone, cut so neat it made a body feel scruffy just to walk past. Next along there'd be just an old fence covered with peeling placards, or a mighty pile of rubbish stinking in the sun. One district we strayed into—though not for long—had missed the gold entirely, being all shacks made from packing cases and calico, or even just coloured paper, so you could see clear through at whoever was inside—usually some woman holding babies—who'd turn and give you a scowl for peeping.

The gold seemed as choosy with townspeople as it was with buildings. There were a good few lucky ones, diggers as I guessed they must be, being wild-looking bodies with long hair and gold rings on every finger like knuckle-dusters. Judging by their chatter they came from most everywhere, and I heard Irish talk, American and all manner of European foreignness, and even some Chinamen with pigtails. The only ones I didn't see were any Australian bluemen, which seemed quite a surprise, too. I'd have expected there'd be scores of the fellows, seeing as this was where they sprang from.

Waiting to catch a few drops of gold from the diggers were scarlet girls aplenty. These looked like they'd been doing well enough, some of them, lounging about as if it was their own town, and dressed so fine they might almost have been proper ladies except for their loitering, and their come-along glances. Why, they had the respectable females looking quite peeved. As darkness fell, I could see the proper ones creeping off home and leaving them to it, and all of a rush the town started tumbling into drink and shouting, as if it was hoping to forget itself till dawn. It was a rough sort of spot, no doubting, and I was glad enough when I finally set eyes on the tavern we sought—a huge palace of a thing with a wooden front three floors high—and saw Kinvig waiting at the corner just opposite.

"I kept a sight on Fields all day," he told us proudly.

"And?"

"I didn't see him chatter to anyone who looked like a uniform. Mostly he was in taverns and liquor shops. I tried to ask about him once, from some old fellow I'd seen him talking to, but all I got was growls and threats and 'What's it to you?' "

That sounded right enough. "Did you find out if there are any Manxmen here?"

"There was a body thought he'd met some, though he wasn't sure if they might've been Irishmen. Either way, he thought they'd gone off to the diggings."

That was hardly much use, the diggings being a proper journey away. I took a glance through the tavern window and caught a glimpse of Fields sat in a corner. He didn't look like a customs pet. "All right. Let's see what price he's giving."

The answer, as it turned out, was a fine price indeed. Why, I could hardly believe my own ears. Fields said himself that there was a proper thirst for good French brandy in the colony, the diggers having caught themselves expensive tastes, but still I had to strain myself not to give a mighty smile. This wasn't pennies he was talking, but a shiny dazzle of jink, a great pouring of the stuff, and enough to quiet Ealisad from a year of sulks. It was all I could do to remember myself and push for some extra on top, which I got so easy that I could've kicked myself for not asking for more. Just a little more chatter and a glass or two of the local brew and it was all settled.

"That was the road to go all right," said Brew, as we stepped back into the noise of the street, grinning as if he'd found a bag of sovereigns in the dirt. "No doubting it."

I can't say I thought any different. There's something in the spirit of Manxmen, though, that doesn't like too much delighting in a thing. "Though we've not seen a penny yet," I warned him, "and, as the man says, there's much between saying and doing."

Brew pulled himself up sharpish to match, giving himself a careful face. "Ah, that's true enough. As the old fellow says, a green hill when far away, bare, bare when it is near."

Then Kinvig joined in. "After the spring tide, neap."

I think we all felt a little better for that. "But it was a middling good price, was it not?" I said, just to put us back a little.

"Ah, that it was," answered Brew, grinning again.

"Seven times good," agreed Kinvig besides.

"Can you spare us a penny or two?" This last, I should tell, was none of us, being a big sprawled fellow slouched against a wall just ahead. There was no mistaking his accent, which was purest low-life Dublin, and drunk too. I suppose I should've just given him a farthing and had done with it, but I felt in no mood for beggars.

"No, we've not," I told him, throwing him a sneery sort of look as we passed.

It was that look must've got him started. "Manxies, are you?" he called out. "I know that Manxy prattle. So what Manxy town are you from, then?"

It was Kinvig played the fool. "Peel City," he answered, all proud.

"Peel?" he shouted, all in triumph. "I've been there. All snots it was, and rotten poor ones at that, with hardly a penny to steal from each other. The smell it had too, all stinking of last year's fish." A wicked look came into his eyes. "Or was that just the Manxy women?"

Kinvig narrowed his eyes at this. There always was fight in Kinvig, being so small. "I'll give him refreshments for that. Go on, Captain, let me settle him."

The last thing a fellow wants, if he's stretching the law tight to bust, is fighting trouble. "Leave him be," I told him. "There's no point in dirtying your knuckles on some yernee yeirk." This last was Manx for an Irishman on the beg, and none too polite, while I took care to speak it clear enough to be well heard, just to answer that chatter about the fish smell. "Besides, we'd best get back to the ship."

I wished I'd kept quiet. "Manxies on a ship, is it?" called out the Dubliner now, delighting at this new fact he'd caught. "And where are you sailing off to then? Off round to some quiet stretch of Port Phillip Bay in the middle of the night, I'll wager."

Trust an Irishman to see straight through to what you least want him to. I was glad we were at the edge of town and there were no bodies about. None of us said a word, but it never helped, as the beggar gave a cry of delight, knowing our silence had been pure yes. "Off you go and sell your dirty, watered contraband rum, see if I care," he shouted out, loud as he could. As if the likes of us would go watering. "And mind you don't catch some bullet through your little cheating skulls from some bushranger or convict or wild man, as they're along the shore in swarms, and will eat up little poxy Manxies for their breakfast."

Bushrangers? I didn't know what they were but they sounded nothing good. For that matter neither did convicts and wild men.

"It's just lies to worry us," growled Brew when we were out of earshot.

The trouble was that those sorts of words will stick in a man's thoughts. By the time we finally set forth in the dark, just a couple of evenings later, we were all thinking trouble, and little Kinvig even had himself a little fighting practice on the main deck, standing like a boxer and throwing little punches at the darkness. Our new friend Harry Fields had scratched us a little map of where we were to go and it wasn't far, being a beach just a few miles from the town. The signal they'd give was to be a light. Swung side to side meant all was well, while if it rose and dropped, then there was trouble and sail off fast as we could. This lamp waving had caught my blood a little, I'll own, being just the kind of thing that was done in the golden days of Man Island, and as we sailed out from the river into Port Phillip Bay by the faint light of the rising moon, I couldn't help but wonder how my great-grandfather, Big Juan Kewley, must've often journeyed through the night just like this. Why, I liked to think he might be looking down even then, proud as punch of his great-grandson, the hard case who'd thought to follow his road.

The breeze kept light but steady, and it was just a couple of hours before I saw the faint glow of a single lamp from the shore, waving crossways just like it should. I had the boys drop the anchor and lower a boat and we were set. Brew I left behind to mind the ship, telling him to dig out the Englishmen's rifles, just in case, while Kinvig joined me going ashore, along with two more to pull the oars. It was hardly a bright night, the moon being only two days grown, with bits of cloud to muzzle her more, but still there was light enough to see the foam of the waves as they broke and the faint shadows of those waiting. Two there were, including the one holding the lamp. That hardly seemed enough to go playing murderer. As I clambered out of the boat, one stepped forward into the lamplight, showing himself to be Harry Fields. "Captain Kewley. You've made good time."

"I dare say." I handed him a cask of brandy that I'd got ready. Pulling free the cork, he had himself a sniff, then took a swig.

"That seems tasty enough." The tobacco pleased him less—he complained it had got a touch damp—but he said he'd take it still. "And the rest's all on the ship?"

"It is."

"Where d'you have it hidden?"

There's questions and questions, and this was prying when he didn't yet have the right. I took the brandy and tobacco from him and dropped them back in the boat. "Where's this gold of yours?"

"Just back here." With that he started walking back across the beach. His helper shone the lamp on the sand by their feet so it was pure night they were walking into.

This I wasn't so sure of. "I'd rather you brought it here."

His voice turned suspecting. "D'you want the gold or not?"

There was a question. There seemed nothing for it, so I called out in Manx to Kinvig, still sat in the boat, to keep a close watch, and then tramped after them, sand sucking at my feet. Their lamp swung upwards once or twice, catching a long row of trees that I could hear hissing in the breeze, and beneath these I glimpsed a kind of shelter. In front of this I could see there was standing a rough sort of body with a bag slung over his shoulder, heavy so he was all lopsided. That seemed right enough, for sure, so on I went. It was only when I was there that I saw the other fellow, stepping out from the trees. That I wouldn't have minded, but the moonlight caught the line of a pistol barrel, pointed nicely at my chest. There was worse. The man seemed to have hardly any head. Then I realized this was just a trick of the dark, from his face being so covered up with black beard, almost up to his eyes.

"If it isn't Captain Kewley," said landing waiter Bowles of the Melbourne customs, "who's only carrying ballast and stores."

Here was a rotten piece of fortune. I almost would have preferred bushrangers and wild men to this sleetch of a customs, all so smug at his own cleverness, like only your Englishman can be. He must have suspected us the moment he'd stepped aboard, sending his little sneak Fields after him to catch us out, which he'd done nice as nip. All these months and miles we'd travelled, and now to finish like this. Why, we'd have been better off getting caught by Captain Clarke, back in the English Channel, rather than fuss our way clear across half the world to no purpose.

Or was it to no purpose, though? What first made me wonder was Bowles himself. Having sprung so cleverly from the trees, he didn't pull out a pair of cuffs, or call out of the words I was expecting, such as arrest or confiscation. No, he just stood there, watching. "There's nobody lands contraband under my nose and gets away with it, I'll have you know," he growled at last. That didn't quite sound like customs talk. I'll own there's nothing like the fear of losing every penny to make a man eager for a chance, but it did make sense. Now I looked, Bowles wasn't even wearing his uniform, but was just in an old jacket. Hadn't Kinvig followed Harry Fields all day and found him company to all manner of dirts and gallows mucks? For all that, this would have to be played careful. It was for him to lead the dance.

"Ah, you have us now, Mr. Bowles," I said sadly.

"I should confiscate your ship and cargo, so I should, as Her Majesty's property."

For all his stern voice the word I heard strongest was "should," and sweet it sounded. "The right you are," I agreed. "Though it does seem a shame, when I'm sure Her Majesty has enough brandy and tobacco to last her nicely."

He should've bit me hard for that, but instead he softened a scran. "This is your first visit to Port Phillip?"

"That it is."

"Hmmm." Down went the barrel of his pistol to point at the sand, as he pretended to have a little wonder with himself. "I should lock you up this instant, so I should. But the fact is I don't like to be too hard on fellows for one mistake. You don't seem beyond reformation."

I followed his lead. "You couldn't be more right, Mr. Bowles. Why, we'd none of us have dreamed of doing such things if our families had not all been starving nearly to their deaths." Was it money he was after? I hoped not, as we had hardly a penny left.

"But even if I could treat you with generosity, there's still the problem of what should be done with your cargo. I must do my duty."

So that was what he wanted. This would be easier. "Ah, the hard it is."

"It's too late to declare it now, as the documents have all been written and signed." He frowned. "And yet I would like to help you out if I can."

"The ones back home would be so grateful to you. Why, they'd be smiling and weeping right down to the littlest poor babby."

Now he was shaking his head and bothering that cheating Englishman's head of his with playing thinker. "I suppose there is a certain party I know who might just be kind enough to dispose of your cargo quietly, just to keep you out of gaol. Though it would be doing you a great favour, and would be more than a little dangerous for me."

Prices. He was talking prices. All at once we were stepping out of the ooze and onto firm land. Before long he'd blurted a number, this being—just by purest chance—the very amount that was weighing down our friend with the sack. This number was hardly good compared to the

glittering sum that Fields had tempted us with, but still it was hardly so
terrible either, being a little more than I'd have expected in Maldon, and
far and above the bagful of nothing at all that I'd been looking at two
moments before. Brandy and tobacco must be fetching handsome sums
in this part of the world.

"I must warn you, though, that this certain party will accept no
bargaining," Bowles growled.

I was in no mood to play greedy. "Whatever you say, Mr. Bowles."

With that we were done. As the five of us began walking back towards the boat, the lamp playing on the sand ahead of our feet, my
thoughts were looking onwards, having a quick wonder at this weight of
gold we'd now be getting—shrunken though it was—and trying to guess
how far it would reach. It would keep the ship afloat and the crew fed for
a decent while, no doubting, and give us a mighty bit of spare besides. Of
course, a ship is hardly much use without cargo. That took me onto
thinking what manner of goods—even legal goods—might be worth carrying from this Victoria, or Tasmania, back to where we'd come from.
Grain, perhaps? There'd be debts to pay, for sure, but if I added in the
last part of the charter fee we were owed by the Englishmen, then it
didn't look so ugly.

I got no further with my wondering. Without any warning all at
once there were fellows jumping out of the dark, and something long—an
oar—swung in to my right, catching Bowles on his head, so his pistol
dropped clean out of his hand. In the same instant Fields was knocked
down to my left. The next thing I knew the lamp had been hurled to the
ground, casting all into nearly full darkness, and I heard footsteps dashing away.

"You all right, Captain?" There was no missing the whine of Kinvig's
voice, which sounded pleased with itself as a voice can be.

He wasn't smirking for long, mind. "You stupid dirt of a one. What
did you have to go and do that for?"

That had him all amazed, like the dog that's been kicked for bringing
back the stick. "They were customs, weren't they?" he whined. "The one
with the beard, and holding a pistol, too."

The little fool that he was. I looked round through the gloom.
"Where're the other two of them gone?"

Vartin Clague, who was Kinvig's helper in this fine cleverness, gave a kind of shrug. "They ran off."

What luck we were having. "Ah," I told him, as if it was a fine proper joke. "So they ran off, did they? The one with the lamp and also the one with the bag full to the brim with gold."

That was news to Kinvig. "Gold?"

"That's right. The gold that our friend Bowles was going to give us till you had the clever notion of batting him on the head." Picking up the lamp, I had a quick glance about the beach but there was no sign of either. They'd be well gone by now.

"I was trying to save us." Kinvig sounded hurt, like the child that's blamed for what baby broke. "Didn't you say we should keep an eye out?"

I had a peer at Bowles and Fields. Both were breathing–which was something, at least–though they were out cold. Even if they came to, I doubted they'd feel like trading now. Still I felt we should tell them it wasn't us had their jink. "Fetch some water."

Kinvig filled the boat's bucket with seawater and dropped it over them. Not that it did any good. Now they were just the same as before but wet.

"We could wait, I suppose," said Clague.

The more I looked at them, the more I saw trouble. What if Bowles turned nasty–as well he might–and tried to arrest us? We'd have to knock him down all over again.

"Perhaps we should just go." Kinvig was looking scared. "Weigh anchor and get away from this place."

Even that wasn't so easy. "What about Mr. Robins, all ready with his cutter and his soldiers and his cannon at the Heads? Won't he find it strange if we come sailing up without our Englishmen aboard? Strange enough to hold us and search us and perhaps ask his chief what to do."

The little gorm had never thought of that, of course. The more I looked at this, the less I liked what I saw. Whatever we did was taking chances, but we couldn't stay here, that was sure. If we could get back to Melbourne and collect the Englishmen, that would be something. Even that would take time, though. "Get some cord," I told them.

In a few moments they were trussed nicely. I didn't want to set

Bowles against us any more than was needed, so I had them dragged back to the shelter and leaned against a wall, where they'd be out of the sun. Even that didn't seem quite enough, though. "Fetch them a cask of water from the boat, and some ship's biscuit too." So we arranged these in front of them, all tidy, like a poor man's picnic. Lastly I wrote a note–unsigned–telling how it wasn't us who had their gold, but the body that had run off, which I put in Bowles's pocket. Then we clambered back into the boat and rowed away for all we were worth. Brew and the rest were leaning over the side with their rifles as we pulled near.

"You've been so long, Captain. Whatever happened?"

"We're raising anchor."

My hope was that Bowles wouldn't think to kick up a fuss, seeing as he'd been cheating himself. My fear was he'd be so riled at us that he'd be past caring (I did wish we'd not thought to douse him with seawater so). Either way it could do us no harm to put a few hundred miles between him and us, and as fast as we might. I dare say there's nothing to make a journey feel slow than knowing a handful of minutes may mean the difference between gaol and freedom, but still it did seem as if everything that might think of holding us back did just that. Raising anchor can be a troublesome business on the best of days, but this time it was as if we'd dropped it into some hole half as deep as hell, and it took an age and a half of shouting and heaving at the capstan before the *Sincerity* was finally freed. Then there was the breeze to fight, this being less friendly to us now we were journeying back the other way. Finally even the moon left us, skulking away behind a cloud, and it got so dark that we were using lead lines to keep from running clean aground. It was nearly dawn before the boats hauled us back up the river. Luckily Melbourne seemed still sleeping, and I saw nobody watching us as we tied up at our berth of the day before. I had half been expecting a crowd of customs and police and such waiting there to shout us hello.

I called over to Kinvig. After his fine cleverness with the oars he'd be catching every piece of rotten dogsbody work that was in, from finding passengers to polishing the pigs' backsides. "Go over to the Englishmen's hotel and catch them back here. Wake them from their beds if need be."

Away he crept, cowed as could be.

After that there was nothing to be done but wait. Having been awake all through the night, I thought I might as well go below and try and catch a few moments' rest. Not that it was easy. The sun was up now, heating the air dank so my clothes clung, while there's nothing like needing sleep to chase it away. Mostly I just lay there, rolling and twisting like a herring landed on the deck. I must have slipped off in the end, though, as I was woken by a loud banging that sounded like something being heaved over the stairs away forwards. There was a good murmuring of voices spilling down from the deck. At first I was well pleased, supposing the Englishmen and their luggage were coming aboard. It was only when I'd got up from the bed and had myself a stretch that I got to wondering. The banging shouldn't have been coming from forwards, you see, as that was the fo'c'sle. I thought I'd best take a look. It was as well I did. The first thing I saw as I clambered onto the deck was Ritchie Moore, the sailmaker, and three others of the crew besides, all stood on the old wrecked vessel we were tied to, with their sea chests at their feet, all set to go. It didn't take book learning to know what was going on here. Like so many rats they were, fleeing away at this little scran of trouble we'd found. What was worse they were cooing at the rest to follow.

"Don't be scared. Come along with us, why don't you, and dig yourselves a fortune of gold."

"Get back here," I shouted.

Ritchie Moore just cackled.

That was when I got another little surprise, which was chief mate Brew. There he was, on the quarterdeck, looking on smooth and calm as if he was the emperor's uncle, and doing not a thing to help. "Why in seven heavens didn't you wake me?" I called out.

He never even looked shamed. "I was just going to, Captain."

I guessed his thinking well enough, besides. The little sleetch was weighing up whether to join the others and run. Here was a fine little prospect. If I wasn't careful I'd lose the whole lot of them, and find myself stranded completely, to be hurled by Australian Englishmen into some gaol, while the *Sincerity* slowly rotted away like all those other vessels.

Not that I was one to give up without a fight.

The Reverend Geoffrey Wilson
DECEMBER 1857

THE CAPTAIN was developing a most unwelcome habit of demanding we leave port at only a moment's notice. On this occasion his messenger was the little second mate, Kinvig, and a most uncivil sort of messenger he was, too, banging rudely on our doors to rouse us. This may have been merited with regard to Potter–and it certainly was for Renshaw–but it was hardly necessary for myself, as, being always an early riser, I was already dressed, and even writing an entry in my diary.

"Another unmissable wind, I suppose," I told the fellow, with some coolness, in answer to his impatient demand that I make myself ready to leave.

"That's it. You're all to come at once."

"What about breakfast?"

"There's no time for that."

A man of gentleness I may be, but there are some matters on which I simply will not be bullied, and breakfast is one such, especially when, as in this case, I would be required to pay for the meal in full whether I had it or not. I dug in my heels, informing Kinvig that I was not prepared to throw good money away merely because of some shipboard whim, and when he continued to protest I settled the question–rather neatly, as it seemed to me–simply by taking my place at the dining table, and letting him know that if he did not leave me in peace I would order extra eggs.

If truth be told the prospect of departure was, for all its suddenness, not entirely unwelcome. Though we had been in port only three days I felt already impatient to leave. The detour caused by the difficult sea currents had been no small one and, in view of Dr. Potter's scheming, I was much concerned by the thought of how many days, or even weeks, might have been lost to us. Nor was it as if our halting place held much charm. I do not believe that I had ever found myself in a spot so wholly lacking in any sense of the spiritual as Melbourne town, where there seemed only one subject that attracted men's attention. When, at dinner in our lodgings, I thought it might be of interest to our fellow guests to tell them of our expedition, their only response was to wonder why I was not remaining in Victoria, so I might apply my knowledge of geology to a search for gold. As if there is not greater wealth to be found than mere mineral. When I endeavoured to explain that my purpose was of an altogether higher kind, they displayed little less than rudeness, turning to one another so they might renew their dismal chatter about prices and diggings.

My two colleagues, astonishingly, appeared to like the town. Renshaw, as ever, vanished on the first evening, and the next (I attempted to have words with him, though he insisted he had merely been enjoying the town's sights, while there was nothing I could prove). As for Potter, he too was rarely to be seen, except impatiently hurrying in or out. I had little notion as to what he was preoccupying himself with until that same morning when the second mate Kinvig came banging on our doors, demanding that we must hurry back to the ship. My breakfast had just been brought when Potter and Renshaw came clumping down the stairs, both looking pale and peeved at being roused from their beds (though I felt full of brightness). The doctor was arguing with Kinvig as he approached.

"But this is quite impossible. I have half a dozen packing cases still to collect, all paid for. Also there is Hooper, my manservant. It will take an hour at least to fetch him."

"Your what?" I must confess to feeling more than a little annoyed. It was typical of Potter to arrange such a thing, without so much as consulting myself, though I was the chief of this expedition. It had been clearly agreed in London that we would all of us forgo the comfort of servants during the sea journey, as neither the size of the ship nor the funds available to the expedition would permit such a thing, and yet, when I reminded him of this fact, he was quite unabashed.

"We've reached Australia, have we not? The sea journey is all but over. You needn't worry, Vicar. Hooper's wages shall be paid from my own pocket."

If I had known he was planning such a thing I would certainly have hired a servant myself, if simply to maintain the dignity of my position as leader. Now there was no time. "That's as may be," I told him firmly. "There may not be quarters for him aboard the ship. No, I will certainly have to raise this matter with Captain Kewley."

That brought a scowl from the doctor, but there was little he could do, being so plainly in the wrong. In the meantime a cab had been sent for the man, and to collect the doctor's packing cases, all of which took no little time, causing Mr. Kinvig to fidget greatly. I had assumed the packing cases would be nothing more than simple luggage containers to ease his travel, but instead no fewer than six wooden boxes appeared, each of them of the bulkiest dimensions.

"What on earth are these for?" I asked.

"My medical specimens."

My patience was wearing thin. "You should have sought my permission before you purchased them. The ship's hold may be full."

Do you know, he even stamped his foot. The man simply lacked all sense of respect. "But we all know it's empty."

I would not be browbeaten. "That we shall have to wait and see."

It was soon afterwards that his new servant, Hooper, finally arrived. Though Potter attempted to sing the man's praises, claiming that he had been in the employ of an eminent doctor colleague of his living in Melbourne, I found him hardly prepossessing. His clothes were poor, while he was possessed of a coarseness, and an aura of thwarted discontent, that led me to assume he had been lured to Melbourne in search of gold and had met with little success. I had found a cart to convey us to the ship, though the packing cases being so oversized, this proved hardly adequate for our needs. Hooper, the driver and second mate Kinvig struggled to load everything aboard, but I'm afraid they did a poor job, and I had to endure a most uncomfortable journey, one of the boxes digging painfully into my back. All in all I was more than a little stiff by the time we finally drew up beside the *Sincerity*.

The ship, I was surprised to see, was entirely prepared to depart, with two boats already lowered, waiting to pull her from her berth. Curiously enough, the wind, which Kinvig had said was so unmissable, was not strong at all, blowing in light gusts. I could only suppose that the Captain had been concerned it might die away altogether. He seemed, certainly, in a most impatient and distracted frame of mind. When I tried to raise the matter of Potter's manservant and packing cases, and make clear my own grave reservations, he seemed hardly even to hear, simply waving me away and ordering his men to load the boxes aboard, which seemed hardly proper. Potter, needless to say, quite beamed.

All in all it had been a tiring morning. As the *Sincerity* began her slow progress down the little river, I felt no wish to remain on the deck, where Potter was instructing his new servant as to the shipboard arrangements, which he did in a quite unnecessarily showy fashion, so I retired to the cabin to rest. By the time I returned to the deck the ship was already several miles out to sea and the town was nothing more than a jumble on the shore. It was as I stood thus, wondering how long it would take us to reach Tasmania, that I observed a most curious thing. The crew were engaged in some commonplace adjustment of the sails, but what was far from ordinary was the manner in which this was being performed. Glancing up at the rigging, I saw that where I would have expected to see ten or more men at work, I could count no more five, one of these being the chief mate, Brew, who never normally ventured aloft. More surprising still, when I looked back to the quarterdeck I saw the wheel was not being operated by one of the crew at all, but by the Captain himself.

"Whatever has happened?" I asked him. "Have some of the crew been taken sick?"

"Not sick." Kewley frowned, seeming quite out of temper. "We left some behind."

It seemed a most astonishing remark, and far from adequate. "Whatever do you mean?"

He peered past me at the horizon. "They weren't needed."

"Whyever not?"

The Captain shrugged. "The ship carries spare ropes and timbers and canvas, does she not? Well, these were spare crew."

CHAPTER TEN

Peevay
1831–35

THE FIRST TIME I heard about the white man's God, who was called GOD, was when we were walking through the forest with Robson. It was interesting, yes, to have some white man here, so close I could even touch him with my fingers, when before the only num I ever saw before was getting speared or killing us. There he was, Robson, leading the way. He was a little fat, and dirty in his white man's dead-skin clothes, but laughing as he took us hither and thither, on and again, fast like there was no waiting in him. All the while he would tell us about God.

"Who made you?" he'd ask, with special watching in his eyes. If I didn't answer he'd say it for me, looking just a little sad, so I felt like I was some rogue and bad fellow. "God made you." Even then he wasn't done. Another few walking steps and he'd start all again: "Who made you, Peevay?" This time I'd answer and quick, just to stop him from getting woeful.

"God made me."

That would make him smile.

Of course, I knew it wasn't really this fellow God who made us. It was other ones who are secret, like everybody knew. I never did say this to Robson, though, as I didn't want to grieve him when he was kindly saving us. Besides, those things weren't for telling to some foreign stranger. Truly Robson's God was one puzzle to confound. Everybody knew where our real ones were, as they could see them every night shining in the sky, but when I asked Robson where God was, he just said, "He is everywhere." He even said he was three people, which seemed some grievous mystery to confuse. Also he told that if we didn't believe

God was everywhere, then God would get angry and send us to some piss-poor place to get burnt, which was heinous, I did ponder. Our real ones never did care if you knew they were in the sky. They were just in the sky.

Except for God, though, those were better days. Three died from coughing sickness, which was a hateful thing, but after this dyings stopped, so most were still alive. Best of all, Mother was, though she was still too weak, needing others to lean on when she walked sometimes, so we must go slowly. Mother did hate Robson still, which was lamentable, and always she wanted us to spear him to death, urging this as often as she asked for water for drinking. Probably she would kill him herself, yes, if she was stronger and us others did not watch her carefully, making sure she never got spears.

The rest of us were pleased with having him, as he was hardly like a num white man at all. His smell was strange, yes, and so were his dead-skin clothes and his "Who made you?" talking, but otherwise he was almost like one of ours. He could speak proper language, and though he made stupid mistakes so it was hard not to laugh, he was the first white scut we ever met who did. He even joined our dancings in the night and played his whistle, which he called FLUTE. He told us he walked two whole summers finding our ones to save, and already he got plenty away to his fine place, where they were safe. Strangest still, when he talked about num he was often angry as piss, as if they were not his ones at all but worst grievous foes. He said they were cruel and hating, with killing in their hearts—which was true—and I pondered this must mean he was ours.

Yes, I did like Robson in those walking-to-the-sea days, better even than Heedeek, though he was like my old brother. Robson would pat my head—I still was quite small then—and say, "Hello, little fellow," and by and by I did like to think perhaps there was some great error long before, and he was my real father, which was some blissful thought. I even had dreamings that one day Mother would stop wanting to kill him, and that they would stand side by side and give me their cherishings both to-gether.

There he was as we walked, now telling us, "Go faster," now asking, "What do you call that tree?" now laughing loud at some muddy place where he slips, just to show he never minds. All of this to save us. Truly he was tidings of joy. Sometimes I was so pleased I wanted to tell others it was me who made this happen, when I burned the forest so he could find us.

It was great good fortune that I never did, of course.

First troubles started at the white men's town. None of us had ever been into any such till now, except those who were with Robson before, like Cordeve's sister, and even they seemed fearful as we stood on some hill looking down at those white men's giant houses, plenty of them.

"What if they don't remember you?" asked Heedeek.

Robson laughed like this was some funniest thing. "They'll remember me."

So we walked in. Well, if those white scuts knew Robson they never knew us, and they stood outside their houses watching as if we were some heinous foolishness, though in truth this was not us but them, with their empty hating eyes and voices screaming like birds. Even Robson looked fearing then, I did observe, and I was glad when we got into a big house made from rocks, whose name was GAOL, where we could be away from those staring buggers. Robson did not stay, leaving us with other num we didn't know, but he did return by and by, looking so pleased, and that was when he said his strange thing.

"You must stay here some more days, I'm sorry, as the ship's not quite ready."

The strangeness, which we did all observe, was that YOU'LL. Where was WE'LL? I did ponder. Heedeek asked at once, "Aren't you going with us?"

"But of course I can't." Robson looked at us as if we were some puzzle to confound not to know this already. "There are all your brothers and sisters still to be rescued, plenty of them." Then he gave us his kindly look. "Don't worry. I'll come back as soon as I'm able. Then we'll have tidings of joy."

So he went away, which was troubling, especially in that num town. There was nothing we could do, though, as our room, which had walls like thin sticks, was strong and the door would not open. Besides, that place with its staring scuts was too fearsome to walk through without spears ready. So we stayed for some days in that house named gaol, eating white men's heinous food, which was hard biscuits and old meat that was salty like seawater, and by and by we pondered if Robson had just tricked us all, ready for killing, though this was so terrible a thinking that nobody spoke it except Mother, who said it often.

Finally other white men came whose name was SOLDIERS, all coloured red and carrying one gun, and they took us past the shouting white scuts to a large white men's boat like I had seen sometimes far away on the sea, that had huge skins to catch the wind. It was fast, that boat, and by and by we were far from the land so we hardly could see it anymore. The boat's white men had guns, plenty of them, and they stared at us like enemies, so we did wonder if this was some trick still, and if they would come quietly in the night to kill us, and then throw us into the sea so nobody ever would know. We did keep watchful. In the end, of course, that boat was no trick at all, and nobody came in the night. Those white men never did any killing to us, just climbing up high to move the huge skins bigger or smaller. No, the cheating trick was ISLAND where we went.

Truly, that was one woeful thing, hateful to behold. I knew most num were bad scuts better speared dead, yes, but I never did think Robson would tell us piss-awful falsehoods. Robson, who said he was our friend and even spoke to us in our own talking to make us love him. Didn't he say we'd go to a fine land? As soon as I saw ISLAND I discerned it was much too small, with only one hill, like it was no place at all. There could be no room for kangaroo to hunt there, or rivers to cross, I did surmise, nor even just walking, which is almost the first thing for being alive. As boat went round I saw a place with huts that was crowded with our ones, more than I ever did see before. Then we got put in a small boat with sticks to push it, and as we stepped onto land our ones watched us like we were some most interesting thing, and their eyes were empty, while even those who knew us from before were quiet in their greetings. So I did guess the whole truth. This was some dying place.

Soldiers took us across, windy sand jumping in my eyes, to meet their chief, whose name was SERGEANT WILKES. He looked old and hating like he had poison in his blood, and was holding one dog animal, very small, so it was like some rat. Sergeant Wilkes never even greeted us hello, but just told soldiers to take us to huts with dirty smell in them. All the while soldiers stared at our women like they were just fresh new food for tasting.

Truly there is nothing more hateful than feeling cheated to death. Worst of all it was me who let Robson find us in the forest, and I did revere him, even till I dreamed him as my own father. Robson, whose name was now FAT SCUT ROBSON. Robson, who was back in the world right now, seeking more of our ones to catch and bring to this heinous dying place. Robson, who I could not even tell to him, YOU ARE SOME LYING BUGGER.

Every one of us of Mother's tribe wanted to go away that day, that very hour, as even being chased and killed was much better than this place, where there was nothing to do but sit and wait for more heinous white men's food, or watch others to guess who got coughing sickness next.

"I told you we should spear him," told Mother, who was pleased by our sad lamentings, as this meant she was right. Mother always loved being right. "You should've listened to me when you had the chance."

That great good fortune about Mother, though, was that she never did despair. No, our new ruination even seemed to make her stronger. When we were woeful and deploring I could see from her eyes that she was already thinking up some new intent. Sure enough, as soon as she was strong again she started going into huts of others who spoke our language, for secret talkings. Several times I asked what was her design, though she would not tell me one word.

"White scuts are your friends," she would taunt. "Go and talk to them."

But it was my craving to join, as after Robson's cheating falsehoods it was some heartfelt desire deep inside my breast to spear that Sergeant Wilkes with his poison eyes, and any of the other white scuts besides. Yes, I dreamed, do those pissers and be away from this place.

It was Heedeek who made her let me join after all. "I need Peevay's help," he said, though really this was just talking.

Mother scowled and said, "If he ruins us then it'll be your fault," but she did permit me. So I learned who was with Mother of our ones—or Palawa as we named ourselves now—and it was plenty of us, as almost everyone she asked did join. Some were hateful of this dying place, others were angry at soldiers and their lustful appetites, as they were always trying to lure our women into their huts with food, or even just pushing them within when Sergeant Wilkes did not see. That was heinous.

Next day Heedeek took me and some others over to other side of the island and I saw how Mother's intent would go. Some others were there already, making spears round a secret fire, put where the wind was blowing away from soldiers and Sergeant Wilkes, so they never would smell smoke. So I started making spears too. Later when the sun was low we buried fire's ashes in sand so there were no signs and came back towards the settlement, holding spears close by our legs so white scuts would not see. Then we put them in a secret place hidden by bushes, where there were already others, plenty of them. Heedeek told that when the next boat came, with more num heinous food, we would have enough spears ready, and could go out quietly in the dark and kill those white pissers, every one. After, we would take their boat and go back to the world again.

Of course the trouble with a hidden intention is that it is fragile like some old dry stick, and just one mishap can snap it broken.

Next afternoon was hot. Soldiers were in their huts, playing with flat painted cards which made them shout loud. Of ours, some were on the other side making secret spears like usual, but Mother said we must not go too many all at once, as we would get observed, and it was my day for staying. So I sat in that dirty hut by and by, throwing some stone at the wall or making dreamings of myself as a brave hero who saved Mother from twenty white scuts with guns. Flies buzzed there, making shapes like sticks in their flyings, and by and by I lost that throwing stone and even my dreamings got tired, so sometimes I got shot or Mother speared me. Finally I got angry with that hut and so I went out and walked up that little hill behind, so I was nearer the fire for making spears, which was exciting to ponder. I was still in that place when Sergeant Wilkes came walking with his dog animal.

This was usual, yes, as he walked with that dog many times every day. He did love that dog animal, which he called FERNANDO, and all of his cherishings went right into it, as he hated us and he hated his soldiers too, shouting at them often. Why he loved that dog was some mystery to confound, as it was too small like a rat and always barking, or feigning to be dangerous, even just at doors banging in the wind. Us Palawa ones never called him Fernando, but MOUSE TURD, and we would kick him too except that Sergeant Wilkes might see. There he was as I watched from the little hill, back and forth, running hither and thither, barking at flowers.

This I did not mind. No, what I minded was where these hithers and thithers were going. All of a sudden he was very near that secret place, with Sergeant Wilkes walking after. That was some worrisome thing. Now he stopped just near, raising leg for pissing. Now he was running back to some other spot for growling at sand, which was quite fine, but tidings of joy were short, as now he was running back, for sniffing where he pissed just before. Worse, now he went further, right to secret bushes themselves. So my heart went pounding deep inside my breast and I hardly could look. Sergeant Wilkes stood waiting, very patient, as Mouse Turd had his shittings right on that very place, on our clean spears. But even this would be all right if he just stopped then, but next he was sticking his arse into leaves for scratchings. Then suddenly I heard that yowl, and Sergeant Wilkes was stooping, peering, then reaching down. All at once he was looking raging and hurrying back to the huts, shouting to soldiers.

I just had enough time to go and wave to those by the fire to get away. Still it was one lamentable misfortune. Sergeant Wilkes made all us stand still for a longest time in front of huts, with soldiers pointing guns at our eyes, and him calling us MURDERING SAVAGES or DIRTY CHEATING BLACKS. After, we must watch as spears that we made so carefully were all put together in some pile and burned. Then Sergeant Wilkes walked very near, staring at our faces for a long time, and asking, "Which of you is the leader of this?"

I suppose he thought we would all say nothing but he was wrong. Mother stepped towards him straightaway, looking like she never cared, and saying, "Me, you bugger," in words of his own white men's language.

That made him turn redder colour with hating, and next he made four soldiers take her to the shore, touching her bubbies and cheeks as they went, so she tried to hit them, and they pushed her in the small boat, very hard, so I could see her leg was hurt, though she never shouted. That was too hateful and I wished I could run out and spear every one of those scuts, dead and dead and dead, like in my dreams in the hut. Afterwards Sergeant Wilkes chose four other of ours to put with her, though one wasn't part of Mother's intent at all but just talked to her sometimes. That was mournful watching boat go away, and pondering they would shoot her and throw her in the sea. What they did was almost worse. When the boat was far, so its skin to catch the wind looked small like some leaf, it reached a big rock that I did notice before sometimes, and that was all alone with no trees or any other thing. That was where Mother and others got put. It was a saddest thing to see them there after the boat left them, looking like tiniest crawling creatures, too far almost to see us wave, though we waved still. That did grieve me and give me woeful feelings deep inside my breast.

That next day Sergeant Wilkes was as if he just forgot them. He never looked towards the sea at all but just shouted at his soldiers, making them walk and stand and twitch with their guns, ever and again. All the while we were watching that rock, hot in the sun. Finally Heedeek and some others went to ask Sergeant Wilkes to fetch them back but he just got angry and shouted that they must go away or they would get put on that rock too. So all day passed, which was mournful. Now I knew Sergeant Wilkes just wanted them killed in this slow, hating way. Being shot was better, yes, I did surmise. They would be dead, too, except that same next morning the boat came from the world with more white men's heinous food. It stopped by Mother's rock, I suppose thinking there must be some accident, and dropped a boat to get them up. When it reached us and Mother and those others were back, Sergeant Wilkes said nothing, but he looked hateful. Poor Mother and those others could hardly walk, being cut like they fell down rocks, eyes huge and closed, skin all broken from sun, and mouths heinous with white stuff from having no water.

That changed many things. Heedeek and me and others put Mother in the best of the huts to be kindly, and though she got better by and by, and she still hated white scuts very much, now she was quieter. Sometimes she just sat in front not speaking at all, and when she talked of killing num white scuts and feeding their arms and legs to dogs she did so in a small voice. Yes, she lost some fighting thing that time, and after that she started getting fat, until she was very huge. I changed too, as I learned something from those days. Now I knew that there was no fighting white pissers just with spears, as they would win each and every time, and we would only die sooner. No, I did surmise, if I was to endure it must be from some other way.

Sometimes it does seem that the difficult thing is just to know that puzzle to confound, and once you know him then his answer comes back quick as can be. So it was. One morning a few weeks after another boat came with new soldiers and their chief. Sergeant Wilkes was waiting as they rowed to the shore, and I observed his smile was stiff like he was angry, which was strange. More interesting still, this new soldier's chief hardly greeted him at all but made them both go into that hut, so we knew he was stronger than Wilkes. So I went round outside to the back of the hut with some others of ours to watch through a small hole in the wood that we knew. Well, here was our surprise. New fellow talked to Sergeant Wilkes loud and shouting as if he was just some low scut and never island's chief at all, telling him he was DISMISSED and other such words. That next day old poison blood took Mouse Turd, walked over to the shore and was rowed away, never to return, and other new fellow, whose name was COMMANDANT DARLING, became our white men's chief instead.

Most interesting of all came just after. By and by Heedeek, who learned some white men's words, like we all did now, asked Commandant Darling why poison blood was sent away, and Commandant Darling told that this was because he tried to kill Mother IN A WRONG WAY. He should not do what he did, you see, but must send her to other white scuts for a great talking. Even then they cannot just put her on a rock in the sun but must hang her with a rope, as this was white men's correct killing way. I did ponder this by and by, and it showed me many things. So I knew that num white scuts had ways they must follow, just like us, though these were so hidden in their cheating falsehoods that I never guessed till now they were there. Well, I surmised, if I learned their thinkings, then I could know how to fight them with their own shit. This was my best intent, I did decide, as fighting them in our ways never worked at all.

By and by Commandant Darling took us away on the boat to another island, whose name was FLINDERS, that was just nearby. This was much bigger and was two days' walking from one end to another, with game to hunt and small mountains to look at, and one that was tall and sharp like spears. Still it was some heinous windy place, with sand jumping in your eyes, so it never was like the proper world, where we knew every rock like old friends. Commandant Darling tried to be kindly, even asking us Palawa into his hut sometimes to eat heinous food with him. He said we must wear clothes like white men, which was hateful, but he also showed us how to grow grass and bushes to eat, which was interesting, and as time passed we got clever at this. So we almost liked him and once we gave him a parakeet we caught which he kept in his hut and called SHAKESPEARE. Then a summer was gone, and another too, and nothing much happened but we stayed on Flinders and more died from coughing sickness, plenty of them. By and by our place, whose name was Wybalenna, got bigger, with new huts for us and for stores, and more num coming there to watch us.

One of these was called SMITH, who said all Palawa children must come to his hut to hear about God who was called GOD. Smith was small with flat hair and little spying eyes, and some other children hated him and just ran away, but I went, because I wanted to learn num ways and words and every other white men's shit so I could fight them. Smith was pleased, and told me if I knew about GOD I would be saved. I never believed him, no, as I learned from fat scut Robson that you never can trust any white man, but still I did go once and again, till I knew more things. Sometimes, and I also spoke to soldiers, as they told me magic words that Mother knew, like pisser, scut, shit, bugger, fucking fucker, cunt and other such. Once I said these at Smith, just to see their magic, and it was strong, as he hated me for them very much, telling me to go away from his hut for a week.

Mother was frenzied by my learning. "Why d'you go?" she asked me. "D'you like white scuts?"

"I want to know them so I can fight them."

"It's better just to kill them," she would answer. "Know them too much and you may get like them."

Not that I listened. Already I was dreaming an intent of my own to get all of us back to the world, so I would be some hero, even to Mother. That was my secret craving.

So another summer passed, and another, and by and by I grew taller and got lustings, so I noticed females in that new way, and their bubbies and fluffs were tidings of joy and filled me with new hungry wanting. Even some of the white women were fine, though they were hidden in their thick dead skins, which were called CLOTHES, and their eyes looked crazed and sad and hard like stone, so I did prefer ours. Not that even ours let me near, as I was still too young, but sometimes they would let me kiss their lips and touch their soft round bubbies if nobody saw. That was great good fortune.

Mostly, though, those were just dying days. People got crook faster by and by, until we were always watching ourselves for signs. That was heinous, as it is too terrible to die hot and coughing and hardly able to breathe. White scuts hardly died at all, of course, and when we got bad they looked at us like this was just some usual thing for blackfellows—as they called us—which I hated most of all. Worst was when my friend Heedeek died, and it was one saddest lamentable day, when he got taken down to the shore and burnt on his funeral fire. That was too woeful.

So it was hard in those long-ago heinous times, and different fellows tried any different way to push days onwards. Some stopped doing anything, just lying down in their despond, like it was their rest. They died quick. Others went away across the island, hunting and so as if these were usual times and nothing flagrant was happening. They lived longer. Sometimes Mother's ones would go away into the bush in the night and dance and talk in old ways. That was best, at least until day came. Some, especially women, talked about Robson and how he would come back soon, and save us, like he said that day in the house called gaol. I never believed this, of course, as if he liked us so then he never would put us on these killing islands.

Other women found a different friend to save them. This was Wraggeowrapper, who was only hateful before and would come at night watching in the trees to make us mad. Now they made a new dance just for him, and they did this in the night and sang songs just to please him. They even lay down with him for fuckings, so some told. Why not? I did ponder. If all the world was just death and dying, for no reason you could surmise, then perhaps it was cleverest to get help from your enemy. At least he was better than some false friend, like Robson.

Sometimes there were troubles. People got wrathful at this heinous waiting, so they did recollect old hatings, of fights from long-ago days. Mostly there were four nations now, as smaller ones got mixed up, and these kept apart usually, but sometimes spears got made and I surmised there must be a killing war soon. Once Tonenweener nation, who were our foes now, came with spears when we were dancing in the night, and they stood all around, watching and shouting they would kill us. In the end, though, there never was any fighting. I suppose death was too easy to make more.

Sometimes new Palawa ones came in the boat, sent by Robson, which was interesting for us but heinous for them. One day Mongana and his mother, Pagerly, came. It was strange to see them, yes, as it seemed another life ago when we lived all together and they hated me with their tauntings. Now they were not angry anymore, but just fearful. They told bad news, that most ones I knew in those long-ago days were dead now, from coughing sickness or white scuts' killing. Worst, Tartoyen and Grandmother were gone. That was a sad thing. Till then I always hoped they might be saved somewhere, just like before, with Tartoyen telling his fine stories and Grandmother sitting by the sea with her long, bony fingers. That always gave me some small hope, even when we were on these islands, and it was woeful to see it taken.

Even that heinous time had some good things, though. Mongana was very fearful at seeing this Flinders Island, so he asked me to help him, which was pleasing as it made me feel cleverest. So I showed him where we waited for our heinous food, and I told him who everybody was and which num white scuts were hateful and which were better. So it was Mongana, my most grievous foe of before, became my fine friend. Another surprise was that his mother, Pagerly, became Mother's friend. Often she would sit with Mother, listening to her hatings of white buggers, and how they should have their heads stove in and such, which she loved to tell. In truth she was Mother's only friend. Some others did smile when they walked near her, and sometimes they even got heinous food for her, but deep inside their breasts they were too fearful to like her truly. Mother always was frightening.

So days passed, nothing much happening. I went to Smith's hut for learning, and every day I did vow to endure. Thus it was when talk came that Commandant Darling would leave us and we would get a new commandant. But this one was no stranger but one we knew.

Robson was coming.

Mrs. Catherine Price, Wife of the Storekeeper, Wybalenna
Aboriginal Settlement, Flinders Island
1835–38

I GUESSED at once that the ship from Launceston, which had been expected for several days, must finally have been sighted. Through the curtains of the front room I saw first the garden overseer, next the chaplain and his wife, then the tailor, and Mr. Dunn, the baker, and more, all hurrying through the rain in the direction of the jetty, their eyes betraying hopes of letters. My husband, Louis, was not long in joining them. I, however, preferred to remain indoors, having another slight headache, so felt not quite in a mood for gatherings.

A while later I heard the front door close and Louis call out, "Have you heard the news, Catherine?"

I had not. Of course I had not.

"The new governor of Van Diemen's Land is coming to pay us a visit, and his wife, too." Though he did not step into the front room to speak to me directly, still his voice sounded kindlier than it had for some time. Then again, it was ever Louis' nature to delight at the prospect of meeting men of influence. Ever since I had first known him he loved to talk of "connections," and the advancement he believed these could bring, though in truth they seemed to have brought him little enough till now. "Think of it," he declared from the hallway, "the new governor, coming all the way here to visit. D'you know he was an explorer in the seas of the Arctic?"

I knew. It was the one thing that was always said about the man, being told and repeated, I assumed, for lack of anything more revealing. I realized that it was a great honour to have him visit us—all the more so as the previous governor had never thought to come—but still I confess I found myself rather less excited than my husband. He did not stay long, the ship's arrival necessitating a good deal of work for him at the store, and I spent the morning teaching the children their letters. Through the curtains I could observe the settlement's wives as they hurried back and forth through the rain to one another's homes, doubtless to discuss the exciting prospect once and again, and perhaps fret over what they might wear for the occasion. I did consider paying a call or two myself. The inclement weather, though, was so very discouraging.

That same evening Mr. Robson called everybody together in the chapel, and as we stood, oil lamps faintly murmuring, he related the arrangements he had devised for the governor's visit. It was the first time I had looked upon his face for almost a week, and I thought he was looking sadly tired. He spoke well, as ever, beginning by admitting that he had been as surprised as anybody by the news, and then urging us all to strive hard to present a good impression of the settlement. As for his plans, these struck me as most sensible. It seemed the governor had, aside from being a polar explorer, a reputation for judging things greatly by their appearance, and so, in the two weeks remaining to us, we were meticulously to clean every building, from the natives' huts to the store-room and the chapel. Our exalted visitor would be given a full tour of the settlement, while in the evening a grand banquet was to be held in his honour, outside if the weather was good, with all of the aborigines attending. His day would be completed with a service in the chapel.

Mr. Dunn, the baker—who can never resist an opportunity to utter some humorous remark—asked if the governor would be fed "the usual quails and suckling pig," or "just roast swan," and, seeing as none of us had enjoyed any but the dreariest of diets since we had arrived upon Flinders Island, this caused a good deal of amusement. Mr. Robson laughed as loudly as any, replying, "After his explorations of the Arctic I imagine even our simple fare will suffice," which won a little applause, causing him to smile, quite as he used to do. When the meeting was finished, though, and we stepped out into the moonlit night, the aborigines watching us from their huts, I was certain I discerned in his face a look of anxiousness. Nor can I say that I was surprised. The governor's visit was a great honour, certainly, but it was not without dangers. Most of all there was the troubling thought of what he might be told.

It seemed already quite an eternity since Mr. Robson first took up his place as our commandant, almost three years before. His arrival, I recall, had come at a time when I was finding life on Flinders Island far from easy. The settlement's location, on the western shore of the island, provided delightful sunsets but also exposed us to the full force of the fierce westerly winds, and these could be a great strain upon the nerves, forever rushing through the trees, blowing sand in one's eyes or causing doors suddenly to slam. A further source of disquiet to me was our unhappy charges, the blacks. While these unfortunate creatures were mostly merely piteous, sadly lingering as disease took its toll ever more upon their numbers, still it was hard not to recall upon the brutality of their history, and the great cruelties they had committed upon innocent settlers. The creatures had only recently been induced to wear clothes, while the loose way they carried these upon their bodies—barely attaining decency—did nothing to reassure one as to their state of mind. When I looked upon them, loitering by their huts, or striding away in a group to hunt, the expressions upon their faces seemed at once so wild and impenetrable that it was hard not to feel some unease. At night I often found the thought of them, dwelling so very near, made sleep hard to come.

Matters were not helped by the paucity of diversions to be found on the island. The supply vessel visited only every three months, making news and letters rare pleasures, and the days passed slowly indeed. Boredom will bring out the devil in men, and in our case its progeny were feuding and rumour. Louis and myself did our best to distance ourselves from all such behaviour, naturally, but this was not always easy. All too often to converse was to be entrusted with unwanted confidences, while to stand aloof from such talk was to find oneself quietly excluded. One of those with a particular love of gossip was the catechist, Mr. Smith, who was a lively man of, it was said, thwarted ambition. While we never encouraged Mr. Smith to call on us, in so small a place it was hardly practical—or wise—to prohibit others from visiting, while he could be most humorous in his retelling of some piece of news, so that even Louis, who was generally inclined to the serious, found him most diverting. After a time his visits to our home became commonplace.

It came as the greatest shock to us, naturally, when we learned that the settlement's commandant, Mr. Darling, was abruptly to be removed, and that this was largely the consequence of critical letters sent to the government in Hobart. Worse still was the discovery that the letters' sender had been Mr. Smith. I knew the two had felt a coolness for one another for some time, ever since the commandant had accused Mr. Smith of wastefulness regarding settlement supplies, but still the action seemed wholly unwarranted. I understood Mr. Smith had accused Mr. Darling of neglectfulness in his religious instruction of the aborigines, a charge that was all the more dangerous for being to some extent true, as the man had hardly troubled to instruct the adult natives save in the most mundane of matters, such as farming. The commandant took the matter very badly, and confronted his persecutor one Sunday outside the chapel, calling him Judas in front of all. It was a most painful incident.

My instinct was to let the matter rest but Louis could not do so. He was much distressed by the commandant's removal, believing Mr. Darling had been about to promote him, and he made it clear to Mr. Smith that he was no longer welcome at our home. The catechist, in turn, behaved quite as if it were ourselves, rather than he, who had behaved unreasonably, directing us haughty, wounded looks whenever we passed. Curiously enough he displayed particular coolness not to Louis but to myself. If I found myself walking towards him in some part of the settlement he would embark on an elaborate and embarrassing charade of turning in another direction, while if I had the misfortune to meet him at another's house he would stare quite over my head. The whole matter became most distressing.

In the event, of course, Mr. Smith's treacherous conduct did have one happy consequence, Mr. Darling's replacement being Mr. Robson. I had heard something about this man, of course, from both admirers and detractors: the famous Robson, who had journeyed for months at a time through the wilderness of Van Diemen's Land with none for company but blacks, that he might endeavour to save their unhappy race. For some reason I had imagined he would be a giant of a fellow, with a look of military severity. How wrong I was! The man I saw sitting in the rowboat, as it made its way from the supply vessel to the settlement jetty, was a most ordinary-looking figure, round and clumsy in shape, whose speech, as he directed the coxswain, betrayed humble origins. Only the lively look in his eyes hinted at the power of resolution that lay within. As to his family, I observed that his wife, sitting beside him, was regarding the island with what appeared to be an expression of distaste, while his sons seemed curiously distracted, showing no sign of the famous determination of their father.

"He has a nice face," I observed to Louis.

My husband, pressing forward that he might be among the first to offer his welcome, nodded in agreement. The blacks likewise seemed greatly raised in their spirits by the sight of this new commandant. He had brought with him a number of their fellows that he had found on Van Diemen's Land, thus inspiring a most touching scene, as siblings separated all these years burst into tearful recognition, and mothers quite shrieked with delight at the sight of children who, doubtless, they had thought lost to them forever. All at once some of the natives began excitedly to babble to him in words of their own strange languages. I had heard that he was able to speak in their tongue, and was looking forward to hearing him reply in a like fashion, but instead he waved his hand with a look of cheerful firmness. "But you must speak English now," he insisted kindly, "only English." Thus he displayed, even then, his resolve to bring improvement to the unfortunate creatures.

He was especially proud of one of those he had brought with him, a slight boy by the name of George Vandiemen, of nervous disposition, who, most charmingly, tried to hide behind his commandant's back. Robson explained, as our large party began walking back towards the settlement, that the child had been found wandering alone by some farmers near Devonport, who had then sent him away to Bristol to be schooled, where he remained long enough to acquire more than a little learning. Robson had discovered him working as a serving lad in the farmers' house, and had induced them to release him only with some difficulty. Thus described, young George was of great curiosity to us all, and as we reached the area of the natives' huts Mr. Robson attempted to coax him into giving a little demonstration of his knowledge. This was not easy, the boy being so shy, but finally he was enticed into uttering a few greetings, which he did with a fluency of language that was indeed remarkable, far surpassing that of any of our own aborigines, winning applause from his smiling watchers, and laughter too, as Mr. Dunn, the baker, observed that the boy even spoke with an audible West Country accent.

The display was, sadly, of short duration. Just as the child grew more confident in his performance he seemed to falter, then uttered some incomprehensible cry in his own native speech. Then, greatly to our surprise, he began impatiently pushing his way between us and ran away towards one of the huts. There, staring at him with the strangest look, was Walyeric: that monster of a creature, undeserving of the title female, about whom such dreadful stories are told, and who answers the kindliest smile with a glower of insolence. It was hard to believe, but I could only assume from little George's excited cries that this terrible woman must be his mother. Though I knew her to be wicked to her bones, still I could not help but be shocked by her behaviour. As he raced towards her, calling out, she simply rose to her feet, then delivered him a mighty slap to his face–though he was her own child, lost to her all these years– and cruelly strode away. Poor George was dreadfully upset, bursting into sobs, and though we tried to coax him back to us, he insisted on scurrying away alone.

It was not long before Mr. Robson's presence among us–striding about, always so energetically–began to transform the atmosphere of the settlement, and greatly for the better. Everybody soon found himself thrown into activity, instantly banishing the devil boredom. Louis was required to rearrange all supplies in the cramped storehouse, as a new and better building was to take its place, this forming only one part of a mighty campaign of construction. The sawyer and bricklayer found themselves in constant toil, their lazy convict labourers lazy no longer, while even some of the aborigines were induced to help in the work. The fruits of these labours were soon evident, as new wooden huts sprang up almost like mushrooms, and a proper brick front was added to one of the double huts, which was to be fashioned into a new school chapel, it being Mr. Robson's stated aim that the blacks should be both housed and led in worship entirely in buildings made of brick.

Mr. Robson's chief concern, it soon became clear, was to mount nothing less than a crusade to civilize the blacks. Louis, who was much impressed by our new commandant, explained how the aborigines were each to be allotted a craft, from shoemaking to animal husbandry, that they would be required to develop as their own. All were to work, although those of lesser ability would be expected only to perform some simple task, such as digging potatoes, or graves for their less fortunate fellows. We both considered this a most delightful notion, which might with time transform them into something like a happy band of English villagers. More ingenious still, Mr. Robson insisted that every one of them would receive a wage for his toil, and announced that a market would be held once each week, where the poor creatures might spend their new wealth on some useful item, such as tobacco, or a new straw hat. His intention was most clear: he was subtly introducing them to that most essential pillar of the civilized world, commerce. There are always grumblers, of course, and some among the officers' wives complained, when we met for tea, that the market—which was, after the first week, somewhat poorly attended—was of little usefulness. I, however, strongly contested such pessimism, pointing out that the market's value was as an example to the natives, and as such it was beyond all measurement.

A still more ambitious innovation was the announcement that the settlement was henceforth to have its own newspaper, the *Flinders Island Journal*, which—with Mr. Robson's help—was to be compiled even by the aborigines themselves. The journal was, it was true, much restricted by the island's lack of a printing press, which required all text to be repetitively copied out by hand by those few natives practised in their letters, and I recall seeing only one issue, whose brief pages were concerned with simple daily occurrences about the island (there being, in truth, little news to relate apart from further deaths among the natives, upon which it was undesirable to dwell). For all this both Louis and I thought the venture a fine demonstration of a new sophistication of settlement life. As I recall, it even won the praise of the *Colonial Times* in Hobart—Mr. Robson having written to the newspaper to tell of our efforts to bring advancement to the natives—which printed a most favourable account of all his innovations.

It never occurred to me, naturally, that I might myself become involved in Mr. Robson's great campaigns, but so it was. This stemmed from the first occasion when I met him to speak to, being one morning when I happened to be passing the site of the new settlement store, just as my husband was showing him how the building work was progressing.

"Catherine," Louis called out, delighted. "Look who is here."

Mr. Robson greeted me with a kindly smile. "Your husband has been doing a splendid job here."

Louis beamed.

"You seem to be changing every inch of our little establishment," I remarked to Mr. Robson in a faintly chiding voice. "What will we have next? I wonder. A railway? A manufactory?"

He laughed with enthusiasm. "I'm afraid I must disappoint you, Mrs. Price. From now I will be concerning myself less with building and more with the natives' learning. Their religious knowledge in particular appears to have been much neglected." Though he did not mention any name I had no doubt it was to his predecessor, Mr. Darling, that he was alluding. "My intention is that every one of the blacks, including the adults, shall be thoroughly schooled. It will be no easy thing to achieve, of course, but it will be done."

It was Louis who produced the suggestion. "But you have taught, have you not, Catherine? Perhaps you should help."

It was a thought that had not occurred to me. "I would hardly call it teaching," I insisted. "I have instructed the children in their letters and sums."

"Then you are nothing less than an expert." Mr. Robson's laugh could be quite infectious. "The truth is, Mrs. Price, we will be in need of all the help we can find. I am planning to take classes myself."

"Go on, Catherine," Louis coaxed. "You would not be required to instruct them in anything difficult."

Mr. Robson gave me a smile. "You would be greatly valued."

I began a week later. What a daunting moment that was, knowing that I would shortly find myself standing before a crowded class of those strange-looking faces, all awaiting my words. Mr. Robson proved a great comfort. "Remember," he urged, "that they are far less acquainted with learning than you are with teaching. Simply start by asking one of them his commandments and you will find all follows from there."

I did just as he suggested and found it most effective advice. Then again, I observed Mr. Robson possessed a quite remarkable understanding of the aborigines, being full of ideas as to how some point of grammar or theology might be explained in simple terms they would comprehend. With his kindly help I soon became accustomed to my new work, and even found I was enjoying myself. After so long spent merely passing time upon this island I suppose I was more than ready for an occupation, and those became times of great hope, there being something about the very process of learning which can instil in all a mood of smiling enthusiasm. The teachers were, it was true, a mixed group—they included Robson's older son, two of the officers' wives and also Mr. Smith, while the educated aborigine child, George Vandiemen, also took a few lessons—but we were kept so busily employed that disagreements were rare, and matters remained civil even between Mr. Smith and myself. As for the blacks, though these continued to seem strange to me, I gradually found I lost my earlier nervousness of the creatures.

Finally there came an evening when, as I was teaching Psalms to a class of children, I saw the door open and, greatly to my surprise, Mr. Robson quietly took a seat at the back, and began observing my poor efforts. By this time autumn had arrived, the nights were long, and I well recall the howling of the wind upon the classroom roof, and the flickering of the oil lamps, as I endeavoured to continue, feeling that my every utterance was foolish and ill chosen. What astonishment I felt when, as my students trooped away, Mr. Robson rose and gently patted me upon the hand, remarking, "Did I not say you would be greatly valued?"

That was a proud moment indeed.

One of the delights of Mr. Robson's leadership was that one never did know what might next occur. Thus it was with the aborigines' names. I had observed for some days that he had been devoting his free moments to what appeared to be a long list, but still I was taken wholly by surprise when he suddenly called all the blacks, and the settlement officers, to gather in the open space in front of the school, where he announced—to the amazement of all—that the natives were to be renamed. It seemed a most bold notion, and as I watched him call the natives up one by one to receive their new appellations—quite in the manner of a general awarding medals to his soldiers—I was full of admiration. I fully understood the significance of his intention. He meant the aborigines to be begun afresh and reborn as civilized, Christian beings.

As for the names themselves, these were quite charming. Some of the older and more exalted of the natives were rewarded with titles of quaintest grandeur, such as King Alpha, Queen Adelaide or Princess Cleopatra. Others were allotted names of purest romance, from Neptune and Semiramis to Achilles. I observed also that Mr. Robson sometimes indulged himself in delightful artifice as—unbeknown to the blacks themselves—he made playful reference to some aspect of their character. Thus a little fellow whose expression seemed always stern now became Cato, while a girl who was dreamy and sad was now Ophelia. This was not only humorous in itself, but made the names easy to recall, especially in comparison with those they replaced, that had been so very long and confusing.

In some cases I was amused to note that a title concealed some clever sting in its tail. Thus the monstrous female, Walyeric, became Mary, and while this might seem innocent enough, I had little doubt as to which murderous monarch was in Mr. Robson's mind. Her half-caste son, Peevay, who had such a curious round mop of blond hair above his little black face, and who insisted on regarding one with such disconcerting seriousness, was now Cromwell, that most sombre of rulers. His friend Mongana, who seemed always to delight in troublesome questioning, was ingeniously reborn as Voltaire, while Mongana's mother, Pagerly, who was often in a state of sinister commune with the dreadful Walyeric, was now Boadicea.

That was a joyous day, and yet it was soon followed by disappointment. Mr. Robson was thorough in his efforts to ensure that the new names would become quickly familiar to everyone, insisting that all teachers and officers henceforth address the natives exclusively by their new titles, and for a time it seemed as if the natives had (with a few exceptions, such as the incorrigible Mary) adopted their new titles happily enough. As weeks passed, however, I became increasingly sure that when they spoke among themselves—using that curious language they had evolved, part English and part native tongues—they secretly continued to address one another by their old, savage appellations. It may seem a small matter, but it distressed me greatly, seeming nothing less than a betrayal of the man, by those whom he had striven so hard to save.

Looking back, I do believe that moment proved something of a turning point, as with every week and month that followed I found myself growing increasingly troubled with doubts as to the success of our great campaign of instruction. Part of the difficulty lay with the other teachers, as, if truth be told, poor good Mr. Robson had not been blessed with the assistants he deserved. Mr. Smith proved as lazy of purpose as he was unkind of tongue, until Mr. Robson was forced publicly to rebuke him, causing no little resentment. Mr. Robson's son proved hardly more able, while his wife, who appeared as dissatisfied with her life on Flinders Island as her first dismal stare at its shore had suggested, quite refused to help. As for the two officers' wives, these seemed of little usefulness, forever loitering about the school–though it was hardly spacious–and distracting Mr. Robson from his work with their fussing.

The authorities in Hobart proved also a great disappointment. Though the Van Diemen's Land governor had been quick to declare his support for our efforts, little was shown in the way of tangible assistance, and Mr. Robson's requests for further books and teachers were met with a succession of excuses. Worse was to come, notably with regard to the business of the seal hunters. These, I should explain, were Europeans of brutal disposition who lived on other islands in the Bass Strait, and many of whom had abducted aborigine women, who they used with abominable cruelty. Some lived close by, and would even visit the settlement to purchase goods from Louis' store, swaggering and uttering vilest language. Our own blacks had long known that their women were held captive by these fiends and were greatly pleased when Mr. Robson announced that he would rescue them from their fate. He made every effort to achieve this, sending letter after letter to Hobart, and yet, hateful as it is to recall, the colonial government quite refused to assist in the matter, claiming the women had borne so many children to their tormentors that it was too late to remove them. The decision was not merely callous and unjust, but also served to undermine Mr. Robson's standing with the natives.

The greatest cause of our difficulties did not, however, lie with white men, but, I regret to say, with the blacks themselves. It may seem harsh and yet I could not help but observe they showed an increasing reluctance to apply themselves to their reformation. There were always a handful, such as the monstrous Mary, who quite refused to attend school classes, but as time passed this number began gradually to increase, almost as if the majority of the blacks had attended only out of curiosity, or boredom, and were now growing tired of this novelty. Even those who continued with their learning would suddenly disappear on some foolish hunting expedition. This made their instruction most difficult, especially in the case of the older ones, whose powers of memory were feebler. How frustrating it was after weeks of practice upon, for instance, the Ten Commandments, to have half a class abruptly vanish, only to return days later, excitably clutching speared wallabies, their commandments all but forgotten.

There was not one among them, if truth be told, who showed a full and enthusiastic devotion to his studies. George Vandiemen himself, the school's finest scholar, who could recite his Psalms so well, would often drift into some troubled distractedness of his own, or petulantly complain that he wished to be taught Arithmetic, though he had been told often enough that it was neither useful nor practical for him to learn. His half brother Cromwell was no better. It was true that he showed a talent for English, surprising some with his mastery of odd and difficult words, yet there was a sullenness about him, so that even when he recited his commandments correctly it was hard to believe he was persuaded of what he said.

Here, indeed, lay the fundamental problem. Though some among the blacks might learn lines of the Scriptures tolerably, they seemed obstinately unable to see the bright light of faith. During Sunday services some would even tie handkerchiefs around their foreheads to hide their eyes, so they might sleep unobserved: this, as the very word of God was being brought to them! It was quite as if they imagined that Christian knowledge had little pertinence to their lives. Sad to say this could hardly have been less true. As time passed, the blacks' numbers were diminishing at a perilous rate. The outbreaks of disease, which had seemed to slow when Mr. Robson first arrived, had grown more frequent than ever, with several deaths sometimes occurring in a single week. The aborigines, who had comprised some two hundred even in the early days, were now reduced to less than half that number, and their huts, whose crowded conditions had caused Mr. Robson great concern when he first arrived, were now all too sadly sufficient. Little by little the settlement began to acquire an aura of sombre emptiness, only the grave-yard remaining busy.

There was, inevitably, much talk as to the reasons for this decline. The settlement surgeon—a man greatly neglectful of his religious devo-tions, so that some doubted his Christian convictions—cited purely prac-tical causes, such as the blacks' lack of exposure to European diseases, and their being restrained in one place when it was in their nature always to be roaming. I, and others too, perceived a greater force at work, however. If the aborigines had only shown greater reverence for the Scriptures I had no doubt that the good Lord would have been moved to protect them from suffering. It might seem unkind, but I could not help but feel that they were reaping the reward for what was, in truth, their own betrayal of Mr. Robson. Had he not risked his own life and health to rescue them from the wilderness? Had he not devoted his every wak-ing hour to their improvement, bringing them new knowledge, and even new names? They had returned his kindness only with indolence and unconcern.

Poor Mr. Robson was much affected by the natives' decline,`natu-rally, and with each new death his sadness became a little more marked. In spite of this he never allowed himself to lose his determination. "If we cannot save them in one way," I recall him confiding in me one terrible day, when two had been taken within only hours of one another, "then we must endeavour to save them in another."

I understood his meaning only too well. It was soon after this, in-deed, that he began his final campaign, which was not so much con-cerned with the education of the natives as with the need to win them away from their pagan customs. A number of announcements were made in quick succession, including a prohibition upon their occasional nighttime revels of singing and dancing, and also upon their hunting expeditions, which were, in truth, often little more than an excuse to evade the scrutiny of the settlement officers. The blacks were also re-quired to discard the superstitious health charms they wore about their necks, which contained, so I heard, bones of their dead relatives, and could hardly have been more barbarously removed from Christian ways.

Sadly these noble intentions proved not easy to put into effect. While Mr. Robson had some success with the charms, the hunting expeditions were undertaken with so little warning that they were nearly impossible to prevent. It seemed for a time that he had made progress with the nighttime revels–several times he sternly marched out into the nearby bush and caused one to cease–but before long ashes of the fire and footmarks were discovered merely further distant, beyond earshot of the settlement. Unchanged and unrepentant, the blacks seemed obstinate in their refusal to be saved. So the life of the settlement continued week after week, month after month, though each was marked with sadness.

Then, one Thursday afternoon, the supply boat arrived, quite as usual, and we found ourselves shaken with news. It had been known for some time that there were plans to establish a new settlement on mainland Australia at Port Phillip Bay, just across the Bass Strait from Flinders Island, and now we learned that Mr. Robson was being considered–and most seriously so–for a position as government protector of the aborigines of this new settlement. If he won the post, as seemed very likely, and he considered it acceptable, which seemed no less so, he would start work there within a few months.

I was most pleased for him, naturally. Having worked so closely with the man, I believe I understood him as well as any. Why, I would even say he was possessed of a kind of greatness. I considered he amply deserved reward for his great toil. The sad truth was, besides, that in many ways his work on Flinders Island was largely complete, his charges being now so greatly reduced in numbers, after all, that their future was unhappily evident. How much more fitting for him to progress to a new land where there was much still to be done. I was saddened, naturally, for those natives who still remained, and who, I knew, would miss him most dreadfully. They had, I supposed, come to rely on his presence, and to presume upon his gentle kindliness. I had no doubt that they would find great difficulty in letting him go. They must, I considered, endeavour to be strong.

As for the Europeans of the settlement, the discovery of Robson's likely departure had, I am afraid to say, a most regrettable effect. The poisonous and malicious atmosphere, that I had thought long banished, soon began to creep back, as I witnessed myself. One late winter's afternoon, only a few days after the supply vessel had come with its news, I was on my way to the school, intending to prepare my lessons for the next day, when I found myself passing the surgeon and the garden overseer as they stood beside the store, sheltering from the chilly wind.

"It's what he wanted, after all," I overheard the surgeon declare. "A fine little career he's won for himself from those blacks."

I stopped. "For a moment, Doctor," I told him in a warning voice, "I almost imagined you must be talking of Mr. Robson, but that would hardly be the way to describe a brave man who risked his very life to rescue the aborigines."

The surgeon assumed a derisive look. "He did well enough from his rescuing, too, as I recall, at five pounds per head."

I could not let pass so wicked an utterance. "That was honourable payment for noble and perilous work," I told him coldly, "and it does you no credit to try and belittle a man whose achievements are so much greater than your own." With that I strode on. The incident continued greatly to upset me, however, and when I reached the school, which was empty, as was often the case in these days of dwindling classes, I sat at one of the desks, preparation work lying unheeded before me, and my eyes filled with tears. Thus I remained for I do not know how long. Finally, greatly to my dismay, I heard the door creak open. The arrival, I knew from the sound of his tread, was Mr. Robson. Though I lowered my head in an effort to hide my distress, I regret to say this was to no avail.

"Mrs. Price. What is distressing you?" he demanded, full of concern.

I could not tell him. How could I when it was he himself and the poisonous remarks concerning him that were the reason? "It's nothing," I insisted, "I'm quite all right." Ever the gentleman, good Mr. Robson offered to get me some water, but for some reason I cannot explain, this caused me only to become more greatly affected. I rose to my feet. "I'm sorry. I must go."

"You still have not told me what is wrong."

I hurried towards the door.

"But, Mrs. Price," Mr. Robson called out behind me, "you do not have your shawl. You cannot go out like that."

I had, in my distress, quite forgotten the garment and yet it seemed somehow too late to turn around. I do believe I hardly cared, such was my upset. Stepping out into the falling dusk, I felt an urgent need to find some quiet place, away from all else, that I might collect my thoughts. I turned towards the sea.

"Mrs. Price," I heard Mr. Robson call out behind me, "your shawl."

I should, I suppose, have stopped, but I simply could not do so. On I strode to the shore, grey waves roaring in the biting wind, until I reached those curious spherical boulders that lie near the jetty, that have red marks upon them, and are so disquieting in their appearance, almost like eyes. Feeling the chill all of a sudden, I found I could go no further. I paused, taking shelter from the breeze beside one of the rocks. Would you believe it, poor, good Mr. Robson had followed me all the way. He hurried to place my shawl about my shoulders.

"Mrs. Price, you risk your health. Whatever is the matter?"

What could I say? "After all the hard work we have done here, all the hopes we have had, I feel . . ." I reached for words. "So very sad."

He regarded me keenly. "You must not despair, Mrs. Price. Our efforts have not been in vain. The situation of the blacks may be wretched indeed, but think how much worse it could be. Imagine them still on Van Diemen's Land, beyond the reach of Christian teaching, harried by wicked men. Even if each and every one of them dies here, at least he will have had a chance to pass to the bosom of the Lord."

His words of reassurance brought, I am afraid, only more tears. "I feel that I have failed."

"You must not permit yourself to think any such a thing. You have triumphed," he declared with a brave smile. "Why, if anyone should feel blame it is me, as commandant."

It was a most unexpected remark. I gave him a searching look. "Do you really think that?"

For a moment his confidence seemed to weaken, and a look of doubt flickered across his face. "It has been hard at times . . ."

My only wish was to comfort this noble, troubled soul. It was this, nothing else, that caused me to place my arms upon his shoulders, and then kiss him gently upon his cheek, just as a sister would to her distressed brother. Nothing more. How cruel men can be. How wickedly can the innocent be made to seem otherwise. All at once I became aware of a faint tapping sound, slow and even, like a woodpecker striking at a tree. Glancing about, I saw that, some distance back along the shore, was Mr. Smith, knocking his pipe against one of the huge boulders as he stared silently out to sea.

Weeks passed. Terrible weeks. There is no disproving scandal generally suspected, however misplaced it may be. Awful were the looks, and of these the very worst were those of Mr. Robson's wife. I had no idea that the human eye could express such malignancy. I did once try to speak to her, and tell her of the terrible misunderstanding that had occurred, but it was to no avail: she simply threw me an icy glance and turned upon her heels. Most distressing of all, I suspected that she and her husband were no longer on speaking terms with one another. It was a terrible burden to think that I might unwittingly have been the cause of such unhappiness. As for Louis, he quite refused to listen to my assurances, treating me with hateful coldness. He demanded, of course, that I cease my teaching at the school forthwith. As if I would ever have thought of continuing.

All the while Mr. Robson was taken with a kind of terrible awkwardness towards me, and wherever possible he attempted to avoid my presence altogether. I could not blame him. Occasionally, when I walked through the settlement I would catch a glimpse of him hurrying away, his noble face sadly troubled. My great fear, of course, was that the unhappy incident might somehow place in jeopardy his chance of taking up the post at Port Phillip Bay. It was a most dreadful thought that he might be denied this opportunity–that he so richly deserved–and would be forced instead to remain with us on Flinders Island.

A month passed, and all the while we were expecting Mr. Robson to be summoned to Hobart to discuss the new position. When the supply vessel finally arrived, however, it brought quite different news. Thus it was that we learned we were to receive a visit by the governor of Van Diemen's Land.

Peevay
1838

IT WAS BAD to watch Fat Robson climb out of his boat that day when he came to Flinders Island, so smiling and adoring himself, but a worse thing was seeing who he brought with him. Tayaleah. I thought my nearly brother was vanished forever, and great good riddance, and suddenly here he was once again. Worse, he was speaking num talk quick like some white man–much better than me–so Fat Robson and others smiled with surprise and gave him cherishings for his cleverness. That was some provocation, as it seemed the little shit was always intending to be better than me, like it was his secret design. So it was pleasing when he ran to Mother and got her grievous blow. Yes, I pondered, how do you like that?

By and by he became Robson's best blackfellow, and if there was any new thing to do, he was doing it. He did CRAFTS and he was FARMER. Then he did GIVING THINGS FOR COINS, whose name was MARKET, and got a hat called STRAW. When MARKET finished–which it did very soon–he did NEWSPAPER, whose name was FLINDERS ISLAND JOURNAL, and which stopped quicker even than MARKET. Mostly, though, he was TEACHER. I supposed he must be pleased at this fine greatness but he never looked so, and mostly he was just sad, like he was some great puzzle to confuse. One moment he was hungry for Fat Robson's cherishings, like these were everything he wanted in the world, but then he got fretful and would try to go back to Mother once again, though all she gave him was more hatings. So then he would be craving at Robson once more, and became like the sea, going up and down, up and down, never stopping anywhere.

Fat Robson was always shouting and walking hither and thither to get new things. There was new STORE, and new house for god who was called god, whose name was CHAPEL, that was made from BRICKS. Later we got new huts that were made from bricks too, and were small and dark with our ones all crowded within and coughing in the night. Also there were new school lessons for knowing about GOD, plenty of them. Mostly, though, everything was just the same, as us

Palawa died just like we did before. Those were heinous times, I do recollect, as we got smaller, like days after summer, till even those who said Robson was our friend started pondering that he never could save us like he promised. Robson said yes, he was our friend, and he looked sad when we died, but he would not let us burn dead ones, which was the correct way, as he said burying was what GOD liked best. That made me hate him more.

By and by our thinking was all sickness and dying. Sometimes it was hard to stay hoping, and not to surmise that we would all be dead soon so nothing mattered anymore. I even grew fearful that I might forget to try and endure, which always was my special skill. When this happened I would just think of my own intent, and I would say it in my head, like one of Robson's prayers that he made us know.

> LEARN WHITE MEN'S SHIT
> GET OFF THIS PLACE
> FIGHT THEM AND FIGHT THEM
> FOR EVER AND EVER

How we would fight them I didn't know, and I hardly troubled either, as just getting away was enough for this time. I was already trying, yes, writing letters to GOVERNOR, who was the chief white scut, in his place, which was called HOBART. I needed help to make these correct and so I went to the only num I ever liked on Flinders Island, whose name was SURGEON JONES, who was kindly and never tried to make us do anything. He told me about writing YOUR EXCELLENCY and helped with spellings, and so I wrote one letter every time there was a boat. Nothing happened, no, but still I did persist, ever and again. Then, finally, one morning the boat came like usual, and though there was no letter for me as usual, Surgeon Jones came hurrying to my hut to say that GOVERNOR, who was a new one, was coming to Flinders Island to visit us. That was interesting, and great good fortune, I did surmise, as I could talk to him, and tell him how he must let us go back to the world, while he must listen to me if I was stood there before him.

Days passed and white men were all hurrying hither and thither to make everything clean for governor, and making tables, plenty of them, for us all to eat governor's dinner. Then one morning I was sitting by the

shore, near big stones like eyeballs, when a surprise happened. This was a favourite place, as I could look at the jetty and dream us all getting on a ship to go home to the world, and so I stayed there, watching birds sitting in the sky, and waves come following, following onto the sand, and as I watched I saw a small boat sailing, one white man inside. By and by he came to the jetty, tied up his boat and walked right past me, going towards the settlement. He was some ugly one, I did observe, smelling of salt and mutton bird and white man's stink, with big scar down one cheek, and no hair, so his head was like some pink stone. Still he seemed no great puzzle to confound, as strange ones like him did arrive sometimes, to get flour and tea and so from the store.

Surely enough, by and by I saw him coming back, carrying two sacks that were heavy so they pulled his arms long. Then, just when he was getting near, a most interesting thing happened. First I heard running, and I knew it was angry running just from the feet. Looking round, I saw Mother, coming fast and holding a waddy stick, and her face was hateful like I hardly saw before, even in her long-before fighting days. White man saw also, and he gave her a strangest look, so mystified, then dropped those sacks very quick. This was clever, yes, as when Mother swung her stick to dash his head with a grievous blow he could cringe, and so she did miss her killing. Next he got that waddy stick too, and so both were holding it and fighting. White scut was stronger, pushing her down so he got her stick, which was worrisome, so I jumped up now to try and save her. But rather than hit her dead, like I surmised, instead he threw that waddy away, then took his sacks and ran away, fast as he could, getting into his boat and pulling at oars to be gone.

Mother was too old for fighting really. She sat there looking angry and rubbing her side where it hurt from falling. "Who was that?" I asked. But she just got up, never saying a word, and walked away.

That was some puzzle to confound, yes, as it was years since she tried to kill anybody, though the answer came soon enough. Later, when I walked back to the settlement, my friend Mongana, who was sitting by the huts, looked up and gave me a hating stare, just like he did in those long-ago small days when he was my childhood foe.

"What's wrong?" I asked.

His answer was angry like spitting. "My mother said she saw your father, walking by the store." Then he looked shamed, as if he did not know what to say. "He shouldn't come here."

So, here, on some usual morning just like any other, I saw Father, who I never beheld before. It seemed strange that I never even guessed him, but just thought THERE'S ANOTHER UGLY WHITE SCUT. But then how could I guess him? When I dreamed meeting him, which I still did sometimes, I made him a fine fellow with a kindly face and hair, rather than some piss-poor one smelling of salt and mutton bird and white man's stink. Still it was interesting, as it meant I had one still. Perhaps I would meet him again, I did ponder, if he came back. Now I wasn't sure if I wanted this or not.

A second strange thing came later on that same day, when I went to school. Today was Smith, and GENESIS again. IN THE BEGINNING GOD CREATED THE HEAVEN AND THE EARTH and so and so and so. I learned it well, you see. But when I went into the classroom Smith was not ready but was just sitting, waiting, and there was Fat Robson, looking troubled.

"Thank goodness you're here, Cromwell. Have you seen George? He should have two lessons here this morning but never came. That is some mystery, as he never misses any. I've looked for him everywhere, but nobody saw him."

George was Fat Robson's name for Tayaleah and yes, it was interesting that he was not here. This was not just some puzzle to confuse, no, this was some impossible thing, as Tayaleah always went to school. When others went away hunting, and even when he got crook, still he would go.

"I haven't seen him," I told.

That made Fat Robson too woeful. I knew why, too. Num chief, whose name was GOVERNOR, was coming so soon, and I surmised Fat Robson wanted to show him Tayaleah's cleverness, to try and get this fellow's adorings. Well, I never wanted to be kind to Fat Robson, as he was my hated enemy, but I was curious to know the answer, especially as it was the second very strange thing this day. Now in my thinking two strange things both at the same time are usually just one strange thing, like two ends of some stick buried in sand.

"I can look for him."

"Thank you, Cromwell." Fat Robson gave me his look. This was smiling and creeping because he needed my help, but it was a little angry too. Then, you see, Robson always gave me a bit of hating, because I showed him with my face that I never forgot he betrayed us so. I supposed he could not endure my thinking that he was not a fine fellow after all, but just some lying, cheating, heinous scut, which he was.

So I went seeking. I never much liked Tayaleah but I did know him and I knew places where he went. Sometimes, when Mother gave him scornings, I saw him creep off towards a hill near the settlement, and so thither I went now. Earth was soft there and good for footprints, and soon I could observe some that were small and thin just like Tayaleah's weakly feet. After that I went carefully, using hunting cleverness to follow on and again, till finally footsteps went into a forest and stopped by a large tree. Up above, through leaves, I could hear some faint sound like sobbing, and so I started climbing. Tayaleah was high where the tree was thinner, and it moved a little in the wind when I reached him.

"What d'you want?" he shouted, angry that I found his secret place.

But it was interesting here. Tree split three ways so it made a seat for him, while he had branches and leaves and such laid all around, so they were a kind of ground, and I surmised he could even sleep here if he was careful. He had pieces of bread, a bottle with water and a cup, a little broken, for keeping sugar. Also there was his man on a horse made from metal whose name was TOY SOLDIER, that I saw before, and which he got from white men's land. I saw he carved num numbers into tree bark, and though some were just small, like eight or twelve, others were too big to read, so they went halfway round the tree.

"Why aren't you at school?" I told him back. "Robson's angry with you."

"Just go away."

His words were fighting but his voice was getting weak, like some old dry stick, and I could see in his eyes that he wanted me to like him. Then again Tayaleah was always so. Ever since I could first recollect, the little scut wanted me to be his friend, which was a mystery to confound, as I never gave him anything but hating. "What's wrong?" I made my voice kindlier, though this was just pretending. "You can tell me, Tayaleah."

That was enough, yes. He just broke, looking at me with pleading like I was his best friend. "I don't know what to do. Mother came just this morning and said she saw your father. She said we must kill him and all the other white men too, and that we must do it now, as soon we'll all be dead and then it'll be too late. She said I must help her, and that this is a last chance to win her forgivings."

So this was the stick hidden in the sand. I suppose it had been some guess in my head, yes, as I surmised she would delight in killing Father. "How does she want to kill them?"

Tayaleah looked away. "She said I must not say it to anyone."

"You can tell me. I'm your brother."

Really he was too easy. He rubbed his face with his fingers, making his eyes hidden. "She said we must spear them when governor visits, at the end of the dinner, when they're all fat and tired. After, we must take the governor's boat and go to your father's island and kill him too. Then she said we can go back to the world. She says if I want to be her son again I must spear Mr. Robson." He sniffed. "But he's my friend."

That was Mother's joke. Mostly, though, this was just some grievous puzzle to confound. Yes, it would be tidings of joy to see Fat Robson get speared, which was his deserving. But this was the first time in so many years when I had hope that I could save us. "Who else is there?"

"Pagerly and three others were with her, and they were trying to get more. Then they were going away to make spears."

It was too few. Even with more I guessed something must go wrong. Probably we would get noticed even before they started killing, and then soldiers would shoot us. Even if we had great good fortune and got that boat we still didn't know how to make it move with those skins for the wind, and probably we would just drown. In truth I doubted Mother cared much if we lived. All she wanted was some chance of spearing Father and other white scuts. One thing was sure. If we tried to spear whites, all my learning and writing letters would become just some fool-ishness, and we never would leave this terrible place. No, I did divine, only I could save us and get us back alive. It was some heinous thing to try and fight Mother's intent, and to thwart her once again, but so I did resolve.

I began to climb down Tayaleah's tree.

"Wait," he called out after me. "What should I do?"

"Do nothing."

William Frampton, Governor of Van Diemen's Land
1838

IT WAS my wife's idea that I should embark on a little tour of Van Diemen's Land, so I might gain a greater understanding of this, my new fiefdom. Her thought had been to visit Port Arthur, the larger towns and settlements and perhaps a farm or two, so I might attempt to establish a useful rapport with some of the island's inhabitants, but I was curious to learn of all aspects of the colony, and it was this that led me to include upon our itinerary the aboriginal establishment on Flinders Island. I had heard a little about the unfortunate history of the natives even before I left English shores, while my interest had grown when I finally reached Hobart and chanced upon the reports sent by the settlement's commandant, Mr. Robson. This officer had been achieving nothing short of wonders in that remote place, as he valiantly struggled to reform the blacks and bring them into a state of civilization. My predecessor had, I noted, suggested Mr. Robson should be considered for a post of aboriginal protector at the proposed new settlement at Port Phillip Bay, and while I had no doubt he would prove more than suitable for the position, it seemed sad indeed that he should have to abandon such promising work. I was greatly looking forward to meeting the man.

The tour began splendidly. We found ourselves blessed with delightful weather, warm and sunny–being, as I was regularly assured, quite unusual for a Van Diemen's Land spring–and as we journeyed northwards across the green countryside of the island, through Oatlands, Ross, Campbell town and Launceston, we received an enthusiastic welcome. All the while I was, with a few exceptions, well satisfied with the cleanliness and good order of the offices and barracks we visited, and the homes and lodging houses where we passed our nights. At George Town we boarded a schooner and set sail across the Bass Strait. The wind was light, so our progress was slow, but when we woke the next morning Flinders Island was there before us. This was largely flat, but supported a few sudden clusters of rocky hills, including one peak that was steep and sharp almost as an obelisk. Within the hour we were being rowed towards the shore.

As to my first impressions of the aboriginal settlement, these were, I must confess, something of a disappointment. In his reports Mr. Robson had given detailed accounts of the many traditional crafts he had had the natives adopt, and it had seemed only natural to assume the aborigines would be clothed in accordance with their new skills. I had, as I recall, been looking forward to finding myself in some form of rustic scene, as might—except for the blackness of the faces—be found in some English village, with ploughmen in their smocks, a blacksmith in his trusty apron and wives in cheery cotton dresses. This, I am sad to report, could hardly have been further from the case. As my wife and I stepped onto the jetty, I observed the blacks gathered upon the shore were dressed in the most dismal of garments, that would not have been worn even by the poorest of the colony's white settlers. Looking upon these unfortunates, indeed—the posture of some of the women being barely respectable—I found myself little surprised that their race had suffered so disastrous a decline.

As to Mr. Robson, he seemed a most decent sort of fellow, who greeted us with warmth. He was a touch nervous as he introduced us to the various officers and their wives—being, as I supposed, quite out of practice with social niceties in this remote land—but became filled with cheerful enthusiasm as he led us forth to begin our tour of the establishment. Hardly were we out of sight of the jetty when he was approached by one of the establishment's soldiers.

"We've searched everywhere, sir, but I'm afraid there's not a sign of either of them."

Our host seemed troubled by this mysterious news. "Then look again."

I could not help but be curious. "Who have we mislaid?"

"Merely a couple of the aborigines, Your Excellency. They can be so naughty. I'm sure they'll be discovered in no time."

I was pleased to observe that the settlement was tidily kept, even if its inhabitants were not. Our visit began with the bakery hut, from which there issued forth an enchanting scent of flour and fresh bread, and walking inside I was happy to note the floor was swept and the baking implements well polished.

"How often do you bake?" inquired my wife.

"Once a week," answered the baker, a fellow with a foolish-looking grin, whose name was Dunn. "Sometimes twice."

"Surely the bread becomes stale?"

Mr. Dunn shrugged a little uneasily. "It keeps well enough, ma'am."

The exchange was typical of my wife, who, I should explain, possesses a quite remarkable talent for chancing upon telling truths. Let her glance upon some stranger for only a moment and she will confidently declare whether he is a good fellow who can be trusted or a cheating rogue, while she seems so often right that I have almost been moved to wonder if she has a sorceress or two among her ancestors. There are times when I find it useful to take note of her opinions, I will freely admit, though I should add that I know also when to treat her with firmness and trust to my own opinion.

After we had examined the bakery we were led to an empty, grass-covered area at the centre of the establishment, that was faced on one side by the chapel, and on the other by a long row of cottages built in the shape of the letter L, which, Mr. Robson explained, were the dwellings of the aborigines. The buildings were neat enough in appearance but the blacks, some of whom stood loitering before their homes, seemed dismal indeed, regarding us with a sullen curiosity. Again I found myself disappointed. Where was their resolution, their wish to improve their lives?

"This is the Natives' Square," Mr. Robson explained. "It has been my hope that one day it may be paved, in the manner of an Italian piazza."

It seemed a delightful notion.

"How charming," observed my wife. "Am I right in assuming this is where the market is held?"

Robson nodded brightly.

"But not today?"

I observed that the commandant looked a touch uneasy. "As it happens, the market is in abeyance just at the moment, but I hope to have it restored very shortly."

"I see." Once again she had struck, and once again it was a complete mystery to me what could have led her to her supposition. I could only consider that, while others, including my own self, marched stolidly forward upon the solid path of logic, she would be carried along upon the swift–if unreliable–flight of womanly instinct.

Mr. Robson led us now into one of the cottages: a tidy enough dwelling, except for a troubling smell of old clothes. It was most noticeable, however, for its sparseness, being divided by no walls, so it formed a single windowless room, which contained nothing except for a few rough-looking blankets folded in the corner. "The natives prefer to sleep on the ground," he explained. "It is their tradition."

"You still have not introduced us to any of them," remarked my wife as we stood glancing about the darkened space.

"That is most easily resolved," Mr. Robson told her with a cheerful smile. "Simply tell me who you wish to meet and it shall be arranged."

My wife considered for a moment. "Then I for one would most like to meet the editor of the *Flinders Island Journal.*"

"Oh yes, your paper," I agreed, pleased that she had thought to remember. On my return from my Arctic journey I once visited a London newspaper and it had been a most exciting sight, with reporters and typesetters hurtling about at the greatest speed, and the printing presses in the cellar beginning their mighty clatter. This would, I supposed, be a much smaller affair, and yet I remained more than a little curious. "I would most like to have a look."

Mr. Robson again frowned. "It's a difficult moment, I'm afraid."

My wife gave him a curious look. "Also in abeyance?"

Do you know, she was right again. Mr. Robson seemed most put out. I even felt a little sorry for the poor fellow. There are moments when even I have myself felt the sharpness of my wife's tongue, while our guide had, after all, been doing his best to be kindly and helpful.

"Perhaps you would be interested in having a look at our school?" Mr. Robson now suggested. "It is just nearby. I have been much encouraged by the progress we have made regarding the natives' Christian learning."

I agreed, naturally, and soon our little party was making its way into a good-sized classroom, doing so quietly, as a lesson was already in progress. This was being taught by an uncertain-looking young man who, Mr. Robson explained in a whisper, was his own son. His students were aboriginal children of varying ages, and a most quaint sight they would have made, sat at their rows of desks with their little black faces, if only they had paid more attention to their appearance. Few if any seemed to have taken proper care of their clothes, while one in the rearmost row was coughing and spluttering in a most unseemly manner.

"Ophelia," the younger Robson called out, regarding a little girl with a sad expression on her face. "What is the First Commandment?"

She began promisingly enough. "Thou shalt have no other gods before me."

"And the Second?"

Here her concentration began to waver. To be fair, I suppose the presence of so many strangers must have proved a great distraction. The younger Mr. Robson made two further attempts to coax the answer from her but without success, and then his father, who had been displaying signs of impatience, stepped up to his side.

"Dear boy, would you mind very much if I took charge of the class, just for a moment?"

His son looked little pleased, but accepted obediently enough, and so his father took his place, regarding the children with a robust smile. "Cato," he called out in a voice full of authority. "What did God make us for?"

It seemed the boy was amply familiar with the question, as, with a sternness befitting his name, he answered without a moment's hesitation. "His own purpose."

Mr. Robson nodded. "Quite so. And what do you love God for?"

"God gives me everything."

"Very good. What sort of place is hell?"

"Burning for ever and ever."

Just when the lesson was proceeding smoothly a very small child piped up from the back, though he had been asked no question: "Does God eat kangaroo?"

For a moment Mr. Robson seemed a little taken aback by this curious enquiry, but he soon recovered himself, uttering a little laugh. "You must understand, Napoleon, that God is not as we are. God is everywhere all of the time. He is watching us every moment."

Napoleon showed a persistence worthy of his name. "Does he eat nighi?"

Before I could enquire what this mysterious substance might be, the sad-looking girl, Ophelia, turned to the questioning Napoleon. "God never eats nighi. God is a white man."

"He's not," called out another little fellow. "God is a ghost."

Mr. Robson evidently felt it was time to call a halt to this little theological discussion, however diverting it might be. He clapped his hands together, shouting out in a cheerful voice, "Quiet! Quiet! Now let us begin again." Then he turned to the stern fellow who had proved so able before. "Cato, who made the earth."

Quick as a flash the little fellow rattled off his answer. "God did."

"Very good." He turned next to Ophelia. "Who made the sky?"

"God did."

"Omega, who made the trees?"

"God did."

Now Mr. Robson was striding about among the pupils themselves, catching their eyes as he went. There was no denying he was a most impressive teacher. "Napoleon, who made the potatoes in the fields?"

"God did."

"Leander, who made the sun?"

"God did."

"Betsy, who made you?"

"God did."

Now he came to a youth in the back row with a somewhat disagreeable expression. "Voltaire, who made me?"

"The devil."

It was a most unhappy moment. Some of Voltaire's older classmates even laughed, and Mr. Robson tried to do so, though he looked quite wounded. It was impossible to know, of course, if the youth had deliberately chosen his answer with the purpose of causing offence—his classmates had, after all, produced some most unlikely statements—and yet, in view of the pattern of repetitive response that Mr. Robson had so cleverly contrived, the correct reply had seemed only too obvious. Whatever the case, the remark had a discouraging effect upon the lesson. Mr. Robson did his best to resume his instruction, cheerfully testing his little observed a number of them consumed only a portion of their meal before rising from their places and quietly slipping away.

My wife remarked on this curiosity. "D'you think something has displeased them?"

Mr. Robson seemed as surprised by their departure as was she. "Milton? Leonidas?" he called out in a cheery voice. "Where are you going?"

They appeared not to have heard, and continued to stride away towards the trees. "The call of nature, most probably," Mr. Robson observed, laughing heartily at this simplest of explanations. "I'm sure that they'll be back shortly."

They were not, as it proved. As the light faded and candles were brought–giving the scene a most charming atmosphere–the number of empty places around the horseshoe seemed rather to increase. Mr. Robson, however, seemed more concerned with other matters. Several times I saw him glance towards the paths that led into the square, and finally he rose to his feet.

"I hope you'll excuse me, but I see my son has returned. He's been helping the soldiers look for the two I told you of."

By then our plates had been collected and before us lay bowls of an ominously stolid-looking pudding that gave off a faint odour of flour and molasses. It was just as I was about to try this dish when I felt a faint pressure upon my shoulder, as someone made their way behind me. This seemed hardly surprising–convict waiters and others had been pushing back and forth throughout the evening–but what was unusual was the folded piece of paper that I now saw had appeared on my lap. I glanced round, but whoever was responsible had already vanished into the dark. Curious, I held the note close to a candle to read.

Your Excellency,
I am most sorry to intrude upon you in this way, but there is something that you must, imperatively, be told, for your own good. I shall be waiting behind the native huts.

More than a little curious, I passed the document to my wife. She was most definite. "You must go."

charges upon their knowledge of the Lord's Prayer, but he was never able to recapture his earlier fluency.

"It is a great shame, Your Excellency," he confided when the class finally ended, "that our two ablest pupils should be absent. You would, I may assure you, be quite astonished by the skills of these young men."

"These are the two that have vanished?" enquired my wife. "Where can they have got to? I wonder."

"Away playing, I imagine. I'm confident they will be discovered in time for our little banquet."

I had been greatly looking forward to this event, which sounded as if it would prove most diverting. Mr. Robson told us how something similar had been held three years before, to celebrate his own arrival as commandant, and he recounted how the blacks had displayed a most delightful exuberance throughout: a prospect that was all the more welcome as, until now, they had seemed such a sombre race. It was to be held outside, in the Natives' Square, which, by the time our tour was finally completed, was already filled with simple tables. These were arranged in the shape of a long, narrow horseshoe, and had been decorated with jugs of spring flowers, giving a delightful pleasance to the scene. The sun was now low in the sky, and as the aborigines appeared, one or two carrying hoes or other farming implements, they were caught in striking silhouette against the reddening sky, making me think, after all, of some rural English scene. As we took our places, my spirits, which had been subdued, began to revive. All those of seniority, including myself and my wife and the Robsons, took our places at the upper end of the table, with the two strands of the horseshoe trailing away before us, and I could not help but remark to my wife how this resembled the arrangement of High Table at an Oxford college.

"Let us hope," she replied, in typical fashion, "that the food also compares."

Sadly this proved hardly the case. The surly convict labourers who were acting as our waiters distributed dishes of a kind of stew, and while every effort had been made to give this a pleasing appearance, with little sprigs of parsley resting to one side, it was evident that the main ingredients were overripe potatoes and very hardy mutton. Even the blacks seemed little pleased with their fare and, somewhat to my surprise, I

Napoleon showed a persistence worthy of his name. "Does he eat nighi?"

Before I could enquire what this mysterious substance might be, the sad-looking girl, Ophelia, turned to the questioning Napoleon. "God never eats nighi. God is a white man."

"He's not," called out another little fellow. "God is a ghost."

Mr. Robson evidently felt it was time to call a halt to this little theological discussion, however diverting it might be. He clapped his hands together, shouting out in a cheerful voice, "Quiet! Quiet! Now let us begin again." Then he turned to the stern fellow who had proved so able before. "Cato, who made the earth."

Quick as a flash the little fellow rattled off his answer. "God did."

"Very good." He turned next to Ophelia. "Who made the sky?"

"God did."

"Omega, who made the trees?"

"God did."

Now Mr. Robson was striding about among the pupils themselves, catching their eyes as he went. There was no denying he was a most impressive teacher. "Napoleon, who made the potatoes in the fields?"

"God did."

"Leander, who made the sun?"

"God did."

"Betsy, who made you?"

"God did."

Now he came to a youth in the back row with a somewhat disagreeable expression. "Voltaire, who made me?"

"The devil."

It was a most unhappy moment. Some of Voltaire's older classmates even laughed, and Mr. Robson tried to do so, though he looked quite wounded. It was impossible to know, of course, if the youth had deliberately chosen his answer with the purpose of causing offence–his classmates had, after all, produced some most unlikely statements–and yet, in view of the pattern of repetitive response that Mr. Robson had so cleverly contrived, the correct reply had seemed only too obvious. Whatever the case, the remark had a discouraging effect upon the lesson. Mr. Robson did his best to resume his instruction, cheerfully testing his little who, Mr. Robson explained in a whisper, was his own son. His students were aboriginal children of varying ages, and a most quaint sight they would have made, sat at their rows of desks with their little black faces, if only they had paid more attention to their appearance. Few if any seemed to have taken proper care of their clothes, while one in the rearmost row was coughing and spluttering in a most unseemly manner.

"Ophelia," the younger Robson called out, regarding a little girl with a sad expression on her face. "What is the First Commandment?"

She began promisingly enough. "Thou shalt have no other gods before me."

"And the Second?"

Here her concentration began to waver. To be fair, I suppose the presence of so many strangers must have proved a great distraction. The younger Mr. Robson made two further attempts to coax the answer from her but without success, and then his father, who had been displaying signs of impatience, stepped up to his side.

"Dear boy, would you mind very much if I took charge of the class, just for a moment?"

His son looked little pleased, but accepted obediently enough, and so his father took his place, regarding the children with a robust smile. "Cato," he called out in a voice full of authority. "What did God make us for?"

It seemed the boy was amply familiar with the question, as, with a sternness befitting his name, he answered without a moment's hesitation. "His own purpose."

Mr. Robson nodded. "Quite so. And what do you love God for?"

"God gives me everything."

"Very good. What sort of place is hell?"

"Burning for ever and ever."

Just when the lesson was proceeding smoothly a very small child piped up from the back, though he had been asked no question: "Does God eat kangaroo?"

For a moment Mr. Robson seemed a little taken aback by this curious enquiry, but he soon recovered himself, uttering a little laugh. "You must understand, Napoleon, that God is not as we are. God is everywhere all of the time. He is watching us every moment."

"D'you think so? I would not want to be a party to some sort of rumourmongering."

My wife smiled. She has, in truth, something of a weakness for intrigue. "It is your duty to be informed about all aspects of the colony, is it not?"

This was true enough, I supposed. It could be easily enough done, besides, and so, making my excuses, I rose from my place and, a candle to light my way, I ventured forth in the direction of the Robsons' house, as if I were intending to visit the privy. The ground behind the natives' huts was much overgrown, and from the direction of a tangle of branches and shadows I heard a rustling, then a whisper.

"Your Excellency, thank you so much for coming. I should not have troubled you, I know."

As I stepped closer, my candle illuminated the face of one of those Mr. Robson had introduced us to that morning: a good-looking woman in her way, with dark hair and a troubled expression. I believe she was the wife of the settlement storekeeper, though the man's name, and likeness, had quite escaped my memory. I had never imagined the mysterious informant would be female and I found myself somewhat taken aback, my concern being far from diminished when, almost at once, she broke into crying. I quite regretted having followed my wife's advice, indeed having no wish to become embroiled in some scene of hysteria.

"I'm very sorry, Your Excellency," she exclaimed, attempting to control herself. "I did not mean to grow upset in this way. I wanted only to speak to you about Mr. Robson. You see, there is something you simply must know about him. He is a good man in so many ways, certainly, and yet it would be most unwise of you to permit him to take up his new post at Port Phillip."

"Whyever not?"

"He has . . ." Words deserted her for a moment. "He has been unfaithful to his wife. He has done so, what is more, with the wife of one of the settlement officers. I cannot tell you who this is, but you must believe me, it is so."

It was a most serious allegation. I hardly knew what to say. "You have proof of this?"

"Proof enough to have no doubts." She gave me a pleading look. "You will not send him to Port Phillip?"

"I will consider the matter most carefully."

My reply seemed enough for the woman, and, without another word, she slipped away into the darkness.

Mr. Robson had seemed a forthright and well-presented individual, and seemed a most unlikely candidate as a philanderer. Was it not possible, I wondered, that the whole matter was merely some form of misunderstanding? The storekeeper's wife had, after all, declined to tell me the identity of the mysterious woman whom he had supposedly scandalized. Whatever the case, it was a most awkward matter, and one on which I was more than curious to learn my wife's opinion. In the event, this proved, for the moment, impossible to obtain. As I returned to the table, I found Mr. Robson waiting for me.

"Fortune has smiled upon us, Your Excellency. I am glad to report that my son has found one of our errant pupils. May I introduce you to Mr. Cromwell."

There before the table, illuminated by one of the lamps, stood a curious-looking young man. He was a half-caste, and while his face was as dark as those of his fellows, his hair was palest blond. Despite the commandant's introduction he seemed hardly very prepossessing, and I observed his shirt was dirty and torn, and was quite blackened along one sleeve, quite as if he had strayed too near a fire.

Mr. Robson gave him a cheerfully chiding look. "Now that you have finally deigned to join us, Cromwell, I hope you will oblige the governor by telling him your Lord's Prayer."

On some previous occasion I had chanced upon an illustrated piece in a scientific book which described what were termed "adulterers' ears," and if I allowed myself to be distracted from the young man's utterances this was only because I was engaged in trying to recall the salient features of these, and to determine whether these were possessed by Mr. Robson. I had cast several careful glances towards the fellow, only to find myself no more decided than before, when I realized that Cromwell was not repeating the Lord's Prayer, as he had been instructed, but instead was addressing my own self.

"We need your help, Governor, I do request you." His delivery was slow and careful, leading me to suspect he had prepared his words in advance, quite in the manner of a formal speech. "We are dying here and if you will not save us from this woeful ruination we will soon all be gone."

For an instant I wondered if the incident had been deliberately contrived, but Mr. Robson seemed no less surprised than I. "This is hardly the moment for such things, Cromwell," he interrupted. "The governor is waiting to hear your Lord's Prayer."

It was as if the half-caste had not heard. "I request you let us go back to Van Diemen's Land, as it is the only way to save us from this dying." He regarded me expectantly. "Please, Governor, will you do so?"

I hardly knew what to say. It was most awkward, and I could not help but feel annoyed with Robson for permitting such a thing to occur. "You must know that everything is being done to help you," I assured him in a kindly voice. "Mr. Robson has been doing all in his power to preserve your people."

Now he stepped up to the table, fixing us with a stare. "You must let us go back," he demanded, in a tone of voice that seemed almost threatening. "If you leave us here you will be killing us."

I confess that I found myself wondering if we were safe, or if he might suddenly pick up some piece of cutlery and launch himself upon us in violent attack. At that instant I believe I began to understand the fears that had been voiced to me many times during our journey across Van Diemen's Land, and remained from those terrible years that were termed the Black War, when fellows such as this Cromwell, whether provoked or not, had devoted themselves to cruelest violence. I even cast a glance to Mr. Robson, wondering if I should require him to call soldiers.

Fortunately this proved unnecessary, the alarm being only short-lived. Help came to us, indeed, from a wholly unexpected source. All of a sudden a heavily built aboriginal woman marched briskly along the centre of the horseshoe of tables. Where she had been hiding herself I could not have said, as I had no recollection of having seen her until then, but she showed the keenest awareness of our predicament. Striding up to the young man Cromwell, another fearsome black matron close behind her, she took him by his shoulder and seemed to quite spin him about, delivering such a mighty slap to his face that he was knocked down. This done, she turned to all of us as we sat watching in wonder, and threw us a most curious look, almost defiant, as if to say, "There, it is finished with!" and in a moment she and her black shadow were gone.

"You may leave us now," Mr. Robson told Cromwell in a warning voice.

The young man regarded us for a moment, but his troublemaking seemed quite beaten from him. He shook his head unhappily and marched away.

"Who was that woman?" I asked.

"The boy's mother."

"An admirably firm parent she seemed."

Mr. Robson laughed a little uneasily. "Quite so, Your Excellency."

My wife was concerned with other matters. "D'you think something has caught fire?" she wondered. "I'm sure I can smell smoke."

She was, as ever, quite correct. We were informed soon afterwards that a bush fire had broken out somewhere to the north of the settlement, though what its cause might have been remained a mystery, as it was in an area that was rarely frequented. It was this, as it happened, that served to bring my official duties on the settlement to a close. Though the fire was still some distance away, Mr. Robson was concerned for the settlement's safety, and the service in the chapel had to be abandoned. I myself joined the party sent to inspect the blaze, and found it a most impressive sight: the flames burned so brightly as to quite dispel the darkness, filling the night air with floating cinders, while some of the trees seemed quite to explode as they ignited. Fortunately the wind swung round to southwards before long, removing all immediate threat, and by morning I was pleased to see that the fire had largely extinguished itself.

It was only as the schooner began its journey back to Launceston, and my wife and myself rested in the privacy of our cabin, that I finally had a chance to tell her of the curious claim made by the storekeeper's wife with regard to Mr. Robson. Rather to my surprise she considered the accusation was likely to be well founded. "Whyever not?" she said simply.

"But that's dreadful," I exclaimed. "I can hardly ignore such a thing. A man of such character cannot possibly be permitted to take up an important post in the new settlement."

She gave me a most curious smile. "Can he not? I would say it is the very thing for him."

It was not the first time I had found myself quite mystified by her words. "What on earth do you mean, my dear?"

"If Mr. Robson is at Port Phillip, then his actions shall no longer be any responsibility of the governor of Van Diemen's Land."

Peevay
1838–47

THAT DAY after governor went away, soldiers found Tayaleah on the ground beneath his tree, broken by falling. Fat scut Robson was woeful about this, though he was lying again, even now. When he saw Tayaleah's secret place in the branches he said he fell just from mischance, but I knew it never was so. I knew he jumped wilfully. Ever since he came to Flinders Island on Robson's boat I saw Tayaleah was like some fellow who is snared between his awake and his dreamings, and is pulled by both, stronger and stronger, never knowing what is true, till he is torn like paper. Tear got too big, so he jumped.

I never did think I would be woeful at Tayaleah dying but yes, it was so. I suppose now he was finished I could not feel hateful, and so he was just my brother and my only one. Besides, perhaps I got accustomed to the little shit by and by. Mother was transported with lamentation, of course, forgetting she did hate him lately. Probably she would detest me anyway, because of fire that burned all her killing spears–which she guessed I made–but Tayaleah's getting dead made her even worse. So it was that from that day she never would speak to me at all, even for hating, and if I came near she got up and walked away, cold like winter wind. Worse, she and Pagerly made others hate me too, telling them I'd spoiled their last chance for going away from this dying place. Even my fine friend Mongana forsook me then, which was bad, I do recall, as I was too alone. So I stayed in a hut that was empty, just spending my time, watching light peer through holes in the roof, or rain drip, tap tap tap, and hearing my own thinkings in my head, too loud.

Soon after then Fat Robson went away to his fine new place, that was called PORT PHILLIP, and though he talked at us of his sad and tender feelings deep inside his breast at leaving us behind, I did observe that his walk was happy, so I knew this was just more hateful, heinous, piss-poor lying. One good thing of his going was Palawa who liked him before could see now that he was just some low, cheating provocation, like I always told. Still it made no difference, as Mother told everyone I was white men's friend.

Days passed too slowly after that, so it was almost like when you've got some heinous pain and moments won't move but sit still like some big stone. Those weeks and months were worst, and it seemed as if they never would stop, so they are woeful to recollect, even now. I still wrote letters to governor in Hobart by and by, for every boat, but I only got one back, and that was short, just saying my desire was not possible, with no reason why. That was some hardship to endure, yes, as I did hope governor heard my words to him that night, so I could be a fine hero after all.

Summer came and was gone, then another. Huts got older and emptier, and it seemed this island was all I ever did know, as walking hither and thither in the world with Mother's tribe was so long ago that it felt as if it never happened to me but to some other fellow. By and by Mongana and Pagerly and others got tired of hating me, which was pleasing, and I could sleep in their hut once more. Mother never forgot, though, and if I went near her she would give me cold-wind looks and turn away, which was heinous. By then I stopped growing taller, as there was no child left in me anymore. I was strong, too, so I would be a good warrior in any spearing war except that they were all finished now. Being grown seemed just some foolishness here, yes, as there was nothing to do with it except sit and wait and push time to go on a little further, or ponder how long I would endure before I got sick like others. Deaths went on, you see, and though these were less often this was only because we were fewer left to die. One day Mongana died, which was terrible. His mother, Pagerly, wailed for days and I wailed with her.

So I got older, till being grown was no new thing but just ordinary. We got new commandants, though they were nothing interesting. All the while num got fewer, not because they died, which they hardly ever did, but because we were so few now that it was easy watching us. By and by they even stopped trying to teach us about God, I do recollect. I suppose it seemed foolish, as we just kept dying anyway. Summers passed, and more summers, and still I was alive, though I couldn't surmise why. Then, quite a surprise, a wondrous thing happened to me. This was Dray, who Fat Robson called Ophelia, who was younger than me, so I hardly did observe her before. Now all of a sudden she was so grown, fine and beautiful, so I liked to watch her sometimes, and if she saw me she looked away in a special way.

One day in autumn I was walking in the forest near Tayaleah's tree, and there she was, so we just lay down, hardly speaking any word, as if it was already said, which was curious. So a new thing started, when I had surmised there could be no new things. I got holding and tasting, and feeling hither and thither, and getting weak and lovely. Later I got more, which was blissful and tidings of joy, and by and by we often went into woods and hills and so, lying in soft grass and getting our great good fortune. She was kindly and soft, and we had some sweetness as wind blew in trees above. This was the first time I had someone who I must preserve from heinous things, and this meant I must live, which I almost forgot till then. Yes, in those days I could believe I found great good fortune after all, and I surmised Dray was my enduring, so even being stuck on that piss-poor Flinders Island seemed hardly of any account.

It is hard, though, to get lovings in a dying place, as sometimes you do feel you are impossible, so you hardly dare let yourself feel your delight. Besides, it was right not to believe. When weather got cold Dray got a little crook with coughing, so we both were too fearful. I tried to do everything, getting Jones the surgeon to look at her once and again, which he did kindly, but it was like trying to stop waves coming higher with your hands. Quite suddenly one afternoon she died.

After that I forgot my talent to endure, as there seemed no purpose to me. I wanted to die also, I do recollect, just like that time all those years before, when I ran off into that forest and lay down by that log. But it is hard to choose dying. Dying chooses you.

That was when Smith gave me his book. I was sitting in front of huts doing nothing, trying to think nothing too, as this was better than thinking something, when he came sneaking up. "I thought this might give you comfort."

I never had read a whole book before, as nobody ever gave me any. I hardly wanted to read this one, no, but there was nothing else to do, so I did begin, and though I was too slow at first, I got faster by and by. Book was called TWO LITTLE ORPHANS and was very sad.

Some family gets stuck on horses in river grown big after rains, and mother and father both get drowned trying to save two sons—very small—who are now the orphans. Mother's drowning is slow, and her last dying thing is to put some interesting CROSS round older orphan's neck. Later the orphans go to another house filled with other orphans, plenty of them, and here they must work hard, as their commandant is cruel and hateful, shouting and giving piss-poor food. One day commandant beats some other orphan very hard, and when our smaller orphan tries to help this other fellow, commandant hits him as well, and with so many grievous blows he is almost dead. In that night both orphans run away to some large town, where they have nothing to eat unless strangers give them coins.

This is a woeful time for the orphans, yes, as weather grows cold with frost and smaller one gets crook. Then one day some kind man comes and gives them money, and as kind man looks he sees that same cross that mother gave to big orphan, which is interesting to him. Kind man says they must wait here while he ponders some other thing, but he will be back soon. Very sadly, though, hateful boys come just after, and try and steal interesting cross, so orphans must flee, and they never can find kind man after. Then weather gets colder by and by, and so little orphan dies, very slow, in a burying place beside some chapel. Big orphan puts him by the chapel door so he will be buried by vicars.

After that bigger orphan is so woeful at dying of little orphan that he gets crook too, and it does look as if he will die too, so everybody will be dead. But then in the night he has some dream, and in this little orphan comes and tells him he must endure, as everything will get better by and by. This gives bigger orphan cheer, and d'you know that same day kind man comes back again and finds him. A great surprise is that in truth he is orphan's own uncle, and he has some fine huge house, though he never knew orphan's mother–who is his sister–all because of other thing. So older orphan gets good food, plenty of it, and cherishings, and even shows new uncle that place where vicars buried little orphan, and they give little orphan a great stone with his name carved so neatly. Finally, at the end, big orphan dreams again in the night, and now little orphan is in heaven, sitting on God's knees with all those ANGELS, and he is smiling as if he is so happy now.

For a time, I must tell, this book was my delight. I read saddest parts sometimes and again, and I did want it to be true. Sometimes I thought yes! I am those poor orphans, and I cried with hungry sadness.

Then, one day, everything changed. Ship came just like usual, with heinous food and letters for white men, but this time it also had something for us. News! News that I hardly could believe. Governor who visited us was finally gone now, and a new governor was arrived instead. Best of all this new governor saw my letters and said we could return to the world.

That day was great good fortune. We were only forty-nine Palawa left now, but still we were some and I did believe we could strive again once we returned. Yes, just thinking of getting away from this heinous, hateful island and going back to our forest and mountains and secret remembered places, that did fill us with delight. Also this meant I was correct, and my intent to fight white scuts with their own cleverness was some fine success after all. Everybody–except Mother–was cheering me as some great good hero that day.

Leaving was swift, yes, as we must go back on that same boat, but still I had time enough to do important things. First I went to the burying place to say goodbye to my poor Dray, and also to Mongana and Heedeek, and to all those many others who were my friends in there, which was a most sorrowful thing, giving me tenderest feelings deep inside my breast. Then I went to Smith's house. Now that we were saved, you see, all of a sudden I could discern what Smith's TWO LIT-TLE ORPHANS book really said. No, it never was some kindness at all, but just a clever trap to catch me when I was despairing and easy. It was shaming to me, yes, that I got so caught. What his book said was, GO ON, LITTLE BLACKFELLOW, DIE SWEETLY NOW, DIE QUIET

AND SMILING AND THANKFUL, AS THIS IS YOUR LAST TASK
FOR US.

Probably Smith guessed my thinking from my face, as he never came
out but just peered round his curtain once, and then pretended he was
too busy getting ready for the boat. But I knew he was secretly watching
as I tore those pages, each and every one, and put them all together. So I
burned those orphans, just like I burned Mother's spears before.

CHAPTER ELEVEN

————◆◇◆————

Dr. Thomas Potter
DECEMBER 1857

The Destiny of Nations (excerpt)

This robust and ever-growing empire that is called British is, as we are told by so-called political theorists, nothing more than the consequence of chance. It is, they claim, a mere totality of small accretions, snatched by traders and adventurers for their own enrichment; a kind of accident of weaponry and greed; some vast yet pilotless engine, whose great hands reach out across the globe, one scattering soldiers, convicts and priests, another drawing in gold.

Such a view could be hardly more misleading. There is, in truth, no finer manifestation of the destiny of men than this mighty institution of imperial conquest. Here we see the stolid and fearless Saxon Type, his nature revealed as never before as he strides forth in his great quest, subduing and scattering inferior nations—the Hindoo, the American Indian, the aboriginal race of Australia—and replacing these with his own stalwart sons. Brave yet unseeing, he little comprehends the unalterable destiny that leads him on: the all-powerful laws of the races of men. Beside him march others, though their step tells of a purpose less resolute. The Roman Type of France petulantly struts southwards across desert wastes, quelling once proud Arab chieftains. The Slav Type of Russia dismally saunters through the icy east, overcoming Asiatics with his every step. The Iberian Type of South America rides across his pampas, lazily extinguishing the savage Indian. The Belgic-Celtic Type plods onwards against island Orientals, stolidly adding to his frail domain. All shall find themselves the unwitting destroyers of their conquered foes, until hardly a subject race, whether African, Australian or Asiatic, remains.

It is when this work is done, and only the strongest Types remain, that another stage in the unfolding of history shall begin. Thus will a new and terrible great conflagration draw near: a final battle of nations, when the trusty Saxon will be required to struggle anew; a conflict of titans; a battle of the Supreme Types, in which . . .

Captain Illiam Quillian Kewley
DECEMBER 1857

I COULD HARDLY guess what Dr. Potter saw in this particular island, as it looked a poor sort of spot to me. Flat and dry as ship's biscuit it was, excepting for a few clutches of mountains huddled here and there, bleak and spiky, as if they might cause injury to careless angels. My own chart, being, as I said, not so very new, showed nothing but the coast and a few peaks, while the rest was pure as virgins, with not so much as a farm or a settlement marked. I had to set a course to a little sketch map drawn by some doctor friend of Potter's, our destination being a cross on the western coast marked "abandoned settlement." Well, to my mind it must have been a pretty poor sort of settlement if it had come and gone so quick.

The Reverend had been all sulks at us stopping here–if only because it was Potter's delight that we should–and moaned that we'd been delayed too much already. The fact was, though, that a short halt at such a spot would suit me well enough. For one thing, the rush we'd had leaving Port Phillip meant I'd never been able to take on a proper supply of water. As to my other certain reason, this was different again, and hardly the sort of thought I'd go troubling Englishmen with.

Now, a handy thing about dropping anchor at some bleak island in the very centre of nowhere was that at least there was no danger of anyone jumping ship, unless, that was, they wanted to go playing hermit. Just nine Manxmen we were now–and no sailmaker–when only days before we'd been fourteen, while even that had been a touch on the thin side, what with the two that had run off from that London sealed dock. It was bad trouble, no denying. We were enough for pretty boating weather, to be sure, but if we struck a proper storm, or even had to unload that certain cargo in a rush, we'd be well hobbled. I'd had to send that old fool Quayle the cook and Mylchreest the steward aloft once or twice, though they were getting too old for such work. It could have been a good scran worse, mind. It took a day and a night to cross Port Phillip Bay and all the way I was wondering if a messenger was riding along the shore, and if our customs friend at the Heads, Robins, would come charging out on his cutter, cannon firing and marines stabbing with their bayonets. But no, he was gentleness itself, having another fine chat with the Englishmen and then waving us on, with never a word about beaches or oars or bodies waking up tied and doused with water. Perhaps we'd been lucky and Bowles had decided to stick quiet after all.

Potter's little scrawl of a map was no use for navigating, but as we passed along the coast of the island just after dawn, we saw a little jetty springing out from the shore, which could hardly be chance, so we dropped anchor and lowered the boat. I watched the Englishmen being rowed away, and waited until they'd landed too–just in case they changed their minds, there being no end to their nonsense–and then went below to find Mylchreest. Down to the pantry we stepped, where I reached for that certain piece of cord and gave it a gentle tug. Then on to the storeroom to that loose wall panel, and those two certain cables behind, that I pulled. Then finally to the dining cabin and the trapdoors beneath the busts of Queen Victoria and Albert, that prized open so neat. I'd been thinking about what that unfortunate little fellow Harry Fields had said that night on the beach at Port Phillip–before Kinvig had had the bright idea of knocking him cold with an oar–when he'd complained that our tobacco was damp. My worry was that the whole cargo might be going. I had no wish to see the *Sincerity*'s treasures, which she'd kept so well hidden from prying customs all this while, go all to rottenness just from neglect. Fortunately when we took a look it proved not so bad as it might have. Mylchreest had a quick poke about and in the end only pulled out a single bundle that had to be dropped over the side.

"We'd be wise to leave all open for a time, mind," he suggested, "and let some of the damp out."

This was easy done, seeing as the passengers were all safely away, and could not return except by the ship's boat. I left the panels open wide as could be, and the door to the cabin likewise, so the air could move freely. By the time I stepped back onto the deck I saw the boat was on its way back from the shore, filled with water casks like she should be, and soon after chief mate Brew was clambering up the ship's side, all smirks. "We found water all right. And something else besides."

He shot a glance at a bundle of tarpaulin that the others were hauling up the ship's side. From their faces it looked heavy.

"What is it? Rocks?" asked Mylchreest as it was sat on the deck before us. Hardly had he spoken, though, when his words were made foolish, as the tarpaulin twitched.

"Near as," Brew told him with a smile. "At least if rocks had fur." He stooped down to untie the rope and all at once a big snubby nose started trying to butt its way out, and with a power of force, too. It was all Brew could do to grab the mystery's shoulders and hold him back.

"What is he, then?" I asked.

"I hardly know. The little fellow Renshaw thought he might be something called wombit."

Wombit? It hardly seemed a proper name for a creature. Whatever he was, he was no kitten, that was clear as glass from all his butting and wrestling to escape. Three of them it took to get him in the boat where we'd kept the swineys, all of them getting in each other's way and tripping on the tarpaulin. Then we had a good peer at our first proper Australian monster. He was hardly a giant, and had the most foolish little stumpy legs, but there was something about his shape that was pure strength, as if he was some kind of hunched stone. He behaved much like a stone, besides. Even as we watched he started bashing his head against the side of the boat, again and again, almost as if it was his enjoyment.

"Some kind of badger, is he?" I asked, as the boat shuddered once more. He was about the right size, though his face was more like some small bear's.

"Something like," agreed Brew. "He was making for a burrow when I jumped him."

Whatever he was, he'd be welcome enough, seeing as we'd never had time at Port Phillip to get any creatures. "We'll have Quayle show us how he tastes with some ship's biscuit."

After that I thought I might as well put a sight on this Flinders Island, and oversee the boys as they loaded up the casks. I left Mylchreest to keep watch over the ship.

The Reverend Geoffrey Wilson
DECEMBER 1857

CONSIDERING THAT Dr. Potter had never shown the slightest interest in this island till now, it was hard not to wonder at his sudden curiosity regarding the place. He claimed that it had been a refuge for aborigines of Tasmania, and that items of value might be found amid the remains of their settlement. I could not help but suspect, however, that this was nothing more than an excuse to delay us further. My fear, indeed, was that he would attempt to have us drop anchor at every empty rock and bay between Port Phillip and Hobart. What was especially worrisome was that Kewley barely troubled to listen to my own objections, reasoned though they were, so I could not help but suspect that Potter had in some way tempted him to his side. It seemed not impossible, seeing as the Manx were great lovers of gold.

The doctor was most assiduous in acting out his pretence of exploration, and as the boat was lowered, he commanded his servant, Hooper, to bring up one of his new wooden packing cases from the hold, for "artifacts" that he claimed he might discover. It really was too much. Then, as we were being rowed towards the shore, a thought occurred to me. What if I were able to prove that the doctor was merely endeavouring to waste our time? That would turn his own weaponry against him, and would deprive the Captain of any excuse from further needless delay. Why, it might even provide me with justification for removing him from the venture altogether: a prospect that was increasingly desirable—purely for the good of the expedition—as his behaviour became ever more malevolent. It would not be easy to do, I realized, being far harder to prove a man is *not* doing something than to prove that he *is*, and yet I had no doubt that it should be attempted.

I considered it would be useful to recruit Renshaw as a helper and witness in this important task, and so, as soon as the boat's crew had dispersed in their search for water and Potter and his servant were out of earshot, I endeavoured to explain the matter. The botanist, who had perched himself, somewhat foolishly, atop one of several curious round rocks that quite resembled giant eyes, proved obstinately uncooperative.

"I'm not playing spy for anyone," he declared in a dreary tone of voice, quite as if his refusal formed some instance of fine virtue.

Further attempts at persuasion being in vain, I was left with no choice but to pursue the two alone. They had, by now, quite vanished from sight, but it seemed easy enough to follow them, there being only one path I could see: an old track greatly overgrown with plants. After a few hundred yards I saw a number of brick buildings ahead, and found myself in the midst of the abandoned settlement. It seemed mostly to have been a poor sort of place. At its centre lay a line of dwellings, ill constructed and resembling slum houses, and I supposed that, if this had been a refuge for aborigines as Potter claimed, these must have formed their habitations. I glanced inside one, but found nothing but bird droppings and a few old rags. There was no sign of the doctor's "artifacts."

Of greater interest to me was the building opposite. This was of a good size and stolidly built, its walls and roof standing proud and well preserved against the ravages of time and the elements. Only the door gave a sense of abandonment, swinging loosely on its hinges, so it banged monotonously in the wind. As soon as I stepped within I guessed this must have been the settlement chapel, being possessed of a lightness and dignity that formed a mighty contrast with the grim dwellings opposite. Knowing that the aborigines of Tasmania had been greatly eclipsed, it was pleasing to reflect that, whatever their sufferings may have been, some had found comfort in the bright light of faith.

It seemed more than coincidence that, as I stepped out into the daylight once again, still gladdened by this happy thought, quite the first thing I looked upon was two pairs of footsteps, clearly distinguishable in the soft muddy ground. There could be no doubt that they were recently made. Much pleased, I began to follow, doing so with care, as I had no wish to reveal myself before I had been able to observe my quarry. The steps led away from the settlement and into woodland beyond. Here, however, a thin carpet of leaves fallen from the silvery trees made them increasingly difficult to discern, obliging me to resort to guesswork, as I looked for gaps in the trees that might denote a track. I found, before long, that the trail had eluded me, but still I struggled onwards. By now I was feeling the warmth of the day, being further inconvenienced by an infuriating cloud of flies and mosquitoes that insisted on buzzing about my head, paying no heed to frequent swings I directed at them with my hands.

It was these same tiresome creatures, indeed, that were greatly the cause of the trouble that was to ensue. I was walking midway along a slope of soft ground, even a steep slope, though the fact seemed of no great consequence. As I swung round once again to fend off the flying insects, however, all at once I felt my footing slip, and found myself suddenly sliding. My attempts to clutch at vegetation proved in vain and, realizing I was passing close by a large tree, it seemed only natural to strike out with my leg to try and halt my progress. This manoeuvre proved most effective, but was not without cost. My foot, which was now shoeless, did not so much as strike the tree as seemed to sink into it, becoming, as I realized, lost in some form of hollow. Distressing though this was, it was nothing as compared to what next followed. Just as, unhappily aware of new bruises, I began endeavouring to pick myself up and pull my leg free, I suddenly felt, somewhere close to my big toe, a terrible, searing jab of pain.

Though I was barely arrived in Tasmania, I was, from my reading, amply acquainted with the fearsome and deadly creatures that were to be found so commonly all across that land, there being, as it seemed, hardly a spider or shellfish or snake that lacked the power to kill. I had not the slightest doubt that I had just suffered a venomous attack, and that, even at that very moment, poison was entering my frail body. Why, I could even feel a terrible numbness begin, as it spread, so swiftly, through my foot, my leg, and into my torso. My heart thumping wildly, I pulled my foot free from the tree stump and peered in, but it was too dark to see any sign of my attacker. Hearing a faint rustling sound, I drew back, having no wish to be afflicted afresh. I tried to get to my feet, only for a wave of dizziness to pass through me, causing me to slump upon the ground, where I struggled to keep from losing consciousness.

It was at this most dreadful of moments, as I wrestled with death itself, that, greatly to my own surprise, I felt myself suddenly filled with profound peace. Thus it was that, lying there beside the tree, I began drifting into some kind of wonderment, a state that was neither sleep nor wakefulness, as I became aware of what I can only describe as a visionary dream. I found myself looking upon a bank of angels, their little wings flapping so prettily, and each giving me a warmest smile as they waved their pudgy hands. Then, as I watched entranced, I observed that they then seemed suddenly to grow saddened, their faces turning to sombre frowns.

Following their gaze, I now saw my own dear loyal wife, sitting in a darkened room, her face lost in silent tears. An opened letter lay by her side. Now the scene changed once again. What was this strange land that I glimpsed next, with its walls of shining stone, its wondrous greenery? I was, I realized, looking upon Eden! This time, however, I heard no voices from the ferns and flowers urging me onwards, and a cold wind blew across this forgotten spot. Worse was to follow. All at once I found myself looking upon a mighty lecture hall, its auditorium filled with innocent faces, eager for guidance. There upon the rostrum sat none other but my own enemies in the war of letters: a row of atheist geologists, the face of each filled with terrible triumph.

I felt myself come to, quite as if I had been in a state of unconsciousness. For a moment I remained beside the tree stump, quietly praying and, in some way I cannot even begin to describe, I simply *knew*, that my prayers were heard. Once again I struggled to regain my feet. This time, miraculously, I felt myself succeed, quite as if some great hand had come to my aid. I took a short step. I paused. I took another. I felt pain. In addition to my wound, the sole of my shoeless foot was exposed to every sharp stone and stinging plant upon the way. Still I pressed onwards. As I hobbled slowly forth, I felt darkness creeping upon me, reaching out with a terrible coaxing. I fought the darkness back. Little by little I advanced by yards, then more. I began to hope that I might at least find strength enough to reach the settlement, where I might be discovered, and given a Christian burial, rather than remain lost, perhaps to be devoured by beasts. It seemed as if an age were passing, but finally, surely enough, I discerned the buildings of the settlement become visible through the trees. Now, wildly, I permitted my hopes to grow greater still, even to the jetty, where others would be found. I persevered. Despair threatened anew, and anew I cast despair away. With each further yard gained I prayed thanks, and I prayed for strength to endure the next. Then, suddenly and wonderfully, I found myself stumbling into clear sight of the sea.

Timothy Renshaw
DECEMBER 1857

THERE WAS little enough to do on that shore, while the sun was shining strong, making it warm in a windy way, and after a time, watching the waves and the seabirds, I felt yawning creep upon me. I had a liedown on the jetty but this was worse than useless, what with the Manxmen forever tramping past with water casks, or kicking up a mighty fuss over the wombat that Brew caught—a foolish-looking creature with vacant eyes—and finally I took myself away to the beach. This was all pebbles, but they were smooth enough, and dry too, so I dug away, till I had made a fine hollow and a kind of pillow too. Stones are awkward, and there was a good deal of adjusting needed, but in the end I had them just about right, and was comfortable so long as I resisted the urge to try and roll over. I was just nodding off nicely, in fact, when I heard footsteps, and suddenly Wilson was shouting fit to wake the dead that he had been bitten by a snake. He looked in a poor way, I must admit. One shoe was gone, causing him to hobble badly, while his trouser leg was torn and the rest of him was spotted with dirt and mud. His face was pale as could be.

"I have not long to live," he faltered.

In a curious way it was all the more shocking because I had always thought him such a bothersome old ninny. There is, I suppose, nothing like a fellow strolling up saying he is about to die to make you feel you should have liked him.

"Where's the doctor?"

"I cannot say." He waved his hand dismissively. "I fear, anyway, that it is already far too late. Just take me back to the ship, so I may find peace."

It seemed a simple enough request, and yet it proved hardly so. I helped Wilson to the jetty, where Kewley was directing his men, only to find that, though he seemed dismayed by this terrible news, the Captain was hardly very sympathetic.

"But we can't go now," he complained. "We're still bringing in the water."

It seemed a most uncharitable remark, and quite unjustified, however irksome the vicar might have been to him in the past. Wilson took it very ill.

"I fear I shall not last much longer," he moaned, with an accusing look.

Thus reproached the Captain agreed to have us rowed back, if with some reluctance. Nor was this the end of his insensibility. As we were in the midst of our journey, and I was endeavouring to help the stricken man lie comfortably, he insisted on suddenly clambering past us both to the front of the boat, so he might hail whoever was still aboard the *Sincerity*, bellowing out with increasing impatience until, finally, the steward, Mylchreest, called out a reply. Even when we came alongside the vessel he made no effort to help carry Wilson aboard, but hurried up himself, mumbling something about finding medicine, though he produced nothing beyond a few grubby rags, that he described–most optimistically–as bandages.

Though I offered to take the stricken churchman down to his cabin, he insisted on remaining on deck, where, as he put it, he might, "gaze upon heaven." I did what little I could, carrying up a few pillows to ease his discomfort, and also a pen and paper, which he wanted so he might scribble a few final instructions for the expedition, and soon he was propped up by the mainmast, quite in the manner of Nelson at Trafalgar. By then his face seemed to have regained a little of its colour, and I remarked on this, hoping that it might give him encouragement.

"The darkness may have drawn back a little," he murmured with a brave smile, "but I fear it will soon return. It is nothing less than a miracle that I have been preserved this long. I can only believe that I may have been looked upon kindly."

I felt there must be something that could be done, and began to rack my brains for any recollection of what could overcome the effects of snakebites. "I have heard that the flesh around the wound should be cut away."

Wilson shook his head. "I fear the poison has already passed within."

"Perhaps you should suck it out?" suggested the cook, Quayle.

The vicar seemed to look more kindly upon this plan. "I suppose it might be worth attempting," he declared faintly, moping his brow with a handkerchief.

The foot had to be cleaned first, being so dirty that I could not so much as see the wound, so I had Quayle fill up a bucket with fresh water and find a soft piece of cloth. I set to work most carefully, but Wilson—though his look was purest bravery—would wince and utter a kind of squeal at my every dabbing. Matters were not helped by distractions elsewhere upon the deck. The Captain, though he had ordered everyone to keep quiet, so that the churchman might be given some peace, then insisted on noisily rebuking the steward, Mylchreest, in a mixture of English and Manx, for, as it seemed, having been asleep when he should have been keeping watch. Hardly had he finished his denunciation when he began all over again, now bawling at the man over the wombat that had been caught, which had, it seemed, butted its way through the woodwork of the boat in which it had been secured, and had vanished, presumably to swim back to the shore.

"I did hear him thumping," Mylchreest admitted, "but how could I know he'd smash it so?"

"If darkness comes upon me," declared the vicar, looking irked by the incessant racket, "will you promise me two things?"

"Certainly." By now I had dirt all cleaned away and could see his wounds clearly. I was surprised, in fact, that they were not worse, being little more than a series of tiny cuts, caused, I supposed, by the stones he had walked upon. His foot would have suffered easily, being curiously soft, almost like a woman's. The bite itself seemed very small. Then again, I supposed, a snake would have only small teeth.

"Firstly, I would like you to seek out my wife, and give her this letter."

I was about to attempt sucking the poison from the wound when one of the Manxmen called out, "There on the jetty. It's the doctor and his servant."

It seemed only wise to wait for the surgeon. The boat was sent at once, and before long Potter was climbing onto the deck, his servant struggling behind him. "A snakebite?" the doctor declared with some interest. "I cannot say it is a field much known to me, but I will do my best." He took my place by Wilson's foot. "Do you have any feeling in the limb?"

"Very little."

I found myself somewhat surprised by the answer, seeing as he had winced and wailed at my every touch.

"Let us try." With this the doctor began a series of pinches, first to the knee, next to the calf and ankle and finally to the foot itself, prompting, with each, a faint yelp from his patient. Potter seemed perplexed. "Did you see what kind of snake it was?"

"I did not see it at all," his patient answered a little impatiently. "The creature was concealed in a tree stump. For all I know it might have been some venomous spider. It is nothing less than a miracle that I have endured so long."

"I see." Potter now examined the foot. "There's no swelling I can see, apart from a few minor bruises. As for the wound itself . . ." He raised the limb so he might look more easily. "It hardly looks like the work of fangs."

By now all the crew were gathered round.

"What then?" I asked.

Potter pondered a moment. "A rodent of some kind?" He peered at the foot once more. "Perhaps some form of mouse."

Someone among the ship's crew let out a faint cackle. I would have joined him, I dare say, had I not felt more than a little resentment at having been induced to show such sympathy. What with the man's wailing and cries for pillows I quite felt as if I had been cheated. Why, I had very nearly had to suck out the imagined poison.

Wilson, needless to say, insisted that Potter was entirely mistaken.

"The pain was such that it can only have been venom," he declared grandly. "A man knows well enough when his life is slipping from him."

He kept to his line all that day. For several hours, as the ship was made ready, the anchor was weighed and we resumed our journey, he remained slumped on his pillows by the mainmast, while he then bullied the carpenter into making him a stick, with which he raised himself up–with some drama–and began hobbling about, casting reproachful looks. By the next afternoon, however, I observed he allowed himself to walk unaided once again. He kept quiet enough about spiders and snakes after that, as I recall.

Captain Illiam Quillian Kewley
DECEMBER 1857

AFTER FLINDERS ISLAND the breeze kept steady northerly, pushing us along well enough, and we put a sight on Van Diemen's Land, or Tasmania, or whatever it was now calling itself, just that same evening. A bleak sort of spot it looked, with a long, flat mountain like a wall. The Englishmen all came up on deck to have a good stare, Dr. Potter all jokes and pointing, while the Reverend said hardly a word, being still all in sulks, I supposed, on account of the mauling he'd had from his mouse. I was grateful to the creature, as it happened, as it was the first cheer we'd had since half the crew jumped ship back at Port Phillip. Hardly an hour went by without some chattering in Manx about lonnags–this being the proper shipboard term for mice–especially if the Reverend should be on deck, and it could be done just in front of his own nose.

Early the next morning we rounded a point on the northeastern edge of Tasmania and from there we had a clear run southwards. The breeze was as good as any we'd had since leaving Maldon, keeping light but steady, and coming from nearly straight behind us, nicely warmed by all that Australia it had blown over, and, seeing as the boys could do with a distraction, I decided I might as well give us a see of what the vessel could do. The topsails and mainsails were already spread, and the jibs and such too, but that still left a good deal more, and I had them put out the royals and skysails, which had her leaping nicely. Even then I felt there was more give in her, and, feeling in a mood for venturing, I told the boys to start roving some studdingsails as well. Studdingsails are awkward creatures at the best of times, perching to either side of all the rest like paupers clinging on to a mail coach for a ride, and, the ship jumping along already at a mighty pace, there were nervous looks all round as, one by one, they and their booms were hauled aloft and put into place. Though Brew and Kinvig never said a word, they both looked as if they were expecting sails to go bursting into streamers and yards to snap like matchwood any moment. I'd judged the breeze well enough, though, and while the spars were straining forward almost like trees in a gale, everything held. The crew even let out a little cheer.

It was the first time we'd had the *Sincerity* under full sail and she looked a fine sight. Snub-nosed though she was, she quite jumped from wave to wave, almost as if she might fly away completely, while the sea roared beneath her bows and washed over her fo'c'sle like a proper river. I had two men at the wheel just to hold her steady, and even then one of them was nearly flung sprawling half across the deck. The wind keeping even, I kept her so through the day and that night too, and we made better speed than any dirty steamship. The next morning the breeze began to back round westerly a scran, so I thought it best to go more carefully, bringing down the studdingsails. It was just as the boys were doing this, in fact, that Potter stepped up on deck with his questioning look.

"It's probably nothing, Captain, but there's a peculiar noise in the cabin. It may seem strange but it sounds almost as if it's coming from the timbers of the hull."

As soon as I heard those words "timbers of the hull" I smelt trouble. All at once I was regretting I'd thought to push the *Sincerity* so, and I was imagining casks shaken loose from their stacking, thumping and rasping. "I'm sure it's nothing," I told him, as cheerily as I could manage, giving a wave to Brew that I was going below. "But I'll have a see."

Down in their cabin the Reverend was sat on his cot reading some theological book, looking far too grand to be troubled by noises, and he hardly paid me a glance, being still in sulks over his mouse. Renshaw, though, had been well caught by the mystery, and was crouching by the wall to listen.

"I heard it just a moment ago."

I took my place next to him. The vessel was still jumping pretty wild and I feared I'd hear the casks grating nicely, but there was nothing. I began to hope the whole thing might be nothing more than English windiness.

"There it is," Renshaw declared proudly. "It's definitely below us, and right by the hull."

Only after some careful listening did I catch it. A curious noise it was besides, being like nothing so much as a faint scratching.

"D'you think it could be some kind of tropical beetle that's devouring the timbers?" wondered Potter.

"I'd be surprised." I was as puzzled as he was. I didn't know much about warm water creepers, but the wood was clean as could be, with not a hole. Worms would leave their mark.

Renshaw laughed. "It almost sounds as if there's some great creature down there scratching at his fleas."

I laughed with him, giving out a proper merry cackle, as the terrible thought came to me. "I'm sure it's nothing to be troubled over," I told them, as calm as I could manage. "Probably it's just caused by the sea flowing past the ship's side."

"Difficult currents?" asked Potter.

For a moment, and a bad one it was, I thought he had seen it all, every last bit, but no, he was serious. Truly, there's no overestimating the foolishness of Englishmen, especially brainy ones like these. There was a moment to breathe careful and be grateful. "That's right. Those currents," I coaxed, and they both nodded, tame as kittens.

After that all I could do was wait as quietly as I could manage. I bided my time through the afternoon, trying not to scare myself with thoughts of beastly yowls suddenly sounding out from the *Sincerity*'s side. At dinner I made sure the Englishmen didn't linger by driving them out with dullness, chattering with Brew about how much things cost in Peel City till I was half asleep myself. Even then it seemed half an age before they finally went. I waited till I could hear snoring, then set to work. Brew stayed on deck minding the ship, while I took Mylchreest to help, and Kinvig too. So I gave a pull to that certain piece of cord above the door to the pantry, banging a few jars as I did so to hide the noise. Next there was that particular loose panel at the back of the storeroom, and the cables just behind. After that I had Kinvig take his place on the steps to keep watch, just in case any passengers started straying. Finally I swung open the trapdoor beneath the bust of Queen Victoria, took up the lamp and peered in.

There, sure enough, a dozen yards off, was the wombit creature, scrinching up his eyes at the light. He must have tramped down when Mylchreest was snoring, and thought the open door was a handsome new burrow. He'd made a kind of nest for himself all out of tobacco bales, and looked as if he'd even been eating tobacco besides. As for his place, he could hardly have judged it more neatly, as I guessed it must be clean beneath the Reverend's berth. Startled by the light, he shrank back into his nest, making a rustling sound, scandalous loud. That was enough to have me close the panel again quick.

It was a tidy little problem. If we left him there it would surely be only a matter of time before he started making some noise that would cause even those dawds of Englishmen to wonder. If we stepped in and tried to catch him, though, there'd be so much din that we might as well just call the passengers into my cabin to take a look for themselves.

"I suppose we could try and get him out sometime in the day, when the Englishmen are all on deck," suggested Kinvig.

It was hardly safe. "There'd be no certainty they'd stay up there. Especially if the creature turned to screeching and such."

"Perhaps we should just hang on till we reach Hobart," said Mylchreest. "It's not so far now."

That seemed worse still. "What about the customs? They're sure to give us a search, while if they hear scratching through the timbers that'll be the finish of us." Their notions were useful in a way, there being nothing like listening to nonsense to help you know your own mind. "What we want is a nice quiet spot where we can drop anchor for a day or two and send the Englishmen landwards, like we did at Flinders."

Kinvig was still worrying. "They won't like that. Wilson kicked up a mighty fuss at our stopping there."

"He'll keep quiet if he thinks the ship might start sinking under him," I told him. "Potter thinks we've got creepers in the timbers. D'you know,

I think he might just be right after all, and proper perilous creepers they are besides. Yes, to my mind we'd best drop anchor and have a search."

I had Mylchreest bring out the chart, and, spreading this out on the table and having a careful look, I couldn't help but feel that luck was finally coming our way. There, just a few miles off from our course, was a little harbour, looking sheltered as could be. As for settlements there was none marked for many miles, the spot being stuck away at the end of a large peninsula shaped like a great flailing hand.

"That'll do, nice as nip. I'll set us a course."

Timothy Renshaw
December 1857

At some early hour of the morning I was woken by the loud thump of a boat running along the *Sincerity*'s side, followed by boots stamping on the deck. As if not already enough, this at once inspired Potter and Wilson to clump from their beds and begin noisily pulling on their clothes. I persevered even then, being no slave to curiosity, and reasoning that if it were anything of importance I would find out soon enough, while if it were something terrible–perhaps some band of Tasmanian pirates–I might as well preserve my ignorance as long as possible. I pulled the pillow carefully over my head, so that both ears were covered but I could still breathe freely–this being no easy thing to get exactly right–and had just begun to doze off nicely when the anchor was dropped. There was, in truth, no more agitating thing the *Sincerity* could conspire to do a poor fellow than this, with its huge clanking roar, causing all to judder and creak, and so, drowsiness being now quite smashed out of me, I resigned myself to rising for the day.

A curious scene I found as I emerged onto the deck. A dozen red-coated soldiers were stood about, leaning on their long guns as soldiers will, while their officer was engaged in talking–or more precisely shouting–at Captain Kewley. "I really find that very hard to believe."

Kewley looked far from happy, though he endeavoured to throw off a grin. "It's every word of it true, Lieutenant, so it is."

Glancing at the shore, I wondered for a moment if we had reached Hobart, though it was surely too soon. Facing us across a little narrow bay was a settlement, and a considerable one besides. Though it was easily large enough to be a town, still it did not somehow seem quite right, and, looking more carefully, I realized there was hardly a single house, but only what seemed to be dozens of sheds or workshops. In the centre stood a huge stone building with row upon row of large square windows, resembling some textile mill. The whole place, indeed, resembled nothing so much as a kind of military manufacturing town.

"Where is this?" I asked Kinvig, who was standing just nearby, looking subdued.

"Port Arthur."

I suppose I should have guessed. I now discerned the soldiers strutting about the shore, and the bands of hunched convicts in their dismal uniforms. I looked with new curiosity upon this place, whose name was so grimly familiar, seeming nothing less than a description of harshness and retribution. Port Arthur: two words that had been usefully employed by scores of mothers on the other side of the earth to threaten misbehaving children.

Captain Kewley, I now saw, was holding what I saw to be a map of Tasmania. "Here we are," he declared, pointing at some part of the chart, which was flapping in the breeze. "See? There's nothing marked at all."

The officer was unimpressed. "You mean to say you've been setting a course to this?"

"It's done us well enough till now." Kewley seemed quite put out.

The officer gave him a diminishing sort of look. "I think you had better come ashore, so you may explain yourself to the commandant."

That had Wilson started. "I cannot believe this is really necessary, Lieutenant. May I remind you that this expedition is of the greatest importance, and our time is short."

Captain Kewley beamed. The appeal, however, seemed to have the opposite effect to that intended. "Very well," declared the officer briefly. "You may come along too."

I found myself included in this invitation. It was not as if I had done anything wrong, and yet it was hard not to feel a certain apprehension as we were rowed towards the shore of this great engine of punishment, watchful soldiers for company. Though we had not been arrested, nor anything like, we seemed hardly free either, being quite marched along beside the yellow-coloured beach. I could not help but feel some sympathy, indeed, for those miscreants who had found themselves suddenly gripped by the scruff of their necks, and deposited in this terrible place.

The establishment's commanding officer was all beard and curled military moustache. "The fact is that we're not normally honoured with unexpected visitors," he informed us dryly. "My curiosity being so greatly aroused, I hope you'll not object if we conduct a little search of your ship."

Captain Kewley did object. "But where's the need? It's not as if anybody'd try to sneak something into a prison town like this."

The commanding officer gave him a puzzled look. "What might be brought in is not our concern, so much as what might be taken out. Or rather who." He regarded us with a kind of warning nonchalance. "The search will only take an hour or two. Unless, of course, something of interest should be found."

Rather than have us pass our time idly waiting, he arranged for the three of us–Kewley being intent on overseeing the *Sincerity*'s search–to be given a tour of the settlement, under the guidance of a brisk-looking fellow in spectacles named Captain James. I was briefly drawn to the grim prospect, but soon found my curiosity vanquished. The establishment was simply too monstrous. As we passed among the sheds and barracks, I found myself unwillingly glancing upon one terrible sight after another: now a gang of convicts, their looks hardened and even jaunty with hatred, and their ankles marked with black sores where their shackles had bit; next a man quietly engaged in cleaning buckets, his torn shirt revealing a mighty pattern of scars upon his back.

Matters were not helped by Captain James. He had, judging by his fluent patter, conducted a good number of parties about the settlement, and seemed to be enjoying his task. The details of every building, every process of punishment, appeared to inspire in him the kind of satisfaction that a collector of butterflies might show at the sight of his display of catches, each pinned neatly in its place. "There is the penitentiary," he declared with comfortable monotony. "It was converted only recently from being a granary, and is the largest building in Port Arthur, being also built of stone. To the right we can see the triangles, used to secure prisoners during punishment, while behind them . . ."

Curiously enough, my two colleagues of the expedition seemed far less affected by the cruelties all around than I. From time to time Wilson would murmur, "Such a shame," and other pious sentiments, but mostly he appeared not greatly interested. As for Potter, he seemed to be enjoying himself, listening to Captain James's description with cheerful attention, and frequently offering questions.

"Has any attempt been made to study the physical features of the criminals here? Or likewise their origins?"

"Not that I am aware of." Captain James preferred to keep to his established chatter. He pointed to a long, low building we were approaching. "This is the Separate Prison, which is often of interest to visitors."

Potter was not so easily discouraged. "You may even have noticed some tendencies yourself. Are there any particular crimes, perhaps, that are peculiar to Scotsmen? Or Irishmen? Or foreigners perhaps?"

"I fear I am not the one to ask," the captain told him brightly. Having reached a low stone building of elegant design, he opened a door and led the way into a long stone corridor. All was silent except for a curious whimpering, emanating from the furthest end. "The Separate Prison," our guide explained in a lowered voice, quite as if we had entered a church, "houses convicts who require further punishment. It is, if you like, a prisoners' prison. It is a most modern establishment and employs the very latest methods of moral reformation. No physical punishment of any kind is used here."

It was a relief to hear this after all I had seen before. My only puzzle was why every convict did not take refuge in this place, where they might escape the lash.

"This has never been a difficulty." Captain James seemed a little surprised by my question. "In fact the Separate Prison is much feared."

I soon began to understand why. As he led us forward, two officers stepped into view, suddenly and quite silently. A little surprised, I realized that both of them were wearing not shoes but some form of slippers, almost as if they were intending to enjoy some restful Sunday morning. They paused to unlock one of the thick metal doors that lined the corridor and, glancing within, one of them called out, as I was surprised to note, not a name but a number.

"Seventeen?"

From the cell there emerged a man clothed in a grey uniform, a large brass badge sewn onto the jacket displaying the number by which he had just been addressed. No less curious was the covering he wore over his face, which concealed his features so completely that nothing remained visible but his eyes. These twitched strangely in our direction as he was led past.

"He's being taken out to one of the exercise yards," the captain whispered contentedly. "There are four of these, and in size they are . . ."

I was beginning to loathe the sound of his voice, which made me think of railway timetables. "What is the mask for?" I interrupted.

He regarded me with something like pique. "I was just coming to that, Mr. Renshaw." He turned to Potter, who was now clearly established as his favourite listener. "The mask prevents prisoners from recognizing one another. The system keeps each man wholly separate from the others' influence, so that their previous, criminal natures may be gradually erased. As you may have observed, even the men's names are not used, and they are referred to only by the numbers of their cells. By keeping them always alone and silent in this way, it is ensured that they are exposed to none but improving influences."

It was, in effect, a life of perpetual solitary confinement. After a few weeks here, I imagined, even a beating would seem like welcome sociableness.

"The convicts are given work to do in their cells so they may learn industry, while the chaplain and schoolmaster visit on occasion to provide morality and learning." Captain James pushed open a heavy door. "In addition they are each of them brought here five times a week for their religious improvement."

It was like no chapel I had ever seen before. The area of the congregation sloped steeply, in the manner of a surgery theatre, and was divided into row upon row of tiny wooden stalls, each of them just large enough to contain one standing man, and separated from its neighbours by doors.

"The stalls ensure that each worshipper can see nobody except for the chaplain, while he has a view of them all," Captain James explained with satisfaction.

"How very ingenious." Wilson appeared quite taken with the place, looking with thoughtfulness towards the lectern. "The preacher must find he has a most attentive congregation."

Potter was more practical. "Has the system proved successful in reforming the men?"

"That is still too early to say. Some of the prisoners have proved distressingly obdurate."

"I imagine there have at least been no escapes."

"There has been one," Captain James admitted, causing surprise to us all. "It appears it was devised in this very room, and that the prisoners sang their plans to one another during the hymns. They were all captured in the end, of course, while measures have been taken to prevent such a thing from occurring again."

It was curious to think of these men, who had not seen one another's faces for weeks or months, singing their plot to invisible neighbours. For all the wickedness they may have committed it was hard not to feel sympathy for their wish to escape such remorseless solitude.

"How were they punished?" wondered Potter.

"We have a pair of chambers known as the dumb cells," our guide explained happily. "Their walls are of great thickness and they have a series of metal doors, so that no light or sound can pass within. A convict can scream and shout for as long as he likes for all the good it will do him. Just a few days there has a remarkable effect on even the hardest of them." He led us back into the corridor, with its sound of faint whimpering.

"What is that crying?" I asked.

"That will be one of the lunatics." A rare frown passed across the captain's face. "Really they shouldn't be here at all, as they quite spoil the silence, but I suppose they must be housed somewhere. They have grown so greatly in numbers of late."

"Where are they from?" I asked.

"As it happens, quite a goodly proportion were formerly convicts of the Separate Prison." Captain James led us along the corridor towards the whimpering sound, which I now realized was accompanied by a number of faint scratchings, clickings and murmurings, all muffled by the thick metal doors. "Sometimes they are noisier even than this. It really is a great shame."

All at once the vicar, who had been looking through one of the peepholes in the cell doors, uttered a kind of delighted laugh. "Renshaw, do come and look."

It was the first time he had seemed so cheerful since the business of the mouse bite and, curious, I peered in as he urged. In a corner of the cell sat a thickset man with the most intense and staring eyes, though he seemed to be regarding nothing but the empty wall directly opposite. As I watched, he reached out with his hand and, without warning, slapped the plaster beside him, as if some bothersome insect were there—though I had seen none—then resuming his perfect stillness. It was not this, however, that was most noticeable about the man.

"Dr. Potter," called out Wilson, "I do believe we have found your long-lost twin."

He was quite right. For all the man's dark-coloured skin and black, lank hair, the likeness he bore to the surgeon was little less than remarkable: his face was of the same shape, while he held himself in the same somewhat stooped way. The stubble on his chin seemed to mimic the doctor's beard, and even in his fixed stare there was a curious resemblance of expression.

Potter was far from taken with the discovery. "He looks nothing at all like me," he insisted crossly.

Wilson would not let him go so easily. "Who is this man?"

"He is known as Black O'Donnell," Captain James told him in his usual monotone. "He has, as I recall, quite unusual origins, being part Irish and part native Maori. He was held in the separate system for some time before being declared insane."

"What were his crimes?"

"I would have to examine the records to be sure, but I believe he bludgeoned his father and uncle almost to death."

The vicar smirked delightedly. "You must admit, Doctor, that there is a strong likeness. Are you sure he is not some forgotten cousin?"

Potter regarded him with coolness. "If you will only look carefully,

Vicar, you will realize there is no real likeness at all, but merely a superfi-
cial similarity, or trick of the eye. Besides, I have not a single Irish relative, let alone any among Maoris."

A glint came into Wilson's eye. "Of course, it is possible to be misled
as to one's forebears."

It was a most poisonous remark, and all the more so for the innocent
way in which it was said: if he had spat it out with feeling I believe it
would almost have sounded kinder. For a moment I quite wondered if
Potter might strike out at the man, but instead he simply turned away,
breathing somewhat heavily. Having, as it seemed, regained control of
himself, he then turned to regard his persecutor afresh.

"It would, I think, be altogether more useful to examine the matter
from a scientific approach, rather than waste one's time with foolish half-
observation." He stepped back with determination towards the man's
cell. "If you will permit me, Vicar, I will provide you with a little study of
this man's cranial features. Afterwards I will do the same for my own self
and"–a thoughtful look passed across his face–"also you yourself, Vicar."

I was anticipating some form of extended insult to the churchman–a
prospect which, I will admit, I regarded with some curiosity–but it was
not to be. Potter applied his eye to the peephole for some time, then
declared in an irritated voice, "Where has he gone?"

"I think," said Captain James quickly, "that you would be wise to
step back from the door."

"Whyever should I?" the doctor demanded crossly, peering still into
the cell.

The answer, as it happened, was only too near at hand. Potter
jumped back with a howl, clutching at his eye. "He jabbed me with his
finger."

Captain James hurried across to help him. "He'll get the dumb cells
for that, lunatic or no," our guide insisted, full of apology.

From the cell I heard another slow slap upon the wall. I could only
suppose that Black O'Donnell had grown weary of being so discussed by
strangers. Nor, in truth, could I blame him.

Captain James insisted that Dr. Potter visit the prison hospital but,
fortunately, a brief inspection of his eye was enough to confirm that no
lasting injury had been caused, though he was provided with a piratical

eye patch. It was then that, to my relief, a messenger brought us news that the search of the *Sincerity* was now complete, the vessel was preparing to depart, and so our tour was at an end.

"I must say I found it a most interesting visit," declared the vicar in a goading voice, as we walked back beside the little yellow beach. Potter scowled from behind his eye patch. If the spirits of one became raised, then those of the other would immediately fall, quite as if they were joined, like the poles of a seesaw. As we stood on the shore, waiting for the *Sincerity*'s boat, I found myself wondering if it was usual for expeditions of discovery to suffer such poisonous clashes, caused perhaps by the confinement of space, or the nature of the personalities drawn to such ventures. Had Captain Cook been grumpy and complaintive? Had Columbus found constant fault with his Spaniards' table manners? Mutinies seemed suddenly comprehensible to me, and I was surprised, indeed, that they did not occur all the time.

"What do they think they are doing?" complained Potter angrily, discharging a little of his discontent. "They must have seen us by now."

It was true that we had been waiting some little time, though several crewmen were clearly visible upon the deck and should have noticed us waving and calling out.

"Hallo there!" called out Potter once again.

It was from another quarter that help came. A skiff containing several soldiers had, as we waited, been passing back and forth between the vessel and the shore—I supposed to discourage convicts from trying to swim their way to liberty—and its commander now took up our cause, hailing the *Sincerity* in the strongest terms. This proved encouragement enough, and in a moment some of the Manxmen clambered into the ship's boat and were rowing, if unhurriedly, in our direction.

"Why on earth didn't you come before?" demanded Potter when they reached the shore.

"Ah, but we didn't see you," chief mate Brew replied, in that peculiarly Manx fashion, at once evasive and yet somehow confiding, as if one were being entrusted with lies. As we took our places and set off, the rowers could hardly have contrived to dip the oars into the water more sluggishly, as if they were not endeavouring to propel us so much as gently stroke the depths.

"I'll go up first and give you a hand," offered Brew as we reached the ship's side, though he did not help us so much as obstruct with his fussing. When I finally clambered past him onto the deck, I at once became aware of a most curious din rising up from belowdecks, as if some violent game of chase were being played in the cabins.

"What's that?"

Brew shrugged. "Must be the Captain looking for beetles, like you wanted."

It seemed hardly the sound for such an activity. Before I could consider the matter further, however, the noise grew suddenly louder and, greatly to my surprise, there leapt onto the deck a wombat–just like the one that had been caught upon Flinders Island–hotly pursued by Captain Kewley and several of the crewmen. They struggled to catch the animal, though this proved by no means easy, as, in spite of his short legs, the creature was quite ingenious at eluding his pursuers, now suddenly changing his direction, now dodging beneath the keel of one of the boats. Just when it appeared he was finally trapped he crashed his way between two of the Manxmen and, uttering a strange grunting sound, hurled himself over the ship's side. As we hurried by the rail, he could be seen paddling patiently towards an emptier part of the shore.

"Wherever did it come from?" demanded Potter.

"The creature?" asked the Captain slowly, as if he might have been referring to something else entirely. "That I wouldn't know." He turned away, ordering the crew to begin raising the anchor.

"But you must have seen," I insisted.

"Ah, he'll have been hiding himself somewhere," suggested Brew thoughtfully. "Probably our checking for the beetles woke him up."

"It seems strange that the search party never found him," observed Potter.

Kewley simply shrugged. "That's creatures for you."

CHAPTER TWELVE

***

Superintendent Eldridge of the Oyster Cove Aboriginal Settlement
to Gerald Denton, Governor of Tasmania
SEPTEMBER 1857

Your Excellency,

As a humble servant of your government I hope I may offer you my own small welcome to Her Majesty's Colony of Tasmania. Might I say that your reputation as a man of ability and fairness spreads before you.

I write to you from the aboriginal settlement at Oyster Cove, of which I am happy to find myself superintendent. In the short time since you arrived from England you will doubtless have been too occupied with matters of government to apprise yourself of our little establishment and I hope I may take this opportunity to acquaint you with it, and also to make one or two small suggestions with regard to its future. The Oyster Cove settlement was founded nearly ten years ago, and for eight of these I have had the honour of serving as its commander, having previously held the post of quartermaster to the Hobart barracks. The settlement was established to house the surviving remnant of the island's aboriginal blacks, who had lately been brought back from Flinders Island in the Bass Straits. At that time, a decade ago, the number of those remaining was almost fifty but, most regrettably, as the years have passed, the unfortunates have, little by little, been taken from us. Even this last winter three more, Princess Cleopatra, Diogenes and Columbus, passed away. A fourth, Cromwell, who is half-caste, having lately been granted permission to move to a cottage of his own, the total number of aborigines dwelling here is presently reduced to eleven, of whom eight are females and three are males, all of them being comparatively advanced in years.

It is in consideration of this unhappy circumstance that I wish to make a request to your excellency. It is, in my humble belief, nothing less than essential that this establishment be moved, and without delay, to some more commodious place, if only for the good of the poor blacks. Oyster Cove was never a well-chosen site, in truth, being greatly subject to damp, so that even during summer months the aborigines are often to be found crouching close about their fire wearing every layer of clothing they possess. I have suffered greatly myself. Of no less concern is the settlement's isolation. The track from Hobart is a poor one and can seem long indeed, especially in the winter, when hardly a soul thinks to visit. This remoteness has also allowed the poor blacks to form easy prey to criminal whites, who–despite my every effort to drive them away–loiter in the vicinity, trying to tempt the natives into exchanging their meagre possessions for liquor (a state of affairs that has obliged me to place repeated requests for further blankets).

My suggestion is that the settlement be moved to Hobart. The town's inhabitants would not need fear such a development, as, even aside from the gentleness of their natures, the blacks are far too few and infirm to pose any danger. They could all of them be accommodated in one of the larger Hobart town houses, while the vicinity of Battery Point would seem particularly well suited, being admirably quiet, and possessing delightful views of the river. Such a change of location would make easier the bringing of supplies of food and blankets–allowing savings to the public purse–while it would be also helpful with regard to my own duties to be within easy reach of Hobart.

If such an arrangement were not thought possible I hope Your Excellency might consider a request of my own, namely that I might be assigned to some other form of service within the colony. Mr. Willis, the storekeeper, having retired from the settlement last year, I am presently the only European still remaining–a situation that can be dispiriting–and, proud as I am of my work at Oyster Cove, I feel that eight years is sufficient time in this place. I would be most content to return to my post as quartermaster for the Hobart barracks, while I would even, such is my zeal to be of usefulness to the colonial government, be willing to consider a position junior to that I held before.

There are some in Hobart, I am sad to report, who may attempt to sway Your Excellency's mind against myself, recounting tales concerning a few stores that were thought lost from the barracks. Such reports, Your Excellency should know, are wholly false, having never been proved in any way, as you may discover yourself from the records. I urge you to avert your gaze from the malicious claims of men who have, for reasons ever unknown to me, long made it their business to try and blacken my own good name. If I may be so bold as to offer Your Excellency advice, indeed, it would be that there is no society on earth more inclined to jealousy and slander than that of a remote island colony, and that Your Excellency should take the greatest care with regard to what he chooses to believe.

I hope you may consider these requests carefully, for the sake of the poor blacks.

Once again I wish you every good fortune as our new governor.
Your humble servant,

Superintendent Eldridge

Pagerly
DECEMBER 1857

ONE EARLY MORNING I was woken by a shout outside the hut, too short, as if something stopped it. Others didn't hear and just kept sleeping but I was curious. Going out, I saw day was reaching out from over Bruny Island like big yellow hands, making light so I could see Walyeric was fallen down, very still. I could guess she was getting new wood for fire as some logs were on the ground just beside. I took her head and her eyes were watching, just a little, so I knew she wasn't dead, which was my great fear, though she looked so bad. Her face was angry with hurt and her breaths were fast as if she wanted air too much. But as we stayed so she did get better by and by, breaths going slower, and she telling that hurt in her chest was getting small now.

Later that morning she was well again and even went swimming in the sea for muttonfish, and got some too. Still I did think about her getting so crook, and after a time I went to her.

"Walyeric, I think you must go and visit Peevay. You must give him your forgivings."

She always hated being told she must do anything. "Why should I?"

There was no use being gentle with Walyeric, as she only noticed fighting. That was her way. "It's bad to go hating your own child so. What if you die? D'you want him to think you hate him always?"

For a moment her look went thoughtful and I had hope, but only for that moment. "I'm not going to his white man's house with all that white man's shit."

She was right about his house, yes, as I saw it, and he had every num thing, just like Superintendent Eldridge's hut. There were table and stools, fireplace and mantelpiece, and also candles, teapot and shelves with a book. Even his clothes were so, like frock coat and shoes and tall hat sitting on the table. A strange thing, though, was that the more num things he had, the less like any white man he got. His hair, which was yellow before, was just grey now, so he might just be any Palawa getting old. Also he got more hateful at white men all the while, so now he was more raging in his talk even than his mother. Then again she hardly cared so much about them anymore, just living more quietly like a fine old lady. I suppose she did kill them when she could, which was pleasing for her, while he never did. Besides, when you get to being some old rotten-bones it's harder to trouble anymore with hatings you had.

Another thing that made Peevay so cross at num was his new house. He never meant to have it, you see, as his wish was to get a fine big place for us all. So many letters he sent to white men that he made us sign, saying we must get land, plenty of it, and also convict white men to grow us food, like other white men got, which he said they must give us after all their cheating hatefulness. Then we would be wondrous fine fellows, so he told. Peevay always was clever with his writing and I supposed he might get anything. In the end, though, all white men gave was that small hut, just for him, with no land and no convict whites either. He was so angry that he said he wouldn't live there. In the end he did, though, so he could go to some place nearby cutting up whale fish and earn white men's coins, as he said money would let him trouble white men more cleverly, till we got our due.

"I'll get that place for you, so I will," he said. "I'll make them give it to us."

Sometimes I thought he was like his mother after all. You see, they both never would stop. I think that was why it was hard to make them be kindly to the other. Yes, they were like two rocks stuck in mud that you cannot push together, and when you try they get stuck deeper. Still I must think of some way before it is too late. I cannot abide them getting trapped in this hating for ever and ever.

Mrs. Gerald Denton, Wife of the Governor of Tasmania
SEPTEMBER–DECEMBER 1857

(Excerpt from *On Distant Shores: Recollections of a Colonial Governor's Wife*, Chapter 27: "A Christmas to Remember")

During one bright springtime of my earliest years I formed a little association of playmates dedicated to the preservation of fledgling birds that had fallen accidentally from their nests. Though our childish efforts proved more wishful than effective, sad to say, the sentiment that inspired them has, I now realize, remained with me ever since, this being a deepest sympathy for those whom life has treated unkindly. It is simply outside my nature to remain unmoved by tales of the wretched of this world, whether they be little children lost in poverty, frail grandparents neglected by their ungrateful progeny or helpless animals suffering maltreatment by a cruel master. In consequence it was no doubt inevitable that, upon coming to this distant colony of Tasmania, I would find myself drawn to the lamentable story of that island's aboriginal natives.

I was aware even before we arrived at Hobart that these has endured a dreadful decline, though I knew few details. Once we had settled at Government House my curiosity grew and I began asking about the matter, first of our housekeeper, Mrs. Murray, and then of some of my new lady friends, the wives of Gerald's officers. To my surprise I found my questions were met with reluctance, even evasion, quite as if it were thought in poor taste to discuss the subject. My interest was not quenched, however, but grew greater, and I next asked Gerald. What shock I felt when he told me that a mere dozen of the poor creatures remained still alive. It seemed that disease and past violence by escaped convicts had taken every one of their fellows, while these few survivors were so advanced in years that there could be no hope of their race enduring.

Greatly moved by this terrible discovery, I tried to think of ways a little solace might be brought to these unfortunates in these their final days. One notion proved especially appealing: to pay a visit to their settlement and bring them gifts. Dear Gerald was also most taken with the thought, though he felt that, for the moment, his duties were too onerous to allow him the time required for such an expedition, the aboriginal establishment being a twenty-mile journey from Hobart, on poorest roads. It was only a few weeks later, however, that he proposed we should hold a social gathering at Government House for Christmas, so we might become further acquainted with those of note within the colony. All at once I became aware of a most delightful possibility.

"We can also invite the poor aborigines!"

Gerald, enthusiastic though he was at the suggestion, felt concern that the blacks might become upset by the commotion of such a grand occasion, being accustomed to a remote and tranquil existence. He was further worried that one among their number might make mischief. This fellow, I should explain, was a half-caste aborigine by the name of Cromwell, being a notorious maker of trouble, who had learned to mimic the ways of an Englishman just well enough to be a perfect nuisance. (Gerald gave a most amusing description of the fellow, strutting about town in an ill-fitting frock coat and a top hat, though his face was black as coals.) It seemed the man's ambition was to lead a life of aristocratic leisure, and to this end he was forever sending whining letters to officers of the government demanding he be given tracts of land, and even convicts to act as his servants. As Gerald pointed out, there could hardly have been a greater contrast between such a fellow, who endeavoured to use his fellows' misfortune to exact gain for himself (though he was hardly even of their kind), and the true aborigines, who showed such a touching resignation as to their lamentable fate.

"The fact is we can hardly invite the others without him, as they insist on regarding him as being one of their number, in spite of his mixed blood," Gerald considered sadly. "Yet to invite such a fellow to a formal social gathering would, I fear, be to ask for trouble."

An idea occurred to me. "What if we arranged for the aborigines to be set apart from the rest of the festivities? That, surely, would answer all our difficulties? They would not be alarmed by the throng, while this Cromwell would have no opportunity to cause a scene."

Gerald was doubtful still, but with my own warm encouragement he eventually assented. Delighted, I dispatched an invitation that same day to the superintendent of aboriginal settlement, a Mr. Eldridge (who Gerald told me was a man of tainted past). I added a further request to Eldridge asking if he might ask his blacks to bring with them objects of their own manufacture, such as bead necklaces, wooden figures or spears, which they might be willing to part with in exchange for simple gifts. My hope, I should explain, was to assemble a small, yet perhaps not unimportant collection of memorabilia of this vanishing race. I could quite imagine the sitting room of our London house in some future time, its walls displaying spears and throwing sticks, and a crowd of savage figurines hunched upon the mantelpiece, forming a delightful and also most touching reminder of our time spent upon this faraway shore.

Within a few days a reply arrived from Mr. Eldridge, who, to my delight, reported that he and his blacks would gladly attend our gathering. Less welcome was the letter of acceptance from the half-caste Cromwell, which arrived shortly afterwards, and was written in a most peculiar style, using long words most strangely, and seemed only too suggestive of a disordered mind. By this time I was already preoccupied with preparations for the coming event, which proved no small matter. The question of food was especially difficult, as it was my dear wish to have each of our many guests take tea, while I had quite set my heart on offering them the same fare that would be found at Christmastime in England. The southern reversal of the seasons made this far from easy, I soon discovered, especially with regard to cakes. There were no plums for plum pudding, nor pears or apples, let alone chestnuts. It was quite as if one were required to devise a harvest festival in an English June.

My troubles did not end there. There was next the matter of a tree—none of the native varieties looking or smelling quite right—while I found it nearly impossible to discover suitable decorations in the Hobart shops. Hardly had I succeeded in arranging a group of choristers to sing carols when I struck new calamity with regard to casting the Nativity drama, as so many of the island's younger persons had left for the Victoria gold rush that it proved nigh on impossible to discover a baby—at least of good family—to play the infant Jesus. When it came to the other roles I found my problems were exactly reversed, as I found that a good part of

Hobart society had a weakness for theatrical drama, so any decision I made was likely to cause great disappointment in some quarter. I was obliged, indeed, to refer several times to Gerald, so I might attempt to avoid unwittingly making dangerous enemies for Her Majesty's colonial government!

As days passed, however, problems were overcome and arrangements made. I had the hallway of the house redecorated, banishing the gloomy hues of our predecessors, and all was given a most thorough cleansing. I then began attending to the garden. I had just chosen a corner where our black guests might be placed–I would have the potted plants moved from outside the stables to provide a screen from the rest of the gathering–when there occurred to me a most delightful idea. I could arrange to have their likenesses taken. It was a notion, I realized at once, as pleasing as it was valuable, for the preservation–at least in memory–of this most unhappy of races. If the results were satisfactory they would certainly earn a prominent place in our London house.

I began to make enquiries that same afternoon and soon discovered the name of the professional I sought.

The Reverend Geoffrey Wilson
DECEMBER 1857

WE WERE ARRIVED! After so many months of discomforts and worries, of struggles and privations, we had finally reached our journey's end. What joy I felt as the *Sincerity* crept gently up the estuary of the Derwent River and there before us lay Hobart town, cheerily lodged beneath the frowning massif of Mount Wellington. Since we had left Port Arthur I had every hour been expecting Potter to demand we drop anchor at some deserted rock or cove, so he might cause us further delay, but, to my relief, he had remained quiet. I could only suppose the Black O'Donnell incident had served to dampen his spirits. If so I hoped the effect would prove of long duration.

The sight of our destination had a most cheering effect upon all aboard the *Sincerity*. The Manxmen grinned and sang as they went about their final tasks aloft, reducing sail that we might proceed slowly towards the port, and Renshaw showed rare animation, quite hanging over the ship's rail to look upon the shore. Even the doctor displayed something like courtesy—a quality I had hardly seen in him till now—and for a brief moment I almost wondered if I had judged the man a little harshly. As for my own self, what excitement I felt as I gazed upon this land that had so long filled my thoughts. The dour peak of Mount Wellington suggested some little-known region of Scotland, but the scent of vegetation drifting across the water seemed exotically unfamiliar, and rich with promise. It was no doubt merest fancy and yet, as I listened to the humming of the wind, playing its strange tunes in the ship's ropes, I almost believed I could hear the faint murmuring of voices, like distant angels, whispering their greetings across the miles of wilderness: "Welcome, sweet vicar, welcome."

Hobart did not tarry long in making itself known to us. Hardly had the *Sincerity* been towed to her berth in the harbour—an elegant arrangement, with grand stone warehouses lining the quays—when there stepped onto the deck a genial-looking man in a straw hat, who introduced himself as a reporter for one of the island's newspapers, the *Colonial Times*, and explained he was seeking information for the shipping announcements. Captain Kewley treated the fellow with some coolness but I saw no need for such reserve, considering we had been presented with a most useful opportunity. Thanks to Jonah Childs's efforts our arrival was already expected in some quarters—including even the governor himself—but still I felt it might be of no small interest also to other, less exalted members of the local population. Thus I endeavoured to explain a little about our expedition to the reporter. I was pleased to observe he showed the greatest interest, quite plying me with questions, and eagerly scribbling my replies in his notebook. I went in search of lodgings with a sense of good work promptly done.

My enthusiasm, I regret to say, did not endure long. The next morning I purchased a copy of the *Colonial Times* only to discover that, behind his friendly demeanour, the reporter was nothing less than a Judas. Alongside the shipping column he had concocted a short article describing our venture, while the tone of this was, I regret to say, wilfully spiteful. He contested my assertion that the Garden of Eden was to be found in Tasmania, though, rather than present his arguments in a man-

ful fashion, he instead chose to treat the matter with a contemtible face-
tiousness. Much of the piece, indeed, consisted of other biblical events
that he suggested might also be ascribed to the antipodes, all chosen for
their absurdity, such as that the Israelites had endured their captivity in
Port Arthur, and had been led by Moses to freedom between the parted
waters of Sydney harbour.

It was not long, however, before my spirits were raised once more.
The next day the three of us called at Government House (there seeming
little point in trying to discourage Potter from attending), where, I am
happy to report, we were received with utmost graciousness by His
Excellency Governor Denton and his charming wife. The governor was
a most cultured man, of good family, who showed the greatest enthusiasm for our venture, and made no reference to the *Colonial Times*. He was
kind enough to invite us all to a social gathering that he and his wife
were holding just before Christmas, and provided me with the names of
various tradesmen whom he felt might be of usefulness with regard to
the final arrangements for the expedition.

The more I set to work on these preparations, the more evident it
became that the ugly cynicism of journalism was not reflected elsewhere
in Hobart society. Everybody I spoke to seemed greatly intrigued, indeed, by the thought that their remote island home was of great biblical
significance, and wherever I went I found myself the subject of curiosity.
Before long a little stream of visitors began to call at our lodging house,
including leading tradesmen and shop owners, all eager to express their
interest in our venture and to discover if we had need of the goods they
sold.

Then again, the more I saw of this little town, the more I was surprised by its unexpected sophistication. It was hard to believe that the
first settlers had arrived here barely half a century ago, as it was already
possessed of a most genteel ambience, recalling to mind some sleepy
Sussex seaside town that has perhaps seen better days. The streets were
quiet and the inhabitants pleasingly courteous, being often in their middle age, as many of the younger generation had ventured away to Victoria to try and make their fortunes from the gold rush. A few were
inclined a little to gloominess, it was true, and I heard many complaints
that trade was poor, especially with regard to the island's whaling indus-

try (it seemed that these foolish creatures, which had lately thronged about Tasmania's shores, had taken it upon themselves simply to vanish away). In the main, however, the Hobartians proved quite as delightful as their town. How pleasing it was to find a place, though it lay on the remotest side of the earth, where everything–from inns and shops to the inhabitants' speech, even to the paintwork of coaches–was unmistakably *English*. Better still, this was Englishness of a charmingly old-fashioned kind, that quite took me back to the days of my own youth, before the railways sent everyone rushing so. How preferable it was to Melbourne, which was so filled with restless clamour and greed. Melbourne had seemed hardly English at all except in name, being quite how I would imagine some brash new settlement of North America.

I wasted no time but quickly set to work to make us ready for the mighty task ahead. My first concern was the choosing of our route, and this was easily decided. I had considered having the *Sincerity* ferry us directly to the western coast, but this would have entailed sailing against the prevailing winds, which might waste weeks of valuable time, and so I concluded that the best approach was by land. I questioned the traders who called at our lodgings, then set about examining the latest maps of the colony, and though the western area of these were absent of any but the vaguest features, the tale they told was amply clear. One of the four rivers that I had identified as being mentioned in Genesis was the Derwent (aboriginal name Ghe Pyrrenne: Euphrates), the very waterway that flowed past Hobart. What could be simpler! If we followed this as far as its source we must eventually find ourselves looking upon Eden.

Arranging the practicalities of the venture proved altogether more troublesome, while matters were not helped by the fact that I received almost no assistance from my two fellow members of the expedition. Attempting to rouse Renshaw from his slothfulness wasted more time than it saved, while Potter was hardly ever to be seen. I tried leaving him notes, detailing any simple task which I had not time enough to attend to myself–such as arranging the removal of the mules' dung–but it was to little avail. Even the Manxmen were uselessness itself. Several times I visited the ship to request that some item from our stores be brought to the lodging house, only to find that Captain Kewley, first mate Brew and second mate Kinvig were all of them away. Finally, losing patience, I browbeat the giant, China Clucas, to tell me where they were hiding, and, with reluctance, he revealed that they were meeting a tidal waiter of the customs and excise by the name of Quine in one of the local taverns. I was a little puzzled as to why Kewley should wish to spend time with an officer of the customs, whose work should have been completed long before, but all soon became clear. Entering the inn, with some distaste, I found all of them, including Quine–a little weaselly man who stood entirely upon one leg, the other tapping about the ground in a kind of secret dance–were speaking not in English but Manx. I was not impressed. While I had no objection to *Sincerity*'s officers reminiscing about their faraway homeland, this seemed no excuse for their neglecting their duties, and I was obliged to rebuke Kewley in strongest terms for his constant absence from his vessel. He was, I was pleased to observe, not a little embarrassed.

Despite such discouragements I managed to make good progress with our preparations. I procured food to supplement our English-bought stores, including quantities of rice, flour, desiccated fruit and vegetables. I found also mules, though this was not easy. The extent of our supplies was such that I had quite to scour Hobart for sufficient animals to meet our needs, while the creatures' owners showed a timorousness hard to credit, and were so fearful that we might encounter some mishap that they quite refused to let us hire their beasts, insisting we purchase each one outright. This absurd demand proved a great burden upon the expedition's funds, a fact that was particularly irksome, as it meant I would not, as I had hoped, be able to hire a manservant of my own. This had been my wish, I should explain, not for my own self, but simply for the good of the expedition, as it would be quite unseemly for the venture's leader to be less well attended than junior members of the party. Seeing as it would be impossible to recruit a new servant, I hoped the doctor might–for once–place the interests of our enterprise before his own petty selfishness, and I left him a note requesting him to relinquish his fellow Hooper. His response was, I regret to say, curt almost to the point of provocation.

Even then I did not despair, and it occurred to me that I might employ one of the mule drivers in this capacity. In the event, however, it proved no easy matter finding any who were qualified even to control the animals, let alone who would be skilled as an attendant. I placed advertisements in the local press, but of the applicants who replied one would be old and frail, the next would be shamelessly drunk, while none seemed possessed of even the smallest piety, and I suspected many were former convicts. Of the six I eventually chose, only one, whose name was Skeggs, had experience of the task before him, having acted as mule driver for an unsuccessful expedition to find gold on the Australian mainland, and, though his manner surly, I supposed this a price worth paying for his knowledge of the animals. The other five had no qualifications beyond a familiarity with horses. Having no great confidence in any, I decided to appoint three to act jointly as my servers, which seemed the least poor arrangement.

More troublesome still was the question of a guide. I knew from the start that this would be a cause of difficulty, the interior of the island being all but unknown, and yet I had hoped that there might be somebody who, if he had not traversed the western wilderness, would at least have ventured a little about its fringes. It was not to be. The few men who answered my advertisements all proved to be charlatans, while my new tradesmen friends informed me that the only significant exploration of that part of the colony had taken place more than twenty years previously, and that the government officer who had undertaken it–a man named Robson–was now living comfortably in England, while even he had rarely strayed from the coast. It seemed this was indeed Terra Incognita. Accepting that there was little more that could be done, I resolved to cast the matter from my mind, and rely upon the benevolence of Him whose will this expedition was intended to serve. If there was no one to guide us, then I would simply have to guide us myself.

Days passed and several times I found myself taken aback by the sight of a gaudy shop display, or by an overheard conversation concerning methods of cooking geese that reminded me that this was December. A spell of unusually hot weather caused the streets of Hobart to shimmer and the men and beasts that travelled them to slow and sag in discomfort, so it was hard to believe that thousands of miles distant–and quite beneath my very feet–Englishmen were lost in midwinter darkness, struggling to keep themselves warm against the elements, as they made their seasonal purchases. I was not so remiss, however, as to forget the governor's approaching party. This was an event to which I had been greatly looking forward, indeed, if only as an opportunity to further the interests of the expedition.

Even as we approached Government House I could see, from the large number of guests arriving, that it was a most grand affair, and sure enough, when I entered the garden it seemed as if all Hobart society was assembled before me, every one of them quite splendidly attired, despite the day's warmth. At the centre of the throng stood a group of singers, red of face as they stolidly braved the sun, who regaled the guests with carols, while behind them a mighty tree, of some curious local variety, had been prettily decorated with candles and angels. Tea was to be found in abundance, and fine cakes too. The only element that might have seemed a little lacking, indeed, was a sense of the spiritual. Though Christmas was still a few days distant it was the true reason we were gathered thus, and, while I learned that a little Nativity drama was to be staged, it would have been pleasing to have a few words spoken, to remind us of the importance of the approaching feast day. It being the purpose of our expedition to discover a Christian significance for this wild land, I would even have been prepared to offer a little discourse myself had such a thing been suggested.

Such thoughts did not of course prevent me from cheerfully entering into the occasion. I wasted no time but endeavoured, with patient perseverance, to press my way through the throng assembled about the governor, that I might offer my greetings. He in turn displayed his usual graciousness, introducing me to several eminent Tasmanians before taking himself away to attend to further duties of hospitality. Thus I found myself conversing with a government servant concerned with tax collection, the owner of Hobart's leading purveyor of ladies' undergarments and the colony's foremost offal merchant. All, I was delighted to find, were greatly interested in my expedition.

"It's just what the colony needs," the offal merchant declared, with a prophetic air. "We want to catch a few eyes right now, to pull us from these doldrums."

"If anything is found, that is," added the shop owner more cautiously.

"You may have every confidence of that," I informed him cheerfully.

"I would hardly have come all this way if I did not believe we will find success."

It was then that my glance lit upon a most curious-looking party passing behind them along the edge of the lawn. The group, which was being led by none other than the governor's charming wife, was composed of black aborigines, a dozen or so in number. Their presence seemed all the stranger as they appeared to have little connection with the event occurring all about them: as I watched, they vanished behind a row of large plants in pots. I had heard that a very few of the native race of the island still survived; even so their presence seemed more than a little mysterious.

"There'd be visitors aplenty, that's certain," continued the offal merchant. "Why, we'd be a place of pilgrimage! A new Holy Land. That'd help trade, for sure."

All at once there occurred to me a most wondrous thought. We needed a guide. What if we were to employ one of these aborigines? I found myself recalling to mind North American Indians who were used by Europeans to help in their explorations of that vast continent. I was surprised, in truth, that I had not thought of it before. Though most of the aboriginal party had looked unsuitable for such work, comprising females advanced in their years, I had observed at least one able-bodied male.

I began making my excuses to my three new acquaintances. It was just as I was setting forth through the crowd that I noticed, with some annoyance, that Potter—who had been loudly conversing with a party of doctors—was doing just the same.

Peevay
DECEMBER 1857

TWO CARRIAGES WENT to Oyster Cove to get our ones, stopping at my COTTAGE to get me too. On their roof sat num COACHMEN and also SUPERINTENDENT ELDRIDGE with his cheating eyes. Those two carriages were too small for us, yes, so I hardly could get inside and that was a heinous journey. Finally we arrived and I could get air to breathe, and governor's wife came hurrying, smiling too much, and saying, "Ah, dearest Eldridge, ah, dearest blackfellows, how fine to see you." Then she was looking round us into carriage to see. "Did you bring crafts and spears like I asked?"

Pagerly told me that Eldridge said we must do these for her, but still nobody did, so I answered, "We don't make those things anymore."

This made her frowning in her smile as if I was hateful. "That is a pity." Then she made us wait a long time outside the door while servants went to find some other white scut called JABLONG, who she told was our happy surprise, but servants never could find him, so her mouth went thin like she ate something bad, and she said we must go into garden. I never went to a num PARTY before and it was a little interesting. This was for Jesus getting born, whose name is CHRISTMAS, and it had singers–looking red and crook in that sun–and also CHRISTMAS TREE, which had candles and shiny stuff as if it was wearing clothes. Mostly, though, party was just white men, plenty of them, all talking loud and smelling hot in their many shirts and jackets and giant dresses and so, some drinking tea if they got any. When they saw us they gave their looks like always, some hating, some laughing, some just watching. Yes, already I wished I never let Pagerly make me come here. It was just fruitless, besides, as I never would end hatings with Mother like she said. Mother was in my same carriage when I came, you see, and I observed she never even looked hello when I came inside, but just stayed watching through her window at any other things.

Still, it was too late now. Governor's wife and Eldridge took us to a table which was hidden behind plants, and in truth this was better, as it meant white scuts couldn't give us more looks. BENCHES were there for sitting, and CAKES and CUPS on the table. Governor's wife stayed standing, looking as if she was eager to go to some other place right this instant, and she sent another servant to find our surprise, Jablong. We sat down and Mother started eating with hungry craving, so I surmised this was the reason she came, and not anything told by Pagerly about ending hatings with me. Mother always did dearly adore cakes, you see, and she said they were the only good thing about white scuts. Then, just as other servants with grey face like dirty water brought tea in TEAPOTS, bushes moved and here came a tall thin white man, nobody I ever saw before, with his small head and too much smile.

"Mr. Wilson," said governor's wife, looking like she was trying to tell him goodbye. "What a fine surprise."

Looking at this Wilson, who was a vicar, I did recollect Smith and Robson from our slow-dying island days. Yes, he feigned his eyes kindly, just like they did. From his twitching I divined he had some greedy wanting from us really, though it was hard to think of anything we had, unless he desired spears and so, like governor's wife. Other one, Potter, was heavier like a fighter, with red hair and beard.

"I wonder if I might be introduced to your charming guests," was Wilson's desire. Thus Eldridge must tell him all our white men's names so Wilson could give us each his little smile, as if we were smallest children, which I hated very much. "The fact is I have some questions I want to ask."

Now red beard Potter started too. "As do I."

Governor's wife gave her hating smile. "I must tell you that I am expecting Mr. Jablong any moment."

So it seemed all these white scuts wanted us now, which was some puzzle to confound, as for years they just wanted to forget us. Vicar Wilson asked to know if we were from the world, which seemed just some foolishness and no mystery to conceal, as where else could we come from? When I answered, "Yes, of course we do," d'you know he was pleased as if this was his greatest good fortune, and his hands went clap as if he was trying to get some small fly, which was praying, like Robson and Smith often did. "Thank thee, Lord, for this tiding of joy," he told God, his face all blissful. "Mr. Cromwell, I must tell you that we are going to that western wilderness. My wish, you see, is to discover Garden of Eden there."

This was most curious of all. Yes, num will think any demented thing if they desire, so I knew, but still this was some great puzzle to confuse. I knew Genesis, IN THE BEGINNING GOD CREATED THE HEAVEN AND THE EARTH, and so and so, but this was nothing of ours.

The one who was interested of our ones was Mother, which was strange too. "Who is Eden?" she asked. Mother didn't know any Bible things, as she never would go to Robson's school.

Vicar Wilson gave her a look as if she was just some humour to amuse, and was going to give his answer but I hated him making her his joke, so I was swifter. "Eden is not a man. Eden is a place. Eden Garden was made by white men's God long, long ago, to put two white men inside, till he got hateful and made them eat special fruit and go away."

Vicar Wilson smiled at me as if I was his best joke now. "That is a most unusual account."

Now Mother was laughing her loud laugh. "But this cannot be. You say God made Eden Garden long ago? Well, everybody knows God never came here till you white men brought him in your boats."

"God was here before us," Vicar Wilson told her in his cleverness. "You see, God is everywhere, and always was."

It was a mystery to confound why Mother was so interested. Now she got PIPE and TOBACCO from her pocket, for smoking, which was a thinking thing with her. "He is everywhere?"

Wilson was surprised by her pipe, but he smiled still. I could see he never surmised Mother at all. "Everywhere. God is in sky and deepest places of the sea. He is in mountains and trees. He is in birds and animals and fishes too. Most of all, he is in us."

Mother lit her pipe. "Then he is in you?"

This he liked very much. "Of course. And he is in every one of you too."

Mother gave her dangerous look. I suppose I divined she must do something heinous soon. "And he is everywhere inside you?"

Wilson nodded. "Most certainly."

"So he must be in your dirty stinking arse, Vicar? Poor old bugger God, isn't he, stuck inside there?"

"Mary!" shouted Commandant Eldridge, but it was too late. Vicar Wilson was strange. First he went staring, eyes wide as if they might go pop, but then he put his chin in the air and tried to smile, as if Mother never said anything bad after all but just kindly words. Of course his blinking, quick quick quick, told everything. Governor's wife went just white in her face, as if she might get sick soon. In truth they were funnier than Mother's saying her magic words, and it was them made me laugh.

So a strange thing happened. Mother heard my laughing and now she looked at me, which was the first time that day. Then she smiled. This was sudden, almost as if it was just some mishap she never did intend, but still it was interesting to me, because it was the first smile I got from her in all those many years. D'you know I think it was the first even since I burned those spears she made to kill Robson, when governor came to our dying island, all those many summers before. I was so surprised that I smiled too. So it was I felt as if some hateful ache stopped, at long last.

The only num who looked like he never cared about Mother's words was red beard Potter, who looked as if he was quite pleased. "Could one of you tell me," he asked, rude in his voice, "how long is it that your females carry babies in their bellies? Also do you know what a number is?"

These were stupidest questions, and some impudence, too. He never got any answer, though, even just scornings, as then another num stranger came. This one looked cross as if ants bit him, and was carrying a thing I never saw before, which was a box made from wood with a blanket on top. Now he put it on the ground so it stood on its long legs like sticks.

"At last," said governor's wife, as if someone gave her food after she was hungry for days and days. "Mr. Jablong has brought a special machine to make lovely pictures of you all. Isn't that splendid?"

Pictures? I didn't know if this was splendid at all. Mother was quickest, though. "You never told us this before."

"But how could I?" answered governor's wife with her laugh. "I never met you till today."

That was just tricks. All at once I saw my road, and it was a fine road, too. So I got up from my place on the bench and sat next to Mother. Thus it was we were two. "Why d'you want pictures of us?" I asked.

Governor's wife gave me her hating smile. "I thought it would be pleasing to you. Just wait and see. It will be your delight how beautiful pictures are."

Mother hit her pipe on the table, very loud. "I won't do it."

"I won't either," I said with her. Then we looked at Pagerly and others of ours to say YOU MUSTN'T EITHER. That made governor's wife wrathful, and she told how Jablong's box wouldn't hurt us, so we must. Eldridge helped her, yes, to try and get her cherishings, and in the end she could make three of ours say yes, which was sad, but at least was not many. So Jablong, who spoke num words strangely, like they went through his nose, got chairs for those three to sit on, which he put in front of STATUE, which was of white scut baby jumping and holding SWORD.

"But I never finished talking to you, Cromwell," said Vicar Wilson now. He was still raging at Mother's magic words, I could observe, but he feigned he was joyous, so I surmised he was pulled both ways, like some dog animal that desires to steal meat from the fire though it is too burning to touch. "You see, it is my fine hope that you might be willing to join our expedition, as our guide." So this was his wishfulness. He wanted me to show them the world. They would need it, too, I divined, being just num strangers, who would get lost or bitten by black snakes. Yes, that was why he came to see us so eager.

Red Beard made a sneering look as if they were foes. "D'you really think that's a good idea, Vicar?"

Wilson never looked at him. "Well, Cromwell?"

Why should I? They should never go there, to the world, which was ours, not theirs. Truly it was hateful to think of them stepping there with their big shoes and greedy eyes, in our own places, with secret names and stories. "No, I won't do that."

So Mother gave me another smile, which was many that day.

Vicar Wilson looked surprised, as if this was a thing he hardly could comprehend. "You'd be paid money. You'd have food, plenty of it, and some comfortable sleeping place."

"I still won't go."

He would not stop. "Please think about it later. Also tell me this. Do you recall ever seeing some strange stones or mountains, different from any others? They might be very pale, or shining."

I would not help him even if I could. "Nothing like that."

"Do try, Cromwell. Think carefully."

But now Jablong was ready with his picture-making box, which was pointing at our three ones sitting on chairs, and holding pipes on their knees, which governor's wife said they must, as it looked so pleasing. "Ready," he said, and he hid his head under box's blanket. That was when I discerned a curious thing. Mother was standing just beside him, watching, very interested, even though she said just before she hated his toil.

"Now smile," said Jablong from under his blanket.

All at once Mother reached out her arm towards the picture-making box. So I divined her great intent, which was so bold. I never did guess, though, what other thing would occur, which was the most woeful, heinous and terrible one of all.

Mrs. Gerald Denton, Wife of the Governor of Tasmania
DECEMBER 1857

HOW RIGHT GERALD had been. From the very moment the half-caste Cromwell arrived he brought a malevolent influence to the gathering. To make matters worse, the rest of his party—the true aborigines—seemed greatly under his sway, none more so than his mother, Mary. Hardly had they taken their places for tea when he induced her to insult poor Mr. Wilson, the exploring churchman, who had come only to pay his respects. As if this were not already enough, when Monsieur Jablon, the daguerreotyper, finally arrived (offering no apology for his lateness beyond an infuriating Gallic shrug), Cromwell immediately sought to play upon the other blacks' timidity and persuade them from having their likeness taken. All the while he cast me accusing looks, quite as if I were seeking to gain some advantage from the exercise, though my only wish had been to perform some small kindness towards his fellows: it being only too evident that their days were sadly limited, I had felt it was nothing less than my duty to try and preserve some touching remembrance of this most unhappy race, before it was too late.

Thanks to Cromwell's efforts I was able to persuade only three of the ladies to overcome their shyness and have their daguerreotypes taken, while even these required no little persuasion. I confess I found it disappointing that they were not wearing some splendid tribal costume (I had presumed they would), as their clothes were dreary indeed, being the sort of garments any poor whites might wear. Their long clay pipes added novelty to the scene, however—one could hardly have imagined a less ladylike habit—and as they took their places I encouraged them to hold these prominently upon their laps. I further suggested that Jablon should afterwards take separate poses of each female, so that as full a memorial as possible be preserved.

Having seen the matter almost to completion, I could not linger further, as I felt I had greatly neglected my duties as hostess: already I could hear voices sailing over the screen of potted plants, informing me that the Nativity drama had begun. I had no wish to seem ill-mannered by my absence, and so made my way about the screen of potted plants with some discretion. Glancing up, I saw that Mr. Phelps, the barrister, Mr. Carey, the harbourmaster, and Captain Dacre of the militia had just taken their places upon the stages—all looking most splendid, if a little hot, in their simple shepherds' costumes—where they were being welcomed by Mr. Henderson of the Hobart Bank, who was our Joseph. I was taking my place at the back of the audience when I heard a curious crashing sound from behind me. This was followed almost at once by a sudden cry. Something about this exclamation suggested more than mere mishap, and so, greatly perturbed, I retraced my steps.

What a sad and terrible scene awaited me. The woman Mary lay still upon the ground, her friends gathered about her, their expressions suggesting only too well their great distress. Also crouched by her side was Dr. Potter, Mr. Wilson's colleague. Seeing my questioning look, he gave a briefest shake of his head.

"I believe her heart has failed."

Mr. Eldridge shook his head at this unhappiest circumstance, which he must have met all too often in recent years. I felt myself suddenly struck with the saddest reflections. How suddenly the hand of fate falls among us! How near, every instant, as we blindly go about our lives, lost in the comfort of routine, lurks the icy embrace of death! One instant this poor woman was stood among us, filled with life, the next she had been cruelly snatched away. My heart was quite breaking for the poor blacks, and I was a little sorry even for the hateful Cromwell as he sat beside his mother, uttering a kind of unbelieving moan, and repeatedly clutching at her arm, as if he believed he might yet call her awake once again.

Not that all present were filled with grief. It may seem hard to credit, but even now, in the midst of such sorrow, there was one whose only thought was to complain, and even to throw blame upon the very poor creature who had been taken from us.

"It is broken," whined Jablon, examining his dreary apparatus, which I saw lay upon the ground near poor Mary. "She did it."

I could hardly credit his words. "How dare you say such a thing?"

"I saw her through the lens. She reached out to push it over, then pof, she fell."

"Your remark is both preposterous and untrue," I informed him curtly. Even then he showed no remorse, embroiling himself in study of his device. The aborigines began moaning to themselves in a most touching manner, though, a little to my surprise, they did not protest their grief noisily—in the manner of some Mediterranean people—but seemed somehow to close in upon themselves, their faces becoming sadly private. Nevertheless, it appeared their cries had caught the attention of the main gathering, as I became aware that the actors in the Nativity play had fallen silent, and curious faces were peering round the bushes. Among the first of these, I was glad to see, was dear Gerald. He nodded gravely as I explained what had occurred.

"How dreadfully sad."

"Please get the carriages now," demanded the half-caste, abruptly returning to his former ill manners. "We must go back. We will take her with us."

Mr. Wilson's surgeon colleague, who had covered Mary's face with her shawl, got to his feet. "Surely it would be more correct for her to be taken to the hospital."

Gerald gave a nod. "I dare say she should."

The half-caste was, as ever, determined to make himself difficult. "She is ours. Give her to us."

"Do not worry yourself," Mr. Eldridge told him, casting a reassuring glance towards Gerald. "I am sure she shall be returned to you soon enough." Despite the man's tainted reputation, I must say that I had found him most helpful.

Ignoring Cromwell, I made every effort to persuade the true blacks to remain a while, so we might endeavour to offer them what comfort we could in their distress, but it was to no avail, and they showed great impatience to leave this sad scene. Reluctantly I called the carriages to be brought, and in a moment their little party was being hurried away. Glancing at their table, cakes still unfinished, tea not yet drunk, it was impossible not to be filled with the most tender and affecting feelings.

The fact remained, however, that the larger gathering was far from finished. The Nativity play was resumed, receiving warm applause, and, despite this terrible event that had occurred, our guests soldiered bravely on with their chatter and eating. I did so myself, feeling certain that poor Mary–who had seemed a most spirited creature–would have wished nothing else. It was some time before our last visitor took his leave, and I am pleased to recount that, poor Mary aside, the party was not without success. I was kept so busy, indeed, that I was quite unable to apprise myself of what arrangements had been made with her regard.

"We put her in the storeroom," explained the housekeeper, Mrs. Murray. "We took her round the garden, so no one saw."

It seemed a sensible choice, being both spacious and cool. "The hospital has been informed?"

"A cart is expected this evening."

It was then that there occurred to me a thought. "Is Monsieur Jablon still here?"

Mrs. Murray thought she had seen him by the blacks' tea table, and thus I found him, still fiddling with his device. I endeavoured to cast aside his earlier shameful behaviour, considering that this might merely have been the consequence of his distress that the machine had become damaged.

"Is it usable?" I asked.

He merely shrugged. I led him back to the storeroom. If Mary had shown a shyness towards having her likeness taken, I had no doubt that, once she had seen portraits of her friends, she would have quite insisted upon having one made also of herself. It seemed nothing less than my duty to try and create some enduring memorial to this most unfortunate creature, who had been so swiftly taken from us: to capture this grand old lady, even at this instant of her being taken from this world. Why, in a terrible way this seemed a remembrance all the more sadly pertinent, seeing as death was creeping ever closer to each last member of her most unhappy race.

"I will try," Monsieur Jablon agreed, "though I cannot say if it will work."

One of the legs of the device had been snapped but he was able to prop it up with a sack of potatoes, and soon he was busying himself with the rituals of his calling: opening the doors wide to admit sufficient light, then fiddling with various sealed containers and pieces of glass, and vanishing beneath the curtain of material. In the meantime I called two of the gardeners to arrange poor Mary into a sitting posture, which I suggested should be done by leaning her against an unseen box of apples. As soon as they attempted this, however, a new difficulty became apparent.

"There's no moving her," the head gardener insisted. "She's hard like a board."

Almost at the same moment there emerged from the mysterious box a host of Gallic curses. "It is quite broken," Jablon declared grimly as he emerged to the world once more.

It was, I confess, a great disappointment to me, most of all because I could not help but feel I had failed poor dear Mary.

Mrs. Emily Seaton
DECEMBER 1857

I WAS SURPRISED to hear Nicholas' step in the hallway. He was not due back from the hospital until the evening.

"I can only stay a moment, Emily," he explained, a little breathless. "The fact is I have a great favour to ask. You recall the doctor we met at the party at Government House? The one who I knew as a student? Potter?" He broke into a smile. Then again, Nicholas always delighted in recalling his years of learning in London: his friends and the many pranks—some more than a little mischievous—that they would play on one another. "He called at the hospital this morning and said how much he wanted to meet us again. The difficulty is that he's going away very shortly, and so I thought it was only right I should ask if he would come and dine with us this evening. It seemed such a shame if he should depart without us having a chance to talk, and remember old times." A nervous look came into Nicholas' eyes. "I know that gives you hardly any time to prepare."

I found it impossible to feel angry with Nicholas. "Don't you worry. I shall manage somehow."

His hesitancy remained. "I rather hoped you might persuade Cook to try her best. I would so like to give a proper impression. The fact is Potter's become quite an eminent fellow."

The man had chosen an awkward time to arrive, certainly: Christmas being almost upon us, housekeeping money was short. I had no intention, however, of permitting our guest to think us paupers. "It will not be easy," I told him, so my efforts would not be taken too much for granted, "but I will see what can be done."

His face quite lit up at my words. Nicholas always has a delightful transparency about his expressions. "I'll go and tell Dobbs to give the carriage a thorough clean. I thought I might bring him from his lodgings myself, so I can give him a little tour of the town, and perhaps point out a few places of interest. He may find himself surprised to discover we are more sophisticated than he supposes."

I was happy enough to set about the preparations, rushed though these were. The children had to look their best, naturally, which entailed a good deal of trouble, with complaints as to hair combing and threats of tears when something pinched. Matters were not helped by Nicholas being late, as the delay caused them to become restless, and all the while my attention was distracted by the need to keep an eye on Cook, who, if left to herself, can be more than a little erratic in her methods. Little Frances managed to dip her sleeve in the applesauce–though fortunately it wiped off cleanly enough–while Toby nearly caused a disaster, pushing Louisa so she almost tripped up Cook just as she was carrying the baked fish from the oven, and this at the very moment when I could hear the carriage drawing up outside. There was barely time to scold him, then to propel them all into the parlour and arrange them in something like a neat line, while Cook flung off her fish-stained apron, straightened her cap and ran to the door.

Nicholas quite beamed as he led Dr. Potter into the room. I must confess, however, that I found myself feeling rather less warm towards our guest. Even at the gathering at Government House I had noticed he was possessed by a curious reticence, while this seemed now more evident, making his cheerful greetings appear all a little forced. Even his compliments seemed somehow too generous, as, in that curious stifled voice of his, he praised by turns first the children, then myself, next the parlour and furnishings, and finally, once the children had been sent to bed and we took our places at dinner, every item of food that appeared before him, even including Cook's soufflé that had risen so disappointingly. If I found this a little excessive, still I was pleased enough to see its effect upon Nicholas, who quite delighted in every word.

Conversation soon turned to student days, as I supposed it must, and all manner of curious nicknames were bandied back and forth. Much of what was said meant little to me, and yet I could not help but notice that, though they clearly had acquaintances in common, the two of them seemed not to have known one another as well as I had supposed, there being as much questioning—which lodgings, which lecturers, which friends—as remembrance. This did not seem to reduce the pleasure each found in their recollections, however, and the evening proved a great success, at least until Dr. Potter caused the mood to be suddenly altered.

"D'you remember old Edwards?" he asked. "The ogre?"

Nicholas laughed, falling into a creaky voice that I supposed must be an impersonation of the man. "That is not an answer, that is a disgrace to the name of Hippocrates."

Potter broke into a mighty guffaw, though there was something about his laugh—as with so much else about the man—that seemed not entirely sincere. "I saw him not long before we left London. I'm sure he mentioned your name, and how able you had been."

Nicholas' eyes quite lit up.

"He'll have been surprised you abandoned us, and slipped away from London. Nor would he be the only one."

Why could he not have simply kept quiet? Nicholas had been so enjoying himself, and now a sad look came into his eyes. He rarely spoke of the months following the completion of his studies but I knew they had been painful ones. To others, who had family money and connections on their side, it would have been no great disaster that a position had not been found, as they could have established a practice of their own, but poor Nicholas had no such advantages and had struggled even to complete his training. To take a post as surgeon aboard a transport ship had been all but forced upon him. In the event, of course, matters had ended well enough, but still the subject was hurtful. I threw our guest a cool look.

He seemed oblivious. "You were wise enough to go, mind. After all, if you had remained in London how ever would you have met the delightful Emily?" He scrutinized his fish and carefully picked out a tiny bone. "But if you returned now I'm sure you would not be allowed to escape so easily."

Nicholas regarded him thoughtfully. "You think so?"

"I know so. We were thrown upon the world at a most difficult time. Why, if you ever thought of coming back I'd be only too happy to help you myself." He then turned to myself. "What d'you say, Mrs. Seaton? How would you like to be a London doctor's wife?"

I was beginning to tire of the sound of his voice. "In truth, Dr. Potter, I am most content as I am. This is my home."

"Quite so, quite so." He laughed, clapping his hands in brief applause, though hardly had he done so when he began to regale us with a lengthy account of London, and how it had changed—or rather improved—since Nicholas' student days. We were told of new theatre plays, of new shops, restaurants and railway stations, of parks where the fashionable would walk, and race meetings where they would gamble. Most of all we were told of the many grand people Dr. Potter was acquainted with, from actors and doctors and members of Parliament even to minor members of the royal family. All the while I could see Nicholas listening entranced. I felt myself increasingly uneasy. I had not the slightest wish to go to London. All of a sudden this man Potter, who I had never liked, and who was eating our food, was threatening to create a division between us—a distance—when there had been none before.

I was, altogether, more than ready when Cook carried away the dessert bowls and our guest finally showed a willingness to leave. "Mrs. Seaton, I am indebted to you for a most delightful evening."

"I'll drive you back to your lodgings," Nicholas offered.

"You will have to get up early tomorrow," I reminded him, having no wish to see him spend more time with the man. "Perhaps I should call Dobbs,"

"Dobbs will be fast asleep by now. Besides, we may talk a little more on the way."

Dr. Potter seemed greatly pleased by the offer. "Are you sure? That would be so very kind."

I did not linger but retired directly. I know it was no more than a quarter of an hour's journey to Potter's lodgings, which were close to the harbour, and so, lying abed trying to catch sleep—my mind astir with dismal thoughts of domestic upheaval and ships lost in storms—I was surprised to see nearly an hour had passed, though Nicholas had not returned. Surprise quickly became alarm, and soon I could not rid my mind of thoughts of the horse, which could be skittish, rearing up and hurling the little carriage upon its side, leaving poor Nicholas lying forgotten by some nighttime wayside. As further moments passed, and still he did not appear, I became troubled by new fears. I did not trust this man Potter. What if he had sought to persuade Nicholas into some terrible foolishness; some attempt to revisit the excesses of student times? Nearby the harbour were several taverns of lowest reputation, where violence and drunkenness were commonplace. There was worse, too. I had seen the women who waited in doorways, even in daylight hours, dressed in their coarse finery, their cheap lace and stockings, hoping to prey upon good men. Nicholas would never so much as glance at such females, I told myself, and yet it was hard not to be troubled, especially having seen the awe with which he regarded Potter.

I was, altogether, more than a little pleased when I finally heard a horse drawing up outside the house. Such relief was short-lived, however, as there followed not the friendly sound of a key in the lock, but a loud knocking. Hurrying down, I reached the door before Cook and found a rough-looking fellow stood waiting.

"Mrs. Seaton? I have a note for you."

The writing, though it appeared to be Nicholas', was more a scrawl than his usual neat hand, and it was a moment before I could decipher the words. He wrote that someone in Dr. Potter's lodgings had been taken suddenly ill, and that it might be some time before he could return.

Returning to bed, I found myself more alarmed even than before. Why was it, I wondered, that this ailment, that he did not trouble to name, took so long to treat? Also why did it require the presence of not one but two doctors? I cursed myself for not having thought to detain the messenger so I might question him further. Thus hours passed and still no sleep came, as I tossed and turned. The dawn broke and I was still wide awake, indeed, when I finally heard the familiar rattle of the carriage returning.

Nicholas was quite pale as he walked into the room. "I'm so sorry, Emily. I had no idea it would all take so long."

I knew his looks so well, I knew his every mood, and now, as I watched him, a terrible coldness seemed to creep upon me. I saw it in his eyes, as clear as if he spoke aloud: a lie. All at once, in that briefest terrible instant, everything in the world seemed spoiled, and I could not even say how or why this had happened. To my own surprise my voice sounded still calm. "Who was it who was taken ill?"

"Some woman staying at Potter's lodgings."

"What was the trouble?"

"An infection."

The patient and illness were both far too vague. "Why did it take so long?"

He sensed my suspicion now, and a wary look appeared in his eyes. "We had to perform a little operation."

"What sort of operation?" I would trap him with detail, even though it would destroy me also.

"Does it matter?" His voice was growing angry. "I'm sorry, Emily, but I'm very tired. I'm going to have a wash."

He left the room but he did not escape. Pulling on my dressing gown, I followed. The door to the bathroom was already closed and I could hear his splashing from within. Cook would certainly be listening after a night of such curious goings-on, but I hardly cared. "Tell me where you were," I demanded in a lowered voice.

"I've already told you," he answered from within.

"You're lying."

"For goodness' sake."

I would not let him hide from me. The lock had never fastened properly, and lifting the door a little, I pushed it open without difficulty. Stepping inside, I found Nicholas had removed his shirt and was stood beside the washing bucket, as he stared at me in surprise. The garment was rolled up in his hand and he was clearly about to plunge it into the water. Darting forward, I grabbed at the thing. For a moment we both tugged, but then he faltered and it was mine.

"Emily, what are you doing?"

There would be rouge and face powder. There would the smell of cheap perfume, cheap flesh, harlot's flesh. Most of all there would be the scent of betrayal.

But, strangely enough, there was none of these. The shirtsleeves were a little marked, brown, with what looked like dried blood. As for smells, I could detect nothing but a faint odour of surgery.

Colonial Times
DECEMBER 1857

ABOMINABLE INCIDENT AT HOBART HOSPITAL
REMAINS OF ABORIGINE FEMALE STOLEN

A MOST DREADFUL and horrific occurrence took place during the early hours of Tuesday morning, when three men made away with the bodily remains of an aborigine female from Hobart Hospital. Suspicions were first aroused when a passerby, Mr. Thomas Perch, who was returning home from the Anchor Tavern, observed two men outside the hospital, who were engaged in placing what appeared to be a human form onto the back of a cart. When he called out to them to stop they did not answer but jumped into the vehicle, while a third man, who was acting as their driver, cracked the reins and drove off at great speed.

Much alarmed, Mr. Perch alerted the Hobart constabulary and Police Officer Richards was quickly upon the scene. Examining the ground-floor windows of the hospital, he discovered that one of these was partly open and that the surrounds were stained with blood. Climbing into the room within, he found a most awful spectacle, with skin and bodily remains lying in profusion upon the ground, suggesting some terrible murderous struggle had taken place. When the establishment's principal, Dr. Lionel Gifford, arrived, however, he explained that the room was used for the storage of cadavers, and that the ghastly discoveries almost certainly belonged to an aborigine female by the name of Mary, who had been brought there only two days previously. Further investigations suggested that the intruders had been able to open the room's window only partially, as it had become jammed with paint, and that they had mutilated the corpse—which was of generous girth—in order to remove it from the room. As to the motives for this bizarre and gruesome theft, it is assumed that the thieves' interest lay in the female's skeletal remains. The aborigines of the colony being so greatly reduced, their bones are known to attract the interest of museums and scientific institutions within Europe.

Mrs. Gerald Denton, the governor's wife, who had been entertaining all the surviving aborigines at Government House when the woman Mary passed away, and who declares herself a great friend of the unfortunate blacks, expressed her distress and anger at the crime, while her husband insisted that those responsible would be discovered and punished. The location of the woman's corpse being not common knowledge, there has been speculation that members of the hospital staff may have been involved, and while Dr. Gifford insisted that this was most unlikely, he confirmed that any physician found to be implicated would be dealt with most harshly.

A full investigation has been promised by Superintendent McBride of the Hobart police. The witness, Mr. Perch, though he saw the thieves only briefly, described the driver as being short but of strong build, while one of those carrying the body was taller and bearded. The third man he did not observe clearly.

Dr. Thomas Potter
December 1857

<u>19th December</u>

<u>S</u> = worse than useless. Quite panicked at vital moment. Self only managed quiet him with strong <u>slap to cheek</u>. Self had little doubt selves only saved from <u>catastrophe</u> by Hooper's quick actions on cart. Most alarming. Consequences re discovery = <u>v. serious</u> re own future prospects + also re prospects of <u>notions</u>. Only hope = <u>interloper</u> = some too far away to see selves clearly.

Endeavoured cast such worries from thoughts. Drove out from Hobart (streets fortunately empty) to quiet area seashore. Built driftwood fire for boiling water, then began, throwing waste into sea. Work = tiring + much <u>slower</u> than self supposed (not helped by <u>S</u> = <u>mewling</u> throughout) so self obliged send Hooper with note to <u>Mrs. S</u> to prevent she falling into <u>panic</u> re his long absence, making enquiries etc. etc. When Hooper returned self had he assist with <u>task</u>. He proved excellent assistant + by end of night he = quite a little surgeon (+ altogether more useful than <u>S</u>). Self growing ever more impressed re his character. He = little educated yet not unintelligent + shows greatest interest re <u>notions</u>, which he understands quite well.

Finally finished at dawn. Self pleased to see specimen = <u>excellent</u> + <u>far</u> better than those from <u>Flinders</u>, which all = damaged or incomplete. Self even able discern faint yet observable <u>characteristics</u> (lack of firmness + proper fibre etc. etc.: cf. hardy Saxon Type). Also found <u>amulet</u> round carcass' neck, made from animal skin + containing some form <u>bones</u>. Good instance <u>savage superstition</u>. So hope all may = worth effort, despite all. Had brought storage materials + placed new specimen within these with greatest care. First wrapped larger pieces specimen in cloth. Then rolled all in several <u>blankets</u> for padding. Next put all in cotton bag on which self wrote <u>Type, name, gender</u> etc. etc. Tied <u>amulet</u> to neck of bag. Finally placed in packing case.

Gave <u>S</u> good scare before sending him home (v. easy): warned he must tell <u>nobody</u> re matter, including even his foolish wife, as = certain to invite disaster for he. Hope + believe he shall do as instructed.

Reached port 7 a.m. Manx showed little interest as = v. preoccupied re own affairs + self had no difficulty taking specimen aboard <u>Sincerity</u>. Returned to lodgings, washed + took well earned rest.

20th December

Weather continuing fine and warm. Purchased copy local newspaper, *Colonial Times*. Worried to find <u>incident</u> = of much concern from <u>foolish sentimentalists</u> etc. etc., some even in <u>highest positions</u>. Most aggravating. If self once brought specimen to England am sure nobody would care from whence it came. Here, though, matter threatens real <u>difficulty</u>. Fortunately description by interloper = poor.

Peevay
DECEMBER 1857

IN THE MORNING white man MR. FORBES came on his horse, like he did sometimes, to ask if I would work cutting whales again that day for MONEY, and when I told him no, Mother is dead now, you see, he looked surprised and said yes, he was so sorry, he read this in NEWSPAPER. Then he looked down, gravely frowning and told a thing that was interesting: "I didn't realize she was your mother. I'm very sorry. I hope they're caught, whoever they are."

This was some puzzle to confound. So I asked him, "Who must be caught?"

That made him shy, I did observe, but I made him tell, asking every question, one jumping from another, till he said it all, every heinous part. So I learned of hospital room, of watching man, of thieves, who were three, and their CART. I learned of window that would not open, and of skin that got cut. This was some discovering. So it was everything in all the world got changed. All those shootings and chasings and babies dropped in the fire, all that waiting on death islands with sand blowing in your eyes, and getting cheated with God, none of this was so bad, you see, as what they did to Mother. Killing was better, yes, as that is being hateful and afraid, which is some esteem, while this cutting and playing was just a scornful thing, odious as could be. That was making her small, into nothing at all, not even dirt. Truly, I thought I got to the end of white scuts' badness but no, there was no end I did now surmise.

Forbes went away, looking worriful, as if he thought I might hate him now, just because he was white like those others who did Mother, which I did a little, yes. So I was alone and my blood ached and I did not know where to go or what to do, as everything was gone bad. I started walking, going towards Oyster Cove, thinking I will see Pagerly and others and talk with them, but what-they-did-to-Mother came with me every step, till I felt shamed, thinking it was all my fault, because I let them take poor Mother away. So I could not after all, as I feared their eyes, and I turned back to cottage. I took and sat outside, watching river and sun going lower, hungry for some quiet thing, but no, it never came, as what-they-did-to-Mother was sitting just beside, so I hardly could perceive any river there. When it got cold, and biting insects hummed, I went inside, but what-they-did-to-Mother got in faster. It was still there when I went to sleep, and in the middle of the night, when all was quiet except for mouses scuffling, suddenly it woke me up and said HERE I AM, as if it was new again.

It was in this dark that I got my first thought. This was THAT'S WHAT WHITE SCUTS THINK OF OUR ONES. That thinking was just quite small, yes, and only took some briefest instant to complete, but little things can grow, like when wind makes tiny hole in hut's roof and then blows ever and again, till hole gets wider and wider and suddenly whole roof flies away. So it was. As I lay there in the night my next thought was I WAS A FOOL TO LEARN WHITE SCUTS' WORDS AND GOD, AS THEY NEVER WERE ANY PISS-POOR USE IN FIGHTING THEM. After, there was I SHOULD HAVE JUST SPEARED SOME AND GOT KILLED WHEN I HAD THE CHANCE. Worst was last, and this was MOTHER WAS RIGHT, I WAS WRONG, AND IT'S ALL MY DOING WE ARE LIKE THIS.

After I had these different thoughts I got up and went to work. First I lit candles so I could see. Then I took TEAPOT and made it fly like a bird to wall and go in many small brown pieces. Next I broke legs off STOOLS and TABLE and hit these against SHELVES, so they fell down, very loud. After, I put pieces of TABLE and STOOLS, together with BOOK and TOP HAT, all in a big PILE, just beside CURTAINS.

Finally I took CANDLES and lit PILE, so it became a fire, very beautiful, that burned down COTTAGE.

When COTTAGE finished burning it was morning. So I sat, smelling ashes smell and watching little smokes climbing up, and I pondered what to do now. It would be blissful to burn more–in fact everything–but rain fell in the night, so I surmised nothing much would catch. Then I thought of killing white scuts–any would do–and though this hardly felt like a real thought, still I walked to Hobart town, as if it might be real after all.

Streets were hot and dusty that day, I recall, and it was interesting going hither and thither, just me amid these white men, thousands and hundreds, all walking in their hurry, or giving me looks as if I was wrong and this wasn't my place. So I tried to divine which day the world became theirs, and I thought probably it was when Mother got sick in the forest, and I burned that tree and showed Robson where we were. Yes, yes, I should have just killed him with my spear, and others too, as it would be easy. Now it was too late. Why, if I killed some it would make piss-poor difference, I did surmise, as there will be so many left.

So I decided to drink RUM. I never drank this till then, no, because I knew it would be my ruination and the end of all enduring. I saw Palawa who did, you see, and it was as if their life got tired and went to sleep, till all that was left inside was getting mad and staggering and wanting more rum. But now I didn't care about enduring as I just wanted to get finished quick, so rum was correct I could divine. Thus I went to INN. This was interesting, too, as I never looked inside any such before. Sun was shining, making smoke from tobacco pipes a pretty thing, floor was wooden and creaking, and on walls were so many bottles, very beautiful, all different colours. White scuts sitting there looked at me as if I was some humour to amuse, but I never minded, and when man in front of beautiful bottles was suspecting I showed money that I got from cutting whales, and he gave me rum just like I asked, in a glass, small and heavy.

Rum was my surprise. I thought it would be like juice from cider gum tree, but no, it had no colour and little sweetness and tasted like metal, or some burning thing. It made me cough, so white scuts laughed, and one of them, with a fat belly, shouted, "Too strong for you, is it, Jack?" but I didn't answer and just drank more, as though it was heinous I wanted to learn it, just like I learned Smith's LETTERS and SUMS and GOD before. So I began to understand rum. I did suppose it would make me feel happy but no, this was never so. It made me feel NOTHING, and this was great good fortune, too, as NOTHING was just what I was seeking. By and by I got another and then another, as I was hungry to get all the NOTHING in the world. But then I learned this rum was more difficult than I knew, as suddenly I was dizzy and feeling crook, so I had to go away, legs leaning like I was on some ship, and white scuts laughing, and when I got outside I was sick and all my beautiful NOTH-ING was gone.

After, I felt so bad and sat by a wall for a time. That was when I grew shamed, and suddenly dying seemed some piss-poor fearful thing, like fleeing in fright, which I never did before. How could I do this when that what-they-did-to-Mother was still here? No, I did divine, dying was not mine to get. Mine was finding poor Mother and giving her fine good-byes, like she must have. So it was that this became my intent. It was no easy thing, of course. Num white scuts took her so the only way I could find them was to get help from other white scuts, while I didn't know any except a few, like Forbes and whale-cutting men, who were quite kindly but no usefulness. So I surmised I must try strangers.

First I washed my face and cleaned my coat where it got dirty from the wall, and then I went to Government House, to see governor, who I supposed was the best one, as he was white men's chief. Servant told that governor was busy but governor's wife could see me, which I sur-mised must do. He took me to some room, very large with flowers here and there, and governor's wife sitting down on her long chair, red and beautiful. She made female servant get tea and then she got tearful, telling how woeful she was that Mother got stolen so. This gave me hope, yes, but only for a short time, as when I asked if governor would seek Mother's stealers she got cross in her tears, saying, "Dear Gerald's doing everything he can," as if I supposed he was doing nothing much, though I never said this. Then she told how she felt so woeful about Mother that she was suffering hardship, and could not sleep well in the night, and thus I divined that governor's wife's tears were not about Mother after all, but were about governor's wife, and what a wonder to behold she was getting so sad. See, now she was looking away through her window and telling, "I'm sorry, Mr. Cromwell, but this terrible thing really is more heinous than I can endure," as if it was her mother, not mine, that got taken and cut. Then she told that I must go and see some fellow called POLICEMAN MCBRIDE, and I knew this meant AWAY NOW, BLACKFELLOW, AS I HAVE OTHER THINGS TO DO.

Still I went to see policeman McBride, just in hope. I could divine he would be no usefulness just from my long waiting on bench outside, with other policemen yawning or watching as if I was some humour to amuse, and surely enough when I finally got to his room he was more interested in wall behind me than my questionings. "Try not to get distressed, Mr. Cromwell," he told, "we're doing everything we can," but his smile said YOU ARE JUST SOME TROUBLEMAKING FELLOW and WHAT DO I CARE ABOUT SOME OLD BLACK WOMAN'S BONES? He said how policeman who was searching was wondrous clever, but when I asked what this wondrous policeman found till now he said it was "still too soon," which I surmised meant he found nothing. Finally he told I must see hospital's chief, who was called DR. GIFFORD, which meant GO AWAY, BLACKFELLOW, just like governor's wife said before.

Gifford was old man, very thin, and touching his head with no hair with his finger sometimes, as if he must know in case new hairs were there now. He was angry at once, as if I called him magic words—which I never did—and told that, though what-they-did-to-Mother was too lamentable, still it was nothing to do with him, but just some woeful mischief by mystery strangers. No, Gifford said, his hospital was great good fortune and num there were all tidings of joy, so I must be happy. But I wasn't happy. In truth I was getting too tired of these white scuts telling me how they were so clever and correct. I wasn't interested in them, I was interested in Mother.

That was a woeful moment. I went outside, sun low but warm still, and I walked, going nowhere, and feeling I was some foolish ruination. Didn't I ever learn anything? White men never would help some blackfellow against other white men. They never did before and they never would. Why, they had all the world now and could keep any mystery to confound they wanted, being like a wall, some parts hating, some parts lazy, but all hiding other white scuts' heinousness. Even kinder ones, like Forbes and whale-cutting men, never would help me against their ones.

It was thinking of Forbes made me ponder. So I recollected him that morning before, coming to my cottage to ask if I wanted to do work, and giving his heinous news. Didn't he say he knew it from story told by NEWSPAPER? I only looked at newspaper once and it seemed just white men's stuff, but now I supposed it was mine, too. Also newspapers were many, so they couldn't be hidden, while I surmised white scuts never cared what was in them, as they didn't think our ones never would see. So I asked stranger num till they pointed to house of COLONIAL TIMES.

This was just rooms, quite dusty, with so many shelves going high up the walls. Just one white man was there and he wondered at me, but finally he went into another room and got that newspaper, showing me PAGE that told Mother's woefulness. So he watched, too surprised, as I sat and read, which num supposed was too clever for our ones. Page was hateful, yes, as I could see newspaper never cared about Mother at all, as if her cutting was their joke, but still it was useful, and better than I hoped. Fruitful things were as follows. First, that some DOCTOR did it, almost sure. Second, about watching man, THOMAS PERCH, and fellows he saw, who were driver, short but strong, and other, tall with beard. This gave me ponderings, yes, but still it was not enough. So I decided I must go to watching man's inn, that newspaper told me was called ANCHOR TAVERN.

Anchor Tavern was loud with white men's singing because tomorrow was CHRISTMAS, but though barman was suspecting, by and by he answered yes, watching man Thomas Perch is here, and he pointed to small fellow with foolish face sitting by window. So I asked him if there was anything he saw that NEWSPAPER never told. He scratched his arm, not sure if he should answer, but then he said yes, he could recollect some such. First he said cart was yellow, which I hardly cared about. Then he told me something that was interesting. In truth I did wonder this already. After all, who was there when poor Mother died, and said she must get taken to hospital?

Thomas Perch said taller man's beard was a RED BEARD.

Dr. Thomas Potter
DECEMBER 1857

<u>25th December</u>
Self just dressing for lodging house Christmas dinner when heard Wilson loudly shouting, "Praise be to God," "Let us thank the Lord," etc. etc. Self supposed = he merely sermonizing re Christmas, but when stepped into sitting room found he = with <u>half-caste aborigine</u> (name: Cromwell) who = at gov's tea party. Self at once saw <u>trouble</u>. Surely enough Wilson excitedly explaining that half-caste had changed his mind + now = willing be our <u>guide</u>.

Self considered this = entirely <u>absurd</u>. He not even pure aborigine, i.e. primitive nature further corrupted by conflicting influence of opposed <u>Types</u> (estimate development in womb arrested after approx. twenty-eight weeks, i.e. <u>eleven</u> fewer than Saxon, <u>two</u> fewer even than other blacks). Analytical faculty = entirely <u>absent</u>. Beyond all understanding to place selves in such hands. Before self could object half-caste asking (in v. <u>primitive</u> English) if self knew anything re <u>theft</u> of <u>body</u> of <u>aborigine</u> <u>Mary</u>, saying she = <u>his mother</u>. Regarded self with <u>strangest look: searching</u> + <u>malevolent</u>. Confess this caused self momentary <u>unease</u>. Self stoutly insisted had no knowledge re matter, then struck back, questioning Wilson as to whether = wise to engage guide at this late stage, suggesting this may = great strain upon stores etc. etc. (half-caste scowling). Wilson = wholly deaf to reason as per usual: insisting = of greatest significance that half-caste appearing on <u>Christmas Day</u>, as this means he = "gift of God," "sign of divine blessing," etc. etc.

Afterwards, however, self <u>reconsidered</u>. Considered own alarm re <u>half-caste's</u> accusing look = wholly <u>irrational</u> as = quite <u>impossible</u> that he possesses <u>logical faculty</u> required to reach such conclusion. Must merely = some <u>random</u> instance of his <u>barbaric</u> behaviour. If his guidance = deplorable (as self = sure it shall) this will = poor reflection on <u>Wilson</u>, not self.

Self now see his employment could = of some <u>usefulness</u> as he certain to provide v. interesting <u>study</u> re <u>notions</u>. May even lead self to further <u>specimens</u> in wilderness.

CHAPTER THIRTEEN

———◆◆◆———

The Reverend Geoffrey Wilson
January 1858

Finally, on this the third day of the new year 1858–a date that would, I had no doubt, be well remembered in future ages–our expedition was ready to depart. What joy was within me as I climbed into the saddle and gave out a cheery shout of "Away!" What wonder I felt as my call was answered with a mighty creaking of packs and the sound of two hundred hooves ringing out, as this Christian venture, of which I humbly found myself leader, bravely set forth upon its way.

Our departure from Hobart was, I confess, a little restrained. I had made no secret of the day and time, and expected quite a crowd would be gathered to bid us farewell, but it seemed the earliness of the hour–I had been determined to make a prompt start–was too much for these lazy Tasmanians. The only people to be seen through the morning darkness, indeed, were a group of fisherman, who seemed mostly concerned with carrying their catch onto the quay, and also a couple of tavern drinkers still remaining from the night before, whose attentions, in truth, we could happily have done without. As we passed through the city streets, however, I was pleased to see our great party was the source of no little interest, causing curtains to twitch and faces to stare out in surprise.

Before long we left the town behind and had conquered our first mile, then our second, our fifth, and the early morning sun was rising above the Derwent River–already I could think of this only as the Ghe Pyrrenne, or Euphrates–that stretched away to our right, so broad and majestic. The land was rich with farmhouses, and often their inhabitants would step forth to ask who we might be, and whither we were journeying. What looks of amazement appeared upon their faces when I answered with a cheerful shout, "We are going to find the Garden of Eden."

Having never taken part in any such enterprise till now, I must confess to being agreeably surprised by the swiftness with which I found I became accustomed to rough travelling ways, as, after only a few days, I felt quite as suited to this outdoors life as any native aborigine. In the morning I would wake with the dawn and wait, with an explorer's patience, as the mule drivers brought the fire to life, so they might prepare a rude breakfast of sugared tea, porridge, biscuits and freshly cooked eggs. As soon as they had cleaned the cooking pots, taken down the tents and packed all away, I would climb into the saddle and lead us fearlessly forth once again. Soon after midday we would stop for the very simplest of meals, this being little more than bread, potted ham or beef and perhaps a few pieces of sugared fruit, and at four we halt again, so we might endeavour to restore ourselves with biscuits and cold tea. Finally, after still more miles had been dispatched, we would choose a place to make camp–hardly caring how wild and remote it was–and, in a triumph of weary limbs, I would sit with my colleagues about our sturdy portable dining table and await a well-earned dinner, composed of boiled rice and Aberdeen hotchpotch or preserved salmon. Renshaw and Potter would quite insist on completing the day with a glass of brandy, and though, needless to say, I took none, I saw no harm in making a little allowance in such circumstances.

A matter on which I was less inclined to show leniency was that of our devotions. Ours being a Christian expedition, it was essential that it should be conducted in a properly Christian spirit, and yet, to my distress, I found that the others showed a lamentable reluctance in this respect. As we walked, I would often break into a rousing hymn, to voice my faith and also to speed us upon our way, only find myself answered with a most ragged and dismal reply from the rest.

More troubling still was the question of our worship. I had, from the very first, endeavoured to arrange an orderly spiritual routine for each day. I conducted a full gathering for prayers before breakfast, as well as after the midday meal, following afternoon tea and also upon any occasion when a short rest was taken from our walking–perhaps after an especially steep ascent–while a lengthier outdoors service was held each evening once we had made camp. These arrangements seemed exactly as was fitting, and it was distressing indeed to observe the hesitancy with which they were regarded by the other members of the party. I was obliged to rebuke the six mule drivers with regularity for their habit of suddenly vanishing away to perform some chore at the very moment when I was about to begin our evening service. Renshaw I had to censure for, among other things, continuing to eat his eggs during morning prayers. The worst of all, however, was Dr. Potter, whose undisguised yawns during morning prayers (despite my reproving looks) were so frequent that they seemed nothing if not deliberate.

Another source of dissatisfaction was our native guide, Mr. Cromwell. I had had no great expectations as to this man's sense of godliness, seeing as he was partly of native stock, but I had supposed he would prove of usefulness to the expedition. Sad to say this was far from the case, and as days passed, he grew ever stranger in his behaviour. From almost the first he quite refused his sleeping quarters–though his tent was easily large enough to accommodate him and two mule drivers in comfort–and insisted on passing his nights in the open air, upon a kind of dreadful nest of branches and leaves. Next, as we progressed further, he became fussy as to his food, quite refusing to join us in our hearty meals, in favour of sustenance of his own discovery, though this could hardly have been less appetizing. I would sometimes observe him digging some mud-covered root from the ground, which he would scrape clean and devour there and then, raw though it was, while in the evenings he would often make himself a fearsome-looking spear or two and then vanish, returning later with some ghastly native rat or ferret, which he would cheerfully skin and cook for himself upon the fire.

If this were not already worrying enough, there was the matter of his attire. The way being sometimes thorny, especially going down to the river to wash or gather water, all our clothes began to suffer a little, but while the rest of us endeavoured to repair them as best we could, our guide seemed wholly untroubled if his shirt became reduced to merest rags. Worse still, as days passed, I observed he acquired a curious odour–

something like old meat—and had a faintly gleaming appearance, all of which mysteries became unhappily clear when Renshaw reported seeing him smear himself with fat from one of the animals he had speared. Though I rebuked him strongly he was quite unrepentant, claiming the substance kept him warm, though this seemed no excuse.

By then I had begun to doubt even his competence as a guide. How many times I attempted to have him cast his mind back to his childhood days and recall any geological curiosities of landscape he might have observed. Remembering the words of Genesis that tell of how the Lord placed a sword of fire to the east of Eden to guard the way to the tree of life, I asked if he had seen some bright beam of light. I am not a man given to suspicion and yet his responses were so obstinately unyielding that I could not help but wonder if he really had journeyed all across the colony, as he had claimed.

Fortunately it soon became apparent we might have little need of his advice. After several days riding along a broad dirt track—the river beside us gradually narrowing from a grand estuary to a wide stream, thence to a hurrying torrent, till the further bank was hardly more than a stone's throw distant—finally we reached a tiny settlement that marked the very edge of civilization, beyond which lay naught but harshest wilderness. As we dismounted, an old man emerged to ask our purpose, and this fellow proved more knowledgeable than any map. Though he had not ventured further up the river himself, he knew a huntsman who had done so and who said it sprang from a distant lake. What was more, it seemed this was not especially difficult to reach, as an old aboriginal path followed the river all the way. Here was a blessing indeed! It seemed only likely that this lake was the source of the Ghe Pyrrenne, and the other three rivers mentioned in Genesis. If we could reach it, then Eden would surely be close indeed, and perhaps even discernible—to a trained eye—from its very shores.

We set forth into the wilderness the next morning.

Peevay
JANUARY 1858

FIRST MY INTENT was just to kill them in some swift rush. How sweet that would be. RED BEARD POTTER, yes. And SERVANT HOOPER. And also MULE MEN, who were hateful at me in their house of cloth, that was called TENT, kicking and giving me magic words, and promising some dread thing would occur to me in the night, so I went away to sleep by the fire. Truly, they must be dead, every one.

It was never so easy, lamentably. They were too many for spears, you see, even if I had plenty of them, while even guns were trouble. Two rifles, new and beautiful, belonged to servant HOOPER and heinous chief mule man SKEGGS, but these could only shoot one white scut at one time. Revolving pistol was more often, but that was red beard Potter's, and he kept it so carefully, giving me hating looks if I got too interested, almost as if he surmised my dear intent. Besides, I never knew guns properly, as I never had one in those long-ago fighting days, so even if I got it, it would just be some grievous mystery to confound. So I resolved just to be watchful by and by, and to hope for some lucky fortune.

By and by we finished num way and went into proper world. It was strange getting back once again, yes, as I never was here since I was small, fleeing with Mother's tribe from fat Robson all those many summers before. It was hateful, too, just me alone with white scuts, and often and again I would think how they shouldn't be here, stamping in their big boots where my ones trod before, or smelling scents of trees and shrubs that filled my mind with strongest remembrance. This wasn't their place, and never could be.

They were stupid here, I could observe. In their Hobart town they always were cleverest, yes, with their sneering looks and knowing every answer, but now it was opposite, and everything seemed some puzzle to confound them. So it was with HORSE ANIMALS. White men loved these, I could observe, sitting on them so tall, but when we went into proper world they were futile, getting mad eyes and shrieking when they saw any petty stirring. By and by we came into a narrow place in rocks, that made them worriful, and when some black snake slid out from his hole, hissing-hissing, one jumped up, throwing small fellow RENSHAW against stones so he nearly got dead. Path was no better afterwards but worse, so Vicar Wilson said one mule man must take all horse animals back now, and everyone must walk, which made them too woeful. Of course I could tell them this must happen long ago, when we first started, but they never asked.

MULE ANIMALS could go on but even they were stupid, yes, plodding tap-tap-tap with their bags. They must all be tied together with ROPES in their long line, never seeing anything except next mule's arse, and getting whackings from drivers often, as otherwise they would just stop. Then again white scuts themselves were piss poor now they must walk, I could observe. Just mud was some puzzle to confound them, and always they were moaning and cursing it with magic words, or stepping some long way around, getting hot and angry so they smelled sour like old roots gone bad. Didn't they know that all the world has mud, and you shouldn't fuss but must just stride on in your quick feet, splash and away? Nor were they better with other world things, like thorny bushes, biting flies, slipping stones or cold rivers to cross.

Truly it was a mystery to confuse how they ever could kill all my ones and steal the world, or even why they wanted it, as it was no place they could endure. Why, they couldn't live here just alone but had to carry some HOBART TOWN with them hither and thither. Every night mule men put up TENTS for sleeping inside, though this was summer now and weather was warm. They had TABLE and CHAIRS for sitting, and CUPS for drinking BRANDY, while mule men made big fires to cook their white men's food on, that came from TINS, and was heinous like usual, all salty and slippy meat. Our ones never carried anything except fire stick, lucky pouch of dead dear ones and stories to recount. Everything else we could find and make upon our way. But who was chief now? Not me, only Palawa here, but them, who knew nothing. They had guns and were many, while I was just some SERVANT. Why, they laughed when I lived in proper ways, sleeping by the fire, under stars I knew, and finding proper food to eat, roots and game and so.

In truth they got more hateful now we were all alone in the world, away from other num. One time MULE MEN came in the night after they drank secret RUM, laughing at me that my ones were all dead now—which was some hateful joke—and telling that I would soon be likewise. When I called them magic words two held me caught while others pissed on my bed of leaves. So it was I began to ponder if I made some dread mistake coming here, and sometimes in the night woeful fears came, that I was in their clever trap, and their intent was just to kill me and get my bones, so they could make me into nothing, just like Mother. So I kept watchful. This was not easy, as I was just alone and they might jump at me any time, but I did try. In the day I kept small knife blade in pocket of TROUSERS all the while, and if someone came near I would grasp this in readiness. At night I told my sleep to be noticing, so I would leap awake at any slightest sound, and I did so, even at wind in trees or mouses scurrying again.

Then a thought came to me. What if Mother was here? It was possible, I could divine, as white men had so many MULE BAGS I supposed they must have everything. So I started looking in the night. First I would listen as they did their moaning talk of THIS IS RAINI-EST TENT or WHO LOST THAT FORK? or NOW WE MUST PRAY ONCE AGAIN. Then, when all was quiet except just snorings and scratchings and fartings so I knew they were asleep, I could begin. Still it was hard, as mules' bags were too plentiful, while I could only search slowly, feeling with fingers in the dark and thinking this is PLATES and FORKS, or NAPKINS, or glass bottles called CHAM-PAGNE, that I saw getting put inside before. By and by I surmised she was not in any easy MULE BAG, but must be in Red Beard's or Hooper's, while these were difficult, as they took them inside their TENT every night for sleeping on as PILLOWS. Still I pondered there must be some way.

Dr. Thomas Potter
JANUARY 1858

<u>19th January</u>
Morning's progress slow + tiring. Day v. humid + <u>mud</u> = <u>worst</u> till now (last night's rain). Mules slipping, selves likewise, till all = greatly

begrimed, boots heavy with dirt. Only one little affected = <u>half-caste</u> (no shoes), who = scampering through oblivious. This = further instance of his speedy reversion to <u>aboriginal savagery</u>. Other instances: return to near <u>nakedness</u>, sleeping <u>outside</u>, eating vilest <u>raw foods</u>, etc. etc. All = v. useful re <u>notions</u>. Definitive proof that <u>when two Types</u> = <u>unnaturally mixed, characteristics of lower Type shall always prevail</u>. Intend call this axiom <u>Potter's Law</u>.

Finally reached drier part + stopped for rest. Wilson endeavouring make all pray, as per usual, when he interrupted by loud shouting. Hooper had taken himself away from party re private purposes + now = returning, driving <u>half-caste</u> before he with barrel of <u>rifle</u>. Shouted out that he just caught him <u>thieving</u>! Had his hand in my own mule bag. <u>Half-caste</u> = wild with rage. Incident = v. interesting to self, as further demonstrated his reversion to <u>primitive</u> state: irresistible instinct to <u>steal</u>. Told Wilson, "Did I not tell you the half-caste = wholly unsuitable to act as selves' guide? Now it = clear. He is nothing better than a savage <u>thief</u>."

Before Wilson could reply half-caste directed self foulest look and exclaimed, "But it is you who are the thief. You were the one who stole <u>my mother's bones</u>."

Confess self = greatly taken aback. Simply could not comprehend how he able arrive at such conclusion. Could not = from <u>rational deduction</u>. Some peculiar primitive <u>instinct</u>? Unless he directed by some <u>malevolent European</u>? Matter = v. awkward: could see Wilson regarding self with spiteful <u>curiosity</u>, Renshaw too. Self insisted this = wildest <u>falsehood</u>, merely intended to distract from his <u>thieving</u>. Fortunately half-caste then made <u>foolish mistake</u> (inevitable): claimed his mother's remains = in mule bag he trying search (i.e. mine) + demanded this be examined. Self gladly agreed. V. amused to see his foolish black face fall as bags = emptied + <u>nothing untoward</u> = discovered. Observed <u>Wilson</u> also looking <u>disappointed</u>. He taking <u>half-caste's</u> side even now. When self demanded he must = <u>punished</u> + <u>sent back</u> Wilson refusing: saying all selves should endeavour forget incident. Typical behaviour of <u>Norman Type</u>: manipulate <u>institutional</u> advantage to thwart <u>truth</u> + <u>justice</u>.

In truth matter = puts <u>self</u> in v. awkward position. Could pose greatest threat re own professional prospects, notions, etc. etc. Fortunate that incident occurred in this <u>remote place</u>. As all resumed progress, self slowed behind rest so could talk to <u>Hooper</u>. His <u>suggestion</u> = hardly acceptable (also v. hard properly achieve) though showed commendable loyalty. Yet fact remains something must be done.

Had not progressed far when heard commotion from front of party, shouts of "Here it is," etc. etc. Shortly after, self stepped through trees to reach shore of long <u>lake</u>, flanked by crumbling grey-brown mountains. Self observed these = little different from others that saw on way, except higher. Self = little surprised. Wilson = stood by water's edge, face quite <u>clenched</u>.

The Reverend Geoffrey Wilson
JANUARY 1858

WHY SHOULD I despair? I did not. Naturally I did not. Annoyance this might be–I had been so sure that I would see Eden's walls glittering in the distance before me–but it was nothing more. How could one small reversal weaken the mighty power of my faith? Why, it was as a mere pebble hurled against a sturdy mountain, an ant blocking the path of towering elephants.

My belief soon won through. After only a few moments of careful thought there occurred to me an explanation as simple as it was true. It is well known that our Lord God will sometimes impose little tests upon His children, so He may be sure of their devotion. Thus it was now: our worthiness was being sought. Why, I even considered that we had been given a kind of blessing. Was this not a wondrous opportunity to demonstrate my own unswerving reverence; to prove my faith was solid as a mighty rock? I would answer this disappointment not with sadness but with joy!

"I have no doubt more will become visible if we proceed further about the lake," I declared to the others.

I could not help but observe Potter and his servant, and the mule men too, casting one another sceptical glances, but none spoke up, so I determined to pay them no heed. Their dismal doubts would be answered soon enough, by the dazzling light of fact. Once we had eaten our simple meal I led us onwards once more, giving forth with a cheery hymn so faint hearts might be speedily restored.

So the shore became too marshy to traverse. So we were obliged to follow the path as it turned inland. What mattered this? We would soon find our way back to the lake, of that I had no doubt. Such difficulties were mere commonplace on the long road upon which I had been journeying. Had I not overcome the false arguments of atheist geologists? Had I not triumphed over the confiscation of our ship, and endured the trials of the ocean? Compared to such struggles this awkwardness of geography was a mere molehill, to be stepped over by my own indomitable belief. Why, my heart had never been so filled with hope. I took every measure I could to help us, of course. Most of all I prayed. I prayed thanks for our preservation. I prayed for guidance in this, our humble effort to serve His cause. I prayed that my fellows might be helped to pray.

I was not so greedy as to suppose these appeals would immediately find an answer and yet, miraculously though it may seem, this is exactly what occurred. Shortly after we left the lake's shore I observed something lying beside the path that caused me to clap my hands in wonder. It was, I must tell, the fallen branch of a tree. To the rest this may have seemed ordinary enough–they showed, sad to say, only a muted interest–but to any who had eyes to see there was no mistaking the object's significance. The alignment of its twigs resembled, with a closeness remarkable to behold, an arrow, while, more astonishing still, it was pointing in the very direction that we were following. This was not all. Within the hour I observed, marked upon a mighty rock, the faint yet unmistakable impression of the letter J, written as finely as if it had been carved for Moses himself, in that other great wilderness. There could be no doubt whose name was signified, nor the glorious hope that shone forth from that stolid stone. Even still there was more. As I stood in wonder, regarding that holiest of letters, I became aware of a faint cry emanating from the forest nearby, of some native bird. I had no difficulty making out the blessed meaning hidden within its call: *E-den, E-den*. I do not believe I have ever felt so greatly blessed.

It was soon after this that the path began to ascend more steeply, climbing through thick forest. This was hard work, the day being so close, yet I banished weariness from my limbs, keenly leading the way. Finally the trees gave way and I found myself upon a saddle of land, with low hills rising up to either side, rocky and crumbling, in the manner of so many Tasmanian peaks. The path, I was curious to discover, now split into two ways. To my left it followed the land down into what looked like another expanse of forest, while to my right it began climbing one of the hills. It seemed we were being tested with another little puzzle.

"We should go left," insisted Potter, though I had not asked his opinion. "Down looks a better track."

I had no intention of being pushed into a decision. "What do you say, Mr. Cromwell? Do you know this place?"

"I don't know it." The guide looked up at the hill, seemingly lost in contemplation. Then all at once he gave a sudden nod. "Up is better. That way is more towards that lake."

Potter did not like this at all, needless to say. "It seems hardly prudent to follow the advice of a thief," he remarked accusingly.

I had no wish to return to that curious disagreement. "What do you say, Mr. Renshaw?"

"Down would save us climbing, I suppose," he answered drearily.

How close I was to waving my hand for us to proceed upon the downwards road. It was as I stood thus, considering the matter, I became aware of a sudden change to this savage scene. The day had grown overcast and the land to the left was hazy and grey, but, glancing up at the hill to our right, I saw this was now bathed in faint, yet glorious sunlight. "There! That is our way."

Potter was still sulking. "A bit of sunshine proves nothing."

My heart was soaring. The best answer to doubters is action, and so I simply called out, "Onwards," and set forth to the right with a hearty stride.

There is mystery in hills. This one had seemed nothing very large from below, but the effect proved deceptive. As we climbed higher, rain beginning to fall, I several times supposed we were just below the summit, only to find another ridge rising into view beyond. Little by little, I realized we were ascending nothing less than a mountain.

"There it is," I exclaimed, catching sight of a line of clear ground just ahead. We had entered another forest and it was quite a game to follow the trail, which had grown playfully elusive.

"Surely that's it, over there?" countered Hooper, his clothes quite sagging in the wet, as he pointed to another line to the left.

Renshaw, as ever, added a dismal note. "Are you sure this is right? They look almost like animal tracks."

As if they could be any such thing. Our guide would certainly have alerted us to such a thing. "This way," I insisted cheerfully, stepping towards a path that was easily the clearest, and on we went once more. As the path rose higher, I caught tantalizing half-views of other peaks, looming through the trees. Who knew, Eden might be just beyond the summit of this very mountain. I could picture the scene with such ease, such hope, that it caused me something almost like pain. There! A mighty cliff of smoothest white rock, rising up steep and clean, a fortress wall of giants' construction. There! A way creeping back and forth upon it, steps hewn from the very stone, to an entrance, perhaps still guarded by the sword of fire. Beyond this, a glimpse of ancient greenery: a scene to amaze the imagination of men, infusing them with wonder, and regret.

One single glance upon that glowing greenery would suffice. That, and a sample of the rock upon which it lay, which would be, I had no doubt, both unknown and resolutely resistant to even the mightiest heat, and would be proof enough to overcome even the most sceptical minds. As I strode onwards, I found myself imagining my opponents in that war of pamphlets, sat in their lonely book-lined studies, blindly unaware of the momentous events occurring on this remote side of the globe. My feelings towards them were not angry but kindly, being those with which a guiding parent might regard his errant child. They would, I was sure, be happier of heart to find themselves proved wrong. Henceforth they would be blessed with new and reassuring certainty, finding in the Scriptures a mighty tree upon which to lean their dismal, doubting limbs. It was these very men, my foes, indeed, that I was endeavouring to save, quite as much as my dearest family and friends.

One glimpse would be enough. Or would it yet? Having been guided hither through so many months and miles, across wild seas and harshest wilderness, I found myself uncertain. It would be wholly improper for lay members of the expedition to enter such a sacred place, I knew, while I myself had no wish to trespass, of course, and yet, as the first ordained churchman ever to arrive at this most hallowed spot, I could not help but wonder if to keep away might be to neglect my responsibilities? There was more, besides. On several occasions during my long journey I had been visited by strange and vivid dreams, each of which followed precisely the same course.

I would find myself walking in that place, awed by the lush magnificence about me. For a while all would be purest enchantment, but then, suddenly, I would be met by a sight terrible to behold. There it would stand, a tree like none I had ever seen before: not large, yet possessed of a kind of awful portent, its trunk black and gnarled, and its branches heavy with glistening, vile-coloured abundance. Even as I looked upon it, in horrified study, I would find myself addressed by a might voice, that filled the air with its wisdom, and breathed purpose into my limbs. As if by magic I would find a golden axe lying in my grasp. So it would come to pass that I, lately a mere pastor of a humble Yorkshire parish, would stride forth, with smiling resolution, towards that hateful growth, and deliver to it a mighty blow, then another, and with each strike I would beg, with all my heart, that forgiveness might be granted for that first and greatest of sins. With a mighty creak, the dread plant would tumble, its deadly harvest smashing upon the earth. Most miraculous of all, hardly had the deed been done when I would observe that the air around me seemed somehow subtly clearer, more innocent, than I had ever known it before. Such dreams might, I knew, be merest fancy, and yet, by their very repetition, they did seem to suggest a significance beyond mere reverie.

Before long the forest came to an end and the path led to the base of a steep ascent, where it vanished away, lost upon the rocky slope. Its tale was clear enough, however, and I did not hesitate. "We must go up."

Potter seemed bent on causing difficulty. "It looks very steep."

His words encouraged the mule drivers in turn to complain, which was, I felt sure, his intention. "I'm not sure at all," Skeggs agreed, with a kind of obstructive satisfaction. "Especially in this wet. Would be better if just you fellows should go up, and we stay here with the beasts."

I glanced at our guide. "What do you say, Mr. Cromwell?"

He pondered a moment. "No, I think it is better if the mules come also. Dark will come by and by, and we cannot stop here."

The half-caste was finally proving of usefulness. "Quite so," I agreed, stepping brightly forth.

I dare say the ascent was a little difficult. As we climbed higher, the slope grew gradually steeper, narrower and more strewn with boulders, while these last were often so close together that one had to quite scramble between them, grazing knees and arms. Matters were not helped by the rain, which was falling ever harder, the sky having grown quite dim, and which made the rocks slippery underfoot. For all this, Skeggs's trepidation seemed excessive. What if the mules showed reluctance? They are creatures well known for obstinacy, and this was no reason to abandon our efforts, yet he complained more than once that we must turn about, and I believe he might have done so had not the way been so prohibitively narrow. Fortunately we were by then almost at the summit.

First among all the party, I clambered over a low ledge of rock and found sky suddenly all about me. I was, I realized, stood at one end of a long ridge, while this was tilted, almost like a sloping house roof. The effect of the slant was, I suppose, a little unnerving, but not unduly so, while it was easy enough to stand upon if one took care. What caught my attention most of all, however, was the view, which made me feel as if I were upon some balcony overlooking oblivion. Making my way upwards to the highest edge, I found myself looking into a deep valley, beyond which rose a vast slab of mountain. Then, clambering carefully down to the lower side, I found a vista more dizzying still: as far as the eye could see, variously hidden and revealed by the dark clouds, lay a jagged sea of cliffs and peaks, of tumbling rocks and desperately clinging greenery, extending to the horizon. Closer below it seemed the mountainside was formed into a shelf, as a line of trees reached up, their tops only a few yards below.

I must, I realized, with greatest excitement, be looking across a great part of the central wilderness of the island. Somewhere here must lie the answer to all my questions. I set to work, paying no heed to the complaints of the others as they gathered with the animals above, but scanning the great expanse before me, hurrying before the sky darkened further. There was the river, where we had walked only that morning, though it seemed already half an age ago. I waited, impatient to my bones, as a swirl of cloud pulled away, revealing the lake, long and narrow. Now, surely, I would see.

"We should never have come here," Potter whined. He was quite crouching beside me, his hands gripping the rock. He gave the view a sour stare. "It all looks much the same to me."

The gall of him. The hateful, plumped-up arrogance. As if he were capable of recognizing what we were seeking, when he had no knowledge of geology. I would not be hurried by such a man. If I had seen nothing unusual beside the lake, as—mystifyingly—seemed to be the case, then it must simply lie in some other spot. What of the part further on, where the cloud had yet to draw away?

"Oh," murmured our guide, who had taken his place at my other side. He seemed agitated, shaking his head as he looked upon the view.

"You have seen something?" I asked encouragingly.

"That mountain." He pointed at one far away—though it looked no different from its many neighbours—regarding it strangely, lost in some kind of savage reverie. "I lived near there before."

"Indeed," I answered somewhat coolly. I had been hoping for something more useful than mere reminiscence. I simply could not understand. For all the drama of the view I could see nothing out of the ordinary in geological terms, either beside the lake or anywhere else. All looked of a similar rock. It made no sense. Had I not been guided here, even from England's distant shore? Had we not been shown kindly signs to lead us along the way?

"You seem disappointed, Vicar."

I should not perhaps have been surprised by the remark, in view of Potter's character, but still I found myself taken aback by the tone in which it was uttered, which contained a faint but audible note of *satisfaction*. It was hard to credit and yet I could not help but conclude that my own momentary discomfort was more important to him than the success of this entire expedition, of which he was himself a part. I was no stranger to malevolent behaviour and yet still I found myself profoundly shocked by this poisonous utterance. "I am not disappointed," I informed him.

"Then you have seen something?"

How strange are the ways of fate. At this most difficult moment help came to me from the very last source one might have expected: even from the doctor himself. Adversity can be a most powerful stimulant to men's wills, and so it was on that afternoon atop some unnamed mountain. I simply would not permit myself to be sneered at in this way. All of a sudden I knew, I simply *knew*, that I must drop to my knees. In a voice that was calm, yet filled with impassioned entreaty, I called out across the great abyss before me.

"O Lord, hear my prayer. Do not turn Thy back upon us now, I beseech Thee, after Thou hast led us so far."

All was still, except for a faint gust of wind tugging at our clothes. Potter coughed.

I persevered. "Please, Lord. My only wish is to do Thy bidding. Show us the way."

Moments passed in terrible quiet. Potter began whistling some low tune, better to show his own impatience. Still I waited, heart pounding.

I did not wait in vain.

What next occurred I can describe only as a true miracle: a revelation as deliberate and wondrous as may be found even in the Scriptures themselves. All at once the sky was a thing ablaze, as there fell across it a dazzling shaft of light. It struck, like some great pointing finger of destiny, upon some place beyond the distant edge of the ridge upon which we were stood, hidden from our view. Signs I had seen that day, but none could compare with this!

"There!" I cried in greatest delight, as thunder roared in upon us. "That is where Eden lies. That is where we must go!"

Even still, Potter was intent on his poison. "For goodness' sakes, Vicar. What else do you expect on a day like this?"

I closed my thoughts to his words, protecting them, as a shepherd guards newborn lambs from a circling bird of prey. Elation filled my being and I would not have it spoiled. I did not answer him, but simply bowed my head in a heartfelt prayer of thanks.

"I saw another like that just moments ago," he whined again. "Actually, I think that was brighter."

"We shall proceed at once," I declared simply, and turned to make my way back towards the front of the line of mules.

Potter scampered after me. "This is madness. The way is far too difficult. I simply cannot permit you to put us all in such risk."

It was a provocation, and a great one, but still I kept my calm. "Do not talk nonsense," I informed him quietly.

I saw his face grow curiously tightened, as if he were in some pain. The words he spoke next were uttered loud and clearly, so there could be no mistaking. "Can't you see, you ninny? There is no Garden of Eden here. There never was. Now for goodness' sake let's get down before you kill every one of us."

How quickly can one's understanding become transformed. The man was possessed of more wickedness, more treachery, than I had ever imagined. He had never believed in this great venture. Why, there could be only one possible reason why he had come here: *to prevent Eden being found*. In a flash all was clear. He had been sent by my foes, the atheist geologists. It made sense enough. Had he not sought us out, demanding of poor, kindly Jonah Childs that he become the expedition surgeon? Had he not done all in his power to cause us difficulties? Had he not sought to take my own place as leader? Now I understood why. There would be no easier way to destroy the expedition than by becoming its chief.

"Judas," I answered him. "Judas revealed. But you shall not prevail. We shall succeed yet, despite your treachery." I did not content myself with words. I took hold of the lead of the foremost mule, that I might turn my fearless words into fearless action.

One might have expected the doctor to show some shame at his discovery, but there is no use looking for conscience in the devil's agents. "No, you don't," he cried out madly, trying to grasp the animal's rope, so he might turn it round by brute force.

His action left me no choice. Calm and dignified, I endeavoured to wrest it back once again. Potter, true to his nature, merely redoubled his efforts.

"Stop that," called out Skeggs. At that moment, however, the animal, which had evidently been alarmed by Potter's reckless tugging, reared up, bucking and kicking so wildly that we both stepped back. As to what occurred next, this was so swift and extraordinary that it seemed not real, but like some slow nightmare. I would have taken the creature's reins to try and calm it, but there was no time. In a moment it had lost its footing, and, striking out in panic, it fell crashing to the ground. It was then that I became aware of a greater movement. The beast's distress had infected its fellows, several of which were now rearing up in fright. As I watched, some hurled off their loads, others were slipping, while those that re-mained still were being pulled off balance by neighbours as they fell.

Skeggs realized the danger. "Untie them," he shouted.

Unfortunately the animals' demented thrashing permitted no ap-proach. I am not sure, indeed, if anybody even made an attempt. It was all we could do to jump clear. Several beasts began to tumble down the slope, legs flailing, and dragging others after them. Thus I watched with a kind of awful curiosity as a wave of animals began sliding and kicking away down the wet rock. It was a mule near the centre of the line that was the first to reach the edge and vanish. The rope that held it to its neighbours briefly tautened, and then they too rolled from sight, quickly followed by two more, till they were disappearing apace, almost like two lengths of string being pulled through a keyhole.

Suddenly all was very quiet.

The catastrophe was so sudden, and so complete, that it was hard to realize. I looked about me and was struck by what a slight party we now made upon this bare mountain. Without a word we all began to creep forwards, picking our way with care over the treacherous rock. Crouch-ing by the edge, I peered over, though I could see nothing but the tops of trees below, their foliage glistening in the wet. The only signs to tell of what had occurred were a few snapped branches, and also a faint braying cry—dulled by the din of the wind and rain—uttered with a kind of terrible mechanical repetition. The cliff below us was as vertical as any wall, and I could see no way down, even from the slope by which we had as-cended.

One might have supposed such a disaster would inspire remorse, but it was not so. All at once there was a shout. "It was him." Potter's servant Hooper was pointing angrily at the half-caste guide. "He brought us up here. It's the blackie who's done for us." Some of the mule drivers uttered a hiss of agreement. Then I watched, aghast, as Hooper took his rifle from his shoulder.

"Stop," I called out.

I would certainly have prevented him, regardless of risk to my own person, if I had only been nearer. As it happened, Renshaw alone was close enough. Before Hooper could properly aim the gun the little botanist knocked the barrel upwards and the shot was fired harmlessly into the air. This, though, was not the end of the matter. The two at once became embroiled in a tussle over the weapon, and as I hurriedly stepped towards them, there was a curious and ghastly sound, like a block of wood striking a hollow stone. All at once Renshaw was tipping backwards. Hooper did try to hold him—nearly losing balance himself—but to no avail. With a kind of amazement I watched as poor Renshaw seemed to lean back into the void, and drop, with what seemed terrible slowness, till he vanished into the trees just below.

Silence visited us for a second time in as many moments.

Hooper was distraught. "I didn't mean to. I tried to hold him."

As if there could be any justification for such horror. How telling it was that this deed had been done by Potter's servant.

One of the mule drivers, whose name was Hodges, peered over the edge and called out, "Mr. Renshaw?" In an instant we had all joined him, yelling with all our might through the soft rain, as if the very loudness of our cries might force a reply. We all fell hushed. No sound came back except for that faint yet terrible braying cry. Though nobody uttered a word I believe all were thinking the same dismal thought.

"Do you think . . . ?" I began.

Skeggs shook his head. "Not from this height."

It was then that I remembered Cromwell. Glancing round, I saw he was already some distance away, scampering back towards the slope we had ascended. "Come back," I called out, but he did not so much as turn his head. I could hardly blame him, I supposed, though it seemed a desperate and ill-advised course. He would not survive long alone in this wilderness. Poor fool! I would have protected him.

So our catastrophe was finally and dreadfully complete.

"This is all your doing, you idiot!"

This remark, I should explain, was uttered by Potter, while, impossible as it may seem, it was addressed actually to my own self. *He,* the traitor atheist, who was wholly and entirely to blame for our disaster, was accusing *me.* This was beyond all reason. "You sought to destroy us," I replied simply, "and now you have."

"It was you made us come up to this terrible place."

I knew what I must do. I rose to my feet, standing straight and tall: a churchman fully roused in just indignation. "By the powers vested in me by Jonah Childs, and by the Lord God himself, I expel you from this expedition. Take yourself away, Dr. Potter, and your murderous servant, too. You are cast out."

The man had no shame. He actually sat down upon the rock, directing me a sour look. I paid him no heed, but, full with dignity, turned to the five mule drivers, summoning up my best speaking voice, quite in the manner of Christian orators of distant eras. "I urge you, do not give in to despair. You must understand that what has happened, terrible though it may seem, is merely a kind of test. A test which has exposed the wickedness of these two men, but which we shall pass in triumph. Let us join together and walk to the end of this ridge so we may discover where our sacred goal lies, and then . . ."

It was Skeggs who answered. "I'm not following you another yard, Vicar."

"Me neither," added another.

It was, I confess, a great shock. I glanced at the other three but each shook his head, even uttering foulest words, to better reveal his betrayal. That was a dark moment indeed. I could only suppose they had each one of them fallen under the spell of my enemy. For all I knew he had been talking to them secretly as we journeyed, ensnaring them with hateful words, filling their minds with his poison.

Still I did not falter. I held my head high. "Very well," I declared calmly, "then I shall go on alone."

"You do that, Vicar," jeered Potter.

Even now, after all he had done, he was filled with venom still. When I began gathering up a few supplies from the mule bags that had been thrown off by their animals, to sustain me in my lonely quest, he at once began bickering most spitefully, insisting on counting everything out, quite as if I intended to cheat him! As it was, most of what remained was of little usefulness, such as table linen, folding chairs or Sheffield cutlery. There were bottles of fine French brandy—all but one smashed— and a shattered box of finest Cuban cigars, its contents turning rapidly to pulp in the rain, but there was not one complete tent. As to food, the sugar, tea and tins of Aberdeen hotchpotch, potted meat and hermeti- cally sealed salmon would not, in the normal way of things, have lasted us more than a few days. Potter counted out my portion with miserly exactness, quite ignoring the fact that, as the only one still determined to discover Eden, I should have more than the others. What was more, he quite refused to let me have one of the rifles, claiming that, as a man of the church, I would have no need of such things. If it had not been for his hateful behaviour I would never have dreamed of placing the extra matches into my pocket when his back was turned, let alone the second bag of sugar that I managed to slip beneath my coat.

So it was that, a mule bag uncomfortably hitched over my shoulder, I turned my back upon them all and started making my way along the ridge. When, some moments later, I glanced back, I saw they were al- ready gone, and all that now remained of the expedition were the vari- ous abandoned cases of stores. In the midst of these was a single chair that had been unfolded during the search for food, and which made a sad and curious sight, looking out upon the wild landscape, as if in readiness for some domestic occasion. Pleased though I was to be away from evil company, I confess it felt strange to be now alone in this wild place. I endeavoured to sing a hymn to cheer my spirits, but the wind was strong and the sound was quite stolen away.

As I approached the further end of the ridge, the landscape that had been hidden began gently to rise into view. The rain had finally stopped and the clouds had lifted higher, and so, by the time I finally reached the outermost point, below which the rock fell away like water, I could see clearly for many miles, with peaks aplenty reaching up to catch the eye. It may seem hard to credit, yet each rock and mountain were of the same crumbling kind that they had been everywhere else. I could see nothing that resembled any sign, nothing to show where I should go. Even then I did not despair. I prayed, shouting the words as loud as I might.

"Please, I beg Thee, Lord, show me the way."

I waited. I prayed. I waited once again. Long moments passed, but there was no burst of lightning, no sudden sunbeam to guide me. The mountains seemed to glower up at me, like some impenetrable maze.

I am not normally prone to doubts, and yet all of a sudden I could feel these creeping forth, like poison dripping into my lifeblood, rendering dearest certainties suddenly frail. Had I been been mistaken from the first? Had all these long years of study and journeying, of writing and persuading, been nothing more than wasted time: a mere delusion? Sensing what now approached, I tried to close my thoughts, to make them into blank nothingness, that I might protect my belief, but my mind simply would not be stilled, and already I could feel my faith grown somehow brittle, no longer the rock which I so needed. All at once I felt myself haunted by a terrible vision, of a world without guidance: a land of emptiness, where all was ruled by the madness of chance. How could one endure such a place, where all significance was lost? I myself would mean nothing, but would merely be a kind of self-invention: a speck upon the wind, calling itself Wilson. I felt my spirit waver, as if it were toppling into the abyss before me.

That I left that dreadful spot was not, sad to say, from purpose, but simply in answer to the elements. Wet and shivering, I knew I could not remain on this windy ridge. Dusk was approaching. I began to go down, following the leftward side of the mountain, which seemed less difficult, though even then I found myself cruelly mocked. Several times my descent was obstructed by some precipice that required me to retrace my steps and try again, and by the time I finally found myself on level ground, I had scratches and bruises in abundance. Weak and forlorn, I tried to find some spot where I might rest, before the light failed completely. The land below my feet was marshy, requiring me to walk back beneath the mountain's shadow until I found a place that was firmer. I did try to light a fire, building a little heap of kindling wood, and expending several precious matches, but it was no use, all being so wet. There was nothing to do but to create a bed of leaves, like those I had seen the guide Cromwell make, though this felt neither warm nor comfortable. Lying thus, I consumed a tin of hotchpotch, which helped at least to revive my body, if not my spirits.

All I sought was sleep. Terrible to say, I believe I hardly cared if I should ever wake again, so black was my despair. In the event, sleep proved hard to find. I was cold, and it was so very loud in the darkness, seeming far more so than when I had had a tent in which to shelter. One moment I would be disturbed by the buzzing of an insect close to my ear, the next a breeze would blow up, scattering drops of water upon me from unseen leaves. Worst were the sounds of faint rustling in the under-growth, full of mystery. Though I told myself these were probably just made by a bird or vole, it was hard not to wonder if some poisonous spider, or snake, were now creeping towards me, or even one of the native wolves that had stripes like a tiger's upon their backs and were known to attack men. All the while my thoughts dismally raced. Was there some failing of which I was guilty? Had I unwittingly committed a great sin? I could not think what this might be. Throughout all my days I had endeavoured only to lead a virtuous life and to serve my Lord. How could He reward me so?

I was still wide awake when I became aware of the faint fragrance of wood smoke, as from a campfire. It seemed a most welcome mystery, if only to distract my thoughts from their mournful course. Gathering up my mule bag, I began picking my way in its direction. Before long I could hear the faint sound of voices. For a wild moment I even wondered if some kindly strangers might be here, from some other expedition, and if I might, by His wondrous intervention, be saved after all. Then, stepping between trees, I saw a little group sat round a campfire, the flames rising nicely. It was Potter, Hooper and the mule men. Creeping nearer, I saw that they were passing the surviving bottle of brandy from one to the next. How dare they have a fire? They should not even be on this side of the mountain. Lost, were they? Or had they come here deliberately to mock me anew?

Suddenly I found that my spirits, which had fallen so low, became revived, if only by the force of my own righteous indignation. Here was the cause of all my troubles, swigging liquor and warming his feet before a fire. Dr. Thomas Potter. I would easily have found Eden by now if it had not been for him. All at once I could understand. This was why the Lord had struck us with calamity. What else could be expected of an expedition that called itself Christian, and sought the holiest of places, and all the while harboured within it a magnet of wickedness? Why, He had been seeking to give me His warning. How could I go in search of paradise with an agent of the devil crawling and slithering at my side? That would be an abomination.

I now knew my task. I would fight him. Eden would yet be found, of that I had no doubt, but it would have to wait for the moment. The devil had appeared before me, and I would not shirk my duty. I would raise the standard of godliness, then join battle and smite him down.

Dr. Thomas Potter
JANUARY 1858

<u>19th January (cont.)</u>

Had supposed selves = finally rid of <u>Wilson</u> but not so. Self just growing warm from brandy when heard his dreadful twittering voice calling through darkness, sermonizing to mule drivers, "renounce this agent of the devil (self) before it = too late. Join me + return to the embrace of God," etc. etc. Skeggs telling he to go away in <u>strongest terms</u>, Hooper throwing large stone. All at once Wilson dashing between selves, <u>stealing</u> two largest <u>firebrands</u> + fleeing away. Self considered <u>pursuit</u> + <u>punishment</u> but in truth all = too weary. Fire quite reduced, so expired during night.

Timothy Renshaw
JANUARY 1858

ENERGETIC EXERCISE WAS not something I had much troubled myself with till now, and there were a good few times when I cursed the day I had allowed myself to be bullied into joining this little jaunt into the Tasmanian bush. Then a morning came when, greatly to my own surprise, I found I had somehow become accustomed to this work of walking. My legs seemed quite to dance across mud and rocks, while I felt myself feeling strangely content of spirit. There was something curiously satisfying about an existence so simple, where all that was required was careful watchfulness hour after hour–to avoid a poor footfall, or an unseen snake—and which was rewarded at dusk with a fine sense of satisfaction at limbs stretched and miles traversed.

Another unexpected pleasure was the land itself. This was quite beautiful in a wild way, with its craggy mountains, its rushing rivers, its forests of pale trees. At dusk I would glimpse the strange creatures that lived here, the kangaroos and wallabies that jumped across the land with such unlikely grace. Even the cries of the birds, which I had at first found harsh, became pleasing to my ear. I would sometimes wake in the morning with a curious feeling, which I could not explain, that I was at home. It was only now, indeed, that I began to realize how greatly I had lacked any such sensation in England.

Then Wilson took us up his mountain.

My last recollection is of struggling, then of all the world vanishing suddenly upwards and beyond my grasp, and of my body being whipped by leaves and branches. After that the next thing I remember is finding myself staring at the sky as I lay, wet to the skin, upon the strangest of beds, being formed in part from tree foliage and in part from dead mules. Only two or three of the animals were still alive, while these were barely so, judging from their faint cries.

I began a number careful experiments of movement, each of which seemed to evince some new and unsuspected injury. By the time I finally risked sitting up I'd learned that I was bad in one leg, in one wrist, in both shoulders, in all ribs, as well as also in my neck, my back, my rear and—last but not least—my forehead, where that murderous fool had had the fine idea of tapping me with the butt of his gun. In truth I hardly knew who to thank most: Wilson for leading us up so miraculously ill-advised a path, Cromwell the guide for not telling him better, Potter for scaring the mule with his tugging, the mule drivers for allowing their animals to go sliding to disaster or Hooper for trying to play assassin and knocking me into this delightful spot.

I was, I knew, very lucky to be alive at all. I could only assume I had benefited from having my fall broken by the trees, and then landing upon the animals. Rising to my feet, I discovered that walking was possible, though it was no delight. Looking upwards at the black line that marked the cliff, I could see no sign of the other members of the party, and though I called out several times there came no answer. It seemed fellow explorers had gone. There seemed little point in dwelling upon such disappointment, however, and so I set about trying to preserve myself. My first need was to make myself a shelter before the light was gone. Fortunately there was a tent in the very first mule bag I chanced upon, and, doing my best to ignore the howling of my various injuries, I put this up, which I did, if not well, at least in a manner that would suffice. Food posed no problem as the ground was quite littered with pots, tins and sacks. Matches and paper I soon discovered, and though gathering wood was more than painful, I managed to light a fire before it became fully dark. So I sat in front of my tent, almost comfortable, eating salmon and duck breast with rice, and drinking a survived bottle of champagne, toasting my still being alive.

I endeavoured to keep the fire alight through the night, hoping that its smoke and smell would help the others to find me. Sure enough, early the next morning, I was excited to hear footsteps approaching through the trees. I assumed that this would be all the party, and so was surprised to see only one. It was the guide, Cromwell.

"Thank goodness," I exclaimed. "Where are all the others?"

He did not answer, but sat down in front of me, directing me a strange, almost quizzical look. "You must tell me this one thing. Why did you fight Hooper so?"

It seemed a strange sort of question. "I could hardly let him shoot you."

A frown passed across his face, almost as if he were enduring some pain, or struggling with confusion. He reached out and, just for a moment, touched my arm with his finger, murmuring, "Renshaw." Then the look was gone, vanishing as quickly as it had appeared. He glanced at my bruised legs and arms. "You can walk?"

"Barely."

"Later you can?"

"I suppose. But you've still not told me about the others. Are they coming?"

He regarded me as if I had asked the most foolish of questions. "Forget them. They're no good."

"What d'you mean? D'you know where they are?"

"Gone away."

"Surely they'll come looking for me."

"They won't come. Forget them." There was something in his look that made me wary of asking further. Rising to his feet, he began loosening the ropes that supported the tent. "This is too near mules. They will smell bad soon."

There seemed mystery in his every remark. "You're not staying?"

He shook his head. "Things to do."

So he began his work, quite refusing my offers of help. He moved the tent further away, close by a tiny stream, then began journeying back and forth, until he had assembled a large heap of pots and tins, and a mighty pile of firewood. Next he sat by the fire and manufactured a number of his spears, which looked light but fearsomely sharp. Taking three of these, he strode off into the trees, returning some time later with a freshly killed wallaby, which he quickly skinned, gutted and began roasting upon the fire, filling its empty belly with hot ashes. To my surprise it tasted very good, all the more so for being the first fresh food I had eaten in many days. Finally, when we had finished eating, he pointed to the remaining spears.

"You keep those in case kanunnah—wolf—comes. He will smell the mules, you see." He smoothed the ground in front of the tent and began scratching with a stick to draw what I realized was a kind of crude map. "When you are feeling better again you must go down here. Path is at the bottom, and you must go so with it, away from sun. Most of all you must make sure always stay this side of the mountain that looks like a skull. Don't go any other way, though it looks easier. So you'll get to other white men." He climbed to his feet. "Now I must go."

"Will you come back?"

He shook his head. "Things to do. You get better, then go back to your ones." Without more ado he turned and was gone.

Dr. Thomas Potter
JANUARY–FEBRUARY 1858

20th January

Morning = bright + warm. Selves made new fire (to replace one
<u>Wilson stole</u> in night) + sat in sun a while, brewing tea, till better recovered from trials of day before. Then considered present situation. All
agreed that <u>self</u> should henceforth act as selves' <u>leader</u>. Next considered
how best try + escape wilderness + save selves. Confess will not be easy.
Thanks to Wilson's <u>deranged</u> wandering + selves' confusion during descent from mountain = far from clear re present position. Neither desirable nor practical attempt retrace steps, as mountain = far too precipitous
(Hodges + Skeggs nearly <u>fell</u>), so decided = best continue along this
valley, following stream. Lie of land suggests best way = S (downstream)
+ then E when opportunity arises.

Set off without delay. Beside stream found <u>path</u>: v. fortunate. Direction not ideal (SSW rather than S) but will suffice for moment. Made
good progress behind mountain with curious shape, like fist or skull.
Later reached open ground where observed selves being followed. Wilson = 1 mile behind. <u>Wilson</u>. When all stopped he also stopping, when
selves resumed he resuming etc. etc. Seems he = determined haunt us
yet.

24th January

Another good day's walking, though self increasingly concerned re
<u>path</u>. Briefly turned E, i.e. towards settled areas, but then veered back
WSW (quite <u>wrong</u>). In afternoon selves attempted cut across country
but driven back by <u>thorny vegetation</u> which = among worst selves have
met: remaining clothes badly torn, skin likewise. Also could observe way
= further blocked by distant <u>mountain range</u>. V. discouraging. All selves
agree = now too late retrace steps, as distance walked = too great +
supplies = too low. Hope + believe path may yet swing back to E.

Dusk attempted hunt kangaroo but no success: animals bound away
so swiftly.

<u>Another</u> nighttime visitation from <u>Wilson</u>. He telling others they

shall suffer eternal damnation, burning etc. etc. because serving "agent of the devil" (self). Too dark to see exactly where he = but Hooper + self threw dirt, stones etc. etc. in general direction.

29th January
River joining second, much larger. Could follow this all way to coast? But which coast? (River veering S to SW.)

Obliged further reduce food ration. All now = permanently hungry. Again attempted go directly across country but again driven back by thorny undergrowth. Better to make progress even if in wrong direction?

No sign Wilson 2 days. Dead?

3rd February
Skeggs shot today wallaby, though only small one. Cooked on fire, all so impatient that ate meat when still half raw. Did not go far between 7 selves. All left feeling hungrier than before.

Wilson again plaguing selves in night, so not dead after all. Now promising have selves prosecuted for <u>mutiny</u> if selves reach Hobart. (If!) Hooper firing rifle in air. Most effective: heard he scampering away.

6th February
Path + river still S or SW. Never *E*. Progress slowing as selves weakened by lack <u>sustenance</u>. Last sugar finished this morning + obliged reduced daily food ration <u>again</u> though this = already v. insufficient. (Self should never have let <u>Wilson</u> take any: he <u>deserted party</u> so abandoned all entitlements.) Selves talking of food every moment, dreaming feasts each night. No sign settlements, roads etc. etc. even in furthest distance. Hard believe any men except <u>savages</u> ever set foot in this <u>cursed</u> place.

Rain during night (3rd time running): shelter of tree branches leaking + selves = (again) v. wet. All now have bad colds. Pneumonia = a fear.

12th February
Selves growing so weakened beginning doubt own judgment. Woke in night convinced could detect faintest smell of <u>meat roasting</u> on some distant fire. Could so clearly imagine fat spitting, skin browning etc. etc. caused self some <u>pain</u>. Yet knew could only = mere figment imagination.

Nobody = within miles of here but Wilson, who has no gun and = no hunter.

13th February
<u>Alarming</u> discovery when packed up after breakfast. Entire main supply ammunition (one large bag) = <u>vanished</u>. Searched everywhere, but to no avail. This = v. <u>mysterious</u>. Ammunition carried by <u>Tom Wright</u>, but he vehement could not have fallen from his bag. But if not he then how? <u>Wilson</u>? Seems unlikely. Yet no doubting = still near. Loss = v. grave. Selves have now only what was in pockets, i.e. 12 rifle rounds + 7 for revolver pistol. Chief hope was better luck hunting game as supplies food now = so low.

14th February
Terrible day. Early morning mule driver <u>Ben Fiddler</u> away to river to get water for tea. Selves waited, waited, but he not returning. Began search, calling out his name etc. etc. but no reply. Finally found empty water pan beside river + stone marked with <u>blood</u> nearby.

Selves = v. angry. Also <u>mystified</u>. He attacked by native <u>wolf</u>? Seems unlikely. Hooper suggesting could be = work of <u>half-caste</u> Cromwell, but self knew this = impossible. Half-caste = wholly lacking in <u>intelligence</u> + <u>hardiness</u> to follow selves here, while would = far too scared by his (Hooper's) actions on mountain. Besides, sure he = already long <u>dead</u> (could not survive without <u>food</u>). If any man = responsible, this surely = <u>Wilson</u>. Unlikely but not impossible. He = here (saw him in distance yesterday) + so <u>disordered</u> of mind could be capable <u>any enormity</u>.

Self decided = time selves <u>sought him out</u>. Found him easily enough, 1/4 mile back along track, hiding in trees. Had not seen he close to + observed he = in poor state: v. fleshless, eyes distracted. His mule bag looking nearly <u>empty</u>. Had <u>cross</u> made from 2 sticks which he brandishing at selves, shouting, "Away devils," etc. etc. When selves approached he scampering back to river's edge + <u>plunging in</u>. This = v. rash (current = fast) but he managing reach further bank, where began uttering deranged taunts as per usual: "Come, come, across the waters, like Pharaoh's cohorts," etc. etc. Self considered following but decided against. Instead shouted out, demanding if he stole selves' ammunition +

murdered Ben Fiddler. He seeming surprised even <u>pleased</u>. Claiming this = "punishment" upon selves + that selves "cannot escape the eyes of the Lord," etc. etc. Self left doubtful he = responsible after all. Also he so <u>thin</u> that = hard imagine could overcome Fiddler (strongest of mule drivers). Wolf responsible after all?

Food too short for selves to linger so continued on way. Self saw 2 wallaby and tried bag they, using revolver pistol, but again they = too quick. Ammunition tally: 4 rifle rounds + 5 pistol rounds. Food tally: 2 teaspoons sugar, 3 full + ¼ tins Aberdeen hotchpotch, 1 full + ¾ tins preserved salmon, 1 full + ¼ bags rice. 12 matches. Have tried carrying burning firebrand as walk, but always becomes extinguished.

15th February

Soon after set out this morning path split. One way SW, other SE. Latter = most promising since left Wilson's mountain! Selves began nervously following but it <u>keeping direction</u>. Must surely lead selves towards <u>settled districts</u>. Only hope = not already <u>too late</u>.

17th February

Most terrible day till now. Selves brewing water (no tea left) for breakfast, Jim Bates away to attend to himself. Suddenly all selves = alarmed by <u>loud cry</u>. Hurried through trees + saw Bates = lying upon ground moaning, long <u>stick</u> (realized = <u>spear</u>) protruding from belly. Self heard footsteps running away. Pursued + caught brief glimpse figure darting away through trees. But not Wilson. <u>Half-caste!</u> Could hardly believe own eyes. Got off shot with pistol but <u>missed</u>.

Left Tommy Wright + rifle with injured Bates + took Hooper, Hodges to <u>hunt</u> he <u>down</u>. In event, this = not easy. Followed footmarks to stream but then <u>no signs</u>. Attempted search further but Hodges growing v. nervous, staring at every bush in fright etc. etc. Confess even self = a little concerned: vegetation = so thick + <u>savage</u> he could be hiding anywhere, ready to fling spears. Decided = best return to Wright + Bates.

Most disturbing. Could only suppose <u>half-caste</u> = following selves all this while (must = he who stole <u>ammunition</u>, murdered <u>Ben Fiddler</u> + = cause of nighttime smell <u>cooking meat</u>). V. hard to credit his survival + pursuit selves = quite beyond intelligence + resourcefulness any of his

<u>Type</u>. He = some <u>freakish exception</u>? Characteristics of his white (Saxon) Type half = unusually dominant? Yet what of his <u>savage</u> behaviour during earlier journey? Unless he possessed of special primitive <u>resilience</u> vs. savage conditions of this land? Confess whole matter = v. perplexing.

Selves obliged continue on way, keeping careful <u>watch</u> all while. Decided half-caste = sure to make mistake. Self hoped he might = attack again, so selves could deal with he. If selves reach settled districts + he follows, selves shall have him <u>arrested</u> + <u>hanged</u> as <u>common savage murderer</u>. Unfortunately selves' progress much slowed by <u>Bates</u>, who = unable walk without much help from other selves, moaning at every step etc. etc. Had to stop early. Made camp by small pond.

After nightfall again detected faint smell <u>cooking meat</u>. This = provocation that simply could not be tolerated. Self insisted selves must <u>follow smell</u>, find fire, deal with <u>half-caste</u> + eat his meat. Hodges scared (as ever), so left he with Bates. Self led way back along path, Hooper + Skeggs following. Difficult in darkness (moon = ¼) but soon saw bright light <u>campfire</u>. Unfortunately this not <u>half-caste's</u> but Wilson's: he in nearby trees, denouncing selves as "devils" etc. etc. as usual. Self v. surprised he not <u>speared</u> by <u>half-caste</u>. Continued further + could soon smell another fire + <u>cooked meat</u> but could see <u>no flames</u>. Searched for some time though troubling to nerves, as so hard to see: moonlight hardly filters through trees. Finally discovered small blaze <u>concealed</u> at bottom of <u>hole</u> dug in ground. Seemed v. <u>devious</u> + <u>cowardly</u> arrangement. <u>No meat</u>. No sign <u>half-caste</u>. Most aggravating. Worse to come. On way back <u>spear</u> suddenly thrown as from <u>nowhere</u> catching Hooper in <u>arm</u> (fortunately wound = slight). Selves attempted pursue, fired 2 rounds, but nothing. Returned to others. Set up system of night <u>watches</u> vs. further attack.

Bates dead just before dawn. Great loss. Though will at least permit small increase in daily ration (selves were seven, now = five).

The Reverend Geoffrey Wilson
FEBRUARY 1858

GOD IS IN my bag of sugar. The devil tries to make me spill grains when I take my meals, but I am careful and he hardly steals any. Though there is little left now it keeps me still, so I know He is there.

I have not seen the devil but I have felt him often, in my headaches, in noises in the dark, in the mud and in my constant dreams of roasting meat. Sometimes he tries to frighten me with thoughts that I am mistaken, even that He has deserted me, but I hold my cross high and do not listen. Most of all, of course, the devil is in Potter and his helpers. Once they were so fast that I lost sight of them for two whole days and, though I could see their footmarks, I feared they had escaped me. That was a dreadful time, and I was haunted by thoughts of Potter sat in some fine dining room, eating roast beef and potatoes, or fish, perhaps a mighty leg of lamb, with peas and carrots, buttered bread of course, and cake afterwards, as he murmured vilest lies, that I was dead and Eden was not here. Then I saw them once more, stumbling forth, looking worse even than me. It was soon afterwards that I learned–and from Potter himself–that He had struck at last, smiting the mule driver Fiddler from the face of the earth. I was not forgotten. In that instant all my faith became restored.

That same night there occurred something so strange that for a moment I hardly knew if I was dreaming. Suddenly, quite as from nowhere, I saw, standing beside my little fire, our guide, Cromwell, who I had thought long dead, several fearsome-looking spears in his hand. He regarded me curiously and for a moment I feared he had come to take my sugar. "What do you want?"

He answered with a question of his own. "Why aren't you with those others?"

"Because they are the devil's agents. They are God's enemies." I held my mule bag that had the sugar tight to my breast, but, to my surprise, he paid it no heed, simply nodding and then turning away. All at once a thought came to me. "Are you His instrument?" I called out. "Was it you who smote down Ben Fiddler?"

He let out a low laugh and I was certain I was right. Sure enough, the next day I heard their shouts, as another of the mule drivers was struck down. As ye sow, so shall ye reap. Had I not warned them they must renounce this devil or be sorely punished? If they had only listened to my words I had no doubt He would have treated them kindly. Why, if they recanted He might even spare them yet, though it was growing very late.

By tearing open their flesh with the spears of His instrument, and snuffing out their tainted lives, He sweetly whispers to me that I am right.

But now I have been frightened again. This afternoon I followed them into hills which were hard upon my weary limbs, though I persevered. Hearing a distant shout, I looked up and saw they were all gathered upon the summit of a ridge ahead and were cheering and waving their arms in excitement. Anything that caused them joy could only bode ill for men of goodness. I did my best to hurry, but it was some time before I reached the spot where they had stood.

There below me, only a few miles distant, lay the sea. How strange it was to look upon it after so many weeks of wandering. So this was the cause of their celebration. For a moment I found myself mystified. The landscape was hard to read, being all steep and sudden hills, while there seemed to be a bay half hidden behind, but I could see no house or road or other sign of men. Or could I? Studying the scene more carefully, I finally observed, half hidden behind the treetops, the cause of the devil's agents' cry. It was a line jutting into the water, nothing more: a tiny shape too clean and straight for any work of nature. I supposed it must be some kind of jetty. Though I could see no buildings, this did not mean they were not somewhere concealed. All at once I became gripped by foreboding. Even now, this moment, they might be talking to strangers, whispering slanders, of errors made and things not here.

I needed strength. My sugar was almost all gone, down to a tiny trail in the bottom of the bag. I ate it all, every bit, and licked the paper too, which helped my spirits revive a little. Then, praying harder than I had prayed for days, I began hobbling down the hillside.

Dr. Thomas Potter
FEBRUARY 1858

<u>20th February</u>

Wondrous, wondrous, wondrous! <u>Sea</u>! <u>Jetty</u>!? <u>Hope of salvation</u>! All selves = stood laughing like children, shouting hurrahs etc. etc. Tom Wright joyfully suggesting selves eat <u>all</u> remaining food this very moment (total remaining: one <u>full</u> tin + ¹/₈th tin Aberdeen hotchpotch) in celebration. Self, though <u>jubilant</u>, remained more cautious, but did permit selves consume the ¹/₈th (¹/₂ teaspoon each).

Hurried down, quite running, even despite <u>feet</u>, as path entered forest, keeping pistol ready in case <u>half-caste</u> appeared. In event, soon slowed as distance to coast = further than appeared from above: dusk well advanced by time selves wearily reached flat land. Selves spirits revived as began observe signs of nearby <u>seashore</u>: ground <u>sandy</u> underfoot, mist drawing in through trees, faint <u>salty smell</u>. Best of all, selves found <u>path</u>! Real path: broad, clear <u>white men's</u> path! Self hobbled onwards, impatient with own weary legs. Then, finally, stumbled onto beach + found <u>jetty</u>, just as thought, vanishing into evening fog.

Confess felt some <u>misgivings</u> even then. All = <u>too still</u>. No sounds men. No lights. Nothing but faint splashing of waves on shore + smell <u>rotten</u> wood. Stepping onto jetty, observed many timbers = broken. None of selves spoke. All began searching nearby, increasingly impatient. But only signs mankind = old beached rowboat (wrecked), staves of burst barrels, long coiled rope, huge pieces <u>bone</u> + stinking <u>carcass</u>. Clear this = a whaling station. Worse, appeared = <u>abandoned</u> whaling station. Despite all evidence selves began suddenly + loudly <u>shouting</u> into mist. No reply. Utter silence. Self felt something like <u>desperation</u>. Nothing harder to endure than high hopes suddenly <u>dashed</u>.

Skeggs = 1st to voice selves fears aloud: suggested this place = further S along coast than supposed, so could be many miles of <u>wilderness</u> between here and nearest settlement. All knew what this meant. Selves have neither strength nor food for further journeying, while also = danger of further <u>attacks</u> by <u>half-caste</u>. Hodges trying voice optimism: claiming some ship might visit but self had no patience for such <u>foolish</u>

<u>delusions</u>. Told he: "What sort of captain would ever bring a vessel into quiet + empty bay like this, where = nobody and nothing?"

Dismal calm descended. Selves drifted back to trees behind beach to prepare for night, more from habit than hope: finding flat ground, building fire (6 matches remaining). Self feeling awful premonition that this shall = last camp and that all selves shall <u>perish in this place</u>. Brewed hot water. Opened final tin Aberdeen hotchpotch: ate $1/2$ teaspoon each (just makes selves feel <u>far more hungry</u>). $7/8$ths tin left. This = <u>total food remaining</u>. Stored carefully in last mule bag.

Deeply asleep + dreaming about to eat feast of beef, roast potatoes, turnips, carrots, peas, onions, gravy, etc. etc. when suddenly woken by <u>screaming</u> and <u>rifle shot</u>. Jumping up saw Tom Wright (on watch: asleep?) with <u>spear</u> through his <u>chest</u>, and <u>half-caste</u> aiming spear at <u>self</u>. Just managed twist out of way so it struck tree just behind. Self reached for pistol but he already fleeing though darkness.

Wright struck clean through <u>heart</u>. Soon <u>coughed his last</u>. This <u>savage act</u> serving to banish selves' lethargy + rouse all to furious <u>anger</u>. Even if selves = to die in this <u>vile</u> spot, at least might now revenge selves re <u>savage murders</u> and deal with this <u>devious</u> and <u>hateful primitive</u>. Must hunt he down like <u>verminous freak</u> he is. Hooper, Skeggs, Hodges + self began search, using firebrands to light way. Followed footsteps through trees but these vanishing on harder ground. Awkward. Selves = wary spreading out in case suffer <u>further attack</u>. Also faint shuffling sounds in undergrowth (birds? mice? half-caste?) = v. <u>distracting</u>. Hodges panicking, tried fire rifle into dark (hammer not cocked) so self had harshly scold he (only 2 pistol + 1 rifle rounds remaining, while if selves fire all then will have <u>no defence</u> vs. half-caste's <u>spears</u>).

Finally returned to fire. None thinking of sleep. Agreed should bury Wright to prevent he being worked upon by birds, wild beasts etc etc. In truth little flesh left on him—just some on calves, thighs, neck + shoulders—but still <u>creatures</u> v. likely be <u>tempted</u>. Took he to beach where sand = softer + set to work digging by light of firebrands. Difficult, as had no spade, so had pull away sand with hands. Soon reached layer roots beneath, so had make do with shallow grave. Placed Wright within + just finishing covering he, when Hodges calling out, "Look. There's someone by the fire."

Self indeed saw man, silhouetted vs. dwindling flames. Appeared = scooping at something with hand. All ran, guns ready. But was not half-caste. There, in full view selves = <u>Wilson, tin</u> in hand, gouging out <u>last mouthful</u> of <u>Aberdeen hotchpotch</u>. Our <u>Aberdeen hotchpotch</u>! Self ran to strike he down but Hooper quicker: knocking away tin, trying recover food from Wilson's mouth (too late, as he already swallowing). Tin = quite <u>empty</u>. He eaten <u>all</u> ⁷/₈ths! Could hardly believe eyes.

Told he, "You <u>vile thief</u>."

He = wholly <u>unrepentant</u>. Claiming this = his "right" as food = given him by "the Lord my father." Claiming it is his "duty" to eat so food will not go to "agents of the devil."

Hooper declaring simply, "Let's hang him."

Self considered this = <u>excellent notion</u>. Could use old rope by jetty. Believe selves would have done so <u>there and then</u> except for <u>Hodges</u>. He whining selves have no legal right hang Wilson. Self less troubled, as considered selves would all be long dead before any lawyers might stray here. Besides, all saw he eating <u>hotchpotch</u>. But for sake <u>decorum</u> self suggested selves hold <u>own trial</u>. Said he must be "tried by his peers" (selves) just like a Lord. All agreed (except Wilson).

Began at once, in broken rowboat. Wilson put in stern, rest facing he on oarsmen's benches. Self = <u>magistrate</u>. Hodges = <u>defence</u>. Hooper = <u>prosecution</u>. Skeggs = <u>watching for half-caste</u>. All = jury. Hooper began questioning: "Did you eat our last tin of Aberdeen hotchpotch and so intend to starve us all to death?" etc. etc. Wilson insisting this not proper legal process but the "devil's law" + saying this whole court = in the <u>dock</u> of "greater court, court of angels," where selves shall receive "higher judgment," etc. etc. Claiming that God gave him hotchpotch "with His own hand."

Self feeling weary. Sky = growing light, selves had been awake through nearly all night. Also <u>cold breeze</u> now blowing, stirring mist. Self eager hang he <u>quick</u> so could rest, and permitted only short summing-up + discussion. <u>Defence</u> (Hodges) proposing selves should not do anything now but wait. <u>Prosecution</u> (Hooper) answering that = no purpose in delay + he must be hanged "as example to others." Then self stood and called out, "The court will now rise and declare its verdict." Asked each one by turn.

Hooper: "Guilty."

Skeggs: "Guilty."

Self: "Guilty."

Hodges: "I still say we should wait."

Self declared verdict = guilty, as agreed by majority + announced sentence, that "the Reverend Geoffrey Wilson shall = hanged by the neck until he = dead." Wilson actually <u>smiling</u> + saying he <u>does not mind</u>, as he <u>knows</u> he shall soon be lodged "safe upon the kindly breast of my father," etc. etc. Self examined rope but realized this = too <u>thick</u> for <u>fine</u> work. Also none selves = sure how make <u>noose</u>. Further difficulty = platform to push he from. Hooper insisting selves can simply tie rope round his neck, sling over tree branch, pull he up, secure other end + let he swing. "It may = less tidy but will work nicely enough, just you see." Hodges, as ever, insisted all = done correctly. Self then proposed constructing simple <u>platform</u> from planks of rowboat, stand Rev. atop, attach noose, then kick away. Selves still examining planks, wondering how do this, when Wilson suddenly crying out, most strangely.

"A miracle! A miracle! Thank you, O Lord! Praise be the Lord."

Self supposed he finally turned quite demented. But then Skeggs shouting, "A ship."

Self turned to follow line of he arm. Mist now much dispersed by breeze. Sure enough, there, at far end bay, beneath cliff, self could just discern faint vertical + horizontal lines. No mistaking these = <u>masts</u>. In fact seemed not one vessel but <u>two</u>.

Self still v. tempted complete matter at hand. Unfortunately already = too late: Wilson jumping from boat, Hodges, Skeggs + even Hooper all = staggering away in direction mysterious vessels. Self had little choice but to follow.

Captain Illiam Quillian Kewley
JANUARY–FEBRUARY 1858

TRULY, A MAN never knew such slowness. First there was Parrick Quine, the Hobart landing waiter, who seemed like gold dust itself, being a Manxman in the customs, but proved a fussing, greedy sort of gold dust at that, being scared that once he gave us the name of that certain kind of trader we were seeking, we'd just do our deal and sail away, and he'd never get his share. Then there was the buyer he finally found, Jed Grey, who was a giant, stooping, worrying sort of fellow, looking as if he'd been bitten by too many low doorframes and was slower even than Quine. His fear was that we were all just some clever policemen's surprise, and that he'd find himself waking up in Port Arthur gaol one bright morning. When he was finally set and had paid a little jink down, there was a good deal of store loading to do, as I was taking no chances this time, our luck being what it was, and I wanted plenty of food and water aboard just in case we got beached on some piece of wilderness, or had to turn tail and flee across oceans. When this was finished there was that southerly breeze that wouldn't stop blowing—cold so it had all the Tasmanians mewling and whining about the rottenness of their summer—and sealing us in Hobart as neat as bottle stoppers. I was even getting to worry the Englishmen might stroll back from their jaunt and thwart us once again, but then the breeze came about to a westerly, which would do, and we set sail that noon, with Quine settling the customs documents tidy and quiet, and one of Jed Grey's men playing pilot.

The wind kept fresh, giving us an easy passage, and the next evening we sailed into the bay we'd picked from the charts, dropping anchor in the shadow of a good-sized cliff. We had to wait another couple of nights for Jed Grey to arrive, as it wouldn't have done for both of us to be setting out on the same tide, but finally his vessel drifted into sight and we started our work, which should have been done at some quiet spot near Maldon, seven months back. Truly, there's nothing like the running trade to murder a man's back. I even had to lend a hand myself, there being so few bodies aboard, though it was hardly proper labour for a ship's captain. First we had to drag the goods from their hiding places and drop them in the main hold. Next we put a rope around them and, tugging at a pulley rigged to the foreyard, we heaved them skywards, swung them out and dropped them down into the longboat that was waiting. Then we did it all again, and again, and more besides, sometimes rowing over to the shore to catch some stones as ballast. It was hard going and we were only half done when the light went and the fog blew in and we had to call it a day. We started the next morning as soon as the mist lifted, and we'd got going nicely, too, when I noticed Brew peering landwards, with a frown bigger than Peel City stuck on his face.

"Captain, look over there on the shore."

Across on the narrow stony beach below the cliff, where there should have been nothing worse than gulls and seaweed, was stood a little group of bodies, ragged as marooned sailors, and each of them waving their arms and shouting as if their lives depended on it, which I suppose they did, too. Well, here was a rotten little piece of surprise. The whole idea of this spot was that there would be nobody here. "Who can they be?"

"Escaped convicts?"

That would be just my luck, to be pestered by runaway dirts. "Get my telescope."

That was when I got my second little shock of the morning. These weren't just any old lost articles, you see. These were our passengers. There was no mistaking them, for all their hair and rags and thinness. There was the Reverend, waving fit to bust, and Potter too, his red beard long and wild as any madman's. There was his servant Hooper, and a couple of others, besides, though there was no sign of Renshaw, nor of that army of mules they'd had. This was far worse than convicts. Why, it was almost as if they'd done it deliberately, just to be awkward. All these months we'd managed to keep everything tidy and quiet–though it hadn't been easy–and now, just when I thought we were finally settled, here they were, plaguing us with some disaster they'd dropped on themselves.

In a moment I saw Jed Grey was having himself rowed over in the next boat, his face worrying fit to burst. My news didn't cheer him one jot, neither.

"They know you? But that makes them even more dangerous. There's no question, Captain. We cannot bring them aboard."

Brew was just as kindly. "It'd hardly be clever to let them put a sight on all of this." He cast a glance to the casks of brandy and sheaves of tobacco being hauled up from below.

They were right enough. To take that gang of fools aboard would hobble us nicely. Whatever they might promise us today they were sure, as Englishmen, to go blabbing to the customs tomorrow, hurling us into all manner of trouble.

Grey was searching for ways to make himself feel easier, looking almost angry, as if they'd done him some wrong. "It's not our fault that they've stranded themselves here, after all."

Brew added a touch of legal neatness. "Besides, the agreement we made never said anything about picking them up from their expedition."

All we had to do was nothing. By the look of them they'd only last a day or two more, at the most. Why, a fellow couldn't have looked for a more perfect bit of murdering. If anyone found them afterwards–which I doubted–there'd be not a thing to say we'd been near. No, it would be easier than spilling milk, with nothing to fear. Apart, that was, from my own recollection of the five of them stood here on the shore, starved and waving and screaming for our help.

I took a breath and called out to Kinvig. "Have the boat go over to the shore and pick up those men."

Grey's voice jumped high at that. "I won't allow it. You'll get us all thrown in gaol."

"He could be right," mumbled Brew.

One of the handsomest things about being Captain of a ship is that you don't have to give anyone a reason for. It's your vessel and that's the end of the matter. "If you don't want them to put a sight on your face, then you'd best get yourself rowed back before they're brought," I told Grey. "I'll put them off at some nowhere spot, to give us a little time, but I'm not leaving them here."

He scowled but there was nothing he could do, and so he slunk away to his ship, to keep his pretty face hid.

Brew was no happier. "Shouldn't we at least wait till the wares are all cleared from sight and we've closed the hatches?"

I couldn't see much point. "They'll have seen enough already from the shore. We may as well just take them aboard and be done with it."

It wasn't long before the longboat was rowing our passengers back. I'd expected them to be all gushing gratitude–which they should, too, considering the trouble I'd be catching saving their skins–but no, they never so much as dropped me a "Thank you, Captain," being far too busy yelling mad accusations at one another. Truly, I'd never have imagined Englishmen could turn so crazed. The Reverend was the worst, and when he was fifty yards distant I could already hear that piping voice of his screeching across the water.

"You must arrest these men, Captain. They just tried to murder me. They're evil, nothing less. You must put them in irons this instant."

Potter was no less sweet. "Wilson's nearly killed us all ten times over, and now he's trying to throw the blame on me. Don't listen to him, Captain."

I could only suppose they'd had no great luck finding paradise after all.

The Reverend hardly glanced at the commotion of contraband as he came aboard, being interested only in his own ranting, but Potter was all eyes at that brandy and tobacco, opening his mouth as if he was about to say something, only to think wiser and close it again. There was trouble, as I'd known there must be. They all of them looked weak and tame as babes, but still I was in no mood for taking chances. I took the pistol that was sticking out from Potter's pocket.

"Mylchreest'll take you below and get you something to eat and drink."

You'd have thought the offer of a good feed would have settled them nicely, but no. "I won't be put in with them," the Reverend quite screamed. "They'll murder me."

The doctor just rolled his eyes as if he'd never heard such nonsense. Still it seemed simpler to let Wilson have his way, and so I put him in the galley. The other four were too many for the sleeping cabins, so they went in the carpentry workshop. I had Chalse Christian take away his tools, especially the sharp ones, and had him fit a bolt to the door, just so they wouldn't go accidentally straying. Mylchreest took them some biscuits and beef, and when he came back with their plates–which were picked clean–he said they were sleeping like kittens. The Reverend was the same, judging by the snores spilling out from the galley. I didn't trouble putting a lock on him, seeing as he was pure fool, but I gave Mylchreest the revolving pistol, and told him to settle down on the stairs and keep watch on the lot of them, just to be safe. In the morning, when they were better rested, I'd have a stab at winning them round. I'd have to admit to our trade, there being no use denying it now, and then appeal to them to keep quiet. It might do no good, to be sure, Englishmen being the kind that love laws sooner than their own flesh and blood, but there was no harm in trying, especially seeing as we'd saved their skins.

What with all this fussing, the goods took longer to shift than I'd expected, and it was late afternoon before it was all finally gone and we had our jink. I counted this out three times and every penny was there, right enough, which was some joy at least, as a tidy sum it made, and more than we'd have seen from that Melbourne customs cheat. Jed Grey didn't linger, having his boys weigh anchor and flee away straight off, but we stayed, having agreed to wait another day to keep us looking like strangers. Brew found a cask of brandy that Grey's boys had missed–though it had been paid for with the rest–and it seemed only right to wet the hour when–seven months late and half a world off course–we were finally rid of that certain cargo.

Dr. Thomas Potter
FEBRUARY 1858

<u>20th February (cont.)</u>

Self never thought <u>ship's biscuit</u> + <u>cask beef</u> could taste so good. Felt quite <u>faint</u> from craving satisfied, though could have eaten <u>thrice</u> as much. As selves ate, ship's carpenter fitting <u>bolt</u> to outside door. He claiming this in case selves = disease. Self = too tired to worry. Fell into deepest sleep among wood shavings on floor.

Dark when self awoke. Others still snoring on bunks. Now self = rested found selves' situation seemed greatly <u>perturbing</u>. Tried door + found bolt poorly done, so able push open few inches: could just see steps to deck, where = legs of sitting crewman. Though could not see head, looked like steward, <u>Mylchreest</u>, while on lap = <u>revolving pistol</u>, confirming own suspicion that selves = <u>captives</u>. Had no doubt as to <u>reason</u>. From sheaves <u>tobacco</u> + casks <u>liquor</u> that self saw on deck before, quite clear <u>Sincerity</u> = deliberately contrived <u>smuggling vessel</u>. This surely also = explanation re other mysteries during voyage, e.g., sudden departures etc. etc. (wombat?). Manxmen using selves all this while to disguise their <u>crime</u>. Own concern = their intentions re selves. They planning cut selves' <u>throats</u> + <u>hurl all overboard</u> to preserve them from discovery, imprisonment etc. etc.? Who would ever know? Would explain presence armed guard on stairs.

Other problem = <u>Wilson</u>. Clear he determined cause <u>ruin</u> to <u>self</u> (wish had not dallied so with trial). Will certainly accuse selves of attempting his <u>murder</u>. If matter ever reached court of <u>law</u> all would rest on his word vs. selves. Could prove perilous re self as he = <u>churchman</u>, while Skeggs + <u>Hodges</u> could = unreliable witnesses. V. <u>perturbing</u>. Little to be done presently, however, as 1st concern = Manx.

Self woke others + told them of own <u>alarms</u>. They also v. concerned. Did what little selves could: removed legs of carpentry stool so have some small means to defend selves if Manx <u>murderously</u> burst within. Then listened carefully for any of their talk that might give clue re their <u>intentions</u>. Heard nothing but faint chatter (useless, as all in <u>Manx</u>). Then heard <u>singing</u>.

Peevay
February 1858

So I FINALLY got my killing war against num, thirty summers late. As I went following and watching, waiting my chance, taking it quickly, I often recalled Mother, and pondered how she would feel tidings of joy if she ever knew what I did now. It was easy, yes, as white scuts were stupid here, never finding roots, and too loud and clumsy to catch game, though food was plentiful with no Palawa left, and I could get fat if I liked. As they got piss poor, I got cleverer, recollecting old ways I knew long before. All I must do now was spear Potter and Hooper and others. Potter was hardest as he was careful, always keeping gun in his pocket, and never straying, but I would get him in the end, I did suppose.

Then, when I was so nearly finished, SHIPS were there and took them from the shore. That was some hardship to endure. It is lamentable when something that you think is in your hand, so simple, vanishes away. Yes, it was hateful to think those heinous buggers, Mother's cutters, were escaped after all, and could just go away somewhere for their fine times, and never get their just spearing at all.

Time passed and I sat so on the shore, getting woeful feelings deep inside my breast. I could not divine what I should do, no, as there was no use in anything. I only came here to get those scuts and now they were gone. By and by day got older, other ship put up SAILS and flew away, but I could observe Potter's still stayed. Even when dark came it was still here. That was a surprise, yes. So I became hoping once again, and I divined one last endeavour I could do. I must try this, yes, even if it was just some piss-poor foolishness, as there was nothing else. So I got fire stick and made new fire, small and hidden behind trees. Next I began making my canoe, in the old way, from tree bark tied with twine I did. This was my first canoe in all these many summers and it went strange, pointing rightwards as if it was trying to go round some corner, but it was done, and when I pulled it into sea it floated, yes. Fire stick I stuck in bark, which held it like fingers, behind me so it would keep secret. Spears went longways under twine, just so.

Thus I went, going carefully, leaning forward and pushing the water backwards with my hands. I never was alone in the sea before, even in day, and it was strange. Moon was down, stars were hiding behind clouds, so only seen things were flickers on water from my fire stick and light from lamps on ship's DECK, swinging hither and thither, first just tiny, then slowly getting bigger. It was as if I was in some huge nothing, with only felt things to know, like cold water on my legs, and little wind on my face. As I went, I could hear white men's noises getting louder, and these were scraping music that is called FIDDLE, and singing too, though words were nothing I could surmise.

Waves got bigger by and by, and though these were not giant, finally there was one that was too big for my canoe that was trying to go round his corner. So I was in the water and trying to know what way was up, which was hard, as everything was the same dark. Then I felt canoe against my back and I pulled till I could climb up and get saved after all. Only then did I see my downfall. My pulling broke those spears, you see, while fire stick's fire was finished, of course. So I pondered if I should just go back to land now, as I was some piss-poor ruination now, you see, and not dangerous, going to fight all that ship full of white men without any killing weapon. But going back to shore, where there was nothing, was too hateful. No, I could not sit and watch Potter's boat taking him far away, happy and gone, winning again, just from my accident. I must try something, though I never knew what.

So I put my hands in water once more, pushing to go onwards.

The Reverend Geoffrey Wilson
FEBRUARY 1858

I WOKE WITH a start, almost as if I had been shaken awake by some mighty hand. Sitting up, I paid no heed to the stiffness I felt from sleeping on the hard galley floor, having but one thought. The Manxmen must be *made* to understand. Evil was come amongst them, and they must know it as evil, look it in the eye as evil, raise their arms and strike it down as evil.

It was dark but a glow shone beneath the galley door and, gently pulling this open, I took in the scene upon the deck, though this was hardly a reassuring one. One crewman was sitting at the top of the stairs they had been taken down, but this was the steward, Mylchreest, who was no candidate for such important work. Even as I watched he left his place to walk over to the rail and slowly spat into the water, though I could clearly see by the light of his lamp that he had left his pistol behind him. Had they not heard my warnings? They should every one of them have been there, keeping guard with every weapon they could find. Instead they were rather at the rear of the ship, drunkenly singing. Should I endeavour to warn them once again? I wondered. The Captain had ignored my alarms when sober, and was even the less likely to do so now, in a state of intoxication.

What I needed was evidence: an irrefutable proof of Potter's evil. There must surely be something that would prove the truth of my claims. My thoughts darted back and forth over our voyage, recalling our life in the between decks with poor murdered Renshaw. A thought occurred to me. His notebooks. He had been constantly scribbling in these, and secretively, too. Here, surely, would be something. He had, as I recalled, worked his way through several volumes, so there must be one in his luggage that had been stored aboard the ship. Peering forward, I saw the hatch to the hold was still open from whatever unloading the crew had been busy with before, and the top of a ladder was visible. Mylchreest had returned to his place at the top of the stairs and had his back to me, as he fiddled with his pipe. Carefully opening the door, I crept outside.

Dr. Thomas Potter
FEBRUARY 1858

20th February (cont.)

Self suddenly heard loud commotion from deck: voice shouting (Wilson?) + loud crashes of <u>objects</u> crunching on deck timbers, frequent almost like rain. Bottles? Stones? Some form <u>contraband</u>? But why falling on deck so? Finally heard boots thumping, Manxmen shouting. Hodges growing fearful, suggesting Wilson = being <u>murdered</u> and we = next.

Self not prepared sit + wait. Also continuing <u>crashing</u> of mysterious objects could = useful, as would drown any noises made by selves. Self pushed at door + peered out, to see Mylchreest = now gone from stairs. This = v. encouraging. Self + Hooper managed to wedge stool legs between door + frame, then levered these, till finally bolt prized away. Door swung open. Selves = <u>free</u>! Began advancing up stairs, v. cautious. Peered carefully through hatch, fearful would find Manxmen waiting above, armed + murderous.

Scene = wholly unexpected. Deck = littered with objects. Sticks + bowls? Hard to see in darkness. Manx = forwards by main hatch to hold. Kewley calling out (sounding <u>alarmed</u>), "What's the meaning of this?" All at once two round objects flying out from hold, dropping onto deck, breaking open, followed by three more. <u>Wilson's</u> voice shrieking from below. "See! See! The devil's work! The devil's work."

All at once self realized terrible truth. <u>Objects</u> = <u>own specimens</u>. Deck strewn with valued <u>instances, ruinously damaged</u>! Large part whole collection! Months of hard + careful work = all <u>smashed</u>.

Self shouting out, "Stop this at once!"

Manx turning to see. Kewley demanding, "What are you doing here?"

Before self could answer <u>Wilson</u> appearing at top of ladder into hold, clutching further <u>specimen</u>, screeching like <u>madman</u>, "Catch him, catch him! Lock him up!" Then raising specimen to <u>hurl at self</u> !

Own reaction more instinctive than considered. Simply could not permit further <u>vandalism</u>. Observed nearest Manxman, Mylchreest, regarding self with foolish look, mouth hanging open, while in his pocket = <u>revolving pistol</u>. Self jumped forward, pushing he back, seizing weapon. Then holding up gun for Wilson to see, calling out, "Stop that this moment."

Wilson lowering <u>specimen</u>. But <u>Kewley</u> now regarding self with harshest look. "You'd best give that to me, Doctor."

Self had not been thinking of he but <u>Wilson</u>. Awful silence. Hooper, Skeggs + Hodges stood on deck beside me, v. <u>unsure</u>. Self felt curious sense of matters slipping away from control. Had never intended matters follow this course. Told he, "I'm afraid I cannot, Captain."

Kewley frowning. "Think again, Doctor. There's some, don't you know, who'd call this <u>mutiny</u>."

Could not go back, so must go on, wherever this may lead. Had crossed own Rubicon. Declared in firmest voice, "I am taking charge of this vessel." Why? Must have <u>cause</u>. "Because I have reason to believe it = being used for <u>smuggling contraband</u>."

Hooper at my side, fidgeting nervously, murmuring, "Are you sure about this?"

In truth self = far from sure. One difficulty = <u>too many Manx</u>. They = 9 (+ Wilson = 10). We = only 4. Also they = ship's crew, we = powerless operate <u>Sincerity</u>. Situation = impossible, yet inconceivable do <u>anything else</u>. All self could do was endeavour <u>alleviate</u> circumstance. Turned to other Manx. "I know you have nothing to do with this crime, rest assured. This = entirely work of Capt. Kewley and Mr. Wilson."

Didn't expect they believe this (nor did they, judging by looks) but hoped it might at least help carry selves through moment + avoid accusing all together. In event, proved of little effect. Kewley raging. "I'm not having anyone steal my ship." Wilson ranting as per usual, "back to hell with you," "agent of devil," etc. etc. But most troubling = giant <u>China Clucas</u>. Hard to comprehend, as he previously always = v. amenable, but he now = looking <u>daggers</u> + stepping forward towards <u>self</u> in threatening fashion. Knew <u>must act</u>, yet could not risk provoking such anger that Manx will respond with <u>recklessness</u>. Aimed pistol above Clucas' head + <u>fired</u>. Fortunately = v. effective. First mate Brew pulling China Clucas back by arm, shouting, "No you don't." Others fall quiet. Even Wilson = silenced.

Self at once acted to consolidate advantage. Ordered Hooper go into hold + fetch 4 <u>rifles</u> that must still = aboard. He nervous but obeying, soon returning with weapons. Selves loaded all. Mood on deck greatly changed now all selves = <u>armed</u>: Hooper + Skeggs = less fearful, Manx watching with looks of grim <u>submission</u>. Self next ordered Kewley + Wilson go below into carpenter's cabin. Kewley swearing and calling selves "pirates," Wilson howling about devils, hell etc. etc. but when Hooper gave Wilson kick they go. Self then ordered carpenter Christian to fix two further + <u>stronger</u> bolts to door. Great relief that numbers = now more even (4 selves, 8 they) but still could not permit crew wander freely. Ordered all into fo'c'sle (saying this = necessary "in case any man has been won over to Captain Kewley's lies"). Then had carpenter, Christian, attach <u>strong</u> wooden bolts to door. He still at work when Hooper called out, "Hey, you!"

He pointing aft at figure. Hard to see he in darkness, but appeared be holding some form of <u>sack</u>. V. mystifying? Thought all = safely locked away.

Self striding aft. "Who's there?"

He stepping across with sack to ship's rail. All at once self recognized he stride. He = murdering savage, <u>half-caste</u>! How he get aboard? Other realization = re sack. This = <u>cloth bag</u>: i.e. one containing own most <u>complete</u> + valued <u>specimen</u>: female <u>Mary</u>. Must be, as = only one stored in thus. How dare he! Self fired pistol but he = already dropping over side. Self took up lamp, ran to rail, saw he already in water, grasping <u>primitive</u> canoe. Attempted fire again but last round expended. Hooper fired rifle but he now <u>submerged</u> in front of vessel, pulling away. Hard to hit.

Considered lowering boat to give chase, but would have release

Manx, while this could = dangerous, as they could foment trouble when selves = distracted. V. aggravating.

Peevay
FEBRUARY 1858

SO I CLIMBED up from canoe, going carefully, and went onto ship's DECK. Climbing over RAIL, I could see Potter + other white scuts at other end, banging with HAMMER, but truth was I hardly took much heed as I was more intent on my surprise, which was terrible. Everywhere was dead fellows, you see, just lying broken hither and thither all around. They were so many, even enough for some tribe. So I stepped among, so sad and surprised, and angry. Who were these? I pondered. Why, they might be ones I knew, I could surmise. Dray, Mongana, Heedeek, are you here?

That was when I saw a bag, only one here, with words written.

BLACK TYPE TASMANIAN ABORIGINE FEMALE (*COMPLETE*)
(SPECIMEN: *M*)
VALUABLE: HANDLE WITH *CARE*
PROPERTY OF *DR. T. POTTER*
LONDON COLLEGE OF SURGEONS

Letter M made me wonder. Looking now, I saw small something tied to bag, and d'you know this was charm Mother kept, with Tayaleah's bone inside, which she wore under clothes so num wouldn't see. So I knew. Bag was just quite light, yes, which was some sad strange thing, as Mother never should be made light, she was too fine. Then I heard Hooper and Red Beard shouting out, so surprised, "Who's there?" and I saw Red Beard's pistol ready, so I knew I must go or get killed, which was piss poor. Even as I got away from his shooting tries, and came back through the water, holding canoe so I would not drown, I was raging. Wrath got worse when I was back on shore, and my dear desire was to return, so I could rescue those poor others, and burn his ship away and scorch him and servant Hooper to ashes.

By and by, though, I knew this was just some vain hope. They would be waiting now, watching for my fire stick, and could kill me too easily. At least I got poor Mother, which was some great good fortune, as I had despaired of finding her anymore. Mother would hate being some playing thing of white shits, I could divine, and this was some small tidings of joy. So I surmised that though I couldn't get everything I sought, at least I got some things, and I must try and make this my peace.

I watched through trees in case white scuts came looking but they never did. Just after dawn ship's sails dropped down, one by one, and it went out from this bay and away to somewhere. So I was left alone, which meant I could give Mother her fine goodbye, and try and dash to pieces all those hateful things that got done to her before. First I went back and forth beneath trees, getting dry wood to make into her burning pyre, like she should have got before, and when it was tall enough I put her on the very top. Then I said my saddest goodbyes and started her fire. Day was warm, no rain, wood was good, and soon all was burning hot and cracking. So, here in the world, which was hers, Mother finally got her correct dignity. Yes, that was some kind of sorrowful jubilation I could divine.

As she went, I pondered the life she got. This was woeful, yes, just fighting and seeking to endure, but I supposed that for this time she lived—most hateful one there ever was—she did it well. No, she could not get her dearest desire to vanquish num white men, and make them go away, because this was some impossible thing, but she had her mob and fought her war, and lived bravely and never cared what anybody else said, which was some wonder. Truly, I wished I was more like her.

By and by flames got strong and smoke rushed up like a big hand reaching. Then, as I watched, a thought came to me, which was interesting. You see, there was one craving deep inside her breast that never got done in all this time, but might still. Yes, in all these many long years and troubles, all these endurings and wanderings, we never did kill Father.

CHAPTER FOURTEEN

——⇒•⇐——

Timothy Renshaw
January–March 1858

So HERE I WAS, bruised and broken, just below the summit of some unknown Tasmanian mountain. At least I was on the leeward side, so the wind hardly troubled me, though it was still badly cold at night and when the rain fell.

Despite Cromwell's warning words I found it hard to believe the others would not return for me, and I was constantly listening for the sound of approaching footfalls. As days passed, my disappointment grew, then turned to sudden fits of anger, though at other moments I would imagine them loyally striding back to the settled districts so they might collect together a rescue party. Often and again I attempted to calculate how many days this would take them, though my guesses were different each time, being sooner when I felt in a good mood, and later when I was caught by gloominess.

The longer I was alone, the harder it became. I found myself often chattering to myself in a solitary way, and I greatly looked forward to the chance appearance of wild creatures, as even the native wolves seemed a kind of company. A pair of these soon stole by, just as Cromwell had predicted–strange loping creatures with dark stripes on their rumps–though fortunately they seemed shy of me, being only concerned with the mules. Wallabies would sometimes come bounding through the trees, and I had regular dusk-time visits by a wombat that would rummage through the vegetation and stop, regarding my tent with blank eyes, then amble away. Less cautious were the possums, with their curious little heads, that appeared at night when I cooked my dinner, which they would steal if I turned my back for a moment. I coveted all, thieving or otherwise. Having food enough, I never thought of using the spears Cromwell had left.

The passing days had at least one use, healing my injuries. I found myself able to walk about my tent ever more easily, though I never strayed far, having a great fear that the others would arrive and I should miss them. All the while my chatter to myself became more drawn to the dilemma before me. "The evenings are drawing in. It's hard to say without a watch but I'd swear it's no later than six-thirty and already the sun is setting. The nights are feeling colder, too. The longer I stay, the harder it will be for me to reach safety, that's certain. But what if they are coming to rescue me after all? Why, they could be climbing up the mountainside this very moment. That is, if they haven't just turned tail and left me for dead. Rotten, treacherous scum. But I cannot believe they would do such a thing as . . ."

So I would go on, round and again, and each time I was a fraction closer to making the hard decision to leave. Finally one afternoon I began assembling what I would need for my journey. The weight of it came as a shock. The tent seemed deliberately contrived to be heavy, with its thick canvas and clumsy wooden frame, while even the pots of food, though each was light in itself, added up to a proper burden. Nor did it help that everything had to be carried in a mule bag, whose straps were all wrong. In the end I decided I could not manage a whole tent but would take only a wide strip of canvas that I would rig up from trees. I took food to last me about ten days, which I hoped would be enough.

I set off early the next morning, clutching the spears that Cromwell had left me, my legs still stiff from my injuries. Several times in those first few yards I stopped, listening, in the hope that I might, even now, hear the others approaching, but the only sound was the breeze blowing the tops of the trees and the faint murmur of insects. Hurling a few foul names into the wind, I turned my back on my lonely home for the last time and went on my way. Cromwell's directions were invaluable, and though the going was not easy—beginning with a mighty scrabble down the mountainside—I soon found the path he had described, which I began following southwards. On the second day I reached the curious skull-shaped peak that he had talked of, which I kept to the east of, just as he had said I must. By the third day the land began to grow less wild, and I felt my spirits revive. I even laughed at my earlier nervousness about setting out, as it seemed it would be no great hardship to find my way to safety.

I dare say one should never think such thoughts. It was that same afternoon that I missed my step and grazed my knee. I cleaned the wound in the river and considered it nothing more than an inconvenience. The next day, however, it began to throb, then to swell, and with time it became so painful that I was obliged to make a crude crutch from a tree branch to help me walk. My progress was greatly slowed, till one morning I woke to find myself feverish, so I could not get up from beneath my poor canvas shelter, and I remained there all day, fitfully sleeping. At dusk I was woken by a rustling in the undergrowth and saw one of the native wolves was stood nearby, regarding me with patient interest. Clambering to my feet, I hurled one of Peevay's spears in the creature's direction, and though my aim was wide indeed, it scampered away. The incident scared me into faint strength and I managed to build a fire, which I made as large as I could, shaping it into a kind of line, in the hope the burning would slowly move, and so last through the night.

At some early hour of that same morning, I came awake, or so I thought. There, stood watching the flames, which were grown very faint now, were my parents and my older brother.

"He has built it very poorly," remarked my father, poking at the ashes with his umbrella. "He should have found more wood, really he should. I cannot think it will last much longer."

"He always was a lazy boy," agreed my mother with a shake of her head.

"If he is eaten, which I suppose he will be, then it shall be entirely his own fault."

My mother glanced towards my brother. "If only Jeremy had made the fire."

My brother, though evidently content with this remark, merely shrugged. "I would have tried my best, Mama, that is all I can say."

"You are too modest, child," declared my mother approvingly.

All at once I felt something welling up inside, like a kind of sickness. "I renounce you, d'you hear?" I shouted out. "I renounce you all. Now just leave me be."

The three of them regarded me with looks of surprise, even indignation. Then, one by one, they turned their backs and walked away into the trees.

I came awake and found dawn was breaking, while, to my great satisfaction, the fire was burning quite well. Though I was still feverish I felt a little better, and strong enough to raise myself up with my crutch. I had not been walking long and had covered no great distance when, stepping from some trees, I was amazed to find myself being stared at by a sheep. It was one of a large flock, and when I took a step towards them they all turned and fled together, like so many startled birds. I yelled and shouted for joy. Though my leg seemed somehow more painful now that I believed I was saved, I pressed on, and before long I came upon a wide dusty track, marvelously scored with marks of horseshoes, some looking wondrously recent. Climbing a low rise, I saw a wooden house, half hidden among trees, smoke trailing from its chimney. Dropping the mule bag, I hobbled forward, until, uttering a kind of giggle, I pushed open a gate and found myself in a garden, all brightest colours, such as I had hardly looked upon for all these many weeks.

How strange it was, though. Everywhere I looked, you see—on walls, atop stones and stood upon the lawn—were winged angels, dozens of them, all regarding me with smiling grey faces.

Dr. Thomas Potter
FEBRUARY 1858

The Destiny of Nations

Chapter 4: On the Future Fate of the Races of Men

The dominating characteristic of the Black Type being savagery, he has no thought beyond preserving himself for the next few moments. His is a mind empty of any comprehension of ideas, of enterprise, or time, and he is content to live his primitive and dreary existence, running naked through wilderness, in search of any form of wretched sustenance that may preserve him a few days longer. As such he may be pitied the terrible fate that awaits him . . .

The Destiny of Nations

Chapter 4: On the Future Fate of the Races of Men (correction)

The dominating characteristic of the Black Type being barbarism, he has no comprehension of ideas, of enterprise, or time, and yet he cannot be regarded as harmless. His dreary existence may seem innocence itself–running naked through wilderness, in search of any form of wretched sustenance that may preserve him a few hours longer–and yet a closer examination will reveal a very different truth. Do not underestimate the savage, for though he lacks any faculty of reasoned thought, he is possessed of a brutish cunning. Worse, he is filled with a malevolent envy of those of races who have–in a fashion incomprehensible to himself–developed the wondrous fruits of civilization. In Australia, Tasmania, New Zealand–and doubtless soon also Africa–the recent history of the Black Type has been one of swift and calamitous decline, even to the point of near-extinction, and in consequence it has become fashionable, in certain intellectualist and sentimentalist circles, to regard the dark-skinned races of this earth with feelings of pity: they are perceived as the victims of cruelest circumstance, suffering at the hands of unfeeling conquerors. Such a view, though doubtless well-intentioned, is dangerously misleading. The truth is that the Black Type, by reason of his flawed and dangerous nature, is largely the author of his own unhappy lot.

No finer instance of this truth can be provided than by that most diminished of nations, the aborigines of Tasmania. This sorry tribe has, ever since the island was brought within the fold of the civilized world, been widely acknowledged as representing the very lowest of all the races–or species–of men, being bereft of the most rudimentary skills, including even knowledge of agriculture, so it may be regarded as holding a place midway between humankind and the animal kingdom. In spite of this lamentable state of advancement, the aborigines' British rulers have displayed great compassion towards their new charges, such sentimentalism being a rare and charming weakness of the Saxon Type (see Chapter Two above). The colonial government made every attempt to improve those blacks who were captured, and to lead them from idleness to civilized ways. One might suppose these efforts would have been received with gratitude, but no, the aborigines showed themselves nothing less than contemptuous of the goodly teaching given them, and, beneath a thin veneer of civilized conduct, they remained quite as savage as before. Even now those few who are left are capable of every form of deceitfulness, violence (even murder) and theft of valuable property.

Such behaviour has all but exhausted the patience even of the kindly and sentimental Saxon, who–though it is not his nature to feel belliger-ence–will never shrink from righteous defence of himself and his posses-sions. There can be little doubt that when there begins the Great Conflagration of Nations, the Black Type will number among the very first nations to perish, and while it is in the heart of men to find sadness in any such occurrence, it may be considered that such an outcome is not without justice.

The Norman Type may by his cunning survive a little longer, but will meet a like fate. The Norman's power is drawn from his stolen seat at the centre of affairs–notably his control of land, title and church–and from his ability to dazzle his Saxon better with the empty spectacle of tradition. Such a state of affairs will not long continue. With every pass-ing day the credulity of the honest Saxon is subtly diminished. With every hour he sees more clearly the empty arrogance. the perversion of godliness that calls itself "noble." One bright morning the Saxon will awake from his slumber and find his eyes opened to the mighty fraud committed upon him and, with one mighty blow, his strong arms will rend asunder the shackles that have bound him thus, casting into obliv-ion the parasitical lords and priests who have fed from his industry for these eight hundred years.

The Celtic Type, by contrast, will endure, though his station will be a humble one. The dominating characteristics of the Celt may be idleness and deceit yet he is not beyond the realms of reason, being generally possessed of a most useful instinct of obedience. It is, indeed, his very failings–his irresolution, his awe of his mightier and cleverer fellows–that will permit him to be preserved. His role will be as a servitor to the Saxon, whether he is waiting at his table, marching in his armies or labouring in his fields, his mills and his ships upon the ocean. The con-nection between the Saxon and Celt will thus be one of mutual advan-tage: a form of compact between superior and inferior, master and slave.

Captain Illiam Quillian Kewley
APRIL 1858

THE MARKS I'D scratched on the wall told their story, and a low, rotten story it was too. Twelve weeks and more we'd been sailing. Twelve weeks locked below in my own vessel, and, worse, put there by a passenger I'd troubled to rescue from his own foolish dying. Twelve weeks of knowing that muck was strutting about the quarterdeck–my quarterdeck–like it was his own. Why, it was like watching some stranger sneak his fingers up my Ealisad's skirts clean before my very eyes. Here was a fine piece of gratitude. I should have left him on that shore to starve, so I should.

The wind had been mostly fair and I reckoned we must be almost at Cape Horn by now, or halfway back to Potter's England, as I supposed must be our destination. There was a pretty thought, and one I hardly could believe. Brew should have seized the vessel seventeen times over by now, in a mighty rush of Manxmen. Why, he could have caused a fine bit of havoc just by doing nothing–which any Manxman can do easier than kicking–as Potter and his three fritlags wouldn't have been able to sail the *Sincerity* two yards by themselves. For a while I supposed he must just be biding his time and waiting his moment, but as days passed it grew harder. The Reverend and me were taken on deck every morning and evening for our visit to the heads–Skeggs and Hodges jabbing us on our way with their rifles–and each time I'd throw scrutineering looks at Brew and the rest of them, watching for a Manx wink or two in return. I got hardly a stare. Well, that sort of thing will set a man to thinking, and I often found myself recalling that old Peel saying, *Never trust a Brew at the Fair*. Or I remembered the little fritlag's countenance that morning in Melbourne, when he'd been weighing up which would pay him better: to stay aboard in the hope of catching his share or to turn traitor and join those runaway dirts looking for gold. Wouldn't it just be my luck if that sleetch was looking to drop all the blame on me–just like Potter had coaxed–and had carried the rest of those useless blebs with him.

A proper lawyer's feast we'd make, for sure, if Potter got us back to his England, with passengers playing mutineer aboard a smuggling boat, and all those skulls and bones besides. How would that play before some crab of a London judge? On the one side there'd be Dr. Potter, educated Englishman, with his three creatures and a boatload of turncoat Manxmen. On the other there'd be Captain Kewley, proud owner of a smuggling vessel, and his fine friend the gibbering vicar, who was turning more crazed by the hour. All in all I could guess who'd be served up on a plate for a long spell in gaol.

That sort of thing will work on a man's mind, and it got so that I was sore tempted to try and make trouble even just by myself, as anything seemed better than just sitting waiting day after day. After a week Potter finally allowed us to have cots to sleep on, rather than just raw floor timbers, and I took a board from mine and had a try at forcing the door. The bolts were strong, though, while the Reverend wouldn't help, being all in a huff now he'd found out I'd been trading in that certain rum and tobacco (I think he was worried my sinfulness might all rub off on him and catch him dirty looks from his fine friend the deity), and though I tried once and again I couldn't even force the board through the door-frame to get leverage. Worse, my work left scars on the woodwork that Skeggs noticed. This brought a visit from Potter, who gave me his snurly look and had Christian fix three more bolts to the door. Our cots were taken away, so we had to sleep on floorboards again, which had the Reverend scowling seven times over. That was the end of my escaping for the while, as the door was fast as iron, while Skeggs and Hodges were careful as lawyers when they came with our food, standing well back when they pulled open the door and not coming inside till they'd had a good sight of us both looking harmless.

So I had the pleasure of Reverend Wilson's company, and by the weekload. That fellow really was the end. Why, I do believe I'd have forgiven Potter his ship stealing if only he'd been kind enough to fling the old article quietly overboard. The man just wouldn't stop. There I'd be, having myself a fine old time counting nails in the timbers, or listening to some interesting sound, you know, just to pass the time, when up he'd start again, wittering fit to rob a man of reason. His favourite was praying, and there wasn't a thing under the sun the old fool wouldn't pray for, from "the souls of our persecutors" to "hope in this darkest hour." Worst was when he prayed for me, as he'd make all kinds of little dirty snipes as he did so, saying how he forgave me for running the brandy, and even for my snoring in the night, which I'm sure I never did. There's few things worse than being forgiven, as you never have a chance of answering back, and if I tried to defend myself he'd just turn all sanity and never-minding. Besides, there were times when I could have done with the odd prayer myself, things being how they were, but I never had a chance with him droning away day and night. It was as if he'd hogged God all for himself.

His other delight was to start fights with Hodges and Skeggs. This was pure showiness—not to myself, naturally, but to his friend up in heaven—and it drove me distracted. Those four bodies had the guns, and the food, and a curious liking for collecting men's skulls besides, so the way I saw it there was no great cleverness in troubling them with taunts, but no, Wilson had to have his way. The moment they came through the door he'd be preaching at them with all his charm, telling how they were a pair of low dirts to go following Potter—who was, it seemed, the devil himself come to call—and that they'd burn in hell for sure. Hodges would take it quiet enough, usually, being a dull sort of body, but Skeggs was another pair of oars entirely, and often he'd be tempted to give the Reverend a batting, which wouldn't have mattered except that I was sure to get a nasty pelt or two myself, though it had none of it been my idea. Worse still was when Wilson started playing martyr, which he did generally on Sundays.

"Take your filthy food away," he'd declare all snurly, though he needed feeding. "I have no need of it. My sustenance is of a higher kind."

It was all very well him being the grand hero but that was my food too, and I wanted it. We were never brought that much, while eating was one of the few joys to fill those empty days. At least he could have asked me before starting up, but no, not him: why should he consult a mere ship's captain when he had divinity cheering him on. I'd have a try at saving my ration, perhaps making a little joke, calling out, "As for me, my sustenance is ordinary as seawater," but it never worked. Skeggs would just have himself a good laugh.

"Just as you like, Reverend." Then he'd take himself a great mouthful of my dinner and offer some more to Hodges.

All in all it was getting so I almost hoped we'd sink, as that would be better than watch Potter smirking in some Englishmen's courtroom as I was led away to gaol. By the looks of it we might be doing just that, too, if the weather had its way. All night waves had been hammering at the stern loud as cannon, and the ship was rolling and pitching wilder than the horse that's trod on the snake's tail. That would fit with what I'd heard of Cape Horn, for sure. If it got worse then, with so few crew aboard, anything was possible.

I'd supposed our gaolers might give our morning visit a miss in such weather but no, there they were just as usual, with our feast of hard beef and old ship's biscuit, and a shrivelled lime besides, all of it flavoured nicely by the dousing of seawater it had had on the way. After we'd finished we were nudged up the stairway for our visit to the heads. This was a proper bit of weather, for sure. One step onto the deck and I was soaked by the spray, while there was a sea roaring over the prow so big that it looked almost as if the ship was playing porpoise and diving down to put a sight on the ocean bed. Our poor Englishmen weren't liking it one little bit. Up on the quarterdeck Potter looked pale as death, and had his arms round the mizzen shrouds as if they weren't ropes but his dear lost ma. As I watched, a great roar of sea came rushing over the stern, knocking him onto his knees. For all that he still had a firm grip on that revolving pistol of his. Hooper must've been waiting to put a sight on us, as the moment the water started emptying into the scuppers he took his chance and skulked away below.

More curious to my eyes than the Englishmen, though, was the crew. For one, there was Jamys Kinred, the body at the wheel, and lashed to it too, to stop the seas from carrying him away. Now, Kinred was a decent enough seaman, no mistaking, but he was no giant. If it'd been me giving orders I'd have had China Clucas at the helm in a drop of weather like this. China wasn't far off, as it happened, being up above, repairing the mizzen ratlines. Well, wasn't that just another fine little mystery? Repairing ratlines is a handy enough sort of chore but it's a fair-weather job and shouldn't be troubled with in hurricanes. Why, to my eye they didn't even look as if they needed fixing. Brew was just below, and d'you know, this time he did throw me a wink. That was enough to get me watchful. It seemed I'd got the little fellow all wrong. He must've just been waiting for a good dose of dirty weather.

Skeggs didn't usually bother himself to shepherd the Reverend and myself forwards, leaving Hodges to do the work while he kept an eye, while today, the wet being so bad, he crept back into the stairway. The truth was it seemed hardly needful to fight our way to the head to piss and shit into the ocean, when the ocean was coming to us. Just as we started on our way the ship plunged down clean into a departing wave, and a rush of water all but vanished the heads from sight. That was enough to start the Reverend whining.

"You can't expect me to go up there," he moaned at Hodges.

I could have knocked him down, so I could. It hadn't escaped my notice, you see, that, despite all the wild dousings he was catching, Chalse Christian the carpenter was stood just behind the heads, where he was fiddling away tightening one of the jib guy ropes, though it looked right as rain to me. Fortunately Hodges just gave Wilson a sharp nudge with his gun, and so we staggered on, stopping to grab the rail and taste some ocean as another wave broke from behind. We were just arrived, and Hodges was standing back to let me open the door, when Christian took a belaying pin from his belt, and caught him the tidiest little knock on his head. I didn't need telling what to do next. Christian jumped on him, and I jumped on him too, and we both tried to get a catch on his gun. Not that our problem was Hodges–who was hardly your fighter–but the next wave, being a proper monster, which struck the vessel so hard that we were all knocked sprawling.

That was when the Reverend started up. "Hurrah!" he yelled, loud as his little nasty piping voice would go. "Hurrah, hurrah! Praise be to God!"

Now, there are times for hurrahing, I dare say, and this was not one of them. Glancing aft, I saw our friend Dr. Potter darting a look at our little mess, and then taking a look upwards. What did he see there but China Clucas, just getting ready to fling a belaying pin at his own sweet skull? A handy sort of look that was, too, as it let Potter dodge clean out of the way, so the pin brained nothing but deck timbers. Potter made a lunge back to the rail before the next sea came, and though Brew's belaying pin knocked him in the shoulder, he didn't lose hold of his revolving pistol, which he fired off at the sky, scaring Brew back. Here was trouble.

"Hurrah, hurrah!" shouted the Reverend.

I'd have hurrahed him myself if I'd not had better things to do. I made a lunge for Hodges' gun. By the time I'd got hold of it and turned about there was a fine proper battle raging. Skeggs had poked his head out from the stairway, only to find himself in a tussle with Tom Karran over his rifle. Meantime Potter was gripping the rail and pointing his pistol at anyone and everyone, his aim looking mighty wild, as the *Sincerity* bucked and rolled over the waves. There were four stood facing him, including Brew and China, and even that old fool Rob Quayle, the cook, all waiting their chance, and I reckoned if he didn't dare fire off a shot it was only for fear that if he hit one, the others would have him.

I might be able to give them a little help. I swung Hodges' rifle round till I had the good doctor nicely lined up in the sights, and I pulled the trigger. Now, it must have been loaded for sure, as otherwise what was the point in Hodges carrying it about night and day? D'you know, though, all I heard was a little click. I could only think it had suffered from getting drenched. There was a fine rotten piece of cheating. Day and night your Englishmen go boasting about how clever they are with their steel and railways and ships that they're saying the whole world wants to have, and now it turned out their rifles couldn't even take a little wet. Did they expect everyone to go fighting Russians and hunting tigers only in fine sunny weather? Truly, it was a miracle to me how they'd ever managed to conquer half the world like they had.

As it happened, that was the end of our little war. In a moment Hooper had darted up from wherever he'd been skulking below and gave Tom Karran a nasty crack on the head with the fat end of his rifle, which in turn ended Skeggs's troubles, and all of a sudden where there had been only one Englishman pointing his gun there were three, which was a power too many. Brew, China and the rest sort of slumped and started backing away. Nor could I blame them. Next Hodges was pulling himself up from the deck and grabbing back his useless weight of rifle, which he used to give me a good jab in the ribs, just to show his thanks. There was a rotten, dirty sort of moment. Nor was it helped any when the Reverend gave me his mad, snurly look.

"If only you had prayed forgiveness for your sins, Captain, as I have many times urged, don't you think matters might have turned out rather differently?"

Dr. Thomas Potter
APRIL 1858

The Destiny of Nations

Chapter 4: On the Future Fate of the Races of Men (correction)

The Celtic Type, like the Black and Norman Types, is fated to become wholly extinguished during the Great Conflagration of Nations. The Celt may try to beguile all with his idle, servile manner, but the stolid Saxon will not be deceived. He will recognize the dominating characteristics that lie beneath that foolish smile: the cunning, the deceit and, above all, the delight in unprovoked and malevolent violence. The Celt lacks even the simplest faculty of reason, and this omission alone shall cause him to perish. The Saxon, provoked ever and again by acts of belligerence and trickery, will reach the limit of his mighty patience, and slap away his foe like some troublesome fly. Thus will the Celt himself be the cause of his own complete and utter destruction, till hardly one will remain upon this earth. . . .

New Rules to govern the ship Sincerity: *Manxmen*

For the prevention of further acts of <u>violent mutiny</u> upon the members of the <u>Force of Command</u>, the following <u>rules</u> will henceforth apply. All rules shall be <u>rigidly enforced</u>.

Rule One

No repairs to the vessel shall henceforth be permitted, from scrubbing the deck to tarring the spars, as it has been observed such work is merely a <u>means</u> to <u>conceal</u> intended <u>attacks</u> upon members of the <u>Force of Command</u>. The only exception shall be daily use of the pumps, while those working these shall always be <u>lashed</u> to their places.

Rule Two

The mizzen mast is no longer to be worked by crew under any circumstance. Mizzen sails are to remain permanently furled.

Rule Three

Manxmen shall not be permitted on <u>quarterdeck</u> under any circumstances except the following:

i. The crewman taking the helm (who will be <u>lashed</u> to the wheel).

ii. The acting chief mate (who will be <u>lashed</u> to the mizzen mast).

<u>Note</u>: Any violation of this rule will be met with <u>harshest punishment</u>.

Rule Four

All crew except the tillerman and the acting chief mate shall henceforth remain locked in fo'c'sle <u>except</u> when Dr. Potter agrees that they are required on deck to work the ship.

Rule Five

<u>Prisoners</u> held below shall henceforth be permanently <u>shackled</u> to their places. Chamber pots will be provided.

Rule Six

The use of the <u>Manx language</u> is <u>banned</u> at all times. Any infringements of this rule shall be regarded as <u>intended mutiny</u>.

<u>Note</u>: Any violation of this rule will be met with <u>harshest punishment</u>.

New Rules to govern ship Sincerity: *Members of the Force of Command*

Rule One

All members of the <u>Force of Command</u> must carry loaded guns <u>at all times</u>.

Rule Two

At least <u>two</u> members of the <u>Force of Command</u> are to be present upon quarterdeck at all times of <u>day</u> and <u>night</u> (see new system of watches).

Rule Three

All <u>four</u> members of the <u>Force of Command</u> must be present on deck whenever the Manx crew are at work aloft (tacking, taking in sail etc. etc.) and must remain throughout such operations.

<u>24th April</u>

Self locked all crew in quarters, but then obliged release they, as storm growing worse (fore topsail and main topgallant both <u>burst</u>). Selves kept watch v. <u>carefully</u> with rifles ready.

<u>25th April</u>

Weather finally calmer. Hooper proposed selves should throw Brew + Kinvig <u>overboard</u> as <u>ringleaders</u>. V. tempting. However, self decided would be dangerous re own circumstances when (if) reach England. Also require they re working of ship. But permitted Hooper give both thorough <u>lashing</u> with all other Manxmen assembled to watch (Hooper made <u>own lash</u> from ship's stores: v. effective). Afterwards sent Brew below with Kewley + Wilson. Had carpenter Christian thoroughly <u>shackle</u> all three to floor timbers to prevent further trouble.

Afterwards self fortified quarterdeck with barricade of crates, ballast etc. etc. Also made use of old <u>cannon</u> from prow. No rounds for this aboard but took gunpowder from <u>rifle cartridges</u> + wrapped in paper to make <u>explosive packet</u>, then made second packet of loose <u>bullets</u>, small stones from ballast etc. etc. Assembled Manxmen on deck for <u>demonstration</u>. Self concerned if had guessed quantities correctly but in event went v. well. Hooper lit fuse (string dipped in oil + little gunpowder), then all watched as cannon roared + fired mighty spray of shot out across the sea. Manxmen pleasingly <u>awed</u>. Self then reloaded + set weapon atop barricade so surveys <u>main deck. Lamp</u> to be kept burning in sheltered part of barricade <u>at all times</u>.

Unhappy fact = mutiny = gravest blow. Self had never trusted they (fortunately) yet had <u>hoped</u> they might = won over vs. Kewley, if only from instinct own <u>self-preservation</u>. Own position now = v. unhappy one. England = better destination than Hobart with its <u>foolish sentimentalists</u>, yet fact remains <u>all destinations</u> now = <u>perilous</u>. Manxmen sure accuse self of piracy. Rev. will attack self re <u>specimens</u> + claim selves intended his murder. Have no doubt that self have acted always wholly <u>correctly</u> yet am aware may be judged with great harshness by <u>ignorant others</u>. At very least self will suffer disastrous <u>scandal</u>. Worst = beyond contemplation. Prospect of own <u>reputation</u> harmed = especially distressing, as would cause terrible damage re <u>The Destiny of Nations</u>. In truth this now = almost of more importance to self even than <u>own prospects</u>. Do believe it = own legacy to this world + = of greatest importance re <u>men's understanding of future</u>. Self simply cannot permit it be <u>slandered</u> + <u>destroyed</u>.

Three fellows also v. disturbed by Manxmen's <u>unprovoked violence</u>. Self have endeavoured convince they that selves = fully justified re seizing vessel from <u>proven criminals</u>. Insist this = not lawbreaking but <u>civic duty</u> + that selves shall receive commendations (in truth self = doubtful re this). Fortunately now = <u>far too late</u> to go back. They = already implicated in this course of action. Selves only hope = to remain <u>resolute</u>.

Other worry = <u>supplies</u>. Had been considering calling at port (Falkland Islands? Argentina) but this now = quite impossible as Manxmen certain to abscond, betray, attack etc. etc. Yet <u>food</u> = insufficient for journey back to England. Self obliged order considerable <u>reduction</u> in Manxmen's rations to ensure remaining supplies = conserved. Besides, self now consider previous <u>overgenerosity</u> may have <u>encouraged</u> they become instilled with <u>rebellion</u>. Rations of food for selves also = reduced though less so, as = imperative selves retain <u>strength</u> to fight off further attempts <u>mutiny</u> (also quite wrong to deprive Saxon Type of vital nourishment). These = v. difficult decisions yet simply <u>will not permit self be swayed from greater purpose</u>. If Manx suffer this = <u>their own doing</u>.

New arrangement watches etc. already = v. wearying. Self much bothered by distressing thoughts + <u>dreams</u>. Attempting find peace in <u>work</u>. Continuing to attempt reassemble + reclassify <u>specimens</u>, though this = v. difficult as destruction wrought by <u>Wilson</u> = <u>terrible</u> + many = too damaged, mixed up etc. to be saved (v. distressing). Self also working hard upon <u>manuscript</u> where can report = making <u>much progress</u>. Chapter on skull shapes of <u>inferior types</u> now nearly complete.

Peevay
FEBRUARY–APRIL 1858

WEATHER WAS BRIGHT as I walked across the world for the last time, trees getting lovely with autumn, but it was mournful to think I was the final Palawa here, and after me there would just be white scuts or no-body. This never could be their place, I did divine. Yes, they could go hither and thither, thinking IT IS MINE NOW, but they never would feel it like my ones did. How could they when they didn't know any-where's name, or how it got there? Num never would have this place deep inside their breasts, no. They would just be dwelling here.

It got hard being just alone. Why, I almost felt sad that hated Potter and so were gone now, as even hating and killing them was some kind of company. By and by lonely madness came to me in the night, whisper-ing that everything was just ruination, and putting aches in my shoulders and bones, as if tears got inside and made them damp like rotten wood. But then day would come, bright and new, and so I would stretch my arms, get up, and endure again. So it came that I left mountain places and I went among white men's roads and farms. I went carefully here, though it was too easy, yes, as they never were watchful anymore. Why should they be, too, when our ones were all gone now? I could see them from my hidden place, going on CARTS or riding hither and thither to make sheep animals run all together, and I observed their eyes looked still and empty, as if there was nothing inside except smallest thoughts, WHAT IS MY NEXT WORK? WHAT IS MY NEXT FOOD? WILL WEATHER BE FINE DAY AGAIN TOMORROW? Yes, these were their delights now that we were dead. I did detest them for this.

Slowly slowly land got flatter till one day I went over some low hill and there was sea, northern sea. I followed shore east until, one good good weather morning, I saw, far away behind the waves, that so familiar mountain, thin and pointed like some spear. Robson's island, where he brought us and watched us die. That was strange to behold like seeing some saddest ghost. Nearer in the sea was a hill, round and low, and I surmised this must be Father's island, as when Mother tried to kill him with her waddy stick that time I could recall he sailed that way. I quick-ened my walk, islands got nearer, and by and by I came to some num place. This was small, with just few houses by a river and few white men near, making sheep run hither and thither like always. River by the sea was muddy and on its mud were two boats, one of them just correct, with two oars and small mast for sail. So I went away to nearby forest, where I made spears, plenty of them, and then I waited. When evening came and white scuts were all gone inside their houses I went to that boat, going carefully, then pushed it into the water, though it was too heavy, and climbed inside and went away.

Night was light enough with half a moon and I put up the sail and I rowed sometimes besides. When morning came hill island was near and world behind was gone in cloud. First I could see nothing, but when I went round all of a sudden I could see houses, six of them, long and low. These were enough for plenty of white men I did surmise, too many for me to fight, which was worrisome, as I supposed they would kill me before I ever could spear Father. Then I observed a puzzle to confound. I could see nobody there, you see, while chimneys had no smoke. Were they all hiding, waiting with their killing surprise? I pulled sail smaller, going slowly, but still no one came to look or shoot his gun, so I went to the shore and pulled boat from the sea. Going to nearest house, spears ready, I pushed door open. Inside were no people but there was TABLE and CHAIRS and smell of mutton bird, while when I went to fire and touched it with my fingers, ashes were still warm. Other houses were just the same, which was interesting. So I decided to observe. I took my boat, very heavy, and hid it in bushes. After that I sat behind, watchful, with all my spears ready in a line.

It was nearly dark and I was sleeping when I got woken by faraway voices murmuring over the water. Lights were shining on the sea, four of them, with little splashes as oars dipped. From lights' movings I knew this was four boats, and though I couldn't see rowers I knew from their voices they were many, which was bad. Still there was nothing to do now and so I remained thus, watching as boats came near, touching spears once and again, to be ready, and wondering if Father had some whole heinous tribe these days.

Captain Illiam Quillian Kewley
APRIL–JULY 1858

EVERY DAY DUSK came just a scran later and the night felt a touch colder. Well, there was no mistaking the story of that. We were getting into northern seas. It couldn't be long now before we'd reach Potter's England. There was a poor sort of prospect to look forward to.

My marks on the wall counted nine weeks since we'd rounded Cape Horn, which was two full months, and I couldn't think of a poorer, more starved pair of months than these. I don't know if it was the scare they'd got, or the cleverness they felt at winning I couldn't say, but ever since our little battle by Cape Horn it was as if frost had got into those ship stealers' veins. Dr. Potter had the sweet notion of chaining Brew, the Reverend and me to the floor timbers, while he even came down himself to make sure it was done to his liking, which meant too tight, so it was hard as could be to catch a proper dose of sleep at night. From then our visits to the heads were traded for buckets, which seemed a vengeful, shaming sort of thing. Even Hodges, who was the softest of the four, started handing out jabs with his gun keen as mustard, almost as if this was a new game that he'd never dared play till now. Hooper was the worst, though. He was the one who gave poor Brew and Kinvig their lashing—which we all had to watch—while he looked like he was enjoying his work, grinning and smirking and taking little runs so he could make more of a mess of their backs. Giving that scelping seemed to give him an appetite for more, and several times I heard him padding down the stairs, quiet as ghosts, hoping to catch Brew and me chattering in Manx, as this was now forbidden under Potter's new laws. Your Manxman may have his faults, I dare say, but he's never sneaking and brutal like that. This was finding a kind of joy in handing out pain.

It wasn't long before he lost his chance to play that particular game. After just a couple of days Potter noticed he didn't have enough Manxmen to sail his vessel, and off came Brew's shackles. That was a shame, too, as I'd enjoyed having some company other than that droning crab of a parson. As it turned out, though, Brew's stay had usefulness even afterwards, as it had showed him where I was chained. That same night after he went I heard a scratching from the wall behind me, faint, like some mouse having adventures, and it kept up all through the night. That caught my interest, not least because I knew that behind the wall was the fo'c'sle. Sure enough, early the next morning a shine of metal broke its way through one of the timbers by my elbow, then vanished away, leaving a little hole, and when I leaned down to listen I heard the sweet sound of Manx. The metal, Brew explained in a whisper, was a teaspoon, this being all that Potter would allow them to eat their dinners with, as it seemed he was afeared that forks and such would make these men of Peel a proper peril against his poor babes that were armed just with rifles.

There was a fine change. All of a sudden I could hear all the talk, and know how things were up on deck. Not that everyone was pleased. Whenever one of the boys whispered hello I could see Wilson turning tetchy, and his eyes would look round corners as if he was trying to hear what they were saying, though it could do him little good, seeing as every word was pure Manx. The man was jealous, though he had not a scran of right to be. It wasn't even as if he was losing my own sweet company as it was days since he'd thrown me so much as a word, preferring to keep all his chatter for heaven. Sometimes when Brew mumbled hello Wilson would start praying extra loud, just to stop me hearing, and I quite feared he'd find some way of blurting about it to Skeggs and Hodges, or making them see the hole in the wall with his staring (I hid it as best I could with my arm). Truly, that vicar was a handsome bit of meanness. We were only equal now, were we not, after all. He had someone to chatter to, in his good friend the Almighty, and now so did I, though, judging by his curiosity, mine was better for telling the latest news.

Not that there was any I was pleased to hear, as it was all bad. Brew said the fo'c'sle was nothing more than the crew's own private gaol, being so fixed up with bolts that there was not a chance of breaking out even with the mighty help of teaspoons, and the boys were kept there except when there was some need for them to man the pumps or work the sails. Worse, by the sound of it they were beginning to lose heart. I tried to urge them on to venture some more havoc–perhaps at night when the Englishmen were tired–but they wouldn't be coaxed. Then again the true fact of Manxmen is that deep down they're purest mood, being the kind that'll fill out and fall slack like sails in the wind. When all's going well and their hopes are high there's no stopping them, but if things once turn sour then the soo will spill clean away, till they've lost all believing in themselves. Getting beat by the Englishmen had knocked the boys badly, while having to watch Brew and Kinvig get lashed, without being able to do a thing to help, was worse again. Nor was this the end of our troubles. Your Manxman is as sensible as cold water most of the time, but certain things will creep under his skin and plague him, and Potter's mystery of skulls and bones was just one. Not that I'm one to pay any heed to such things myself, but I'll own it had got some of the others a touch nervous, and there was talk that Potter had *certain ones* on his side, so he'd never be caught out, however clever we were. That sort of notion did bring a body low.

The ship was getting into a poor way, too. Potter's new madness of forbidding all repairs soon started to take its toll, especially when we reached those doldrums, where we were caught for two weeks and more. That was all hot sun and sudden windless squalls, just the sort of thing to spoil a sailing vessel, and by the time a breeze took us away I could hear the sound of the *Sincerity*'s aching spilling down through the deck timbers. It was there in the screeching of the metal blocks, too shrill and scanky to be right, and in the thuds of the boys' boots on the deck planks, which should've rung out dull and solid, but instead were getting a touch hollow, as if they were dancing on some cheap fellow's coffin. Most of all it was in the slushing sound of water down below, which was getting gently slower and deeper—like a tin bath that's beginning to fill—and it was in the squealing of the pumps as they were worked, trying to keep the ship's belly dry. Any ship that's been a year or two afloat will need pumping now and then, but this was different. There seemed hardly an hour, day and night, when they weren't going.

It was no mystery what the trouble was. We were falling apart. Very slowly, as it happened, but falling apart still. Starve a sailing ship of mending and she'll soon set about turning herself into so much rotten wood, torn ropes, rusted metal and rising seawater. Without their daily dousing and caulking the deck planks will shrink and let in rainwater to slosh about the bilges, and start a little rot besides, and sure enough I began to notice wet seeping down from the deck during squalls, till spots of damp were springing up along the walls. Brew said the ropes were fraying and going slack, as Potter was too suspecting to let them be tightened regularly. If he wasn't careful the masts themselves would go, as without fresh tarring there'd be nothing to stop them turning rotten and brittle. Little by little the *Sincerity* was trying to reach that fine state that every wooden vessel is always hankering to become: a wide spread of driftwood and canvas decorating some empty stretch of ocean.

There was a low, dirty piece of vandalism. My own *Sincerity*, that I'd had built from wrecks, almost with my own hands, and kept trim as could be, brought to ruin by ignorant mutineering dirts. Why, it was like having someone go pissing on your favourite child. I'd have almost been pleased if she'd just gone completely and sunk, but we didn't even luck enough for that. Brew said that, for all her leaks, she was still high in the water. For a time that had me puzzled but then I guessed the why. It was the contraband holds. They must be acting like two great floats, holding us on top of the ocean. I suppose it's no easy thing to send a vessel to the bottom when she has two hulls to preserve her.

The shame was that us poor Manxmen didn't have a second hull to save us. Ever since our Cape Horn battle Potter had cut our rations right down, till we weren't getting enough hardly to famish a mouse. Soon all I could think of was eating, and that ache that gnawed at my gut and wouldn't stop. It soon showed. The Reverend had been thin enough to start with, and by the time we left the doldrums he was a proper skeleton, while I could see my own arms and legs getting bonier by the day. Brew said the boys were getting so light and fleshless that their faces were looking like so many dead men. All the while I was pleased to see the Englishmen were keeping themselves nicely fed, and I could have sworn Skeggs put on a new inch or two on his fat belly.

He wasn't so lucky with the scurvy, sad to say. I knew this must come, as I'd not seen a lime since before the doldrums, and I was already getting a mad hunger for vegetables. Skeggs was the first it caught, for all his meat, turning pale and weary—which I thought a fine improvement on the man—till his mouth began to swell so there was no question left. After that Brew's news was scurvy and more scurvy, who'd got it, and who thought they might next. I caught it like the rest, and I can't say it was a pleasure, neither. First it took me with a tiredness strong as death, so it was hard to imagine doing so much as a thing, and then my gums and mouth became raw, making it rotten painful to eat. I knew where it went from there. Next a fellow would go blotchy like he had seven plagues, then his teeth would start working loose, till finally he'd find himself wrapped in a slip of spare sailcloth and dropped quietly over the side to puzzle the fishes.

Wouldn't you know who was the very last one aboard to get struck? The Reverend. How he managed it I just couldn't say. Perhaps he'd found a way of stealing limes. He loved that, of course, and hardly an hour went by without him praying more thanks to the Lord God his Father for making sure he, the Reverend Geoffrey Wilson, was still fine as fiddles, when all us other poor dirts were bloating up like corpses and feeling our teeth go slack. The relief I felt when he finally fell sick too. Not that it made much difference. Why, I do believe he got worse. He wouldn't rest quiet even for an instant, and if he couldn't think of anything to say to his friend the Almighty, then he'd just start humming, or making strange little put-put-put noises with his lips, or drumming on the floor timbers with his knuckles, just to play pest. The jink I'd have given to be loosed from my shackles, so I could coax him into quiet with a good honest pelting.

All the while the evenings grew longer and the air cooler. A day came when Skeggs stopped coming on his errands, and Hooper came to give us our scraps of food instead. Brew said two of the boys were so hobbled they could hardly stagger aloft to work the sails. Still we sailed gently on. Storms? Why, I hardly knew what this ocean was playing at. Since our wetting by Cape Horn the Atlantic had been shaming itself, giving us hardly anything worse than pretty boating weather. Cape Finisterre, Bay of Biscay, with all their bragging of ships smashed and sent to the bottom. Why, they should've been ashamed of themselves.

Finally, one morning, as I was feeling a tooth coming loose from my mouth, there came a whisper from Brew through the wall that I didn't want to hear.

"We passed Ushant last night."

We'd be well into the Channel by now. We were almost back in Englishness.

Kinvig guessed my thoughts, though I never spoke a word. "Don't you worry, Captain. I've had a thought. We're not finished yet, so we're not."

The Reverend Geoffrey Wilson
JUNE 1858

LORD MY FATHER who art in heaven, these cool nights tell me we are nearly returned. Another man might feel despair at the ordeal I have endured: hungry, shackled, suffering from sickness, forced to suffer the company of a trafficker in liquor, and to watch my persecutors–Thine own foes, the agents of the evil one–strut in triumph. Another man might feel abandoned, and even cruelly *betrayed*. Another man might be filled with *rage* at the seeming futility of his great quest, that he embarked upon with such high hopes, and endured so bravely, all merely to serve *Thou thyself*.

I feel no bitterness. I cast no *blame*. Lord my Father who art in heaven, I valiantly preserve my faith still. I only ask that if Thou hast some great design for me still–as I can only assume Thou *must*–then *let it be soon*. I am more than ready, and watch every moment for Thy smallest sign, though there has been *nothing till now*.

Was Eden here, in England, all along? Is this the answer? Has all of this great venture merely been some kind of grand test? *But then why didst Thou send me all that way?*

Lord my Father who art in heaven, at least couldst Thou ease this hunger that I feel. Surely that is not so much to ask? I have such a strong longing for apples, and see them often in my dreams. Even the miracle of an *onion* would be greatly welcome, or perhaps a raw potato.

Dr. Thomas Potter
JUNE 1858

MANXMEN = <u>treacherous</u> even to v. last. Self heard Brew (lashed to mizzenmast as per usual) instructing helmsman to steer NNW. When self questioned he re this he claiming we = carried into <u>Bay of Biscay</u> by difficult sea currents + must set course to avoid Breton Peninsula. He pointing to distant point of land to NNE, claiming this = Brittany. Self = doubtful. From own inspection of charts had supposed we = already further <u>N</u>. Also could see several distant vessels journeying <u>E</u> or <u>W</u>. These = entering or leaving <u>English Channel</u>? If distant land = not Brittany but <u>Cornwall</u>, then NNW course would take selves into Irish Sea + to <u>Isle of Man</u>. Brew hoping lead selves into trap + wreck ship on some Manx shore, so his Celtic Type <u>compatriots</u> may <u>murder</u> selves? When self accused he his reply = <u>weak</u> and <u>unconvincing</u>. Evident own suspicions = <u>well founded</u>.

Self considered only most radical action will answer this latest attempt <u>subversion</u>. Cannot jeopardize selves by continuing entrust ship to <u>lying</u> + <u>conniving criminals</u>. Decided selves must take <u>complete command of vessel</u>, including <u>navigation</u> + control of <u>ship's wheel</u>. Cannot be so difficult if even <u>Manx Celtic Type</u> = can manage, while selves have = observing Brew, Kinvig etc. etc. long enough to gain ample understanding re their craft. Self acted at once. Had Brew unlashed from mizzenmast + thrown off quarterdeck. Self announced henceforth self will act both as <u>captain</u> and <u>chief mate</u> + crew to take orders <u>directly from self</u>. Brew whining protests, prophesying disaster etc. etc. (of course) but self <u>determinedly ignored</u>. Likewise dispensed of China Clucas at the helm, replacing he with <u>Hooper</u>. Hooper worried that he = too weak (scurvy) but self assuring he that = not far now to go. England = within sight.

Issued own first order = "loosen more sail." Wind = light while self suspecting Brew = deliberately attempting <u>slow vessel</u>. Brew claiming more sail = dangerous, saying wind will strengthen + masts = weak from lack repair. His complaining only serving <u>strengthen own resolution</u>. Ordered <u>more sail still</u>! Crewmen v. <u>slow</u> in performing duties aloft, so self = obliged fire one round from revolving pistol into air. V. effective. Self at once proved <u>correct in judgment</u>. Sails held, ship making better progress. Self had crewmen returned to fo'c'sle or lashed to pump, as before. Set course ENE.

Self feeling v. tired. Decided go below for rest, leaving Hooper (helm) + Hodges at watch. Looked in on Skeggs. He v. bad. Own mouth + hands painful with scurvy, so difficult even write this entry. Find self filled with <u>most unhappy feelings</u> re shore of <u>England</u> that selves = approaching. Am greatly troubled by <u>fears</u>. Must land or die, though this means self will suffer <u>accusation</u>, if not <u>arrest</u> + <u>imprisonment</u> by <u>ignorant men</u>. One comfort = that have now completed <u>Destiny of Nations</u>.

Whatever own fate may be, do hope + believe this work shall = <u>my child</u> for a future (+ wiser) age.

Captain Illiam Quillian Kewley
JUNE 1858

I WAS WOKEN by the sound of creaking wood, though it wasn't like any wood creaking I'd heard before, being sort of slow and huge, as if half a forest was falling on its face. Just as I sat up there was a mightiest crash and all at once it seemed as if some kind of guts had been slit, with great lumpers of things spilling down from above all in a rush, filling the air thick with dust. Something dropped onto my lap, dull and heavy as a dead body, knocking the wind clean out of me, and in the same instant I could feel the whole vessel rolling sharp to larboard, as if some great hand was tugging her over. She started righting herself, only to swing right back. Had the keel gone? If she capsized, then seawater would come seeking a road through every hole and rottenness and take us to the bottom fast as could be. I'd never fancied drowning, but it's not up to a body to choose his way, while there was little I could do. I counted seconds, and more, and though the ship rolled on, still we floated. Finally she calmed into a sharp lean, and I decided I wouldn't be breathing seawater just yet.

I gave a spit as mouth was dry with the stink of tar and paint dust. Looking down at my lap, I saw I hadn't caught anyone's corpse after all, but just a big coil of rope. By then the air was starting to clear a little, showing me how our gaol now had a brand-new piece of furniture, this being a proper tree of wood that was skewed clean across the place, and had smashed the door to pieces. There's a magic about things that have got into their wrongest place and it was hard to think this was one of the yards that on an ordinary day would be sat halfway up a mast, with a length of sailcloth dangling from it to trouble the wind. A proper show it made, too, spearing through the floor timbers, with its fuss of canvas and ropes cluttering up the cabin. I was glad it had chosen to drop in slant-wise, as it happened, as straight down might have knifed me along with the boards. There was no doubt how it had got in. Glancing up, I saw the hole it had fingered through the deck timbers, which was wide enough to drop a cow or two, and told a tale on that rain tickling my face. I could just make out part of the mast it should've been fixed to, which was now lying along the deck. Beyond I could see sky, all prettiest pink with the dawn. And a good morning to you, too.

Here was a fine piece of rottenness. My poor *Sincerity*, ruined by dirts of Englishmen that should never have been allowed near a sailing ship. It was hardly much of a surprise, as Brew had said Potter had piled on a madness of canvas. On another vessel he'd have suffered nothing worse than a burst sail or two, but not this one. Thanks to his wrecking, the bands and bolts would've been rusted through, the ropes would be slack and the mast itself would've been half rotten and aching to split into so many spillikins. All that was needed was a good puff of wind and over she'd go. Then I found myself in puzzles, though. This could only be the mizzen, as the others were too far forward, yet, as I recalled, Potter had said in his rules that no sail was to be set aft. Then why had it come down?

I pushed the coil of rope off my lap, like some old dog that's got too comfortable, and had a try of my arms and legs, finding that though I had some fine bruises nothing seemed actually broke, which was something. I could hear voices calling out from up above, and from their direction I guessed they must be the pair lashed to the pumps. I was glad they'd not been smashed to death by the mast. Though I couldn't catch their words for the wind, they sounded raging as could be. As it happened, the reason came soon enough. All at once there was a mighty thump from the ship's side, jarring the whole vessel. That little noise told me that not one but two masts were down. The main must have pulled the mizzen with her. Worse, while the mizzen had dropped along the deck, nice and tidy, the main had sheared clean over the side, where waves had just battered it against the hull. If the mast kept scelping her like that, it was only a matter of time before it poked a hole clean through the ship's timbers and down we'd sink, nice as nip.

"Thank you, Lord, for preserving me from disaster," mumbled the Reverend into the dust, catching, as ever, just the wrong moment.

It was then I noticed another interesting change. The fact is that if a body happens to find himself shackled to the floor for a few months, he soon comes to know every little habit and mood of his chains, almost better than he knows his own wife. The fetter between my wrists, being small, had a mean and nagging feel, rattling at any fuss, while the larger one, which was held to a ring bolted to the timbers, was more heaviness, tugging me back with a start like it bore some grudge. Now, though, I realized that this last seemed a touch lazier than usual, giving just a scran before it hauled at my arms. I soon saw the cause. The yard had smashed a mighty rent across the timbers of the floor, which had cut nearly through to the metal ring. Here was a welcome piece of curiosity. One of the ring's bolts was quite loose, so I could pull it free without trouble, and though the other was stuck, that was a fine start. Fingers trembling at this chance of not getting drowned after all, I set about trying to work it from the floor. This wasn't easy, for sure, but little by little the wood began to splinter, till I could feel the bolt loosening nicely, like a bad tooth. Finally I crouched above it, gave a mighty tug, and out it jumped. There was a fine sweet moment. I was free! Aside, that was, from the half a hundredweight of chain still trailing from me.

Now I was wondering what was happening up on deck. "Is anyone still in there?" I called out through the hole in the wall.

"Every one of us," Brew's voice called back. "And all right as rain except that we're about to drown."

Here was a rotten piece of wonder. I'd assumed Potter would let some of them free so they could cut away the mast. What did he think he was doing? "I'll get you out of there, don't you worry," I promised, though it was more wishing talk than anything known.

"Captain Kewley, you must help me."

It was so long since I'd heard the Reverend speak to me rather than to his friend in heaven that I almost jumped. So he wanted rescuing, did he? The gizzard of the man. All these weeks he'd hardly troubled himself to tell me the time of day and now, when he needed some help, he was all talk. I was sore tempted to leave the troublesome article to rot, which was all he deserved. The fact is, though, that if you've been shackled next to a fellow for a power of time it is awkward to just step away and leave him to breathe seawater, however low and useless he may be. Before you know it you're wondering how you'd feel if somebody did the same to yourself, and that's the finish of your rushing. I kicked away the leavings of the door and was about to step outside into the passage, but then I turned back.

"All right, Vicar." The surprise I got when I put a sight on his chains. Would you know it, he was hardly held to the floor at all, if only he'd bothered himself to look. The timbers by his feet must have taken more rainwater wet than had mine, as they were flaky with rot, while the mast had done the rest. All it took was a bit of a tug and he was settled. However much time we had left, and whatever I might have to do, I couldn't see myself doing it with a weight of chains to carry, that was sure. Just along the passage was the boatswain's locker, where, in normal times, there was kept an axe, just in case some rope needed snapping in a rush. Normal times these weren't but the axe was there nonetheless.

"Stretch your chains over the there," I told the Reverend hurriedly, pointing at the yard that had dropped on us.

He obeyed with a kind of giggle, and so I brought the axe down, aiming for the little ring that held them all together. My strength being half gone with scurvy, it took four tries, but in the end the ring snapped, so the main chain dropped away and the smaller one was sheared in two. His hands free, Wilson picked up a long nail from the floor and began fiddling at the rings round his wrists.

"There's no time for that," I told him quickly. "Here." I handed him the axe and started gathering up my chain, hoping he had a good eye for chopping. I never did discover, of course. I suppose I should have learned my lesson by now, as the fact is there's no doing favours to Englishmen. Rather than show a proper bit of gratitude, like a body might have expected, the evil old article just murmured, "I have work," and then, while I was still trying to guess his joke, he started clambering onto the yard and up towards the deck. There was a low, dirty piece of helpfulness. I managed to catch one of his feet, but d'you know he gave me a nasty kick with it right in the eye, while, the chains still tugging at me, this was enough to knock me clean over. There's words for that sort of thing, and I called him them, too, but it didn't stop him scampering away. Truly, that fellow really was the end. As I watched, he was already trying to pull himself through the hole in the deck timbers.

All at once what little time I'd had was robbed from me, and my troubles—which had been more than enough before—were doubled and trebled and doubled again. It's a clever man indeed that can shear a chain between his wrists with an axe that he's holding himself. Worse again, there was the question of surprise, this being the one solitary thing that I'd have had on my side in whatever wild, desperate something I'd have do against the Englishmen. With the Reverend scrabbling through the hole to the deck, my surprise would be as fresh as last month's kippers. Still, there was no use in staying here and waiting, so I reckoned I might as well venture something, however desperate. Gathering up my chains in an armful and picking up the axe, I hurried back along the passage and up the stairs.

So it was I found myself putting a sight on a world that I hadn't seen for a good little while, and a rotten sort of world it looked, too. I knew those dirts had made a mess of my vessel but still I never supposed it would be so bad as this. A proper ghost ship she seemed, with her paint flaking and her deck timbers buckled. Why, she was worse, as even a ghost ship will have a full quota of masts. The *Sincerity* had lost two, just as I had supposed, leaving a pair of stumps, like dead trees, while the foremast looked lonely as could be. Why, she was hardly like a sailing vessel at all anymore, being all sky and mad strewn wreckage. A tangle of ropes pulled taut over the side told me where the mainmast was, though I hardly needed telling, as that moment another wave sent it thumping into the ship's timbers. That little mess would have put paid to the rudder, and leave the ship drifting like a dead thing. All in all we were now nothing more than a big wooden lumper of wreck, waiting to sink.

This took me to my next little piece of rottenness, which was quite the king of them all. At a moment like this any normal seaman, whether angel or pirate, will have only one thought, and that's to save his vessel. Inside half an instant he'll pick up the nearest axe and start chopping at wreckage before it sinks her. What was going on here was rather different. The Englishmen were all busy as beavers, for sure, but their delight was all in trying to lower the main boat. All in all it seemed they weren't eager to clutter themselves with Manxmen, preferring to keep this a private ride just for themselves. I could see the shore, with a prettiest line of surf breaking, and though it was a few miles off it looked near enough to suit them nicely.

What a fine case of Englishman's murder this was. Murder by *doing nothing*, which is your Englishman's favourite, I'm sure. Shooting or bludgeoning a shipload of men to death is such a dirtying sort of thing to do, as well as being legally awkward besides, so what could be prettier than to quietly set out for the shore and leave all this untidiness behind, handy as kittens drowning in a bucket. All my friend Potter needed to do was shut his eyes for a moment, dream up a smart little story to tell the curious, and, with a little gentle rowing, all his worries would be gone. He must, I supposed, be quite hugging himself beneath his beard. No wonder the two bodies at the pumps were raging and screaming so. The boys in the fo'c'sle must've heard them, as they were hammering and shouting fit to burst.

Not that the Englishmen were doing so well in their murdering. Truly, you never saw a gang of dirts less fit for messing with ships than these. All they had to do was lower a boat, which is hardly your most difficult piece of seamanship, but a proper pig's ear they were making of it. The boat was hanging over the ship's side, but only a foot or two, as it was nicely jammed. As for the Englishmen, Skeggs–who looked pale as death–was lying inside it with his head propped up on one of the rowing benches, while Hodges and Hooper stood beside him tinkering with the blocks, and Potter was facing them over the rail from the deck, a pile of guns and a leather carrying case at his feet. Was that our gold in there? Our gold that we'd sailed clean round the world to earn? The low mucks.

An ill-tempered gang of dirts they were, too, yelling at one another like drunks raging over the last swallow from the bottle. I suppose they were getting scared they mightn't escape after all, and would accidentally murder themselves along with everyone else. The poor babes. If only they'd thought to ask, I could've told what was wrong, as I could see it with one glance. The blocks were nearly solid with rust while the ropes holding the boat were fraying like sheep's hair. This was their own fault, too, seeing as it was them that had brought the ship into such a handsome state of ruin in the first place.

"We must cut the ropes," shouted Hooper.

"But that's madness," Potter yelled back. "The boat could capsize when it hits the water."

If only I could get to the fo'c'sle and free the others, then we might have a chance. It wouldn't be easy, though, with chains to carry and a heap of guns lying at Potter's feet. I was getting ready to have a try when I heard a shout of "Lord God who art in heaven, I pray to Thee, smite down thine enemies." Strange to say I'd almost forgotten about the Reverend in these last moments. Here he came, striding across the deck, bold as brass. For a second I feared he might give me away, but no, he didn't cast so much as a sneer in my direction, being far too intent on his own madness. It was high time he made himself somebody else's nuisance for a change. Why, he might even come in handy, giving Potter somebody else to stare at.

"Get back from here," Potter shouted, as if he'd seen a ghost.

I didn't wait but darted out from the stairway fast as I could, to the stump of the fallen mizzenmast, which I reached without getting shot even once. Getting to the fo'c'sle would be harder. I gave a wave to the two poor skeletons at the pumps to keep quiet.

I could hear Wilson droning behind me. "I must have this boat."

"I'm telling you to get back." Potter should have known better than to try giving orders to the Reverend.

"God says it is mine."

"God told you wrong."

Glancing back, I saw Potter waving his pistol at the Reverend. Not that it made any difference, as the only way he could've persuaded that old article was by putting a bullet through him. He must've wished he'd done just that, too. The next thing I knew Wilson uttered a kind of piping yell, then took a rush at the rail, and sort of scampered and hurled himself over, quite your flying vicar, landing himself nicely in the boat. The surprise, though, was what came next. The weight of him can't have been much, being all skeleton like he was, but it was enough for those frayed ropes. One held and one gave, so the thing dropped down purest vertical. How Wilson held on I couldn't say, but he did. The rest were less lucky, or less wilful. All of an instant Hooper, Skeggs and Hodges– and the oars too–were sprinkled nicely onto the ocean with pretty little splashes. I heard them wailing up from the water, already getting fainter, as the wind was carrying us away. Here was a wonder. Why, I could've shaken the Reverend by the hand for vanishing three quarters of Potter's Englishmen quietly away like this. I didn't wait but took my new chance. One more dash and I was standing before the fo'c'sle door. Dropping my chains in a heap, I started pulling bolts free. A proper army of the rotten, murdering things there were, too, half of them tight with rust.

"How dare you," Potter shouted at the Reverend. Casting a quick glance back, I could see he looked undecided, now looking over the side, I suppose in the hope he might save his friends—though I could see no sign of them—now throwing a raging look at Wilson, as if he was trying to work himself up to shooting the old article. If that was his notion he was too slow. The second rope will have been straining nicely, having the whole of the boat's weight to carry, and all of a sudden it snapped, dropping the boat with a mighty splash. That turned Potter's face redder than his beard, and he leaned over the rail and fired his pistol empty. I couldn't see if he'd had any luck, the boat being too close to the ship's side, but his aim looked wild.

Not that I had time to dwell on such things. Finally I had the last bolt free, the fo'c'sle door was being pulled back open from inside and familiar bodies were staring out. Though, in truth, they were only just familiar. If I thought I was bad, they were seven times worse, as I'd never seen men so starved. Their faces looked like masks, while their arms and legs were hardly more than bones with a little scran of skin wrapped about them, like skeletons in stockings. Even China Clucas seemed half wasted away. If I needed any more rage inside me—which I didn't—that gave me a fine dose. I was amazed they were all able to stagger out at all, especially the two that were half killed with scurvy. Then again, I suppose there's nothing like being locked away and left to drown to give a man a bit of eagerness. In a moment we were freeing the pair lashed to the pumps.

Potter looked all raging amazement at the sight of us, shouting out, "Get back in there." How fat he was compared to the rest of us.

I never gave an order, but it was as if we all knew what to do. We started stumbling towards him, the sick giving a shoulder to the worse.

"One step nearer and I'll shoot," Potter yelled.

We were too raging to care. As we tottered closer, he grabbed up all the rifles from the deck, slinging three over his shoulders and grasping the fourth in one hand, while he had the revolving pistol in the other, so he looked a proper medical bandit. Here was a fine little battle so it was:

on one side nine Manx skeletons, one in chains, two hardly able to walk, with hardly a toothpick for weaponry among them; on the other a single Englishman pretending himself a whole army.

"I will shoot." He waved his rifle back and forth along the length of us, but it seemed as if we were just too many to choose from. For a moment he reached into his pocket, I guessed for more bullets for his pistol, but then sort of yelped, like a kicked dog, and, grabbing the leather carrying case, he darted away, guns clattering, to the stairs to the officers' cabins. His rifles nearly stopped him, catching the hatch with a proper jarring that made him spit curses, but he managed to scamper down before we could reach him. "If any man steps down here I will shoot him," he promised kindly. I could hear a scraping sound, of boxes being moved, so it seemed he was trying to make some kind of nest for himself.

I let him be, having more urgent worries. "The wreckage," I called out. I hardly need have troubled myself, as China Clucas was already reaching for the axe. In just a few moments the mast and its mess were cut loose and drifting away, and Vartin Clague had the wheel to steady us. I took a quick glance over the rail at the timbers. A nasty sight they made, too, as the mast had scraped and bashed them something terrible, so I could only hope they wouldn't cave in at the next big wave. Nor was this the finish of our troubles.

"We'll never get past that," growled Brew. All this while that we'd been playing our games with the Englishmen the wind had been pushing the ship straight at England, and we were drifting nicely into a bay. Brew had his eyes on a long point jutting out into the ocean to larboard. "Even if we put more sail on the foremast, and it held, too—which I doubt it would—the wind's too far round."

The sad thing was that he was right. Not in a thousand tries would we slip round that big chunk of rock. It seemed those Englishmen had done for my poor *Sincerity* after all. The rottenness of it. Halfway round the world she'd taken us, and the other half, too, and now she was to be broken on rocks of their own muck of a land. All that was left was to hope we wouldn't go down with her. Spreading my chains over the fallen mizzenmast, I had China Clucas set to work with the axe, which he did neatly enough, then snapping the rings off with Christian's chisel. That was something, at least. After all this time shackled my arms felt light as air, so they kept sort of floating up without my intending.

"Look, there's the Reverend," called out Kinvig.

Sure enough, there he was, sitting in the longboat a hundred yards distant, his hands clasped together for another bit of praying, just in case God was feeling neglected. His vessel being low in the water the wind seemed to be leaving him in peace, and he was drifting away with the current. By the looks of it he'd even clear the point. That fellow had the devil's luck, no denying. Though I couldn't believe he'd last long in the open sea, especially without oars. There was no sign of the other three.

We had none of his fortune. I took a look at the rest of the boats, but the fallen spars had done for them nicely, smashing two to splinters and giving the third a handsome crack stretching clean across her bow timbers. It seemed we'd just have to take our chances as best we could. We might be half an hour, we might be more, but it would be soon enough. It was hard to see how savage we'd have it, but the way surf was jumping at the shore looked hardly friendly.

That was when Brew came up with his question. "Where's the gold?"

What a fine little question that was. I'd thought those Englishmen had used up all their nuisance, but no, the doctor had found a sweet way of riling us even now. The rotten thief, with his leather carrying case. Glancing down the hatchway, I could see he'd blocked up the door of the dining cabin with a heap of packing boxes. A rifle was sticking out from a hole in the middle.

"Keep away," he shouted. "One step nearer and I'll shoot."

Taking a run down there wouldn't be clever, that was clear as glass.

"We could lower someone over the stern," suggested Brew.

"He'd be sure to see, and put a bullet through him."

"How about the cannon?" wondered China Clucas, in a grim sort of voice. "We could just blast him."

One look put paid to that. The mizzenmast had landed clean on top of the thing, squeezing it flat as a rat in a mangle. But I had an idea now. "What about the contraband holds. Does he know about them?"

Brew wasn't sure. "He must know they're there."

There was a sight of difference between knowing they were there and knowing how to get in, as the London customs had proved nicely. It would be a risk, for sure, especially seeing as we had no guns, but what was risk when we were about to go smashing into a rocky shore. "We may as well have a try."

"Let me come," offered China Clucas, picking up the axe.

He'd do as well as any for a jaunt like this. I took a belaying pin and we were all set. Aside from the dining cabin, the other way in was from the hold, so we opened up the main hatch. A proper lake of bilge water there was down below, slooshing through the ballast and licking at the empty store casks, and giving me a good soaking as I clambered down the rope. Fortunately it hadn't reached those particular timbers on the wall. I heard a faint click as Kinvig pulled that certain cable, making them twitch, and they prized open nicely enough. Lighting a candle and peering in, I learned for sure why we hadn't sunk or capsized. D'you know the contraband hold was all but dry, with just a little wash of water dribbling about in the bottom. We couldn't have built the *Sincerity* a better pair of floats if we'd wanted.

In I climbed. I could see no light shining in from Potter's end, so the hatch to the dining cabin must still be closed, which was something. Unless he'd guessed us, of course, and was waiting his moment. Whatever he was doing, we couldn't afford being heard, that was sure, so I whispered to the boys to take themselves aft and pester him with all the noise they were able. Before long I could hear them shouting into his den, calling him names–which is a fine skill of Manxmen–and China and me started our little journey.

This wasn't easy. We had to drop down to where it was narrower and more slanting so we'd not slip, and even then it was hard to feel a way ahead–our legs being all sort of twisted with the timbers–while all the time we were trying to keep from scraping the axe and the belaying pin, and so giving ourselves away. The further we went, the darker it got, and the stronger was the smell of brandy and tobacco. All around me I could hear the timbers creaking, to remind us that we were lodged in just a little slip of air, with seawater by the ton pressing in from both sides. I'd chosen the side that hadn't been battered by the mast but it wouldn't make much difference, as if the timbers went the *Sincerity* would dive down quicker than porpoises. My other worry was that some bit of England might suddenly come smashing through the side, as our surprise. As we went, the sounds of the boys' tauntings changed and changed again, growing louder and softer, harsher and muffled, as they found some different way to seep through the ship's woodwork. Finally there was a loud bang that was answered with laughter and told me they must have riled Potter into wasting a bullet. It seemed they'd found the right names for him, then.

By then we'd finally reached the end. We wedged ourselves between the timbers like a proper pair of chimney sweeps, then prized our way upwards, till finally I felt the touch of the cable that sprang the trap. I could hear no sound apart from the shouting of the boys. If Potter had stumbled upon the entrance–as he well might have, squatting in my cabin for all these months–then he'd be ready as rabbits, but there was nothing to do but try. The hatch had never creaked before and I hoped it hadn't got into bad habits. Gently as could be, I pulled up the cable, holding the catch to stop it clicking too loud. Jump it went and the hatch came loose. I waited a moment–for no reason at all, you know, except to put it off–and then, very gently, I pushed it upwards, holding its weight, so Queen Victoria swung over nice and gently.

Out I peered, quite dazzled by the light. There was Potter, or rather his back, crouched with all his guns behind a proper wall of his packing cases, as he stared away down the passage. That was a piece of luck. One of the boys must have just said something, as even while I looked he pointed his pistol and fired it off. That was more luck again. My ears were ringing like seven bells and his would be worse. Belaying pin ready, I was just about to pull myself up through the hatch when all of a sudden I felt myself tugged back. Would you believe it, that big gorm China Clucas was pushing me out of the way, so he could clamber up himself. For a bad moment I quite feared he meant to warn Potter–after all, he'd quite worshipped him for healing his pig gash–but no, I couldn't have been more wrong. By the time I poked my head up through, Potter was twisting round–must have heard him coming–though he was too slow. I'm sure China didn't mean to do for him, as he didn't use the axe blade but gave him a tap with the metal back of the handle. Then again there's nothing to get a man's rage going like admiration gone sour. He caught Potter on the head, just above his eye, making a strangest sound, like a barrel being staved. That was enough. Down went the doctor, all clattering guns and flying mess.

I pulled myself through the hatch and had a scratch of my chin. "That's that then."

China looked sort of sheepish. "I didn't mean to . . ."

I shook my head. "Don't you go troubling your conscience with that one, China. He's not deserving." I called out to the boys through the hole in the packing cases. "It's all right now. We're finished here."

Brew's face peered down the stairway. "You'd best get back up here, Captain. We're getting close to the land."

That was when I noticed a curious thing. There on my shelf, just where I'd left it all those months before, was our same bag of gold that I'd got from Jed Grey for our brandy and tobacco. Potter had just left it. It looked like he'd never even troubled himself to open the thing and see what was inside. What a strange body he was. But then what was in his leather carrying case? It must be valuable, or he'd not have been clutching it so keen.

"Hurry up, Captain."

China had cleared the packing boxes out of the doorway. I grabbed the gold, and the leather case, too, and hurried up towards the deck.

So we finally had our disaster at sea, and a curious one it was besides. Your traditional shipwreck is all noise and wind and bodies getting landed against rocks, but this was nothing like. The sea, which had been a little choppy before, was calming nicely, while there was even a bit of sunshine to warm our bones. We didn't so much as founder on rocks as get wedged between two of them, the *Sincerity*'s timbers grinding and creaking something terrible, as the waves pushed at her once and again. Well, we didn't wait for fortune to go changing her mind, but lowered a rope onto a big flat chunk of stone below, and dropped ourselves down fast as fright, all giving a hand to the two that were so gone with scurvy.

I hadn't thought beyond these rocks. Why should I have? It was good, and better than good, that we'd not all been drowned after all.

Now we were actually here, though, panting and gasping on this miracle of solid ground, I could see all sorts of new troubles raising their nasty heads.

It was as well we hadn't dawdled. Hardly had we sat down and caught our breath when there was a crunching sound, and the poor *Sincerity* gave a mighty shudder. The timbers that had been battered by the mast must have gone, crushed by those rocks, as all at once there was a wild sort of gurgling and she was sliding back down fast as could be. The contraband holds had no bulkheads, so they'd fill as quick as a sieve dropped in a well, and sure enough her poor battered hull slipped down so she was gone in hardly an instant. The foremast poked up above the water for a short while but soon even that was tilting to one side, and then disappeared. She'd gone down whole.

That was bad as well.

Here was a hard sort of moment. Saying goodbye to the *Sincerity*, the first and only vessel I'd ever owned. I'd still felt she was my ship even during all those months I was stuck below, with Potter playing captain and making a wreck of her. Why, she'd saved our lives, keeping us afloat just long enough. Not that that was all my thinking. There was also the little matter of what was still in her–or rather who–waiting to be found. I quite wished I hadn't taken China Clucas along for that jaunt. Mind you, what else could we have done?

"Is that the jink, then?" asked Brew, pointing at the leather case.

I'd clean forgotten about the thing. Mind you, it was a proper waste of time as it turned out. There I'd been, dragging it off the vessel like my life depended on it, and when I opened it up all I found was paper. Where was the use in that? From what I could see it was purest gibberish, too, being all about types and characteristics and other nonsense. I couldn't think why Potter had been hanging on to it so.

China pointed at the sand dune behind us. "Someone's coming."

Following his look, I saw two bodies on horseback riding towards us. Rescuers, that was all we needed. From their clothes they looked like farmers. They were good and shocked at our being so starved.

"What on earth happened to you?"

It was questions that would hang us and this was the first. "We've come from Tasmania. We ran out of food."

That was enough to quiet them, at least for now. "I'll fetch the cart."

The only safe thing would be to get far away, and soon too, before it was too late. It might be salvagers, or scavengers, or just some Englishman with a curiosity. Any would do. After that it wouldn't matter a spit that we'd been in the right. It's never being *right* that matters, after all, it's being *believed*, which is another animal entirely. One quick study of the ship would spring enough mysteries to put us in some Englishman's court of law, being called smugglers and murderers. All the while bodies with letters after their names would be remembering what a fine respectable fellow Dr. Potter had been.

Wouldn't that just be my luck, to spend all these months battling against the old scriss, and then, just when I thought I'd won, to be hanged by his own dead corpse.

CHAPTER FIFTEEN

——➤◆◄——

Timothy Renshaw
MARCH–APRIL 1858

I FOUND MYSELF in a plain sort of room, yellow evening sunlight shining on the bedclothes. A young woman I had never set eyes on before was looking at me, smiling as if I had made some joke, though I was sure I hardly could have.

"Well, well, and good afternoon to you."

I felt dazed. "Where is this place?"

"Dad's farm, of course."

"Have I been here long?"

"Nearly two days." She smiled again. "We have been curious. You looked as if you'd walked clean across the whole bush. Have you got a name?"

"Timothy Renshaw."

"I'm Liz. Liz Sheppard."

Recollections were returning, though they seemed long ago, and not quite real. "I saw angels."

The smile dulled. "That's right. Dad carves them. They're all over the place."

It was another month before I heard the full truth about the angels. That morning Liz's father was away getting stores and her brothers were out checking fences, while Liz and I took ourselves away to the barn. She'd let me unbutton the top of her dress, and loosen her corset, and though I could have done with more loosening still, it was sweet enough for now. I was just enjoying myself nicely, in fact, when her mood suddenly changed.

"That's enough," she said crossly, pushing me back and hiding away those neat round breasts. "You've no right, really you've not."

I was quite put out. "What's wrong? You were happy enough just now."

She threw me an accusing look. "You don't care about me. I'm just some plaything for you."

Females have a way of growing serious at the very poorest time. "That's not true," I told her, though I dare say a good part of me was just hoping I might warm her into loosening herself once again. Instead she started crying.

"I don't know why I let you near me. You'll only cause me hurt." A look came into her eyes, almost hunted. "You'd never have looked at me if you'd known."

Here was something new. "Known what?"

"About Dad." Her voice, which was usually strong and without concern, fell hushed. "He was a Port Arthur man. All he did was take some fellow's bag at a coaching inn because he was hungry, and then hit back once when he shouldn't, but that was enough. It was at Port Arthur he started his stone carving. He made sculptures for the governor's wife's garden."

I suppose I had begun to wonder. The previous Sunday I had finally been well enough to join them going to church–a little shed of a place with a tin roof–and I had seen the neighbours' looks.

Now she was angry. "Go on, then. Run off and don't come back. After all, you wouldn't want to be seen walking with a convict's daughter."

I kissed her, and then she kissed me back, hungry. After that she loosened nicely, till I had almost the whole story, and a handsome sight she made, too, lying back on the hay.

I'd already been helping a little on the farm by then, and that afternoon I saddled up the horse to check on the sheep down by the river, where Liz's father said he'd seen a native wolf prowling. It was a fine day, the trees changing their colours for autumn, and it felt good to be riding across the land, a broad hat on my head for the sun and a cape on my shoulders in case it turned wet. There was something about this place that made me feel alive, in a way I never had done back in London.

It was hard to think of Mr. Sheppard as a Port Arthur man. With his sloping shoulders and his shy, startled look he seemed quietness itself. So I had kissed a convict's daughter. What would my mother say to that? It would hardly be the kind of news she would want to tell her society friends. Why, just thinking of Mother made me want to go back to the house there and then and loosen Liz again. It was none of their business what I did anymore. They had sent me here, and nearly killed me, too, so now everything was mine to decide. Why shouldn't I stay? I liked the life well enough. The farm didn't seem to make a great fortune, but the land wasn't bad, and Liz's family were able feed themselves without breaking their backs. Why, I even liked plants here. In London they had been just a chore that I had been pushed into studying, but here they were useful. The farm had several fields of wheat, as well as the kitchen garden, and a little apple orchard, too, while I had been able to give a few useful pieces of advice. And Liz? Even aside from the fact that she had nursed me back from death, she was a tempting-looking female, nicely curved, while she had shown me more affection than I'd ever received from my own relatives. Yes, I might even marry a convict's daughter if I chose.

I saw one of the lambs had got through the fence and was out in the bush beyond, thinking himself so clever. He'd change his mind quick if a native wolf jumped out to take him for dinner. I went after him on the horse, though he gave me a good chase, dodging back and forth and landing me in the dirt once, before I finally caught him and dropped him back with the others. After that I mended the fence where he'd slunk through, and it was almost dusk by the time I finally returned. Liz was still working in the kitchen garden and saw me riding by. She seemed recovered from her earlier upset.

"Look at you," she called out with a laugh. I suppose I'd picked up a good bit of dust. "You look like a real Tasmanian."

Mr. P. T. Windrush
1865

<u>Wonders of the Isle of Wight</u>

<u>Chapter 6: An Island of Eccentrics (excerpt)</u>

It is just beyond St. Catherine's Point, however, in the little village of Chale, that one of the island's most remarkable characters is to be found. Pay a visit to the delightful old church, from where one has such a fine view of the coast stretching away to westwards, and one may well discover, sitting just inside the porch, the cheery, ragged fellow who is known all across the island as the Messiah of Chale.

He was found by the village innkeeper on the shore beneath the dark and crumbling cliffs that typify this part of Wight. He was fleshless almost to death and looked half drowned, while how he came to be there is a mystery that is much discussed in Chale to this day. A number of timbers from what appeared to have been a rowing boat were nearby, but these were without lettering of any kind, while the poor unfortunate himself could offer no enlightenment, being too bereft of wits to repeat his own name. Whether this was his nature, or a consequence of some ocean ordeal–some have suggested he succumbed to drinking seawater– will doubtless never be known.

The innkeeper and his wife endeavoured to nurse him back to a state of tolerable bodily health, though sadly his mind remained lost, his chatter being greatly excitable yet all but without meaning. From the first he displayed a simple and most touching wish to visit the nearby church, whose bells he could hear ringing from his sickbed, and such was his enthusiasm for this house of God that, as soon as he was recovered, he quite insisted upon making his home in its porch. What a happy idiot he proved, smiling and uttering foolishness to any who would listen, and urging passersby to pray for their souls. Even left to himself he would talk volubly, looking to his right quite as if some invisible phantasm was sat beside him, whom he would inform of any small piece of news, from a change in the weather to the fact that a leaf had fallen upon his lap. Ask who he was speaking to and a strange look would come into his eyes, while his reply was always the same. "My father. My father who art in heaven." It was this that inspired his nickname.

There was always somebody who would offer the Messiah a penny or a crust of bread, so he kept himself well enough. He was not, however, welcomed by all. He had, from the first, showed a great antipathy towards the vicar, Mr. Roberts, whom he would denounce on occasion as "Beelzebub's fiend." Eventually Mr. Roberts was moved to suggest he be removed to an insane asylum. It emerged, however, that the Messiah was not without friends of his own, including a local farmer of nonconformist views, who was generous enough to offer him a place to dwell, being an empty outbuilding upon his land that had previously been used to house animals, which would seem only suitable for a Messiah. He lives there to this day, spending his hours sat upon the churchyard wall, cheerfully chattering to his father the deity. His fame has spread, even attracting the curiosity of those elsewhere upon the island. When visitors appear the Messiah delights in showing them a little overgrown patch of land, close beside his simple home, where the pigs used to bask in the sun, which he quite insists is the Garden of Eden!

Another mystery about the man is his knowledge of stones. Though he cannot so much as remember his own name, he knows these perfectly, and show him any piece of rock or mineral, however rare, and he will name it at once. He is never wrong.

Peevay
1858–70

SO I GOT my surprise. As I looked from my secret place at these fellows coming in their four boats, then pulling them ashore and taking out STORES they brought, I saw they never were like Father at all, but all different. Lamp lit one like a white man–white face and pale eyes like any such–but there, just beside, was another who was dark like Mother. Others were mixed like me, pale skin with Palawa's nose, or black face but red hair. Even those white ones weren't like any usual num, no, as they never made themselves proud like white scuts did. No, these weren't foes, I could divine. I got up from my hiding place and called hello, making them turn about at this mystery to confound.

So I got my second surprise. You see, these weren't some strangers but my own brothers and sisters. Brothers and sisters that I never even supposed till then, plenty of them. Not that all were Father's, no, as other white men also lived here before, catching seals and mutton birds like him, but many were mine. Truly that was great good fortune and tidings of joy, better than any I ever had before. So I was not just alone after all. I had some whole family I never did divine, yes. These were PEEVAY'S MOB.

Father died five years before, so they told me that night. His dying was nothing interesting, no, but just going away in the boat to Robson's dying island to get STORES, getting drunk, falling asleep outside the STOREHOUSE in a cold night and coming home with fever. After, he went to bed and got found dead. He was the last white man left here, and the most hateful, and nobody was sad. They put him on the other side of the hill so they wouldn't have to look at his burying place except sometimes. Mothers, who were all Palawa, stolen like Mother was, and who were also all dead now, got put near houses, so people could give them greetings every day.

So Mother lived longer than Father, though she never knew. She would like that, I did ponder.

Strange thing was that though stories about Father were all bad—drinking too much again, or striking grievous blows for piss-poor thing—still I could not hate him only. Yes, he was some heinous scut with no good in him, but good came from him, even if this was just some foolish mischance he never did intend. See, he made me, and now he gave me my tribe, too. That was some mystery to confound.

So I am in this place, my place. Sometimes I awake in the night and it is some new puzzle to confuse that I am here, so lucky, just living and going with others hunting seals and catching mutton birds and getting eggs from their holes in the ground. The only time I see white men is when we go to Robson's dying island to sell things and get more stores. STOREKEEPER smiles, as he desires our trade, but I can see his eyes full of scornings. White scut farmers—they got that island now—are worse, laughing and shouting magic names if they get drunk. Truly, though, this is a useful thing, as it makes me remember to be fighting. My new ones don't know much about the world, you see, or even about themselves, as Father never told them any, so it is my fine purpose to give them teachings. I tell them writing and LAWS, white men's tricks and BIBLE CHEATING and more. They must know everything so they can endure. Who knows, perhaps one day they can fight those heinous pissers back. This is my dream. This is my heartfelt desire deep inside my breast, and I will strive for it every day.

Captain Illiam Quillian Kewley
1858–59

IT WAS JUST a week or two after I got back to Peel City, and Ealisad's scoldings were still ringing in my ears, when I heard the news. It came from the *Sincerity*'s insurers over in Douglas, and was as bad as bad could be. They'd had a letter from a certain Mr. Jonah Childs, who told them he wanted to have the *Sincerity* salvaged, which he'd do with his own jink, seeing as there was no cargo aboard.

That sent us all scurrying. Most of them took themselves off to Whitehaven or Liverpool, looking for any kind of ship work that would take them far away. Brew got a second mate's berth on a vessel bound for South America, Kinvig vanished onto some dirty steamship voyaging to New York, while China Clucas went off to play giant on a tea trader sailing away to, of all places, China, which was fitting, I dare say. I would have followed them, too, but I just couldn't find the wish in me. I don't know if it was that journey back, with all its starving and worse, or if it sprang from what happened on that last morning, but it was as if all the soo had drained away. There seemed no point in fleeing halfway round the world, as I felt they were bound to catch me in the end. There's only so many Manx sea captains, after all, while there's nothing like a shout of murder to set fellows all across the globe watching.

I couldn't just wait, mind, and one day I took a passage across to Dublin. My journey back was more roundabout, being first to Liverpool, then over to Douglas town, and finally back to Peel City, which I

did in the night, walking quietly over the hills. From there I went
straight to cousin Tobm's house, and stepped quietly into his basement,
where I stayed, quiet as mice. I can't say that was much of a delight,
but at least it was keeping alive. The damp I could manage, and boredom too, as you get used to such things aboard ships. Cousin Tobm
paid a visit every day, and Ealisad came once a week just to taunt me
some more. No, it would have been all right except for Tobm's cat. All
there was for windows was a few chunks of glass jammed in the pav-
ing at the top of Tobm's garden. When the sun was high it shone
through these nice as nip, making lovely bright squares on the floor
near the table, but that's just when Tobm's cat liked to flop down his
great body of a self and blot all to darkness. I suppose the glass was
warm for him to lie on. I tried shouting, and hitting at the ceiling with
a chair leg, but it made not a scran of difference. Animals always know
when you're helpless.

Summer turned to autumn, then Christmas came with its damp,
leaving me coughing and cursing this private gaol. All the while I was
puzzling and fretting why those certain ones still hadn't brought themselves over from England, like I knew they surely must, sleetching about
with their fishing eyes, asking for Illiam Quillian Kewley. I'd have heard
soon enough if they'd come, for sure, as cousin Tobm kept his ears open,
while a stranger in Peel is news within the hour. It wasn't that I was
missing them any, but there's nothing to bother a man like mystery.
Besides, the longer they didn't arrive, the longer I was stuck waiting in
that cellar.

Finally winter turned to spring, and d'you know on the very first day
the sun was strong enough to feel, that cat flopped himself down in his
place, eclipsing me all in darkness. It was just after then that Ealisad
came with a letter that had arrived, which was from Jonah Childs himself. Inside I found a prettiest little invitation, and even tickets for the
train and the steam packet.

> *You are invited to an exhibition at the London College of Sur-*
> *geons of the collected artifacts of the much lamented Dr. Thomas*
> *Potter, eminent explorer and writer, assembled during the recent*
> *journey to and exploration of Her Majesty's Colony of Tasmania.*

I knew it was a trap, of course. I didn't care. I'd had enough of hiding in the dark, month after month, shivering and waiting for trouble. If I was to be hanged, then on with it. So up I climbed, giving that cat a nice little kick on the way, back into the world. Soon I was steaming across a springtime Irish Sea, watching the passengers fuss and pewk at the little scran of weather we met. Next I was on a train rushing out from Liverpool that was whistling and screaming and daubing everyone with soot. Then suddenly I was back in that mad rush of London, that I'd never thought I'd set eyes on again. A ride in a cab and I was stood in front of a grim sort of building that was the London surgeons' nest, where the porters gave a nod at my invitation, then pointed me up some stairs.

I half expected to find nothing more than a mob of London policemen waiting to grab me, but no, there really was an exhibition. I stepped into a giant of a room that was busy as beetles, with all manner of grand London snots strolling back and forth in their Sunday best, chattering and shouting their hellos. Right in the centre was a fine portrait of the good doctor himself, smirking away. And good evening to you, too. All around were glass cases filled with the bones and skulls he'd collected, some all fixed back together on stands, leaning back with their arms by their side as if there might be hope for them yet. So the ship had salvaged well enough. That just added to the mystery of why no one was jumping out to put me under arrest.

"Captain Kewley!" This was Jonah Childs, showing all his teeth as if we were old friends. "I'm so glad you were able to come, and from so very far, too. But let me introduce you."

Before I knew it I was shaking hands with some major out of the English army–a huge fat sort of body, who Childs said had gone exploring deserts on a mule, though he looked like only an elephant would carry him–and also a pair of Potter's doctor friends. These two and Childs had organized the exhibition.

"But it's Captain Kewley we should thank as much as anyone," said Childs, giving me a wide smile. "If it had not been for him, after all, Dr. Potter's book would never have been preserved for us. If anyone deserves our gratitude, it is you, Captain."

This was all news to me. "What book?"

He just laughed. "But you must know? *The Destiny of Nations.* You were the one who brought it ashore."

I could only suppose it must have been that packet of gibberish in the leather case.

Childs was grinning at this fine joke he'd found. "Really, Captain, you should be proud of yourself. You saved a work of greatness. People are talking of nothing else. The printer cannot keep up with new orders."

For a moment I wondered if this was some kind of trick. Had there been something in there, hidden among the gibberish, calling me criminal? Yet Jonah Childs and his doctor friends were all sweetest smiles. I had to ask, though it was tempting fate, sure as sure is, "So the salvaging went well, did it?"

Childs gave a little piping laugh. "You joke, Captain. Why, I've never known such a trial. First there was the weather that could not have been worse, though this was supposed to be high summer. Then there was the fact that the vessel had sunk deeper than was supposed. Then there were the treacherous salvagers, who suddenly took it upon themselves to vanish away to Devon to another operation that offered greater payment. It was more than four months before it was done."

I was that far down the road now I had to finish. "Did you find any surprises?"

D'you know, he gave me a troubled sort of look, as if *he* was the one who was being suspected. "I assure you, there was nothing there aside from Dr. Potter's stores. If there had been anything else I would certainly have informed your insurers."

"I'm sure you would, Mr. Childs." Had the tide taken him away? I wondered. It was possible she'd broken up on the sea bottom, and he'd been dropped clean out. I could feel a smile brewing, and a mighty one it was, too. Then again there are few cheerier things to do of an evening than to find you're not to be hanged after all.

"But there are others here you should meet," cooed Childs, all trying to please. "I never supposed the exhibition would attract so many eminent people. That tall man with grey hair is a member of Parliament, while that fellow just by the door is a writer of philosophy, whose works are greatly admired. The one beside him . . ."

I didn't much care who they were. All I wanted was a bit of quiet room to enjoy my own news. "If you don't mind I'd like to take a look round the exhibition. I wouldn't want to miss it."

"Quite so, Captain, quite so."

So I started taking a little stroll round the room, though I hardly looked at the exhibits very carefully, being far too busy following my own sweet thoughts. I was free. Why, I'd never even needed to lock myself away in that basement all this while. The mad stupid foolishness of it.

I was barely halfway round when I found myself looking at another set of bones, all arranged on a handsome metal frame, and spliced together tidy as could be. I didn't think anything of them at first. Then I noticed the skull had a big hole just above the right eye. It was probably just chance, but wasn't that the sort of spot where China Clucas had gone tapping with his axe? On the frame was a little brass plate, all carved with neatest writing.

UNKNOWN MALE PRESUMED TASMANIAN ABORIGINE
POSSIBLE VICTIM OF HUMAN SACRIFICE

Just nearby was a little glass case, and in it was a little scran of what looked like skin.

ABORIGINAL WITCHCRAFT CHARM

There was no mistaking the hairs, which were were short, just right for someone's beard, and a fine shade of red.

He'd not been washed away. He'd been picked clean. Of course. Four months would have been long enough for sea creatures to have themselves a fine little feed.

For a moment I quite expected Jonah Childs and the others to come up and haul me away to gaol, but none of them did. They all just carried on with their hellos and politeness and making little jokes, like before.

Nobody seemed very interested.

EPILOGUE

ALL FICTION—and nonfiction—changes and concentrates what it portrays. This is one of its first purposes. Having said this, I have tried to represent this era as truthfully and precisely as possible. All the major events of the Tasmanian strand of the novel follow real occurrences, from the stealing of aboriginal women by sealers to the massacre on the cliff, the bizarre cruelties of the convict system, the fiasco of the Black Line and the terrible farce of Flinders Island. Likewise some of the characters are closely based on people of the time, including Robson, the various governors and their wives and also Mother (Walyeric). She was inspired by a formidable woman named Walyer, who fought the whites and was greatly feared by them. She knew how to use firearms, was reputed to have cut a new path through the bush to facilitate her campaigns and would swear fluently in English as she launched her attacks. She was eventually captured by the British in late 1831, and at once began trying to organize fellow aboriginals in a rebellion. She died not long afterwards.

Another character based on a real figure of the time is Tayaleah, or George Vandiemen. The real George Vandiemen was a Tasmanian aboriginal child who was found wandering close to New Norfolk in 1821, having become separated from his family. His aboriginal name is not recorded. His discovery came to the attention of a recently arrived settler, William Kermode—oddly enough, a Manxman—who decided to have him sent to Lancashire to be educated. The boy did well in his studies, and was sent back to Tasmania in 1828, only to fall sick and die soon afterwards. His short history was soon forgotten.

Now I'd like to jump forward a little. During the 1850s a quiet revolution was occurring in England. Prior to this time Europeans had frequently treated other peoples with great cruelty–the worst example being, famously, slavery–yet there was little or no attempt in educated circles to justify such behaviour. The biblical notion that all men are roughly equal may have been ignored, yet it had remained largely unchallenged. This was all to change. In 1850 a disgraced surgeon named Robert Knox published *The Races of Men, a fragment.* This was in many ways a precursor of Hitler's *Mein Kampf,* insisting that all history was nothing more than a process of racial conflicts (rather as Karl Marx, in his *Communist Manifesto* of three years earlier, had declared all history was merely a struggle between economic classes). Knox was among the first writers to claim that the various races of mankind were actually different species (a ludicrous notion in modern scientific terms), while it will come as little surprise that he proposed that the Saxon, of England, was among the most exalted. His book was an immediate best-seller. For the first time it became acceptable, even fashionable, to see the world in these terms. Though such ideas were strongly opposed in some quarters they continued to gain influence, forming a kind of ugly background music to the latter part of the century. Their impact since then is infamous, and we are living with it still today.

If only the Victorian British had troubled to look a little more carefully at the evidence before them. It was widely accepted throughout the later nineteenth century that the most inferior of all races had been the aborigines of Tasmania–how else could they have so foolishly permitted themselves to be exterminated?–who were often depicted as being a kind of halfway house between men and apes, wholly lacking in faculties of reason. Another presumption of the time was that the highest and rarest form of reason was mathematics.

I would now like to include a factual document from that time. This is George Vandiemen's final school report, written by his teacher in Lancashire, John Bradley. I have reproduced it in full.

Mr. Kermode,

You will perceive, in George's ciphering book, the easy manner that has been pursued in teaching him Arithmetic, a branch of education that he was supposed to be incompetent in, but this supposition, I am persuaded, could only have arisen from want of method and experience in those who attempted to teach him, and not from want of faculty in George. His abode with me has been but short, but I am convinced that his good memory, which you will perceive in his repetition of the Psalms and other things which he has got off, must certainly enable him to go through common Arithmetic with as much faculty as boys do in general.

I feel much gratified in having had this boy with me, tho' but a little time, as it confirms me more in the opinion that I have long cherished: that Man is on all parts of the globe the same; being a free agent, he may mould himself to excellence or debase himself below the brute, & that education, government and established customs are the principal causes of the distinctions among nations. Let us place indiscriminately all the shades of colour in the human species in the same climate, allow them the same means for development of intellect, I apprehend the blacks will keep place with the whites, for colour neither impairs the muscles nor enervates the mind. We know that a black horse can match a white one in the race and that Hannibal and his black Africans contended gloriously with Rome for the Empire of the world. May the revolutions of mind establish the empire of reason and benevolence over the ruins of ignorance and prejudice. But I fear, sir, that I am running from the subject, which is by your desire to say the method that I would recommend to be pursued in the passage.

Arithmetic may be followed up by selecting the easy examples out of a printed one (?) which he has with him; but care should be taken that he do not disfigure his ciphering book, as it may be shown to the Governor, so that if he should write down any sums let it be on common paper, these may be at some future time transcribed, if it should be thought necessary.

The Psalms. Repeat one daily so as to keep in most those which he has already got off.

Read a lesson daily in the Juvenile Reader and commit a portion of it to memory.

Say the multiplication and pence tables frequently, also a portion of the Geography and write a lesson out of the Orthography & get the Rule connected with the lesson.

I refer to your judgment for the next. May the Giver of Intellect bless your endeavours and make you happy in the exercise of benevolence. I also pray that our Nation may be just as it is great and secure to George a portion of the land *that gave him birth, that our Rulers may in this instance be governed by justice, let the Native have what the voice of reason and equity adjudge to him, and not let power supersede right.*

Accept my wishes for your own and George's prosperity & a pleasant voyage to the other side of the globe.

Your humble servant,
John Bradley

THE ANGLO-MANX DIALECT

THE MANX SPOKE a Celtic language closely related to Irish and Scottish Gaelic. It gradually declined during the nineteenth century, and the last native Manx speaker died in the 1970s (though recently there has been a move to teach it in Manx schools). As the old language faded, there grew up what became known as the Anglo-Manx dialect. This was a form of English but was peppered with Celtic words and thoughts, and grammar was often a literal translation from Gaelic. Thus Manxmen would not say *he has a new hat* but *there's a new hat at him*, and the definite article (*the*) could be used for emphasis, as in the phrase *the hot I am.*

Sad to say, the Anglo-Manx dialect has, like the old Gaelic language before it, largely vanished now, apart from the odd word or phrase, but fortunately a full record was made when it was still widely spoken, at the beginning of this century: *Vocabulary of the Anglo-Manx Dialect* by A. W. Moore, Edmund Goodwin and Sophia Morrison, which offers an intriguing picture of past Manx preoccupations. The sea, herring and superstition all figure strongly. So do various types of character, all of them viewed with disapproval. Smooth, slippery people are represented by no fewer than nine words (*Creeper, Click, Clinker, Cluke, Crooil, Reezagh, Shliawn, Slebby* and *Sleetch*). Showy, boastful people get ten (*Branchy, Filosher, Feroash, Gizzard, Grinndher, High, Neck, Snurly, Stinky* and *Uplifted*). Large, blundering people get fifteen (*Bleih, Bleb, Dawd, Flid, Gaping, Glashan, Gogaw, Gorm, Hessian, Kinawn, Looban, Ommidhan, Slampy, Sthahl* and *Walloper*), while peevish people–especially small, scolding women–get as many as eighteen (*Borragh, Coughty, Crabby, Cretchy,*

Corodank, Gob-mooar, Gonnag, Grangan, Grinnder, Grouw, Huffy, Mhinyag, Pootchagh, Scrissy, Scrowl, Smullagh, Spiddagh and *Targe*).

There is also a wealth of words concerned with beatings, inheritance and small amounts of money. Most of all, though, the dialect gives an impression of a people who delighted in playing games with language. I have used it sparingly, so it does not become too much of a distraction, and have tried to make the meaning of words apparent from their context. In case any have proved puzzling, though, I offer a glossary.

Anglo-Manx Glossary

Baarl	Manx name for the English language
Babban	Baby
Bat	Hit
Big	Denoting anyone of importance
Black Pig	Sulk: *He had the black pig on his back*
Bleb	Fool
Boaster	Someone from Ramsey town
Body	Commonly used for person
Branchy	Boastful, showy, spreading oneself out
Brave	Smart/intelligent
Canokers	A beating
Clicky	Crazy
Cob	Short, stout person
To Cog	To beat down a price
Cretchy/Cretch	Querulous, infirm/querulous person
Crooil	Crouching, deceitful
Crust	A frail old person
Customs	An officer of the customs
Dawd	Dull, awkward person
Derb	Wild, intractable person
Dirt	No good person/bad weather
Fritlag	Worthless person/rag

Gizzard (to have)	To be conceited
Glashan	Big hulking boy
Gorm	A lout
Grouw	Glum, sulky
Guilley	Boy, fellow
Hard Case	Someone with daring
High	Proud, fine, loud
To be Hobbled	To be in difficulties
Huffy	Ill-tempered
Humpy	Humped/hunchbacked
Jerrude	A state of forgetfulness/dreaminess
Jink	Money
Lonnag	Sea name for a mouse
Lumper	Anything of a good size
Mhinyag	Short person
Mie	Good
To Molevogue	To punish
Morrey	Morning
To Murder	To ill-treat
Pay Wedding	Wedding at which each guest pays a share
To Pelt	To thrash/skin
Pommit	Sea name for a rabbit
Power	A large number
A Raddling	A beating
Rank	Keen/eager
Refreshments (give)	To beat
Rile	To beat/to salt and shake herring
Sainty	Saintly/Sanctified
Scanky	Shrill
To Scelp	To smack
Scotch Grey	Louse
Scran	A scrap/any caught fish not herring
Scranch	A rending sound
Scrape(r)	A miser
Scrapings	Savings

Scrawley	Parsimonious, mean
Screeb	Scrape, scratch
Scriss/Scrissag	A mean person/scolding woman
To Scutch	To whip/lash
Shliawn	Smooth, slippery, sly
Slampy	Flabby
Sleetchy/Sleetch	Slippery or deceitful/slippery person
Slewed	Drunk
To Snurl	To turn up your nose in disgust
Soo	Juice, energy, substance
Spiddagh	Small sharp person
Stink	Pride
Stob	Short fencing post; stumpy figure
Swiney	Sea name for a pig
Thrail	Walk slowly
Throng	A crowd/to crowd
Yernach	Irish
Yernee Yeirk	Irish beggar

ACKNOWLEDGEMENTS

I WOULD LIKE to thank the following people for their great help during the long time I have been trying to write this book.

In Tasmania: Jenny Scott, Phillipa Foster and Damien Morgan and, most of all, Cassandra Pybus. Thanks to the Archives Office of Tasmania for the use of George Vandiemen's school report.

In mainland Australia: Gerard Bryant and Jacqui Boyle, Meredith and John Purcell, Maggie Hamilton, Judith Curr.

In the Isle of Man: Alan Kelly.

In Wales: John and Edna Fernihough and all in and around Grosmont, Gwent.

In England: Deborah Rogers, David Miller, Maggie Black and Pamela Egan.

This book is dedicated to Victoria Egan.